Praise
Santa Mor

'Original, suspenseful and intriguing'
RACHEL HORE

'Remarkable and compelling'
JULIAN FELLOWES

'Fantastic, moving and beautifully written'
TRACY REES

'Enjoyable and engaging, I loved it!'
BARBARA ERSKINE

'A love story to break your heart!'
LIZ FENWICK

'Mystery, love story and time travel fantasy, it's an irresistible blend'
NICKY PELLEGRINO

'Beautifully written, haunting and enchanting'
FIONA VALPY

'Irresistible! Full of passion, love and loyalty'
CAROL KIRKWOOD

'A sweeping, romantic mystery I couldn't put down!'
ANTON DU BEKE

'A spellbinding story that shimmers with mystery and intrigue'
EVIE WOODS

'Totally absorbing, just brilliant'
JUDY MURRAY

SECRETS
OF THE
STARLIT SEA

SECRETS OF THE STARLIT SEA

Santa Montefiore

ORION

First published in Great Britain in 2025 by Orion Fiction,
an imprint of The Orion Publishing Group Ltd.
Carmelite House, 50 Victoria Embankment
London EC4Y 0DZ

The authorised representative in the EEA is Hachette Ireland,
8 Castlecourt Centre, Castleknock Road, Castleknock, Dublin 15, D15 XTP3,
Republic of Ireland (email: info@hbgi.ie)

An Hachette UK Company

1 3 5 7 9 10 8 6 4 2

Copyright © Santa Montefiore 2025

The moral right of Santa Montefiore to be identified as
the author of this work has been asserted in accordance
with the Copyright, Designs and Patents Act of 1988.

All rights reserved. No part of this publication may be
reproduced, stored in a retrieval system, or transmitted
in any form or by any means, electronic, mechanical,
photocopying, recording, or otherwise, without the
prior permission of both the copyright owner and the
above publisher of this book.

All the characters in this book are fictitious, and any resemblance
to actual persons, living or dead, is purely coincidental.

A CIP catalogue record for this book is
available from the British Library.

ISBN (Hardback) 9781398720053
ISBN (Export Trade Paperback) 9781398720060
ISBN (eBook) 9781398720084
ISBN (Audio) 9781398720091

Typeset by Input Data Services Ltd, Bridgwater, Somerset

Printed in Great Britain by Clays Ltd, Elcograf, S.p.A.

MIX
Paper | Supporting
responsible forestry
FSC® C104740

To Jo De Poorter and Geoffroy Van Hulle,
with love and gratitude for our very special friendship.

I don't solve crimes
That's too easy
I settle souls

Pixie Tate

Chapter One

2014

The Aldershoff Hotel, New York

It was midnight when the four ladies made their way purposefully through the Aldershoff Hotel's lobby towards the Walter-Wyatt drawing room, which lay on the other side of an imposing pair of white double doors. Light bounced off the marble floor and threw into relief the original French-inspired mouldings that adorned the ceilings and walls, and the grand sweeping staircase, once one of the finest in New York, that dominated the hall. If one was unaware of the time, it could easily have been the middle of the day, owing to the brightness of the electric lights and the various guests who sat in the comfy velvet chairs dotted about the lobby, staring into their smartphones. The slick young man at Reception did not detain the women, for Mr Stirling, the owner, had made it clear that they had important business to attend to and were not to be disturbed. The drawing room, therefore, had been reserved exclusively for their use, even though it was unlikely to be in high demand at this time of night.

Alma Aldershoff-Blanchett-Carrington, granddaughter of the great William Aldershoff who had built this faux-seventeenth-century French chateau in 1872, moved surprisingly fast for a woman in her late nineties. She supported herself with a silver-handled walking stick personally designed for her grandfather by Thomas Brigg & Sons of London back in the 1890s. Petite in both stature and bone, her demeanour however was far from frail. Dressed in a perfectly tailored black trouser suit, heavy gold chains at her throat and wrists, Alma had the air of a recalcitrant queen, shoulders back and chin held high, for as a child she had raced over this very floor and scampered up that very staircase, and she still felt a deep sense of ownership. Although her mother had sold the grand house after her father's death in 1931, the fifteen-year-old Alma had never really got over its loss, or how the developers had, in her view, ripped out the very heart of her family home. Renovated, renewed and remodelled over the subsequent eight decades, it had morphed into a private members' club, a museum, and, finally, this hotel – The Aldershoff. If the great William Aldershoff had been alive to witness such an affront to his masterwork, Alma was sure it would have done him in.

Alma was still striking. Her hair, once a luscious brown, was now completely white and fastened into a loose updo held by a diamond comb once belonging to her grandmother, the famous doyenne of Gilded Age society, Mrs William Aldershoff, known to her friends as Didi. Besides jewellery, with which Alma adorned her person in a feverish desire to connect herself to the past, and the heirlooms that she crammed into her small Brooklyn apartment, Alma had inherited the formidable Aldershoff chin and piercing blue eyes, and the strong, uncompromising will to go with them. She was accompanied by her daughter, Leona Croft, a fey and mousey woman of sixty-four who had inherited few of the Aldershoff genes and was meek and compliant, with an over-anxious desire to please, and her two dear friends, Phyllis de Vere and Bonnie McAllister, who trailed behind her like a pair of aged bridesmaids.

Alma strode into the drawing room and stood before a sturdy

round table fashioned out of polished walnut, which had been cleared of the floral display and glossy decorative books for her clandestine purpose. She appraised the room with a critical gaze and inhaled contemptuously through her aquiline nose. It had once been her father's library but was nothing like it used to be. They had long since taken out the bookshelves and covered the walls in green silk and what she considered, disdainfully, 'fashionable' art. She didn't think much of the modern décor, but nothing could compare to the Gilded Age when her grandmother had bought antiques from Paris and Vienna with which to embellish her magnificent home. Alma could see her father now in his immaculate three-piece suit, tailored at Kaskel & Kaskel, seated behind his desk in a tall-backed leather armchair, ink pen in hand, papers piled high. He had worn spectacles and a grave expression – Walter-Wyatt Aldershoff had rarely smiled, burdened alas by the weight of his inheritance and the responsibility that had come with it.

'Put the box here,' Alma said, gesticulating at the table with a hand more used to commanding staff.

'Are you sure you want to do this, Alma?' asked Phyllis nervously, small brown eyes watching Leona put down the faded blue box she'd been carrying reverently through the hotel as if it contained the Ark itself.

'Of course I'm sure,' Alma replied curtly. For a tiny woman she had the voice of a giant. She sniffed her approval, for Mr Stirling had done as requested and arranged four chairs around the table and put a candle in the centre. The candle was of the utmost importance. Alma had been quite specific, although she hadn't disclosed what she intended to do. She didn't imagine Mr Stirling would understand, being a pragmatic man. She'd simply told him that she was bringing her daughter and two friends to partake in an old family tradition, which she always celebrated at this time of year, at this precise hour and in this particular room that had once belonged to her dear father. Mr Stirling had not questioned her further – after all, she wasn't asking for the moon, simply the use of one of their drawing rooms, and he had only recently bought the hotel, so he had no reason to doubt that she was telling the truth. Who was he to deny an old lady such a simple request? Besides, he was impressed that she was the granddaughter of the great William Aldershoff, no less. *That* had given her great authority. She had reminded him that she had grown up here as a child and he had immediately respected her ties to the place. Satisfied that she was going to get away with it without anyone discovering the true nature of her purpose, she lifted her chin and tapped her stick on the carpet with impatience. 'This is a last resort, Phyllis, and will not be discussed outside of this room – is that clear? I won't have anyone thinking me a fool.'

'Of course,' said Phyllis.

'No one would think you a fool, Alma,' Bonnie added.

Leona said nothing; she knew better than to challenge her mother.

Alma noticed that Mr Stirling had also seen to it that the curtains were closed, shutting out the night and any prying eyes that might be curious to see what the ladies were up to. If she remembered rightly, the curtains had been made of a rich red velvet in her father's day.

At the memory of those curtains, Alma felt a sudden stab of anguish and put a hand to her breast. Oh, the opulence! The grandeur! The sheer splendour of the mansion as it had been then – the crystal chandeliers, the paintings by the great Italian and Flemish artists, the sculptures, ornaments, furniture, imported from all over the world as far away as China. Gone now. Sold at auction years ago. Vanished with a vanished world.

These days, the names Vanderbilt, Astor and Rockefeller – and, indeed, Aldershoff – were merely legends of a bygone age of elegance and excess that had emerged after the Civil War and risen to greatness like a magnificent phoenix out of the ashes of conflict. Alma felt its loss keenly for by the time she was old enough to appreciate the power and influence the name Aldershoff carried, the new world with its desire for change had robbed it of its gilt.

'Close the door, Bonnie,' she said, pulling out a chair and sitting down. 'And dim the lights.' She handed her daughter her walking stick and watched her lean it up against the wall – a wall that had once been an impressive library, the envy of New York. She couldn't recall what had happened to all the books; perhaps they had been sold at auction with all the other beautiful and valuable things that had once embellished her life. It was awful to think about it, but the Aldershoff millions had dwindled over the decades following the introduction of income tax in 1913 and the subsequent dividing, wasting and unwise investing by Alma's two late husbands, older sister and cousins. In three generations, William Aldershoff's fortune had all but disappeared. Leona's daughter and grandchildren had nothing, not even the name.

Alma waited while Bonnie and Phyllis seated themselves. Bonnie, full-bodied and big-breasted, groaned like a rusty old hinge, but Phyllis dropped her behind onto the seat without so much as a gasp. The three women looked to Alma to tell them what to do next.

'Light the candle,' she commanded. Obediently, Leona struck a match from the green glass match-striker Mr Stirling had considerately placed beside the candle, along with a small ashtray for the match. The flame flared momentarily, lighting up the apprehensive faces of Alma's loyal acolytes. Their fearful eyes fell upon the blue box, fashioned out of wood like an ordinary paint box, as they waited with uneasy anticipation for the contents to be revealed. They knew it did not contain paints.

The candle was lit. The match discarded in the ashtray. Alma placed her hands on the box and spread her bony fingers, upon which inherited jewels glinted sharply. She inhaled through dilated nostrils and closed her eyes, as if basking in the sanctity of the moment. 'This belonged to my grandmother, Didi Aldershoff, Leona's great-grandmother,' she said at last, and her voice was soft and low as her mind drifted down the well-trodden path into the past, which was bathed in the eternal, untarnished glow of nostalgia. 'There was always great ceremony in its opening, for one must not play with these things. She would light a candle and say a prayer, wrapping us in angelic protection against dark entities who would take pleasure in doing us harm.'

Phyllis glanced at Bonnie, whose round eyes widened at the thought of dark entities. As if sensing collusion, Alma lifted her heavy lids and looked at them in turn, a fierce glimmer in her blue gaze. 'It's good to be a little afraid,' she whispered. 'It adds a suitable reverence to the ritual.'

Bonnie bit her lip as Alma flicked the two brass clasps and lifted the lid. Inside, the Ouija board looked innocuous enough. It certainly didn't give the impression that it was about to leap out and bite them. However, it was painted in the muted colours of its time and the bold black numbers and letters were in a curvy font, which gave it a magical air. On the inside of the lid was a yellowed label that stated the name *Haversham 1891*, and the words *The Mysterious Cabinet*. Leona had seen it before, but Phyllis and Bonnie had not. They didn't know what to expect and hoped Alma knew what she was doing. Stories of teenagers playing with Ouija boards did not on the whole end well.

Carefully, Alma lifted out the board. Leona put the box on

the floor beside her chair, for it would not be needed. Alma slid the board into the middle of the table as her grandmother used to do. Bonnie and Phyllis studied it curiously. Painted in an arc was the alphabet and beneath it the numbers 0 to 9. Under the numbers were the words *Goodbye* and *Hello*. In the top-left corner was *Yes*. In the top-right corner was *No*. The planchette was made out of wood in the shape of a giant teardrop, with a circular hole carved into the fat end within which the number or letter chosen could be viewed. The idea was for each person at the table to lay a finger lightly on the planchette and wait for it to move around the board, spelling out words and numbers as the spirit communicated from the Other Side.

Alma was ashamed that, in her youth, she had condemned her grandmother's interest in spiritualism as absurd, following her mother's lead like an obedient sheep – Alice Aldershoff had only been interested in things she could buy, and which preferably shone. Having been raised in the Christian faith Alma believed in some sort of afterlife, but she did not believe in spirits, much less in her grandmother's ability to communicate with them. However, as she approached the end of her life and the question of where she was headed grew increasingly more pressing, she had begun to open up to the possibility of surviving death in spirit form, and even perhaps being capable of returning to keep an eye on those left behind. Certainly, she hoped to be reunited with the people she had loved in life who had gone before her. She very much hoped to communicate with the dead now.

'Alma, are you sure you know what you're doing?' Phyllis asked. She knew Bonnie felt the same anxiety but was too scared of Alma to voice it. 'I mean, this was something your grandmother used to do. Don't you have to be a spiritualist or something to work this board?'

'Anyone can use a Ouija board,' Alma replied with a sniff. She had already explained this, so why were they getting nervous about it now? 'Even children play about with them.'

'And get into trouble,' Phyllis said with an uneasy chuckle. 'I don't want things to start flying about the room.'

Alma shook her head. 'My dear Phyllis, nothing is going to fly about the room.' Of course, Alma didn't really know anything about Ouija boards, but she didn't remember anything untoward happening when her grandmother had used it.

'Mother, perhaps now would be a good time to tell Phyllis and Bonnie what you intend to do with the board?' suggested Leona gently. She couldn't reveal that she thought the whole operation ridiculous. Leona didn't believe in life after death. In her opinion, when you died, you just became earth.

'Very well,' Alma replied. She took a deep breath, aware that what she was about to say was going to sound crazy. The Ouija board was one thing, what she intended to do with it was quite another! 'I need to contact my father,' she said. Bonnie and Phyllis did not seem surprised to hear this – after all, the purpose of the board was none other than to communicate with the dead.

'What do you need to ask him?' Phyllis enquired.

Alma's nostrils flared as she readied herself for disbelief, or worse, ridicule. 'You are my two dearest friends,' she said carefully, looking at each woman with a steady gaze, as if challenging their devotion. 'That is why I have invited you here, because I trust you.' She paused, feeling exposed suddenly. Alma was not known to be a sensitive woman, but she was feeling sensitive now. Recent events had cut her to her core. She felt as if she'd shed a skin, leaving her vulnerable. She did not want to be laughed at. 'I need to ask my father where he hid the Potemkin Diamond.'

Bonnie, who was a shy woman, did not allow her face to show surprise. But she *was* surprised. Phyllis was bolder. 'The

Potemkin Diamond?' she repeated, her face ablaze with astonishment. 'Treasure hunters have been searching for that for years.'

'Which is why I need to ask my father directly,' Alma said. A vision floated to the front of her mind: her father kneeling before her and opening his hand slowly, as if he were a magician doing a trick. Cradled in his palm was a sparkling pale-pink diamond, the colour of candy. The many smooth facets caught the light and shone brightly. It was the size of a date. She blinked the vision away. 'He died young and without sons to pass it on to,' she continued, another memory rising like damp to sully the recollection of that rare, tender moment with her father. 'You know how he felt about daughters. He would never have left it to my elder sister, or to me, the final longed-for child who should have been a boy. No, he kept the secret as his father had done before him, and waited for the heir that never came. Oh, what a disappointment I was. All I have is this key, which he always wore about his neck.' She pulled from her blouse a tiny gold key that hung on a chain. 'I need to know where the lock is.'

'But why now?' Phyllis asked. 'What does it matter?'

Alma caught her daughter's eye. 'I need to sell it,' she said tightly, shuffling uncomfortably on her chair.

At last Bonnie spoke up. 'But you're in your nineties, Alma. What would you do with all that money now?'

'I have something very specific I want to do with it,' she replied cagily. 'A dying wish.'

'You're not dying, are you?' Phyllis exclaimed in alarm.

Alma laughed, a rare flash of humour on this dark night. 'I'm approaching a hundred, Phyllis,' she replied wryly. 'I'd say I'm on the home stretch, wouldn't you?'

'So, let's get on with it then,' said Phyllis. 'If you're on the home stretch, we mustn't waste a moment. How do we do it?'

Alma felt better now that she had shared her purpose with her friends, although she wasn't confident it would work. 'A Ouija board is all about the law of attraction,' she said, recalling what her grandmother had told her. 'If you go into it with the intention of playing a game and causing mischief, you will attract a mischievous spirit. That's why we say a prayer and ask for protection prior to using it.'

'That sounds very sensible,' said Bonnie, who looked really quite nervous.

Alma nodded. 'So, let's do that now.'

She closed her eyes. The others followed her example. The room was silent, except for the rumble of traffic outside on Fifth Avenue, and the more distant droning, like the low buzzing of bees, of a city in constant motion. Alma took a deep breath, as she remembered her grandmother doing. It was important to follow Didi Aldershoff's example to the letter. Alma didn't want to admit that she had never attempted to use the board on her own. The last time she had been included in a seance was back in the 1930s when she had gone to stay with her grandmother, who was by then in her late seventies, on Rhode Island. The countryside mansion, referred to ironically as a 'cottage', was an obscenely large Italianate palace facing the sea in fashionable Newport. That, too, had eventually gone the way of the house on Fifth Avenue after Didi passed away in 1951. It was simply a case of economics – and the death throes of that once magnificent phoenix. But a covert fascination in the board had stayed with Alma and remained at the bottom of her consciousness, like a sleeping serpent she was afraid to awaken. She had saved the box from the refuse collectors when her mother had gone through Didi's possessions following her death, but had never had the confidence, or courage, to open it – until now. Desperate times called for desperate measures! She was now going to look the serpent dead in the eye.

'In the name of God, Jesus Christ and the Angelic Realm.' Alma tried to remember what her grandmother used to say. 'Please surround us with your protection and your light as we endeavour to communicate with those in spirit. Please protect this board, this house and all the people in it. Amen.' She sniffed self-consciously. She was aware that she hadn't recalled her grandmother's exact words – she was sure there had been mention of Archangels Michael and Uriel, and something about the forces of evil, but she wasn't certain. It had been a long time ago and, to be fair, she hadn't really listened. She now wished she had. In any case, she had asked for protection and expected it to be given. There were, after all, only so many ways to bake a cake!

The women repeated, 'Amen,' and then opened their eyes expectantly.

'That should do it, shouldn't it?' said Bonnie eagerly. 'No dark entities will be allowed through, right?'

'Right,' said Alma. 'We're all set. Are you ready?'

'Ready as I'll ever be,' Phyllis replied with a sigh. 'I never thought I'd be playing with a Ouija board in the middle of the night.'

'We're not *playing*,' Alma corrected irritably.

Phyllis looked contrite. 'I didn't mean playing. Of course, I didn't mean that.'

Alma's face took on a self-righteous quality in the flickering glow of the candlelight. She rested a finger on the planchette. The nail was coated in claret-coloured polish, the knuckle swollen with arthritis. No amount of jewellery or paint could disguise the ageing body, but Alma had standards and she resolutely stuck to them.

Bonnie inhaled sharply, as if about to plunge into a cold pool, and placed her finger beside Alma's. Phyllis joined her, and, finally, Leona. The room seemed to hold its breath. Alma, when she spoke, adopted the tone of a priest in the pulpit. 'Now, I solemnly call out to my father, Walter-Wyatt Aldershoff, to come forward and make himself known.'

The women did not look at each other but focused their attention on the planchette, alert to even the slightest movement, should it occur. It did not occur. Alma could feel her heart beating hard in her chest, the force of it reverberating into her neck and throat. If she remembered rightly, when her grandmother had summoned spirits, it had sometimes taken a few minutes to get a result. Being an amateur, Alma presumed it might take longer for *her*.

'I repeat. I summon my father, Walter-Wyatt Aldershoff, to make himself known to us.'

Still nothing.

Bonnie relaxed her shoulders; she would prefer it if the planchette didn't move. Phyllis, on the other hand, was now hoping something would happen. They had come this far; it would be disappointing to go to bed without having received a message from beyond the grave. Even a simple 'Hello' would be worth the inconvenience of staying up late.

A few minutes passed. The planchette remained still. Leona dared not look at her mother. She couldn't bear to witness the disappointment or to reveal her scepticism. Alma wanted so badly to communicate with her father, but Leona knew it was futile. The dead were dead and couldn't speak.

Alma wondered whether one had to believe in the board, in which case the chances of it working were slim. She *hoped* her father might communicate through it, but deep down she didn't *believe* that he would. Nonetheless, it was a last resort. The Potemkin Diamond was in this building, somewhere, she was certain of it. The various renovations to the property had not brought to light anything significant, so the Potemkin Diamond must, surely, still be here. Alma knew that her grandfather, being a playful man, had incorporated into the architect's plans secret compartments here and there in which to hide his valuables – he'd never have settled for anything as obvious or pedestrian as a safe. One of those 'clever little hiding places', as he liked to call them, which his wife and son had known about, had been an invisible cupboard built into a decorative pillar in the bar. In there he used to hide his glass of whisky from his wife when he heard her approaching across the hall. Eventually, the bar had been destroyed by developers and so had the secret compartment. But Alma knew there were others, among them the *very* clever little hiding place where he had concealed the Potemkin Diamond. After his death, only his son had known its whereabouts. However, Walter-Wyatt died suddenly of a heart attack at the age of fifty-six, taking the secret with him. He had not concealed the fact that, like his father before him, he had intended to share the information with *his* son, but destiny had not allowed it for he had only had daughters. He had died before choosing an heir.

The only clue Alma had was the tiny key. She had found it the previous week when sorting through her things – she didn't want to leave Leona to have to deal with drawers and cupboards full of useless knick-knacks when she died. Among those useless knick-knacks was a velvet-lined box containing an assortment of buttons and beads that had belonged to her mother. Alice Aldershoff had loved to collect pretty things. Alma had run her fingers through them, wondering why she had forgotten all about them, for they might have done nicely for her own dresses and jackets. She had been overcome, suddenly, by a wave of nostalgia, for she could see in her mind's eye her mother choosing buttons with her dressmaker, Mrs Varga, when her fingertips had settled unexpectedly on the key. Alma had recognised it at once for her father had always worn it beneath his shirt and took pleasure in taking it out and showing it to her. 'This is the key to the clever little hiding place where I keep the Potemkin Diamond,' he would say, and he would tease her, telling her that if she was clever enough to find the hiding place, he'd give her ten dollars. Of course, she never found it. Her mother must have put the key in the button box for safekeeping, even though without the lock the key was useless. But now she had found the key, all she needed to do was find the clever little hiding place the key unlocked. If only her father could come back from the dead and tell her where to find it.

Alma blinked. Her jaw stiffened, her chin lifted, the air was drawn into her nose as she contemplated failure. And then, something happened.

The planchette moved.

Very slightly, but clearly with a force that had nothing to do with their fingers, it shifted. Bonnie gasped. Phyllis opened her mouth in astonishment. Leona's eyes narrowed – she wondered which of the old ladies was making it move. They all stared at the planchette. Suddenly the candle flame began to sizzle and jump wildly on the wick. It seemed to grow, throwing dancing shadows over the walls. Bonnie glanced at them in alarm. They looked like demons released from captivity below ground.

The planchette slid to the word *Hello*. It was so swift and certain, Alma, Phyllis and Bonnie were in no doubt that Walter-Wyatt Aldershoff had, indeed, chosen to make himself known.

Alma blanched. 'Hello, Daddy,' she said in surprise. She blinked hard at the unexpected stinging of tears at the backs of her eyes. She hadn't anticipated feeling emotional, or teary; Alma Aldershoff didn't *do* tears. But at once she was a child again, in the presence of her father, hoping for approval, longing for affection that never came. 'Is that really you?' she asked. Hope flared in her chest. Did her father's soul live on? Was he coming now to speak to her through this magical board? Could it be this easy?

The planchette vibrated. Bonnie's face contorted with fear, but she was more afraid of Alma's wrath were she to pull her finger away than of the spirit now communicating through the planchette, so she left her finger where it was.

With another sweeping movement the planchette slid onto the word *No*, taking the four fingers with it.

Alma gasped. 'You're *not* Walter-Wyatt Aldershoff?' she asked in a small voice.

The planchette vibrated once more and then shuddered. But it remained most determinedly on the word *No*.

Alma's throat grew tight. The temperature in the room plummeted. It was suddenly very cold. She cleared her throat. 'Then who are you?' she managed to say.

At that moment, the candle went out. Bonnie whimpered in panic. Then the table began to shake. 'If it's you, Phyllis, stop it at once!' Alma demanded, glaring at her friend accusingly through the semi-darkness. 'It's not amusing.'

'It's not me,' Phyllis replied as the table shook more violently.

'Nor me,' Bonnie added. 'I wish it was.'

Leona felt the hairs stand up on the back of her neck even though she couldn't bring herself to believe that a ghost was doing the shaking. 'Well, it's not me, neither,' she said.

'Then who is it?' Alma asked in a tremulous voice.

The planchette began to make large circles on the board. Round and round it went, with the ladies' fingers circling with it.

'Enough!' Alma shouted, taking her finger off the planchette. 'Leona, turn on the lights at once!' Leona was only too happy to bring the seance to an end. She made her way across the room, illuminated weakly by the streetlights outside that shone through the gap between the curtains. She found the switch and flicked it. The lights lit up the terrified faces of the women and the rattling table that showed no sign of stopping. Leona looked at it closely, certain that either Phyllis or Bonnie was the culprit.

'What's moving it?' Phyllis asked, lifting her hands off the table to show that it wasn't her and leaning back to look beneath it.

'Well, it's not my grandfather,' said Leona. 'I'm sorry, but if it's you, Bonnie, I think you should own up. It's not fair on Mom.'

Suddenly everything began to move. Books, paintings, lamps, ornaments, chairs, even the floor appeared to tremble as if an earthquake were rumbling beneath Manhattan. Bonnie cried out. 'Alma, what have we unleashed?' Leona reached for the walking stick and thrust it at her mother.

'I don't know.' Alma seized the stick and heaved herself off the chair. 'I don't know what I did wrong.'

'You did nothing wrong, Mom. It's an earthquake, quite obviously.'

'We need to leave at once,' said Bonnie, pushing out her chair and making for the door.

'Wait!' Alma exclaimed. Bonnie froze, hand hovering above the knob. 'Leona, the box. Put the board back in the box. No one must know what we were doing.'

'We can't just leave it like this,' said Phyllis. 'We need to tell it to go away.'

'You're right.' Alma pulled back her shoulders, drawing on the unfailing Aldershoff mettle that coursed through her veins. 'Be gone!' she commanded, thumping her stick three times on the floor. That sounded like the sort of thing her grandmother might have said and three was traditionally a magic number, was it not? 'Be gone, bad spirit. This is no place for you. Go back to where you came from at once.'

But the spirit wasn't listening, or more likely it didn't care. It felt as if a cold wind was blowing through the room, causing everything to shake, and it was getting more violent. 'It's not going away,' said Phyllis in a wobbly voice. 'In fact, it's getting angrier.'

'Maybe it'll go of its own accord, if we leave it alone,' said Alma hopefully.

Bonnie nodded. 'Let's get out of here.' She turned the knob and the four women burst into the hall, shutting the door firmly behind them.

The slick young man behind the reception desk looked at them in bewilderment. The ladies appeared as if they'd seen a ghost. One or two hotel guests looked up from their smartphones and stared. Concerned that something had not been to their liking and aware that Mrs Aldershoff – she insisted on being called by her maiden name – was an important person, the young man crossed the room to speak to them.

'Is everything all right, madam?' he asked in a low voice, directing his question at Alma.

Alma took a breath and lifted her chin. She was about to tell him that everything was perfectly fine when she faltered. She couldn't bring herself to lie. It wasn't in her nature. And, besides, she couldn't silence the din coming from the other side of those double doors or pretend that it had nothing to do with them. The young man frowned and looked past her. It sounded as if they had left someone in the room, a furious someone who was now on the rampage.

There came a smashing noise. A lamp, or a vase, shattering on the floor.

Alarmed, the young man strode to the doors and opened them. What he saw made him cry out in horror.

Chapter Two

Henry Stirling, proprietor of the Aldershoff Hotel, was none too pleased to be awoken in the middle of the night. He had ignored the ringing of the telephone the first time. But when it rang a second time, he assumed that it must be urgent and answered it. Clayton Miller, the night manager who'd made the call, was not the kind of man to panic in a crisis, nor to bother Mr Stirling about it. He certainly wasn't the sort of man who dragged his boss out of bed and begged him to travel all the way across town to give him assistance. The very fact that he had, on this occasion, done exactly those things, was great cause for concern.

Mr Stirling was a meticulous man. He never did anything in a hurry, even when the occasion demanded a certain amount of haste. He was measured, moderate and methodical, always. His alarm went off every morning at exactly ten minutes past six. His pressed grey suit, white shirt and subdued tie, which he had chosen the night before, were hanging on a wooden hanger on the hook he'd screwed into the door of his wardrobe specifically for that purpose. His black shoes were placed on the floor beneath them, polished to such a degree that they shone like onyx, and his underwear and socks were laid out on the upholstered chair in front of the sash window. His bedroom, decorated tastefully in pale greys and creamy whites, was as tidy as a hotel room, and just as impersonal. Mr Stirling liked everything to be just so, and just so it was.

At the age of forty-two he was a handsome man. He had not been attractive in his youth – his features had been too large for his face – but age had worked to his advantage. His forehead was high, denoting intelligence; his deep-set grey eyes conveyed sensitivity and humour; his pronounced nose and full lips expressed strength of character, and his chiselled cheeks and jawbone were indecently good-looking. He knew he was a catch, but Henry Vincent Clarence Stirling was a confirmed bachelor. Love affairs he had enjoyed a few, but he was much too possessive of his independence, freedom and orderliness to share his life with anyone. He simply couldn't cope with the mess.

Now Mr Stirling dressed in unusual haste. On a normal morning, he put his clothes on with great care, checking himself in the mirror to make sure he was elegant and well-groomed, taking his time. He always permitted himself one flourish of colour: a bright silk handkerchief with white polka dots – he only ever wore *spotted* handkerchiefs – stylishly poking out of the breast pocket of his jacket. But at this early hour he was in such a terrible rush that he didn't allow himself the luxury of choosing a silk handkerchief and left the apartment without even straightening the bedspread.

As he sat in the back of a cab looking impatiently through the window at the passing lights of shop fronts and street lamps, he wondered with rising panic what the exact nature of the drama could be. Clayton had not been able to find the words to describe it, only that it involved Mrs Aldershoff, who, in Mr Stirling's opinion, was something of a termagant. Coming from England as he did, where he had rubbed shoulders with the aristocratic world, he did not consider Mrs Aldershoff quite the duchess the Americans believed her to be – or that she believed *herself* to be!

Naturally, the name Aldershoff still carried weight, but, rather like the other once-famous families who'd presided over New York society during the Gilded Age, they had run out of money. In these modern times, money spoke louder than class.

Mr Stirling arrived at the hotel a little after half past one. The façade of the building, faced with pale-grey limestone ashlar, had not been altered since it was built in 1872 in the French Renaissance style, and still gave him a frisson of pleasure every time he laid eyes upon it. It was sublime, with its gothic arches, colonettes and pretty foliate reliefs around the windows. The high mansard roof, covered in grey slate and adorned with dormer windows, turrets and pinnacles, endowed it with elegance and grandeur. It was one of the few Gilded Age mansions to survive into the twenty-first century. Mr Stirling could not understand how the city had condoned the destruction of such staggeringly beautiful art and architecture, not to mention the waste of money. It had cost William Aldershoff the equivalent of seven million dollars in today's money to construct his home. The Vanderbilt palace, the largest private residence ever built in Manhattan, had been pulled down in 1926 to make way for the department store Bergdorf Goodman. Really, how on earth had they been allowed to do that? he wondered. In England, the historic buildings were protected, which, in Mr Stirling's opinion, was a very good thing. A city without a respect for history was a shallow and superficial place.

The lights glowed golden as Mr Stirling walked briskly up the three wide steps that led to the big front doors, making an effort not to reveal how flustered he was. Above him, from an ornate stone balcony, the American flag was motionless, for tonight there was no wind to enliven it.

Clayton Miller awaited him in the foyer, rubbing his hands together anxiously for he did not know how to deal with this extraordinary situation. When he saw his boss, his face relaxed, for now the responsibility would not weigh on his shoulders alone. He could defer the problem to the higher command. If anyone could sort this out it was Mr Stirling, in his calm, unflustered way.

'This had better be good,' said Mr Stirling in a low voice. He took in the young couple sitting at a low table in the far corner of the foyer, and Mrs Aldershoff with her daughter and two friends at another table, drinking what appeared to be whisky, or something similar. They looked sheepish, which immediately raised his suspicion. He had never seen Mrs Aldershoff looking sheepish before. She usually had the air of a general in command of an army.

'I think you'd better come and take a look,' said Clayton. He didn't wait for Mr Stirling to agree but made his way swiftly to the drawing room. He hesitated a moment in front of the double doors. 'Hear that?' he said to Mr Stirling, who was right behind him. A shadow darkened Mr Stirling's face as he listened to the strange shuffling sounds coming from within.

'What the devil is going on, Clayton?'

'That's the trouble. I don't know,' Clayton replied with a shrug.

'Well, open up,' Mr Stirling commanded. It wasn't like Clayton to be so feeble.

Clayton put a trembling hand on the knob and opened the door a crack. The shuffling stopped. It was eerily quiet. Clayton stood aside for Mr Stirling – he wasn't keen to enter the room again. Mr Stirling strode in, typically no-nonsense. Whatever it was, he didn't doubt he could sort it out, and swiftly.

But nothing could have prepared him for the terrifying sight.

It was as if a raging bull had been confined in there, creating havoc. He blanched. His beautiful hotel had been brutally vandalised. The sight of the devastation cut him deeply. How had Mrs Aldershoff and three other elderly ladies managed to cause this much destruction? Lamps were shattered on the rug. Chairs were broken. The table was on its side – that alone would be much too heavy for four old women to move. Almost all the paintings had been thrown onto the floor. Even the curtains had been pulled off the pole. It was pure vandalism.

He was considering how to confront Mrs Aldershoff and demand that she pay for the damage, without descending into rudeness, when there came another loud crash to his left. The last remaining painting, one he had personally chosen at auction in London, crashed to the floor, joining the others in a pile of broken glass and wood. His heart sank. Then he frowned in bewilderment. The nails were still on the wall and, glancing at the wreckage, the hooks were still on the back of the frame. What had caused it to come off the wall? He hadn't noticed any earth tremor.

Mr Stirling took a deep breath. Nothing would be achieved by panicking. With studied calmness, he stepped out of the room and closed the door softly behind him. He looked at Clayton's anxious face. 'Have you spoken to Mrs Aldershoff?' he asked quietly.

Clayton slid his eyes to the four women and dropped his voice. 'She's claiming that she doesn't know what happened.'

Mr Stirling narrowed his eyes. He didn't believe that for a moment. 'I will go and speak with her now,' he said. She had requested a private room in the middle of the night for her and her small party, and demanded that they not be disturbed. He hadn't asked what they'd needed the room for. Well, he was going to ask now.

Alma stiffened as Mr Stirling walked across the hall towards her. He looked very serious. 'Oh dear,' she whispered to her daughter and friends. 'I think I'm going to have to come clean.'

'That would be a good idea,' said Bonnie, who was finding it hard to stay awake. 'Then we can go home to bed.'

Mr Stirling stood before them. 'Ladies,' he said. 'May I sit down?'

'Please, Mr Stirling,' said Alma grandly.

He pulled up a chair between Alma and Leona, then knitted his long fingers and looked steadily at Alma. 'With all due respect, Mrs Aldershoff, I think you owe me an explanation.'

Alma looked small suddenly. Not the grande dame who threw her illustrious name about and expected everyone to fawn. There was something frail about her, as if the veneer of stateliness had fallen away to reveal a frightened little person behind. She lifted her crystal glass to find it empty. 'Might I have another glass of whisky, please? On the rocks. Make it double.'

Leona protested. 'Mother . . .'

'If ever I need a double, it's now!' Alma retorted fiercely. But the fight had gone out of her.

Mr Stirling waved at the manager and delivered her request. The young man, only too happy not to be directly involved any longer, but clearly curious to know what had gone on in that room, hurried off to pour another glass.

'I'm afraid I have unleashed a ghost,' said Alma. She cleared her throat as Mr Stirling stared at her in puzzlement.

'You have unleashed a ghost?' His eyes moved slowly over the faces of the three other women, who nodded in agreement. He wondered whether he was, in fact, dreaming because the whole situation was beginning to feel very surreal.

'It's the board, you see,' Alma continued.

'The board,' said Mr Stirling. 'What board?'

Alma's shoulders dropped further, and she lifted the blue box off the floor beside her chair and placed it on the table in front of them. Her hands were trembling. She was embarrassed to have to admit such foolery. 'The Ouija board,' she said, tapping it with her dark red nails.

'You were playing with a Ouija board?' he asked, incredulous.

'Not playing, you understand,' she said defensively. 'We were trying to make contact with my father, Walter-Wyatt Aldershoff.'

In all the years Mr Stirling had worked in both England and America, he had never heard anything so outlandish, and yet he didn't disbelieve it. Only a fool believed truth was simply what one saw with the eyes. 'Well,' he said evenly. 'You have clearly upset him.'

'No, no.' Alma was quick to respond. 'It's not my father. He made that very clear. It's someone else. Someone else entirely.'

Mr Stirling arched an eyebrow. 'Did they say who?'

'No, they just went crazy.'

Now the proverbial cat was out of the bag, Phyllis cut in excitedly. 'The planchette was moving all over the board. It was possessed by something horrible. Then the table started jumping about.'

'And the candle went out,' added Bonnie.

'It might have been an earthquake.' Leona rashly decided to inject some pragmatism into the discussion. 'Let's not rule that out.'

'It was not an earthquake,' snapped Alma, and the sharp tone of her voice reminded Leona of why she usually chose not to contradict her mother.

The young man returned with Alma's glass of whisky. She put it to her lips and took a gulp. It burned all the way down to her belly, but quickly took the edge off her distress. She inhaled deeply, feeling a little better. 'I told them to go away,' she said.

'Perhaps you should have been a little firmer,' said Mr Stirling.

'What are you going to do?' Bonnie asked, eyes wide and fearful. They all turned to the proprietor expectantly.

'I am going to speak to someone who knows about the paranormal,' he said. 'I am certainly no expert on the subject.' He couldn't help but shuffle uncomfortably on his chair as he said the word 'paranormal'. It wasn't the sort of thing he liked to admit to believing in. But he *did* most certainly believe – he had experienced one or two unexplainable phenomena himself when he'd lived in England. However, he certainly wasn't about to publicise the fact that there might be an unwanted entity lurking about the hotel, especially as Tanya Roseby, the CEO of Manson & Roseby, was due to arrive in a few days. Tanya was the most sought-after PR guru in London and he most keenly wanted her public-relations company to represent the Aldershoff in the UK. Having only recently opened the hotel – and put everything he had, both materially and emotionally, into it – he really needed to raise its profile and encourage people to come and stay. Right now, the place was by no means full. 'This must remain strictly between us,' Mr Stirling added gravely, imagining word of ghosts leaking out and putting people off making reservations.

'Are you going to seal off that room so it can't get out?' Leona asked. She would have offered to pay for the damage, but she didn't have the money, and neither did her mother.

'I will seal off the room while we repair the damage. I doubt very much that we are insured against rampaging ghosts, but I will think of something. If it is, indeed, a ghost, it can surely penetrate walls, so trying to contain it is not an option. I just hope it doesn't intend to do damage anywhere else in the hotel.'

'I'm very sorry,' said Leona, because her mother would never offer an apology; at no time did she believe herself to be in the wrong.

Mr Stirling nodded. No one was sorrier than him for having allowed these women to tamper with things they knew nothing about. Could Mrs Aldershoff not have tried to contact the dead in her own drawing room? 'I suggest you all go home,' he said wearily, getting up. 'I will keep you informed.'

'Maybe it will go away by itself,' said Phyllis hopefully. 'Now it's had its fun.'

'Let's hope,' said Mr Stirling. 'If fun is all it's after.'

He looked at his watch. It was now two o'clock, still time to get some shut-eye. He told Clayton to lock the door of the Walter-Wyatt drawing room and then went home to catch a few hours' sleep. He'd deal with the poltergeist on the morrow.

The following morning, Mr Stirling awoke to rain. It had been a hot September of sapphire-blue skies and sticky humidity, but the streak had broken just before dawn and the heavens had finally opened. He wondered whether this had something to do with Mrs Aldershoff and her Ouija board.

He had barely slept. He dragged himself out of bed and went through his usual routine with a heavy head and an anxious spirit. He had dealt with many crises in his long career, but never one to do with the supernatural. It seemed absurd. Now, in the murky light of a dreary day, he questioned whether he had been too quick to believe Mrs Aldershoff and her friends' version of events. However, three things were crystal clear: the damage to the room was undeniable, the elderly ladies were too old and frail to have caused it themselves, and there was no sign of damage anywhere else in the hotel, which ruled out an earthquake. Something otherworldly was the only explanation, unless they had smuggled someone else into the room with them, someone strong and hot-tempered.

As soon as he arrived in his office, he tracked down a reputable medium through a chain of discreet friends. Hamish McCloud came highly recommended. Getting rid of earthbound spirits was something he apparently did on a weekly basis, there being so many souls stuck on the earth plane, unable or unwilling to move into the light. It all sounded a bit woo-woo for Mr Stirling's liking, but he was desperate – he could not afford for this to come out. Not simply because it would injure the hotel's reputation, but because it would injure *his*. The very fact that he believed Mrs Aldershoff's story would make him a laughing stock. That aside, Tanya Roseby was the best in the business and the UK market was important to the Aldershoff. Mr Stirling didn't want her to be put off and choose to represent one of their rivals instead.

Hamish McCloud arrived at the hotel at eleven. He wasn't at all as Mr Stirling had imagined him – he'd always assumed people in that world to be hippies, pagans or just plain weird Hamish McCloud was none of those things. He was short and stout with a cheerful round face, intelligent brown eyes and curly auburn hair encircling a bald head in the shape of a dome. He wore a raincoat over a pair of beige chinos, a blue cashmere V-neck sweater and a check shirt. On his feet he wore brown suede lace-up shoes, wet from the rain. There was nothing about him that distinguished him from anyone else coming into the hotel. He did not fly in on a broomstick or wear a wizard's cloak. Mr Stirling was relieved.

Hamish McCloud looked concerned when Mr Stirling told him about the Ouija board. He shook his head and rubbed his cleanly shaven chin ponderously. 'Not good,' he said, a faint Scottish accent lacing his Brooklyn vowels. 'Not good at all.'

'The lady in question was trying to contact her dead father,'

Mr Stirling added, hoping more information might be helpful. 'Her grandfather built this very building, you know.'

'She might have tried to contact her father, but she attracted a mischievous spirit in the lower astral instead.'

'The lower astral?' Mr Stirling wasn't quite sure where that was. It sounded like a planet from the Superman movies.

'A place where dark entities lurk. The Ouija board can act as a portal to allow them into our dimension. People shouldn't play with these things. They're not toys. They can be dangerous. But let me see what I can do. Perhaps I can encourage it to go back to where it came from, or, better still, to go to the light.'

'If you can't?'

Hamish looked at Mr Stirling with sympathy. 'Then you'll need to find someone who can.'

Hamish entered the room with Mr Stirling, who closed the door behind them. No one had been in to clear up the mess. Mr Stirling wanted to make sure that whoever – or whatever – it was who had made the mess, had gone. He did not want his staff upset by objects moving about on their own.

'Well, it certainly had a party in here,' said Hamish, putting his hands on his hips and looking over the wreckage in dismay. 'I sense a very dense and angry energy,' he added darkly. 'A male energy. Let's see if we can tell him to go. Might I have a chair, Mr Stirling?'

Mr Stirling bent down to pick up one of the four chairs that had been turned over and was lying on its back on the floor. 'Where would you like me to put it?'

'Wherever you can find space,' Hamish replied. 'Then you can leave me to my work. It's not going to be easy, I'm afraid. But I'll do my best.'

Mr Stirling went into the hall, leaving Hamish McCloud

settling onto the chair, closing his eyes and taking some deep breaths. Mr Stirling imagined the medium would need all the energy he could muster if he was going to get rid of this nasty presence. He wondered how he was actually going to do it and what special talent was required. Was it simply a case of being able to speak to the dead, or did he need to do something else?

Just as he was crossing the foyer to go to his office to check his emails, he noticed a kerfuffle at the hotel entrance. He stopped and watched with a sinking heart as the doorman and two porters rushed to open the doors and escort none other than Mrs Aldershoff into the hall. She cut a delicate but energetic figure as she marched purposefully towards him. She was dressed in her usual black as if she had never come out of mourning. A diamond brooch sparkled on the lapel of her jacket and rings glittered on the bony white hand that clutched the silver dog's head of her trusty walking stick. 'Mr Stirling,' she said when she reached him. 'Just the man I want to see.'

'I'm afraid I have no news yet,' he told her, irritated that she was troubling him for information so soon. Hadn't she troubled him enough already?

Her lips twitched with impatience and she sniffed. 'Might it have gone of its own accord?' she asked.

'I don't know.' Mr Stirling lowered his voice. 'There's a medium at work in there as we speak.'

Mrs Aldershoff slid her eagle eyes to those double doors across the hall and nodded. 'How long will the medium take?'

'Your guess is as good as mine, Mrs Aldershoff,' he answered. 'He has only just started.' Then, reluctantly, because he knew he wasn't going to get rid of her until Hamish McCloud had finished, he offered her a cup of tea. 'Perhaps you'd like to sit in the dining room. It's quieter in there.'

Mrs Aldershoff looked at the double doors again. 'I hope he gets rid of it,' she said and there was a tremor in her voice. 'You know, I didn't sleep a wink last night. Not a wink. I think I was in shock. I was hoping to contact my father.' She sighed crossly. 'If he had tried to come through, he would have been eclipsed by whatever it was that destroyed your room.' She turned her sharp eyes back to him. 'You know, it might not be human. It might be a demon, in which case perhaps you'd better call a priest.'

Mr Stirling was losing patience. 'Allow me to escort you into the dining room, Mrs Aldershoff. Perhaps a nice cup of chamomile tea will calm your nerves.'

She nodded. 'I'd prefer English Breakfast,' she said, glancing one final time at the double doors before following the manager into the dining room.

The dining room at the Aldershoff was one of the most beautiful rooms in Manhattan. With high, vaulted ceilings decorated in rococo *trompe l'œil* in the prettiest shades of dusty pinks and blues, it retained much of its original opulence. If Mr Stirling had thought he could just leave Mrs Aldershoff there, he'd been over-optimistic. 'Sit down, Mr Stirling.' She waved her hand at the empty chair on the other side of the round table. A waiter attended her and before Mr Stirling had had the chance to request tea, she had already ordered it – she was a woman who was used to being in control. 'You know, when I was a girl, this was a sumptuous drawing room.' A dreamy look settled upon her eyes like mist. Mr Stirling had heard this before, of course, but Mrs Aldershoff never tired of telling him, or anyone else for that matter who was prepared to listen. 'I remember it like it was yesterday. The oriental rugs, the gold-framed mirrors and giant palms. In those days they stuffed their rooms with all sorts of treasures. Really, it was like a museum with the wealth of antiques they collected from all over the world. My grandmother, the celebrated Didi Aldershoff, imported treasures from as far away as India and China. Her favourite city, of course, was Paris. But then she did have exquisite taste. Most of the things she bought came from there. This house was the envy of New York. Even Mrs Astor was impressed.'

'I'm sure it was marvellous,' said Mr Stirling, but secretly he was not as impressed as Mrs Astor. As magnificent as the building undeniably was, when compared to the great historic houses of England, a faux French château built only one hundred and forty years ago and crammed with objects bought to create a sense of ancestral history fell woefully short. But to Mrs Aldershoff it was a veritable Versailles.

'I was hidden away, of course, being just a girl. But I spied from the top of the staircase when my parents entertained. And they did entertain, Mr Stirling, most lavishly.'

A waitress brought tea for two in a pretty china teapot decorated with pink roses and green leaves, with matching cups and saucers and a small jug of milk. Mr Stirling poured while Mrs Aldershoff reminisced. She appeared to enjoy talking about the past a great deal more than she enjoyed living in the present, for when her mind travelled back down those old, familiar paths, her whole face softened and her thin lips quivered as if slowly remembering how to smile. At length, Mr Stirling decided she was mollified enough to perhaps be more forthcoming about the reason why she wanted to make contact with the spirit of her father.

'Mrs Aldershoff,' he said when she had finished telling him about the moment her mother had given her her own personal lady's maid. 'Might I be so bold as to ask why you decided to try to communicate with your father now?'

Her eyes, which only a moment ago had been lost in the past, snapped sharply back to the present. She lifted her chin and sniffed. 'You may not,' she replied.

It was a relief for Mr Stirling when a member of his staff came hurrying across the floor to inform him that Hamish McCloud had finished. 'Bring him to me,' said Mrs Aldershoff as Mr Stirling rose from his chair. 'Whatever he has to say regards me as well, so I might as well hear it from the horse's mouth.'

Mr Stirling reluctantly nodded his approval to his member of staff and sat back down again. He would rather have talked to Hamish McCloud on his own, but Mrs Aldershoff was not going to allow herself to be marginalised. A moment later the medium was shown into the dining room. Mr Stirling could tell from his serious face that he had not been successful. His heart plummeted and a wave of despair washed over him. He didn't know any other mediums. If Hamish McCloud couldn't sort this out, who could?

Hamish shook the old woman's hand and then accepted the chair she grandly offered him and sat down. Mr Stirling asked him if he'd like a drink and he requested a double espresso. Mr Stirling noticed that his hands were trembling slightly.

'Is it a demon, Mr McCloud?' Mrs Aldershoff demanded. 'Have I unleashed the devil?'

Hamish looked disconcerted by the old woman's directness. 'Not a demon or a devil, no. But a very angry earthbound soul,' he replied, withering slightly beneath her hawklike gaze. 'By playing with the Ouija board, you've given him a door into our dimension. He's likely excited to be perceived after years of being ignored.'

'Is it still there?' asked Mr Stirling uneasily.

'I'm afraid it is.'

'Is it confined to that room or can it . . .' Mr Stirling barely dared utter the words as the vision of a demon of destruction creating havoc all over the hotel took his breath away. But Hamish finished his sentence for him.

'It can go anywhere. It really depends on its state of mind. It is imprisoned by its own thoughts, you see. If it thinks it can't get out of that room, it will stay there. If it believes it has the run of the building, it might make trouble everywhere. Its reality is a mental construct and we don't know exactly what that is.'

'Where do we go from here?' Mr Stirling asked, struggling to maintain his composure. It was very unlike him to feel rattled.

'Well, if we can find out who it is, we might have a chance of reasoning with it.'

'How do we do that?' Mrs Aldershoff asked.

Hamish looked pleased to be able to deliver something. 'I did manage to get a name,' he said. 'I hope it might help.'

Her eyes widened and she leant forward in her chair. 'What is it? What's the name?'

'Lester,' said Hamish.

'Lester.' Mr Stirling was none the wiser. He looked at Mrs Aldershoff.

'Lester Ravenglass,' she said slowly, pulling that name out from the distant past like a long-buried treasure. 'Well, I'll be damned . . .'

'Who was he?' Mr McCloud asked.

Alma frowned. She hadn't thought about Lester in a very long time. 'He married my sister, Esme, who was twenty-two years older than me,' she said. 'He was an Englishman, Viscount Ravenglass, with a grand estate in Hampshire. You might know it, Mr Stirling. It's called Broadmere. But my sister swiftly divorced him, moved back here and that was that. They didn't have children and we never heard of him again.'

'What was he like?' Mr McCloud asked.

Alma shrugged. She'd never met him. 'Apparently he was dapper,' she replied, recalling what her grandmother had told her, for after the divorce, her mother had never mentioned his name again. 'He wore bright, flamboyant clothes, which were in stark contrast to my father, who was conservative and traditional. I remember my grandmother using that word,' she added wistfully. 'Dapper.'

Mr Stirling arched an eyebrow. 'Do you have any idea why he might be so cross?'

'None at all,' she replied. 'My family lost touch with him after the divorce.' Her frown deepened. She sat back in her chair and folded her hands in her lap. 'Then he died. I wonder why he's come back into the world?'

Mr McCloud looked at Alma steadily. 'I think you'll find, Mrs Aldershoff, that he never left.'

Chapter Three

It was with great regret that Mr Stirling escorted Hamish McCloud to the front door. 'What do you suggest I do?' he asked him as a damp wind swept into the hotel.

Hamish turned to Mr Stirling with a face full of pity. 'I'm afraid some spirits don't *want* to leave.'

'And you can't make them?'

'Not really. Not if they refuse to go. You've got a stubborn spirit here, Mr Stirling.'

'But if he creates havoc in the hotel, the guests will leave. We'll be out of business within the week.'

Hamish scratched the dome of his head. 'You could dabble with priests and shamans, but I doubt they'll make a blind bit of difference in this case.' Mr Stirling's heart sank lower. 'However, there is someone who might be able to help you. She has a reputation of succeeding where others have failed. But you'd have to fly her over from England.'

'I'd fly her over from Australia if I thought she could get rid of it.'

'I think she's the only person who can. She's rather extraordinary. You can contact her through the College of Psychic Studies in London. Her name is Pixie Tate.'

Mr Stirling nodded. 'Pixie Tate. I'll think about it. Thank you, Hamish.'

'In the meantime, I suggest you leave the room as it is and lock the door. People going in and out might make the situation worse, and, if you're lucky, the spirit might stay in there.'

'I will do that.'

'Good luck.'

Mr Stirling watched Hamish disappear up the wet street and then went straight to his office and wrote down the name *Pixie Tate* so he didn't forget it. He'd bear her in mind. But he wasn't sure the situation was bad enough to fly someone out from England. Perhaps this Lester chap would leave of his own accord, if he existed at all.

Alma returned by taxi to her small apartment in Brooklyn. She went straight to her sitting room and sank into her favourite armchair where she stared into the half distance, lost in thought. Ever since hearing the name Lester she had been feeling a little sick. For a start, the fact that the medium had mentioned that particular name proved to her that the soul lived on, because if Hamish McCloud had been a fraud he would not have come up with the name Lester. Who was called Lester? No one but the famous jockey, Lester Piggott, and Lester Ravenglass. That should have been reassuring, but it wasn't. It was unsettling. Sure, she wanted proof of an afterlife, but not from Lester! Then there was the question of why Lester had come through when her father had not? Surely, Lester couldn't help her find the Potemkin Diamond. Lester was a menace, clearly, or he wouldn't have destroyed the room. What did he want? She had specifically called out to her father – why had he not responded? Why had Lester barged his way in? She had *not* invited *him* to the seance!

As far as she was aware Lester had lived and died in England, so why had he turned up here in New York, on Fifth Avenue? She knew he had come out to New York before she was born to court her sister, Esme. Her parents had been thrilled that their daughter was going to become a viscountess. The Aldershoffs had had enormous wealth, but they'd lacked pedigree. By marrying their daughter into the British aristocracy, they'd secured their place at the very pinnacle of New York society, which had been more important to them than almost anything else. The most important thing, of course, as Alma remembered bitterly, had been having a son, but at the time of Esme's wedding to Lester they'd no longer held out any hope of that happening. Then Alice had got pregnant at the age of thirty-nine and Alma had been born, to great disappointment all round. She pushed that painful thought aside and focused instead on Lester. But she knew precious little about him for just as soon as Alma had been old enough to ask questions, her sister had been divorced and back in New York, and Lester's name had no longer been mentioned. Well, she wasn't going to get any answers now. Anyone who knew anything was dead.

She could, however, find out when and how Lester had died. Her granddaughter was good at technology. As a member of the British aristocracy, his death would surely be documented. She'd call Leona and ask her to get Gemma to do some research for her. However, research wasn't going to help her find the Potemkin Diamond, nor was it going to get rid of the ghost. Alma knew she could just walk away – after all, there was nothing *she* could do to help poor Mr Stirling. But the diamond was in the building somewhere and she needed it. She *desperately* needed it. Finally, she had the key in her possession. If it was the last thing she did on this earth, she would find the lock! It would be the only unselfish thing she had ever done in her life.

*

Mr Stirling decided not to tell any members of staff the truth about the incident in the Walter-Wyatt drawing room. He instructed Clayton to fob them off with a story about a group of young people who'd had a drunken party in there and made a great mess of the room. Until it was repaired, the door would remain shut and the room out of bounds. In spite of the readiness with which they seemed to accept the lie, they exchanged whisperings and suspicious glances, and tossed about various conspiracy theories in low voices when out of earshot.

The drawing room was quiet. Mr Stirling hovered about the double doors every now and then anxiously listening out for movement, but there was nothing. Just silence. He was relieved. Perhaps it had been a small earthquake, after all. Nothing to worry about. Panic over. By lunchtime he was beginning to feel a little foolish for having believed Hamish McCloud and for listening to the ranting of four elderly ladies.

But, one by one, small signs that whatever had created havoc in the drawing room was now working its way around the hotel began to occur in the most alarming fashion. At lunch in the dining room, new arrivals Mr and Mrs Sanchez, who had travelled all the way from Spain, were celebrating the first day of their honeymoon when Mrs Sanchez noticed her champagne flute slowly sliding across the table. At first she laughed, thinking it was something to do with a sloping floor, but, then, when she felt what she later described to Mr Stirling as a 'cold breath' on her neck, she screamed and ran out of the room, followed by her extremely concerned husband. Mr Stirling managed to calm her down, explaining that the floor was indeed a little uneven (it wasn't) and that the window was open, thus creating a draught. The young woman took a while to be convinced, but convinced she was in the end. They decided they wouldn't move hotels after all, and returned to the dining room where nothing else untoward happened.

But Lester, if it was Lester, had not finished being mischievous. That afternoon, a couple of children who were running up and down the corridor outside their parents' room were terrified out of their wits when a ghost suddenly materialised at the end of the corridor and screamed at them. They both saw it – a misty white apparition with a big mouth, before it apparently disappeared. That report sounded a bit exaggerated to Mr Stirling, especially as the more attention the children got the wilder their description of the ghost became, but it did not make easy listening. Something was going on.

Mr Stirling could ignore Lester no longer. The children were gleefully racing about the lobby telling everyone their story and some of the guests were beginning to look a little concerned. Lester's mental construct, as Hamish McCloud had called it, was obviously not confined to the Walter-Wyatt drawing room. He was now on the move around the rest of the hotel. Something had to be done. Mr Stirling decided to call the College of Psychic Studies and ask about Pixie Tate.

He was left frustrated, however. The college told him that they would contact Pixie Tate and get back to him as soon as they had spoken to her. He hoped they'd be able to give him her telephone number so that he could call her himself. He explained that this was a matter of the utmost urgency. The woman at the college was very understanding but did not oblige – he imagined they received panicked calls all the time and thought nothing of it – but really, they couldn't imagine what he was dealing with over here. He waited until evening, but they didn't call back. Fortunately, there was no further evidence of Lester bothering the guests, but Mr Stirling had a very uneasy feeling. For one, the hotel had begun to feel distinctly cold. Not a normal cold, either, but a kind of damp cold. The kind of cold one might expect to feel in an old house that hadn't been lived in for a long time. An *unfriendly* cold. He told himself he was just being paranoid, but when an elderly guest complained of it and a bullish man demanded he turn down the air conditioning, he realised he wasn't the only one. The Aldershoff, which only the day before had been hospitable and welcoming, was beginning to feel distinctly resentful. He left that evening with a heavy heart.

That night when he went to bed, he laid his head on the pillow, closed his eyes and tried to think of something else. But he couldn't relax and he couldn't get Lester Ravenglass out of his thoughts. He expected the telephone to ring at any moment and for Clayton to beg him to come to his aid. He imagined Lester tearing through the hotel, terrifying the guests, destroying all the furniture and defacing the walls. In the lonely midnight hours where small worries grew into giant anxieties, Mr Stirling imagined the worst and allowed his fear to feed upon it like a ravenous beast.

Alma stood by her apartment window and gazed out onto the balmy September evening. The light was fading over Manhattan, turning the skyline pink and plunging the streets below into shadow. In the park some of the trees were already beginning to turn, but it wouldn't be until November that they would really start to change to the rich yellows and fiery reds for which Central Park was so famous. She remembered kicking the leaves there as a little girl and was assaulted suddenly by the smell of damp earth and decaying foliage, and a dizzying wave of nostalgia. There was something poignant about the memory, for that time was lost in the past, along with the innocence of childhood and the unbridled joy derived from simple things.

She realised then that she had forgotten how to find joy in simple things.

As she lifted her eyes to the sky, she found a startling beauty in the vast canopy of blue and in the pink candyfloss clouds that drifted somnolently beneath it. Alma was sad suddenly at the thought of leaving the world. There was no point trying to pretend otherwise. She was ninety-eight, the sand in the hourglass was running out. She looked back at the long road she had travelled and saw it as a ribbon meandering into the faraway mists of time, marred with flaws and errors and bad decisions, but also lit up with moments of joy and laughter. She had lived a long time and experienced a great many things and yet, she had never dared ask herself what it was all for. It had been easier to just live rather than to think too hard about the meaning behind it. But she was thinking about it now. Lester turning up had really unnerved her. He was angry. He wasn't resting in peace, at all. Perhaps he had been unhappy in life. If he hadn't been happy, he probably wasn't very nice. And if he wasn't very nice, had he been turned away from the gates of heaven? Alma was scared. Might she be turned away too? She wasn't always nice, either.

But she was trying to be nice now. She was trying to make amends. If she could only find the Potemkin Diamond then she'd be in a position to put things right. She did not want to leave the world without putting things right.

In the sunset of her life, faced with leaving behind everything that had defined her, most notably her name, she wondered what she would take with her. What did she have? And, in a bewildering flash of inspiration, she realised that all the things she'd thought were important, were of no importance at all. None of it. It was quite a revelation. None of it mattered. Least of all her name.

So, what *did* matter? Could it really be such a simple thing?

She dared not look too hard, because, for Alma, love had never been simple. But she realised now that rather like the light at the core of an atom, love was at the core of life. She'd been much too consumed with the wrapping to notice it, or to give it the importance it deserved. Yes, she'd been much too consumed with the wrapping.

But she was considering love now and like a rosy sunrise, it was dawning on her consciousness with the innocence and unbridled joy of a child. She had changed. Honestly, she would have thought she was much too old to change. But change she had, and quite profoundly. The cause of that change had been the devastating and heartbreaking death of her great-grandson, Joshua, who had recently died of a brain tumour. His loss had cut her deeply and the pain she suffered because he was no longer in her life was unbearable. She loved her daughter, Leona – of course she did, even though their relationship had never been close – and she loved her granddaughter, Gemma, too – but there had been something about the love little Joshua had given to *her* that had been unique. It was as if he had come into the world loving her. And the version of her that she'd seen reflected in his eyes had had all the wonderful qualities that she had never possessed. Selflessness, generosity, kindness, patience, tolerance – really, the list could have gone on. In Joshua's eyes she'd been perfect, and, consequently, he'd inspired in her a desire to fulfil that vision.

But now his eyes were closed.

Alma stifled a sob. She pressed her hand against her chest and waited for balance to be restored. She hadn't been able to help Joshua, who had suffered terribly, but she could help others in his name. If she found the Potemkin Diamond, she could help thousands of children just like Joshua and make up for all the selfish things she had done in her life.

She went into her bedroom and opened the bottom drawer in the fine walnut chest of drawers that had followed her from the mansion on Fifth Avenue to their cottage in Newport and finally to this resting place here, in Alma's modest apartment. Among the few treasured items that had not been sold off to pay debts and to sustain Alma in her dotage, was her grandmother's Ouija board. Alma sat on the edge of her bed and placed the box on her knee. She unclipped it and lifted the lid. Another wave of nostalgia washed over her. In her mind's eye she saw the round table in her grandmother's extravagantly upholstered drawing room, the candle burning brightly in the centre, Didi Aldershoff's striking green eyes reflecting the flickering flame in dancing specks of gold. Alma blinked and the vision was gone. Here she was now with the board and none of the skill required to use it. Had she really opened a door for Lester's spirit to come through and wreak havoc? And, if she had, from where had he come? What exactly did earthbound mean? She wished she had asked.

Just then the box began to vibrate in her hands. She gasped in fright and stared, horrified, as the board itself started to tremble inside it. She knew she wasn't making it happen, but whatever it was seemed to be using her body, rather like the spirit had used their fingers to move the planchette.

She felt the blood drain from her face as if it was falling all the way to her feet, leaving her lightheaded with fear. The air around her chilled. It was icy suddenly, and strangely damp. She shivered. 'Is that you, Lester?' she asked in a trembling voice.

The vibrating stopped.

Alma's heart was beating so hard in her chest that her entire body was vibrating with the force of it. 'If that's you, Lester, tell me what you want?' she said more courageously.

The box shook again, to such a degree that Alma lifted her

hands, and the entire thing bounced off her knee and onto the floor. The planchette flew across the carpet and landed by the door. Alma took a sharp breath. 'What do you want?' she asked. But everything was still. The chill disappeared and the room was warm again, as if the window had just been closed, shutting out a winter's night. She remained on the bed, running her eyes over the furniture, waiting for Lester to make himself known again. But he didn't. He was gone.

Alma bent down stiffly and picked up the board and the box, and then went to fetch the planchette. There was definitely a connection between the spirit – Lester – and the board. Of that she was no longer in doubt. With shaking hands, she put it back in the box.

Suddenly the telephone rang. She nearly jumped out of her skin. She put a hand on her chest where her heart raced beneath her narrow ribcage and went to answer it. It was her daughter. 'Hi Mom, it's Leona. I've got some information about Lester Ravenglass.'

It was a dull, overcast morning when Mr Stirling arrived at the hotel. The air was hot and stifling, as if the thick cloud above Manhattan was preventing it from going anywhere, leaving it to stagnate. Even the usual breeze that blew in over the Hudson had died. To Mr Stirling's disappointment, Clayton reported that a French couple had come down for breakfast enquiring whether there had been an earthquake in the night. Apparently, a picture had fallen off their bedroom wall, but the hook had remained on the back of the frame and the nail had still been in the wall. The floor had trembled and everything had trembled with it. Mr Stirling was relieved to hear that nothing had been broken, but the couple were upset. When the wife had brought up the possibility of a haunting, for she could have sworn that she'd seen a shadowy figure walking about the room, Clayton had been quick to reassure her. 'I told her that we occasionally experience tremors,' he recounted to Mr Stirling. 'And the shadowy figure was surely a trick of light. I think I managed to convince her.' But Mr Stirling was alarmed. How long before others reported disturbances? Would they manage to convince them all that Manhattan was being shaken by earthquakes, when earthquakes in New York were almost unheard of? He thought of Tanya Roseby having a nocturnal visit from Lester and shuddered.

By midmorning, Mr Stirling had gone against Hamish McCloud's advice and summoned the team of builders to begin the task of repairing the damage in the drawing room. He couldn't leave it in such a state. The interior designer, the esteemed Nadia Kovach, also came to see what needed to be replaced. Mr Stirling repeated his lie, a little more embellished this time, telling them that a rock star who could not be named had entertained guests in there and, under the influence of too much alcohol, had thrown everything about the room, as rock stars were wont to do. The builders shrugged and got on with their job – they'd seen it all before. But Nadia was appalled that anyone could desecrate her beautiful work and looked as if she might cry.

Just as Mr Stirling was leaving the drawing room, he was confronted by Mrs Aldershoff and her daughter, Mrs Croft, making their way through the hall with purpose. The old woman had a determined look on her face, while her daughter trailed beside her seemingly under duress. 'Good morning, Mrs Aldershoff. Mrs Croft,' said Mr Stirling, forcing a smile, for there was no way of escaping them.

'Mr Stirling,' said Mrs Alderdshoff, striding towards him and pounding her stick loudly on the black-and-white marble floor.

'What can I do for you ladies?' he asked.

Mrs Croft looked typically apologetic. 'May we have a quick word?' she said.

'It won't be quick.' Mrs Aldershoff cut in sharply.

'You may have a slow one, then,' said Mr Stirling agreeably, hoping to extract a smile from her daughter. 'Let's go to the bar, shall we? Perhaps you'd like a cup of coffee.'

'Yes, I would,' said Mrs Aldershoff, striding past him with the usual proprietorial air.

'Thank you,' Mrs Croft added softly. She had the expression of a beaten dog and Mr Stirling felt sorry for her. Growing up in the shadow of Alma Aldershoff could not have been much fun.

Mrs Aldershoff stopped suddenly in front of the stair and rubbed the silver dog's head of her walking stick with her thumb. Mr Stirling thought she seemed a little agitated this morning. 'You know, my mother had a problem with that staircase,' she said, nodding at it. 'She insisted it was unsafe. I had to walk down it with my hand on the banister, one step at a time, even when I was no longer a small child. Of course, when she wasn't looking, I'd race down it, basking in the knowledge that I was breaking a rule. I liked doing that. It was fun being naughty. I never knew why that was. She didn't take any interest in me at other times. Only on the stair.' She chewed the inside of her cheek. Mrs Croft put a hand beneath one elbow, cradling it gently, trying to draw her away. 'Funny the things one remembers.' The old lady sighed and yielded to her daughter. 'This house provokes the strangest memories. I can't remember what I did five minutes ago, but I can remember every time I came down that staircase.'

They sat at a table in the corner of the bar and Leona took her mother's walking stick and laid it behind her on the banquette. The silver dog's head growled silently up at the gold ceiling. Mrs Aldershoff settled into an armchair as if she were presiding over a board meeting. She put her hands on the table and linked her bejewelled fingers. The bar was another sumptuous room, modelled on Marie Antoinette's boudoir at Fontainebleau. However, instead of the silvers and golds of that famous room, Nadia had chosen apple greens and flamingo pinks, and hand-painted scenes of fountains and birds rendered within the wood panelling. The effect was flamboyant, luxurious and fanciful. Even Alma had to admit that they had cleverly kept the integrity of the original home while masterfully reworking it to suit its new purpose. 'In my day this was a drawing room where my mother liked to play cards with her friends,' she told them wistfully, and Mrs Croft and Mr Stirling feigned interest for it would have been impolite to let on that she had already told them that numerous times. 'She had a friend called Elizabeth Harding who was famous for her sleight of hand,' she added with disapproval.

As they drank their coffee, Mrs Aldershoff told Mr Stirling what her granddaughter had discovered by digging about on the internet. 'Lester Ravenglass died at the age of forty-nine in nineteen thirty-seven, at his country estate in Hampshire, England,' she said. 'He passed away seemingly from natural causes, but he was a dreadful alcoholic and goodness knows what else besides. He and Esme, my sister, had no children, and by the time he died he'd run out of money entirely – her money, I might add. I imagine he only married her for her money. The estate was sold and the money vanished settling his enormous debts. Gemma, that's my granddaughter, says that he was a gambler and a reprobate, and very unhappy.'

'As alcoholics tend to be,' said Mr Stirling. 'So what, might I ask, is he doing here?'

'That's a very good question,' Mrs Aldershoff returned.

'What do *you* think, Mrs Croft?' Mr Stirling turned to her with the intention of bringing her into the conversation

– she rarely got a chance to speak – but her mother continued regardless.

'I think he wants to tell us something,' she said ominously. 'So, I think we should listen.'

Mr Stirling's phone buzzed in his jacket pocket. 'Excuse me, ladies.' He got up and looked at the screen to see that it was the college calling. His heart thumped with anticipation. To his intense relief, the woman informed him that Pixie Tate and her partner Ulysses Lozano could come to New York immediately. She gave him Ulysses' number. 'He's awaiting your call,' she said. Then she added kindly, 'I do hope they manage to sort out your problem.'

Mr Stirling couldn't have agreed with her more.

He returned to the table in the bar. Mrs Croft and her mother dropped their conversation and looked up at him expectantly. 'That was the College of Psychic Studies in London,' he told them. 'I'm enlisting the help of a professional.'

'I was under the impression that you already had,' said Mrs Aldershoff tartly.

'Hamish McCloud was not up to the task. But he recommended someone who is.'

'Well, now we know it's Lester, we might be able to reason with him,' said Mrs Aldershoff. 'Why don't I try to do that before you fly somebody all the way over from London?'

'Mother . . .' Mrs Croft protested weakly.

Mrs Aldershoff was already pushing herself up from the chair and there was no deterring her. Her jaw was set with resolve. 'My stick,' she demanded, putting out her hand. Leona obeyed and passed it to her. Alma wrapped her fingers around the silver dog's head and lifted her chin defiantly.

'I'm not sure it's a good idea to go back into that room,' said Mr Stirling, who didn't want Mrs Aldershoff creating any more trouble.

But Mrs Aldershoff was determined. 'Lester was my brother-in-law,' she reasoned, even though she had never met him. 'I think it's only appropriate that I try and find out what he wants.' She strode past Mr Stirling and out into the hall. *Could it be*, she thought to herself, *that for some inexplicable reason, Lester knows where the Potemkin Diamond is hidden?* Was it possible that he knew her question and had come through to answer it? She had never given him a chance.

Mr Stirling followed Mrs Aldershoff into the drawing room. 'Would you give us a moment, please,' he said to the builders. 'Perhaps it's a good time to have a coffee break.'

The builders put down their tools and left the room. Mr Stirling closed the door behind them. He nearly jumped out of his skin when Alma banged her stick three times on the carpet. 'Lester Ravenglass, is that you?' she asked, once more adopting the voice of the pulpit. 'Lester, come out from wherever you are hiding. It's me, your sister-in-law Alma Aldershoff.'

Mrs Croft looked terrified. She stood with her arms hanging stiffly by her sides. Only her eyes moved warily about the room, as if anticipating something to suddenly start flying about. When Mrs Aldershoff banged her stick on the floor again, her daughter's whole body flinched.

'Maybe we were too quick to pack away the board,' said Mrs Aldershoff, almost to herself. 'If I'd only given it a minute, then Lester might have managed to communicate with us. I reacted too swiftly.'

Mr Stirling was keen to get the women out of the room. He didn't want a repeat of the other night. He certainly wasn't going to allow Mrs Aldershoff to have another go with the Ouija board. 'Let's let sleeping dogs lie, shall we?' he said smoothly, making for the door.

'Lester, Lester . . .' Mrs Aldershoff continued with increasing fervour. 'Come on, Lester. Make yourself known to us. What is it you want to say?'

But nothing happened. Everything remained still and silent.

Mrs Croft, looking relieved that the entity hadn't made itself known, hurried out of the room. Her mother banged her stick another time in frustration and then gave up. 'I should have asked him what he wanted,' she mumbled, regretfully following her daughter into the foyer.

'I'm sure Pixie Tate will be able to tell you that,' said Mr Stirling. 'Now, if you will please excuse me, I must arrange her trip.'

'Very well.' Mrs Aldershoff conceded with a sigh. 'Call in the professional from London and let me know when she arrives. She will want to speak with me, of course.'

'I'm sure she will,' Mr Stirling replied, but he hoped she wouldn't. He smiled sympathetically at Leona Croft. 'Good day to you, Mrs Croft.'

'Thank you, Mr Stirling,' she replied, and she looked at him apologetically. 'I hope Pixie Tate is able to sort it out for you.'

'So do I,' Mr Stirling answered, then he watched her escort her mother to the door.

He went to his office and telephoned Ulysses Lozano to make the travel arrangements. He was surprised when Mr Lozano requested business-class seats, but Mr Stirling was in no position to argue – he needed Miss Tate and Mr Lozano, and he needed them fast. He was pleased to hear that they could come out the following day, arriving at the hotel by late afternoon. A couple of nights would be sufficient. Ulysses couldn't say how long it would take, but, after listening in confidence to the details, he sounded pretty certain that Pixie could fix the problem quickly. 'She's everyone's last resort,' he said with a laugh. 'But they should really come to her first.'

It was only when Mr Stirling put down the telephone that he realised that Tanya Roseby and her assistant, Lara Montesino, were flying out on the same flight. He felt a cold sweat ripple across his body and prayed to a God he didn't believe in. *Please don't let Tanya Roseby bump into Pixie Tate.*

Chapter Four

Pixie Tate grasped Ulysses' hand as they settled into their business-class seats on the aeroplane. She was terrified of flying. Given the nature of her business, this was surprising. She was comfortable travelling out of her body, and, indeed, through time, but trusting a man-made machine to carry her safely into the sky was something she was deeply uneasy about. She simply couldn't understand the physics of it. However, she was much more afraid of her mother. The very idea that the woman was now out of prison and hoping to make contact was so appalling that when the College of Psychic Studies in South Kensington had reached out to Ulysses about an earthbound spirit in a hotel in Manhattan, she'd immediately agreed to the job.

Pixie did not want to think about her mother. She'd torn up the letter she'd received a few weeks ago and thrown it in the bin. She hadn't been able to breathe easily since. Thoughts of her mother induced a crippling anxiety, stirring up memories so dark and frightening that she was reduced to a trembling child again, struggling to make sense of what had happened. No, she most certainly did not want to dwell on that.

New York beckoned to her like a life raft unexpectedly and blessedly floating by a drowning woman, even when that life raft was, in itself, decidedly unappealing.

'Champagne, madam?' A smartly dressed air steward with immaculate hair and big white teeth held out a tray of glass flutes filled with the sparkling golden liquid.

'Don't mind if I do.' Pixie leant over and took two, knocking them back one after the other. She grimaced as the champagne fizzed its way down her gullet. The air steward's eyes bulged.

'Do you really need that, Pix?' Ulysses asked, settling into his seat with a contented sigh. He nodded his thanks at the shocked steward and reached for a flute of his own.

'I absolutely do,' she replied. 'I hope it'll knock me out, so I wake up when the plane lands.'

'I don't know what you have to be nervous about. Planes rarely crash. You're safer in a plane than in a car. In fact, you're safer in a plane than crossing the road. You're much more likely to—'

'Okay, I get it. I don't like feeling out of control, thousands of miles above the earth.'

He frowned. 'You who travels through time as easily as most people breathe.'

'That's different. That's perfectly natural. It scares me to think of the great weight of the plane, full of people and luggage, taking off. I mean, how does it do it?' She shuddered and glanced at her empty glasses. 'I think I need another one.'

She made to get up, but Ulysses put a hand on her arm. 'No, you don't, Pix,' he said softly. She looked at him and he saw the genuine fear in her eyes. He took her hand again and squeezed it reassuringly. 'We're in business class, Pix, and I'm with you all the way. Trust me, you're going to be fine. Next stop, the Aldershoff Hotel. Isn't it exciting! We're going to New York!' He let go of her hand and looked out of his pod into the aisle. 'Now I'm going to go and make amends with that rather dishy air steward you've frightened something terrible.'

Pixie shut her eyes, muttering under her breath. With any

luck, she'd fall asleep before take-off. She didn't notice the other travellers lifting their eyes off their devices to stare at Ulysses as he walked past, so devilishly good-looking and golden, like a film star.

'Excuse me?' Pixie heard a woman's voice. She opened her eyes, frustrated that she had shut them for barely two minutes and already someone was disturbing her. The voice belonged to a chic blonde woman who was sitting in the pod opposite her. She had intelligent blue eyes and a full and generous mouth that looked as if smiling was its natural repose. Her English accent was cut glass, but her obvious warmth softened it. Wrapped in cream-coloured cashmere, she exuded elegance and comfort, like a luxurious cat.

'I couldn't help hearing that you're staying at the Aldershoff Hotel,' the woman continued. 'That's where we're headed, too. My assistant Lara and I. It's a very special place.' She gestured at the tall, leggy girl who was striding towards them in a sharply tailored black trouser suit, holding a couple of wine glasses. 'There she is.' The girl gave her boss one of the glasses and put the other on the ledge in the next-door pod. She flicked her long flaxen hair off her shoulders, sat down and switched on her iPad. 'I'm Tanya Roseby, by the way.' Tanya put out a graceful hand.

Pixie sat up, her irritation evaporating immediately. 'Pixie Tate,' she replied, reaching out to shake it. 'What a coincidence!'

'Isn't it.' Tanya smiled. 'Of all the hotels in New York and we're heading to the same one.'

'Have you been before?'

'Only once, for the opening party in the spring. It's an old Gilded Age mansion that's been converted into a rather special hotel.'

'That sounds interesting. Do you know anything about its history? I've never been before and I have a thing for old buildings.'

'It's my job to know its history,' Tanya said. 'My company represents some of the most magnificent hotels in the world. We're going to look at a couple of very unique ones that are vying for our services. The Aldershoff is one of them. It's particularly famous, and infamous, of course.'

'Oh, do tell.' Pixie leant forward eagerly, forgetting her fear of flying at the thought of learning something about the building that harboured the earthbound spirit that refused to leave. She knew at once that there was nothing coincidental about this chance meeting.

'Well, it was built in eighteen seventy-two by William Aldershoff, a Dutchman who came to America as a young man to seek his fortune. He made a massive amount of money in railroads and built a wildly extravagant mansion, as all the new rich did in those days, on Fifth Avenue. At that time there was no inheritance tax and no income tax, so you can imagine how wealthy they became. William's wife, the notorious New York socialite Didi Aldershoff, famously spent over a quarter of a million dollars in today's money on flowers for her debut party.'

'That's a lot of flowers!' Pixie exclaimed.

'Sure is. Their lives revolved around society and money, and nothing was more important than being invited to the right parties and knowing the right people. But the Aldershoffs were, in old New York's eyes at least, new money like Vanderbilt and Carnegie, so the old families like the Astors looked down their noses at them. To the snooty "Old New York", the *nouveaux riches* were very common. So, William Aldershoff bought the famous Potemkin Diamond, which impressed everyone.'

'What was that?'

'One of the most valuable diamonds in the world, more valuable even than the Koh-i-noor. It was given to Catherine the Great of Russia by her lover, Prince Potemkin. William

Aldershoff displayed it in a glass case in the mansion and showed it off to all the grandees – no one declined an invitation to their house after that, not even Mrs Astor. But following an attempted robbery, he hid it, confiding the hiding place only to his eldest son, who inherited the diamond upon his father's death. Unfortunately, Walter-Wyatt died before telling anyone where it was hidden. No one has ever found it. It's been a mystery ever since.'

'Oh, do you think it might still be in the house?' Pixie asked.

'Well, the building has gone through various renovations and no one has found it. William Aldershoff also built a big palace in Newport, by the sea, which is now a museum, but the diamond has never turned up there, either.'

'I love a mystery,' Pixie murmured thoughtfully. She wondered whether she'd be able to find it with a dowsing crystal. 'Are there any Aldershoffs left?'

'Only one of note. Alma, Walter-Wyatt's second daughter, who in spite of having married more than once, still goes by the name Alma Aldershoff. Must be in her nineties. I remember seeing her in Cipriani's in the late eighties. Big hair and shoulder pads and lots of gold jewellery, surrounded by the rich and fashionable. You know the type. They seem to constantly be divorcing and marrying someone else. I'm not sure how many husbands she's had, but it must be at least four.'

'Sounds like quite a character,' Pixie mused.

'Formidable, I should think.' Tanya laughed.

'So, when did the house become a hotel?' Pixie asked.

'In the late nineties. It was owned by a big hotel chain. Before that it was a museum and a club. The lovely thing is that Henry Stirling, who owns it now, has kept the integrity of the original home, so it's unusual. It doesn't feel like a hotel. All the bedrooms are different and incredibly beautiful. The bones of the house haven't changed. He opened four months ago after five years of renovations.'

'That's a long time.'

'Well, he wanted to restore it to its former glory and was meticulous about detail. I'd say he's pulled it off beautifully. One really does feel one's in the Aldershoffs' home.'

At that moment Lara appeared over the top of the divider that separated her pod from Tanya's. 'Can I jump in here?' she asked.

'Of course,' Tanya replied, raising her wine glass. 'Come and join the party!'

'I just want to add that the Aldershoffs were quite unusual. Immensely wealthy, of course, and upwardly mobile like they all were. But what sets the Aldershoffs apart from other Gilded Age families, is their lack of charity,' she said. Pixie noticed the yellow flecks in her washed-denim-coloured eyes and was reminded of a wolf. 'While Carnegie, Rockefeller and Astor gave to the city in a big way, the Aldershoffs hoarded their wealth. It was as if they were afraid of losing it.'

Tanya chuckled. 'But they lost it in the end all the same,' she said.

'They didn't lose only their money,' Lara continued. 'Alice Aldershoff, Alma's mother, had many miscarriages after her daughter Esme was born, which is why there are twenty-two years between Esme and her younger sister, Alma. Some people are just unlucky, I suppose. I read that Alma's great-grandson recently died of an inoperable brain tumour.'

'That's awful,' said Pixie with feeling.

'Luck is something money can't buy,' said Lara philosophically.

'Well, William Aldershoff clearly had luck when it came to making his fortune and building his palace – not to mention the mansion in Newport and the Potemkin Diamond,' said Tanya. 'As so often happens, it's the subsequent generations that squander the wealth. Perhaps they lack the appreciation that comes from having worked hard to make it.'

'Very true,' said Pixie, wondering about the Potemkin Diamond and whether it was hidden somewhere in the hotel.

The captain's voice sounded over the speaker, announcing take-off. Lara sat down and fastened her seatbelt.

'Well, enjoy your flight, Pixie,' Tanya said, draining her glass then pulling a silk eye mask and neck pillow from the enormous bag at her feet. 'I'll leave you alone now, but it was lovely talking to you.'

'And to you both,' Pixie replied, smiling at Lara, too.

'Oh, and I find a good podcast is just the ticket if you're feeling nervous about flying. It's the perfect distraction, that and a couple of glasses of something strong,' Tanya added, with a wink.

Pixie laughed and fastened her seatbelt. She noticed that Ulysses still hadn't returned. She twisted her head round and spotted him in front of the curtain dividing business class from economy. As expected, he was with the air steward from earlier, who was now looking decidedly happier, his cheeks flushed as he flirted with Ulysses. As usual, Ulysses basked in the attention, flicking his hair and seeing how far his charm could get him. From the eager expression on the steward's face, and his obvious delight in Ulysses' pleasure, it would get him very far indeed. Pixie watched as Ulysses brushed a fleck of invisible lint from his uniform, leaving his hand lingering on his chest a touch too long. She knew that he had the steward in the palm of his hand and had no doubt that the poor man would now make it his personal mission on this flight to ensure that Ulysses was as comfortable as possible, as if he were a Hollywood star.

Ulysses was the last to return to his seat. He plonked himself down with a satisfied sigh and grinned at Pixie. 'Miss me?'

'No,' she replied. 'I've been making friends of my own.'

He reached across the aisle and gave her his hand. She took it. 'You're going to be fine,' he said firmly. 'We're going to have a *very* pleasant flight.'

Pixie squeezed his hand as the plane's engines roared and then propelled them up the runway. With a rapid lift the wheels left the tarmac and the plane soared into the sky. Pixie concentrated on her breathing, in through the nose, out through the mouth, until the plane eventually levelled out and the overhead signs were switched off. Feeling calmer, she let go of Ulysses' hand and rolled her eyes as he pretended to nurse it.

She pulled out her headphones and tried to follow Tanya's advice by listening to a podcast. But she couldn't concentrate for long – her mind was whirring with everything that Tanya had told her about the Aldershoff Hotel – and so eventually, she gave up the struggle and switched to music instead. Yet, in recent weeks, whenever she allowed her mind to wander, she ended up following it into the past, and, inevitably, to Cavill. She'd never forget the first time she saw him, the jaunty way he had skipped down the stairs, in a blue morning coat and shiny leather boots, toying idly with a black top hat. His brown hair had been tousled, his handsome face softened by a confident smile and his cornflower-blue eyes had twinkled with amusement.

Beside her, she heard Ulysses snort slightly as he fell asleep. In a way, it was a relief to be alone with her thoughts for a while, no matter how painful they were. She had fallen in love. *That* had never happened before and it had knocked her for six. She knew that Ulysses didn't understand her feelings for Cavill Pengower. How could he possibly understand? The man who had so totally and completely conquered her heart had died in 1943, seventy-one years ago.

To Pixie, though, it was as if he had been gone merely months, not decades, and she still pined for him – absurd though it was, her heart ached for him as if it had suffered a deep and searing wound that would never heal. In a strange way Pixie didn't want it to – that pain connected her to him and made him feel real to her, when her head insisted on trying to convince her that it had simply been a dream. Only Ulysses and Avril Merivale, her teacher and mentor from the College of Psychic Studies, knew that she had a unique gift – not only was she a gifted psychic, but she was a timeslider. She was able to slip through time and possess the body of another person. Her last slide had taken her back to Victorian Cornwall and into the body of a beautiful young governess called Hermione Swift. It had been when she'd been Hermione that she had met and fallen in love with Cavill Pengower. Cavill, in turn, had fallen in love with Hermione not knowing that it was *she*, Pixie, who'd looked at him through Hermione's eyes, and that it was *her* heart that had loved him. Even now she was tormented by the question of whether Cavill had noticed a difference in Hermione when Pixie had left and returned to her own time. Did he love Hermione still? Or had the part of her that he had loved disappeared with Pixie. Pixie would never know.

Even though she had explained timesliding to Ulysses, she knew that he would never fully get his head around it. She could *explain* the paradox of time, but she couldn't make him *comprehend* it. She could tell him that time did not exist, that there was only ever the Now, which meant that, technically, everything was happening all at once – no past, no future, only ever *this moment*, but, having no experience of it, he could only take her word for it.

Pixie had been a small child when she'd first slipped out of her body. She'd heard her parents fighting in the kitchen downstairs, their sharp voices cutting each other to shreds. She'd curled into a ball beneath the covers at the bottom of the bed, squeezed her eyes shut and willed herself to be somewhere else. And, just like that, she had risen out of her body and found herself in a peaceful meadow where she'd been all alone. Where no one could hurt her. There'd been only flowers and bees and sunshine there. Distracted by the beauty around her, she had basked in the serenity of this secret place that had become hers and hers alone, whenever she'd needed it. Only later had she learnt that she hadn't travelled to another place, that she was, in reality, in exactly the *same* place, only decades prior, before her house had been built, when it had simply been a field. When she'd realised what it was, she'd coined a word for it: timesliding. She had her parents to thank for that. Without their vitriol, she would never have had to find a way of escaping. The fact that they had always made up – until they didn't – was irrelevant. Their fights used to terrify the life out of her.

In those days she had travelled as herself, but without a body she had only been able to observe the goings on, and for a brief space of time. Later, with the help of Avril Merivale, she had discovered that by linking into a person's energy via an object and making clear her intention, she had been able to possess the body of someone else and live for a longer duration in the past. At that point things had got more interesting and she had discovered a use for it: helping settle lost souls stuck between worlds to move into Spirit.

There were, however, unwritten rules that made her task more complicated. A timeslider carried an enormous amount of responsibility. It was paramount that she tampered as little as possible with time to avoid altering the future. What might seem a small change could possibly result in something massive later down the line. It was known as the Butterfly Effect – one small flutter of a butterfly's wing on one side of the world could cause a hurricane on the other side. Pixie knew that when she'd met Cavill, she'd broken that cardinal rule: to leave the past how you'd found it. She had interfered. She had fallen in love and altered the course of his life, and his heart. Who knew what she had set off?

As she lay listening to music with her eyes closed, she wondered yet again whether he had noticed a change in Hermione when Pixie had ceased to possess her. Had he found her lacking? Or had he loved her as much. How deep had his love been? These questions troubled her, but they were futile and a total waste of energy, because she would never learn the truth.

And what did the truth matter, anyway? She would never see Cavill again. It might as well have been a dream.

Chapter Five

Mr Stirling looked at his watch. It had just gone four in the afternoon. The plane would have landed by now and his guests would be well on their way to the hotel in two separate vehicles he had deliberately arranged to keep them apart; he didn't want Pixie Tate to divulge to Tanya Roseby the reason for her visit. He hoped she'd get rid of the ghost – if it were such a thing – before it had a chance to put Tanya off. He very much wanted her to represent the Aldershoff.

It was a relief, therefore, when the first sleek black Lincoln Town Car drew up outside the hotel and the bellhop opened the passenger door for Mr Stirling's most important guest. After a moment's pause, one patent black stiletto alighted onto the pavement, then the second, and Tanya Roseby, in a pair of dark sunglasses and a soft white coat, emerged into the light.

Mr Stirling appreciated glamour and Tanya Roseby did not disappoint. Wrapped in luxurious pale cashmere with an expensive designer tote bag hooked over her arm, she was the epitome of fashionable London. Accompanied by her young assistant, equally elegant and polished, they made a glossy pair. Mr Stirling introduced himself with enthusiasm, shaking their hands firmly and escorting them into the hotel. He politely enquired after their journey and asked whether they would like something to drink while they checked in from the comfort of a pair of purple velvet armchairs. 'A Bellini, perhaps? Or a cordial. It's not too late for a cup of coffee.'

'I think Bellinis would be nice, don't you, Lara?' said Tanya, taking off her coat and draping it over the back of the chair. 'Let's start as we mean to go on, shall we?' she added with a smile. Mr Stirling was charmed. Her smile was the kind that could infect an entire room with a party spirit.

Tanya Roseby was used to being fawned over by hoteliers but had never allowed herself to grow spoilt or jaded from the attention. Fawning hoteliers were always a delight, and she settled herself into the chair with a contented sigh. Mr Stirling summoned a member of staff from Reception, giving orders that she show them to their rooms as soon as they were checked in. 'The Bellinis are on their way, Miss Roseby,' he said. 'Please, make yourselves at home.'

Satisfied that his most important guest was happy, he turned his attention to his two other guests who were now making their way into the foyer. It was a relief that their car had arrived a decent time after Tanya Roseby's. Mr Stirling was immediately struck by Pixie Tate's unconventional appearance. With her long black crocheted coat and pink hair, she cut a bohemian figure. In fact, if she'd been carrying a broomstick in place of her carpet bag, it wouldn't have surprised him. His skin bristled with the fear that he'd flown a charlatan all the way from London, and in business class too! However, his dismay at Miss Tate turned swiftly to wonder when he laid eyes on the excessively handsome man who eclipsed her. In fact, he didn't think he'd ever seen such an attractive human being. Ulysses Lozano, Mr Stirling deduced with mounting enthusiasm – the person he had spoken to on the telephone.

'Welcome, Mr Lozano,' he said, turning to the man with

a fresh and eager gaze. 'How kind of you to come so quickly, Miss Tate,' he added. He shook the young woman's hand and was disarmed momentarily by the surreal shade of her blue eyes. They really were an extraordinary colour, like lazulite. With tact honed over many years in service, Mr Stirling ushered them to the other side of the room where he could speak with them without the fear of being overheard. 'We are in dire need of your assistance,' he said in a low voice after enquiring politely after their journey. The three of them sat down on the plush armchairs arranged around a low table. 'I sought the help of a medium I found here in Manhattan, but he was unable to get rid of the disturbance. I'm very much hoping, indeed, I'm praying, Miss Tate, that you can succeed where he failed.'

'Please call me Pixie. I'll do my best,' she said, folding her hands in her lap. 'Tell me what happened.'

Mr Stirling would have felt uncomfortable discussing such a whacky subject with anyone else, but these two subscribed so wholeheartedly to the world of whacky that he launched into the story betraying not a whiff of his doubt. He filled them in on Alma Aldershoff's disastrous attempts to contact the dead with a Ouija board and confessed that, had he known what they had intended to do, he would never have given them permission to use the room. 'I'm not sure what they were playing at, she and her accomplices, but they seem to have attracted a spirit that they believe is Mrs Aldershoff's brother-in-law, Lester Ravenglass.' He coughed to disguise his unease. Really, the whole thing sounded ridiculous. He inhaled sharply. He was committed now and had no alternative than to fully embrace it. 'Mrs Aldershoff later came back with more information. Lester died an alcoholic in nineteen thirty-seven, aged forty-nine.'

'Did he die here?' Pixie asked.

'No, he died in England.'

'Okay, so something has drawn him back here. Either Alma Aldershoff herself or this building. Can you take me to the room where the seance took place?' she asked. Then added, to Mr Stirling's dismay, 'It would also be helpful to meet Mrs Aldershoff too.' Mr Stirling did not relish the idea of involving Mrs Aldershoff any more than she had already involved herself.

Mr Stirling glanced warily at Tanya and Lara, who were now being shown across the hall to the elevator. Once they were safely out of sight, he hastened to the double doors of the Walter-Wyatt drawing room, turned the glass knob and strode in. The builders had left for the day and the room was quiet. The broken picture frames and pieces of furniture had been taken away and the place looked tidy once again. He closed the doors behind Pixie and Ulysses, and folded his arms with a shiver. In spite of the seasonal warmth outside, the air in the room was cold.

Pixie immediately sensed the presence of a confused and miserable soul. It was as if it was coiled up in the corner like a snake, watching them suspiciously. As she tuned in, she managed to see a murky energy, rather than a human form, building like thickening smoke. 'I think you'd better leave me to it,' she said, anticipating another rampage. Mr Stirling was only too pleased to abandon the room.

'Shall we wait in the bar?' he suggested to Ulysses, who followed him into the hall.

Ulysses smiled and Mr Stirling found him so full of charm and mischief that he smiled back like a schoolboy experiencing his first crush. 'I never pass on the opportunity to enjoy a cocktail,' said Ulysses, his Brazilian accent transforming his words into music.

'Good,' said Mr Stirling, and his unease lifted at the prospect of enjoying a quiet moment alone with this captivating man. 'I have a feeling your friend Pixie is going to see off the ghost,' he added, keen to ingratiate himself.

'Oh, she will,' Ulysses replied with confidence. 'One way or another, she always does.'

Pixie sat down on one of the upholstered chairs that had escaped the rampage, closed her eyes and focused. She took a few deep breaths. She felt the energy in the corner of the room growing thicker as the earthbound spirit, consumed by distress and confusion, gathered enough power to make itself known. It wasn't easy for disembodied souls to grab the attention of the living due to the difference in vibration, theirs being so much lighter, but this spirit seemed to have mastered it somewhat. The energy grew into a mud-brown funnel of smoke, like an uncurling snake, at least that's what it looked like to Pixie's clairvoyant eye. It then began to move towards her. *Are you Lester?* asked Pixie in her mind, sensing the drop in temperature and the alarming weight of negativity the spirit carried. This was not a nice spirit, she realised, but a very troubled one. 'Lester,' Pixie repeated, this time out loud. She opened her eyes. 'I'm here to help you move into the light.' The energy whooshed past her, brushing her cheek and shoulder, and causing the curtains to billow behind her. 'Lester, is that you? Are you Lester, or are you someone else? I'm here to help you, whoever you are. You're stuck and I can help you find your way out.'

Pixie was surprised that the spirit didn't respond. They usually did. On the whole they were eager to make contact and relieved to be seen after having languished between worlds, invisible and alone. But this spirit was mute. Pixie tried a few more times to communicate, but either the spirit didn't want to, or it couldn't. She closed her eyes again and sat a while without making any further attempts to converse. She linked into its energy. She picked up the vibration of a man in middle age, with a long, chiselled face and deep-set, dark eyes framed by heavy eyebrows. His hair was a light-brown colour and tousled, falling slightly over a high forehead. He was wearing a white collar sticking up at his throat, a tie and jacket. Clothing appropriate for early Edwardian society. And then, as faint as a whisper on a breeze, she heard two words. 'Yes. Lester.' The name was unmistakable. He was, indeed, Lester Ravenglass. The question was, why didn't he want to leave?

Ulysses and Mr Stirling sat at a table in the bar, deep in conversation. Ulysses was enjoying a Martini, but Mr Stirling, aware that he was on duty, was simply drinking sparkling water with a slice of lime. When Pixie walked in, they stopped talking and beckoned her over. 'It *is* Lester Ravenglass,' she said, pulling up one of the velvet armchairs and sitting down.

Mr Stirling couldn't help being sceptical. If he hadn't told her that Mrs Aldershoff believed the ghost to be her brother-in-law, would she have come out with a different name?

Pixie continued. 'But he doesn't want to move on, or he can't. I need to find out why. That's going to take a little more time. I suggest I leave it for tonight and give it a proper go tomorrow morning. Might Alma Aldershoff be available to talk to me? It would help to know a little bit about him.'

Mr Stirling sighed. Although he didn't want to involve that woman, he was prepared to tolerate her if it meant there was a better chance of getting rid of her dastardly relation. 'I can give her a call. She lives in Brooklyn,' he said, inwardly grimacing at the prospect of her coming back and taking over. 'However, she confessed that she never knew him. He might have been her brother-in-law, but he was a good twenty-nine or so years older than her. Plus, he lived in England. Her sister divorced him and returned here. They had no children. Little else is known about him. I'm not sure Mrs Aldershoff is going to be that helpful.'

'Lester must have come here at some stage,' said Pixie thoughtfully, biting her thumbnail. 'Something is drawing him to the house.'

Mr Stirling shook his head and pursed his lips in irritation. 'That woman and her Ouija board.' He sighed again.

'Yes, she's given him a portal into our world. But we can encourage him to go to the light.'

Mr Stirling wasn't too sure what 'the light' meant. It sounded rather trite to him and once again he felt his stomach lurch with doubt. His cheeks burned with embarrassment. Was he being taken for a fool? 'If he doesn't find the light, maybe he can make himself useful and tell us where the Potemkin Diamond is hidden,' said Mr Stirling with a nervous chortle. 'I assume you've heard the story of William Aldershoff's famous diamond?' he added.

'I have,' said Pixie.

'Well, while you're in conversation with him, perhaps you might ask him.' He meant it as a joke, to make himself feel less foolish, but Pixie took him seriously.

'It's certainly a possibility,' she replied, looking at him earnestly. 'As a soul still attached to the earth plane, any avarice and materialism would remain part of his character. He would be the same, only without a body with which to indulge his desires.' She lifted her tapestry handbag off the floor and delved inside. The bag seemed full of things and Pixie rummaged about to find what she was looking for. At last, she pulled out a small suede pouch and poured an amethyst and chain into her palm.

'This dowsing crystal will tell us if it's in the house,' she said with a grin. Mr Stirling noticed her crooked teeth. But her smile had a sweetness to it and he felt himself warming to her. She placed her elbow on the table and let the crystal dangle on its chain from her thumb and forefinger. 'Let's ask whether the Potemkin Diamond is in this house, shall we?' She trained her blue eyes on the amethyst with intent.

Mr Stirling did not believe in dowsing crystals, but he was willing to go along with it – mainly because Ulysses thought it a marvellous idea. 'How much is the diamond worth in today's money, do you think?' Ulysses asked Mr Stirling.

'Around four hundred million, apparently,' Mr Stirling replied. 'At least, the last time I read about it, that was the figure.'

'Bloody hell!' Ulysses gasped, mouth opening wide with astonishment. 'That's a hell of a lot of money.'

'Those Gilded Age tycoons were indecently rich,' said Mr Stirling.

Ulysses nodded. 'I'm surprised no one's torn the house apart to find it.'

'Trust me, they've done their best. You see, William Aldershoff had a quirky sense of humour. He boasted that he'd hidden it in such a clever place that no one would ever find it. After his death, jewels and other treasures were found in odd places – for example, they discovered that the ornamental wooden ball at the bottom of the staircase was capable of being opened. He'd hidden some valuables in the hollow cavity there. A secret compartment was found in one of the legs of the large sideboard table in the dining room. There was a hidden drawer in his desk where he'd concealed papers. It seems, he did not believe in a safe. He used to say, apparently, that the least safe place in a house was a safe, because that's the first place a robber will look. I think he took great pleasure in devising clever hiding places that would fool the most seasoned thief. The trouble was, he and his eldest son, Walter-Wyatt, took that knowledge with them to the grave. I don't suppose Walter-Wyatt expected to die young.'

'No one does,' said Pixie. She was staring into the crystal and it was beginning to quiver.

'What's it saying?' Ulysses asked, leaning forward.

Mr Stirling shook his head. This was getting stranger by the minute. What was Pixie going to pull out next? A crystal ball? A deck of tarot cards? As much as he was thrilled to be in the company of Ulysses, he was rather wishing he'd given his impulsive invitation to Pixie Tate a little more thought. He was beginning to fear she was a total fraud.

Pixie gave it a moment, silently asking the question: *Is the Potemkin Diamond in this building?*

'No,' she replied firmly as the amethyst began to circle in an anticlockwise direction. 'Definitely not. No point tearing the place apart then. It's not here.' As much as Mr Stirling doubted the power of the crystal, and Pixie Tate, he couldn't help but feel disappointed with the result.

'That's a shame,' said Ulysses, pulling a sad face. 'I was hoping you'd find it, Pix, and make us both rich, for surely with such a find there would be a reward.'

She laughed. 'I don't know why you assume I'd share my reward with you.'

He grinned. 'Because you love me?'

Pixie rolled her eyes and dropped the crystal back in its pouch. She glanced at Mr Stirling. 'The trouble is, everyone does.'

Mr Stirling smiled at Ulysses. He could quite believe it.

The Aldershoff was the most exquisite hotel Pixie had ever seen. With its grand marble staircase, panelled walls and doors, oriental rugs and gold-framed paintings, it felt more like a private home than a hotel. 'It was my most ardent desire to restore this building to its original magnificence,' Mr Stirling told them as he gave them the keys to their rooms. 'My intention is that you feel as if you are back in New York's Gilded Age, but with all the modern conveniences of the twenty-first century.'

'I think you've done a great job,' said Pixie, gazing around her in wonder. However, there was something about the staircase that caused her to stop at the foot of it and gaze up ponderingly. It might have looked golden to the naked eye, but to Pixie's psychic eye it looked as if it languished in the shade. Everything around it shone with a gilded radiance, as if the sun were shining upon it. But the stair was dull, as if the sun could not reach it. Something had happened there that had left a decidedly negative energy. She didn't know whether it had anything to do with the earthbound spirit. But she would certainly find out.

Mr Stirling, taking her interest in the stair to be admiration, added, 'This staircase was one of the finest in New York. It was designed by the architect Richard Morris Hunt in imitation of the Château de Blois in the Loire. The style is Louis the Twelfth. He also designed the stair for Mrs William B. Astor's mansion, but I believe *this* stair surpasses the beauty of even that.'

Pixie and Ulysses took the elevator to the second floor. Every one of the thirty-six bedrooms was different, as Pixie discovered when she left hers to find Ulysses in his. Pixie's room was papered with graceful hummingbirds and pink beebalms, while Ulysses' depicted peacocks perching on the delicate branches of a magnolia tree. She flopped onto the sumptuous bed with a sigh. Ulysses, who was hanging up his clothes, even though he was only staying for a couple of nights, knew what she was going to say from the woeful tone of her sigh. 'You're going to have to slide, aren't you?' he said.

Pixie put her hands behind her head and pulled a face. 'I really don't want to. I don't think, after the last time, that I have the energy.'

'Of course you do,' Ulysses said encouragingly. 'You need to move on from the past and from Cavill Pengower. In fact, here's an idea, Pix – you need to fall in love with someone *living*. The best way to get over a love affair is to have another one.'

'Easy for you to say.'

'Of course, because mine are just affairs.'

She laughed. 'You wait. One day someone will break your heart and then you'll know what it's like to suffer in love.'

He shrugged. 'I don't think I'm cut out for love. I'd rather avoid it, to be honest. You're not exactly giving it a good review, are you.'

'If suffering is the price I have to pay for loving Cavill, and being loved in return, I am happy to pay it ten times over. I'd rather love and lose than go through life with a cold heart.'

'Oh, Pix. You're so dramatic. There's more to life than love.'

'That's where we differ. You see, I think life is all about love. That's what we're here for.'

'Then I'm in the wrong place.'

'No, you're not. You're just sleeping. Someone will wake you up eventually and then you'll realise what you've been missing. What you've been hiding from.'

'You concentrate on what you're here to do, Pixie, and leave my heart, or lack of one, to me.' From the serious expression on his face, Pixie knew to change the subject.

'This Lester person is a real linguini,' she said, using the word they had coined for an earthbound spirit who lingered and refused to move on. 'He's not going anywhere and he's not talking to me, either. God knows what's keeping him here, but he has no intention of leaving and he's bent on creating havoc. I wish people wouldn't play with Ouija boards when they know nothing about them. Mucking about with the paranormal is a dangerous game. If I don't move Lester on, he's going to destroy this place. Alma Aldershoff has no idea what she's unleashed.'

Ulysses took his leather washbag into the bathroom and she watched him lining up his cosmetics and creams in tidy rows. 'I think a new slide will do you good,' he shouted. 'Consider it a holiday. You slide back to when this was a private house, preferably in summertime, and swan about in luxury.'

'That's all very well if I slip into the body of a wealthy lady, but what if I slip into the body of a kitchen maid?'

'Or an *old* maid!' He chuckled.

'By the law of attraction, I will slip into the body of someone with a close match to my own vibration. That's what I've learnt so far about timesliding. It is, of course, a work in progress and I'm still learning. So, old women are out, as are men. Of course, an object will link me to a person, but if they don't match me vibrationally I'll slip into the body of someone close to them. My point being that even if Alma Aldershoff gives me something of Lester's, I won't slip into him. That's just not possible.'

'That's a shame. Wouldn't it be interesting to discover what it's like to be a man?'

'Perhaps. I'd come back and understand *you* better!' She laughed at the thought.

He emerged from the bathroom and looked at her fondly. 'You know, if you were telling anyone else about this, they'd think you were crazy and put you away.'

'I know, which is why you're the only person I can tell.'

'I'd love to time travel. I'd like to slip into the body of someone really hot!'

'You don't need to time travel for that,' she replied with a grin.

'Just think of the mischief I could get up to.'

'You get up to enough mischief here. Anyway, you'd have to be careful. You can't change the future and you have to be mindful of the person you've taken over. You can't leave them in a mess when you slide back. You have to have as little impact on the past as possible.'

'But you fell in love, Pix. If that isn't impacting the past, what is?'

'I know. I didn't mean to. I couldn't help it. I'm not saying I'm especially good at this. It's a learning curve. Which is why I'm scared of sliding again.'

'Why? Because you might fall in love?'

'No, that will never happen,' she retorted firmly. 'I don't think I'll ever fall in love again, in the past or the future. I'm just scared of finding myself in a situation where I'll want to change things but can't.'

'You see, that's what I find hard to digest. You go back into the past, which doesn't exist any more. Everyone is dead. And yet, they're all going about their business not realising that where you come from, they no longer exist.'

'That's the paradox of time,' said Pixie. 'If there is infinity, there is no past and no future, only the eternal present, which means everything is happening all at once.'

Ulysses shook his head and closed his suitcase. 'Okay, Pix, my head is spinning now. Enough of time and space talk. What are you going to do?'

'I don't want to, but the only way I'm going to get rid of Lester is to slide back and find out what happened in the past that is preventing him from accepting his death and moving on.'

'Good. Then that's settled. Let's go downstairs and have dinner, I'm ravenous!'

Chapter Six

Alma gazed at the photograph of her great-grandson and her chest suffered the usual stab of pain, for even though her mind knew that he had gone, her heart was resistant to the truth and, therefore, every time she contemplated his face, she experienced the same sense of disbelief and bewilderment that his death had at first aroused.

Joshua stared out with big brown eyes full of innocence and wonder. The world had been new and exciting to him, the road ahead abundant with possibilities. He could have been anyone, done anything. He might have made something of his life or he might have squandered the opportunities, but he hadn't been given the chance to find out. He'd lived only five years, but in that short time he had shared more love than many shared in a lifetime. He had touched the hearts of all those he met, with his courage, with his peculiar and baffling wisdom, with his joy and enthusiasm that shone even when his small body was weak and suffering. Even then his love never dimmed and he still found more to give. It had awoken Alma, as if from a deep slumber; igniting in her a light that she now recognised for what it was: love. And she was sorry that it had taken nearly a century to discover it.

Alma had known loss, lots of it – her father had died when

she was fifteen, her sister Esme had left the world thirty-five years ago, and Alma had buried two husbands, but none of those deaths had impacted her in the way that little Joshua's had. The power of her reaction astonished her, being as it was so visceral. She grieved for her great-grandson with all her heart, and in so doing she grieved for the love she hadn't given. Because now she knew what love was. She regretted her failure to love her daughter and granddaughter, her husbands and her friends, in the manner that they'd deserved. That's not to say that she had never felt affection or tenderness; she had in her own way – cautiously, distantly – but the love she had felt for Joshua and the pain at losing that love had rendered all other shades of it inferior. Joshua had inspired in her a deeper affection that was totally selfless. For the first time in her life, she'd loved someone more than she loved herself, unconditionally, and it hurt. Oh, how it hurt, right to the marrow of her bones. Real love hurt.

When she looked back to her own childhood, the memory that shone brighter than all the others was the one of her parents coming to kiss her goodnight. She'd pretended she'd already been asleep and, believing that their daughter wouldn't hear, her father had said to her mother, 'What a tragedy it is that she was not born a boy.'

And her mother agreed. 'I so longed for a boy,' she said mournfully. 'And now it is too late.'

Alma never cried. She had wrapped her heart in an iron shield to protect it from the ache of not feeling wanted and she had retreated into herself, growing selfish and inconsiderate of others. She had never *allowed* herself to cry. But she had cried when Joshua had left the world and she had cried a lot since. And she had tried to make sense of life and her purpose here on earth. As she faced her own death, for surely it wasn't far away, she scrabbled about in the dark for answers. What was it all for? Would she be reunited with Joshua? Would she be reunited with those who had loved her? Would she be given the opportunity to say she was sorry; she just hadn't known how to love and she hadn't dared trust it when it was shown to her.

Joshua had been Alma's only great-grandchild. The moment Alma had looked into his crib and those misty eyes had stared back at her, a spark of recognition had ignited within her, like the striking of a match that had never before been lit. The effect had been momentous. She'd *known* him. Of course, that wasn't possible. She couldn't know someone she had never met before. But she'd recognised him on a deeper level, in the love that had flooded her heart and filled it with something warm and sticky, like honey. She had felt love like that once, she was sure of it, because it felt so familiar, but she couldn't say when or for whom she had felt it. Nevertheless, in that moment of recognition, a veil had been lifted and she had crossed into a world where love and pain walked hand in hand – for with the discovery of love came the fear of losing it.

As soon as Joshua could speak he called her Mamie, even though his mother had tried to give her the name Great-Granny Alma. Joshua had invented a word that had been his alone and Alma had basked in the fact that it was special and unique, and created only for her. She was his Mamie and that name seemed to have a touch of magic because every time he uttered it, the honey in her heart warmed and spread into every corner of her being.

Joshua hadn't been more intelligent than other toddlers and he hadn't been quicker to learn to speak or read or walk – in fact in those respects he'd been quite delayed. He'd shown no signs of being especially brilliant. But he'd had enormous charm and a strange, otherworldly wisdom that had revealed itself when he'd become sick with an aggressive brain tumour. He'd only been four years old, a frail little thing in an oversized bed with his head bald and his skin as thin as tissue paper. But he'd looked into his great-grandmother's stricken face and smiled beatifically. 'Don't be sad, Mamie. I'm going home,' he'd told her.

Alma had been so taken aback, she didn't know what to say. He added, squeezing her hand to comfort her, 'I'll wait for you there.' When Alma told Leona, her daughter thought she was making it up – no four-year-old child would ever say such a thing. But Alma wasn't making it up. And Joshua said many other strange things that belied his tender age and limited experience. He was certain he was going home and very confident of what he would find there. 'Do you know, Mamie, the colours are very different. There are colours you haven't even seen before. You wait. You won't believe it.' And those were not the words of a little boy, but a wise old man, and Alma believed herself in the presence of an angel.

She spent many hours at his hospital bedside, playing with the finger puppets he made, and precious moments stroking his brow and telling him stories when he was sent home to die; when the pain got too much, when it was so much bigger than him and he struggled to bear it. Never once did he lose courage. Alma did. Watching him suffer was torture and she wished that she could have borne it for him. But Joshua endured it bravely and always managed to rally and surprise everyone with a smile. In fact, the closer he got to leaving the world, the more light seemed to shine out of him. The more serene he became, and expectant. Indeed, he welcomed death like a familiar friend who was once again coming to escort him home. 'I'm not scared of dying, Mamie. There's nothing to be scared of. You aren't scared, are you, Mamie? Because I'm not.' And Alma didn't share those words with Leona. She kept them to herself and ruminated on them long and hard.

And she wanted to believe in heaven too. In a place where she and Joshua would be reunited. But a worry simmered in the pit of her conscience. A worry she couldn't articulate to anyone else, because she was too ashamed. What if she didn't deserve to go to heaven? She wasn't even sure she believed in God. That's why she needed to find the Potemkin Diamond. She had a grand scheme, but she needed the money to pull it off. It was her only hope. Her only hope of redemption.

The telephone rang. Alma put the photograph in its silver frame back on her bedside table and answered it. 'Hello?'

'Mrs Aldershoff . . .'

'Mr Stirling? Have you news?'

'Pixie Tate, the woman I was telling you about, has arrived and would like to meet you, if you're able to come by.'

Alma's heart gave a skip. 'Oh, yes, I can come by.'

'Perhaps tomorrow morning. Shall we say ten?'

'That would be fine. Has she said anything? Has she communicated with Lester?'

Mr Stirling cleared his throat. 'Only to say that it is, indeed, Lester Ravenglass who is haunting the hotel. I'm confident that she can see him off, but it would be helpful if you could come and tell her a bit about him.'

Alma didn't have much information, but she would try to dig out a photograph. 'Very well,' she said. 'I'll see you at ten.'

She turned her eyes to the photograph of Joshua and her thoughts focused once again on the Potemkin Diamond. She felt for the little key that hung about her neck and rubbed it between her thumb and forefinger. 'Please,' she whispered, thinking of her father. 'Tell me where it is.'

Tanya lay propped up against fat white pillows in the sumptuous bed of the Didi Aldershoff suite, the most expensive suite in the hotel. It comprised a large, harmoniously proportioned bedroom and sitting room, complete with fireplaces and the original white marble chimneypieces, a lavish bathroom and a walk-in wardrobe. The ceilings were high and embellished with elegant plaster cornices, the walls covered in hand-painted chinoiserie wallpaper depicting cherry blossom and hummingbirds. The floor-length curtains, fashioned in a delicate blue silk, were drawn to shut out the streetlights, the windows closed to mute the noise of a city buzzing with activity, but Tanya got a delightful taste of what it must have been like to have lived at the turn of the last century, when this had been a private house. Mr Stirling had, indeed, done an excellent job in restoring the building to its original grandeur, or at least in giving that impression. What a pleasure it would be promoting the Aldershoff to the UK market. She wondered whether she should cancel the second hotel she was going to look at because she couldn't represent both, due to a conflict of interest, and her heart was already set on this one. With its history and unique charm, it would have little competition. She smiled with satisfaction and closed the novel she'd planned to read, placing it on the bedside table along with her reading glasses. It was nine o'clock American time, but two in the morning UK time and she was exhausted.

She turned to switch off the bedside lamp. Just as she did so, her attention was caught by a shadow moving slowly across the wall. She blinked. She must be seeing things. She recalled the margarita cocktail she'd had in the bar and the red wine, more than one glass, she'd enjoyed with her dinner. Certainly not enough to give her hallucinations! She closed her eyes and rubbed the bridge of her nose. Then she looked at the wall again.

The shadow was still there.

She stared at it, anticipating it moving again. It had no defined shape. It was like a cloud or a smudge, and the size of a scatter cushion. As she stared at it, her heart thumping frantically in her chest, it shifted. She caught her breath and sat up sharply. She looked around. She decided it must be a trick of light. What else could it be? She blinked a few times and focused on it again. To her astonishment, it began to grow. Her eyes widened and her mouth opened in disbelief. Surely, she wasn't drunk enough to be seeing things? She really hadn't consumed that much alcohol. Had one of her drinks been spiked?

Just then the shadow seemed to morph into the shape of a figure. It began to take on a human form. A head, arms, legs. Tanya climbed out of bed, awake and alert suddenly. She walked slowly towards the wall to get a closer look. Her first thought was not that it might be a ghost, but that it was the effect of a breeze coming through the window and moving the curtains to make it *look* like a ghost. She put her hand against the wall and the shadow stopped moving *beneath* it. It defied logic. Tanya was baffled. It appeared that the form was not created by something moving in front of a light, but was in the wall itself.

For a moment, both Tanya and the shadow remained still. The hairs on the back of her neck stood up and a cold draught encircled her ankles. She felt as if she was being watched. Did she see the dark form of a hand in the wallpaper, reaching towards hers, or was it simply her own shadow? When she stepped away in alarm, it vanished.

Pixie stood by the window and gazed out into the night. The lights of New York shone brightly and she sensed the excitement in the heightened energy of this city built on rock. It had a unique resonance that vibrated up from deep in the earth and into the soles of her feet. She knew she wasn't going to sleep much; the energy was too invigorating.

It was thrilling to be in New York. Pixie had never travelled this far from home. When she'd been a child, living with her grandmother, they'd gone once to France. She remembered white sand and pink shells, and burning, because her English skin was pale and unaccustomed to such strong sunshine. Then, when she was at Manchester University, she and Ulysses, whom she'd met at a society for students interested in the paranormal, had made a trip to Bruges and stayed in a quaint little hotel on the canal. She remembered sitting in a café in Burg Square and talking for hours over cups of coffee and chocolate cake. She didn't remember much about what they'd talked about, but she remembered the silences in their conversation very well, because they'd been comfortable. The silence that settled softly about two people who were totally at ease in each other's company. She'd only ever experienced that before with her grandmother. Pixie had never had a friend before, being so different to everyone else, and the sudden realisation that Ulysses liked her, perhaps not in spite of her eccentricities, but because of them, caused her instinctive mistrust to evaporate. She'd experienced a dawning, like the blush of a first love, and at that moment she had allowed Ulysses into her heart, where his affection had expanded into the cold, dark corners and infused them with warmth and light. He had done much to assuage her fears, old fears from a childhood scarred with unhappiness, but he wasn't enough to dispel them completely. No one could do that but her, and she wasn't ready to face them.

Her thoughts drifted then to Cavill. His gentle face floated into the window of her mind and she closed her eyes to see him better. His tender gaze, the colour of cornflowers, the jocular curve of his lips, the angular line of his jaw, the contours of his features over which she had run the tips of her fingers and committed to memory. He came back to her, like a melody whose chords were at once familiar and unique, and she felt his energy as if he were standing before her. A sharp pain stabbed her chest and she put a hand there to relieve it. What had she done to deserve such an impossible love? Now, having experienced it, she was certain that she would never find anything close to it in her present life. She could tell herself a thousand times that he'd died decades ago, that she could scour the world and never find him, for he was gone for ever, and yet there persisted still a fragile flame of hope that no logic could snuff out, however rational. For Pixie knew that if there was no time, if everything was happening in the now, then surely they weren't separated at all. It was only perception that kept them apart. But how to shift her perception and find him, she didn't know. Was she mad to think it could be done?

She drew away from the window and climbed into bed. Tomorrow was going to be testing, she knew that. She didn't feel ready to slide. The last one had ended so traumatically, she wasn't sure she had the strength to go through something like that again. Yet, she knew she had to help Lester find his way home. She couldn't leave him, or poor Mr Stirling, whose business Lester threatened. And no one but she could do it.

She switched off the light and lay in the semi-darkness, gazing up at the ceiling. She did not want to be disturbed by Lester, but she knew there was a good chance that he would come; sensitives like Pixie were bright beacons of light to lost souls like him. Most came seeking help, but Lester appeared not to want help. He appeared to want to create havoc, which was clearly a result of his unhappiness. Now that he had been brought into this dimension, perhaps he was keen to explore the possibilities and see how far he could affect the living, who, up until now, had been unaware of his existence.

She lay awake and alert for some time, expecting Lester, but Lester did not come.

When she finally slept, she expected Cavill. But Cavill did not come either, not even in her dreams.

Chapter Seven

The following morning dawned over Fifth Avenue with bright sunshine and cobalt-blue skies. The rumble of traffic and sporadic wailing of sirens reminded Pixie of where she was, and what she was here to do. She climbed out of bed with a heavy heart and opened the curtains. New York appeared to her as the concrete jungle it was known to be. Skyscrapers rose high above the treeline, their glass cladding reflecting the light and shining sharply. She wondered how it had looked in Lester's time. Smaller, certainly. But she didn't feel ready to find out.

She was not looking forward to slipping through the veil of time and sliding back into the past. Even though she was in New York, she'd find herself in Cavill's time once again. He'd be older, of course, for he'd been in his late-twenties in 1895 when she'd fallen in love with him, and he'd be far away in Cornwall. Still, to know that he was on the same planet as her would be agony. So close and yet thousands of miles away, and no chance of meeting him. What would be the point, anyway? She would be someone else entirely and he would be married to Hermione. Hermione, whom she had possessed for those two weeks. Oh, if she could be Hermione again, even for a moment, just to feel his arms around her once more.

As she showered and dressed, she wondered how long this

slide would take. How much time would she need in the past to set Lester Ravenglass free in the present? When she had travelled back to St Sidwell Manor to find out what had happened to Cordelia Pengower, she had needed eleven days. Due to the elasticity of time, what had been nearly two weeks for her had been merely a few hours for Ulysses, who'd kept watch to make sure that she had not been disturbed out of her trance. Those ten days had taken their toll, not only because she had fallen in love with Cavill, but also because she had grown fond of little Felix Pengower too. His death had affected her deeply and she had carried that sorrow with her into the present. It had altered her profoundly. How could it not? She wasn't sure she could take another blow like that, for even though those events had happened a long time ago, Pixie had had to live through them and her experience had been very real. It would take every ounce of courage to slide into the past again. She hoped it would be quick and less traumatic. For certain, she would make every effort not to get emotionally involved this time. She would slide in, do her job and slide back, like she had done lots of times before, and not allow herself to be affected in any way.

She knocked on Ulysses' door. A moment later it opened. He stood before her with his hair wet and swept off his forehead, in a blue shirt and jeans. 'Did anything go bump in the night, Pixie?' he asked, grinning at her mischievously.

'Thankfully not. I don't think I need to ask you the same question.'

'I gave up trying to see spirits many years ago.' Which was true. In spite of joining the paranormal society at Manchester, and joining in every workshop and lecture, Ulysses had never once had any unearthly experience. 'Are you ready for your slide?' he asked.

'No.'

'But you're going to do it, right?'

'I have to.'

'Then you need a full stomach. Come on, let's go and check out the breakfast. It's not every day that we get to enjoy a free banquet in a five-star hotel!' He slipped past her and set off down the corridor.

The dining room was busy. As they followed the member of staff through the tables Pixie was aware of the usual stares as Ulysses' beauty drew eyes off smartphones, iPads and newspapers, and her long pink hair caused a few curious looks. She knew that they made an incongruous couple.

They were seated at a table by the window and ordered coffee from the waitress who seemed only too delighted to take Ulysses' order. Then they looked at the menu. 'Okay, Pix, what's it going to be?' Ulysses asked excitedly. 'Pancakes with maple syrup, waffles, bagels, bakery basket with Vermont butter and homemade preserves, eggs – in a dozen different ways – yogurt, granola, oatmeal—?'

'You know I don't eat breakfast.' Pixie scanned the menu indecisively. 'But it does look tempting.'

'When was the last time you ate breakfast in a place like this?'

'Never.'

'Then make the most of it and order a feast. I know I will.' The waitress returned and Ulysses ordered more than any human being could possibly eat, and Pixie asked for the bakery basket.

Ulysses was tucking into scrambled eggs and smoked salmon on toast when Mr Stirling appeared, debonaire in his suit, purple tie and matching silk handkerchief in his breast pocket. 'I trust you slept well,' he said, looking hopefully from one to the other and clearly not failing to appreciate how handsome Ulysses looked, fresh from the shower.

'Very well,' Ulysses replied.

'Me too,' said Pixie. 'No visit from our resident troublemaker.'

'Then I will leave you to enjoy your breakfast.'

'Oh, I'm certainly enjoying mine,' said Ulysses with a laugh, piling as much scrambled egg onto his fork as was humanly possible.

Mr Stirling was relieved. He hoped the ghost had gone. Clayton Miller had not reported any paranormal activity in the night and, so far, no one had complained of any disturbances. Tanya and Lara were having breakfast in their rooms before their meeting with him and his marketing team at eleven. The only disturbance came on the dot of ten when, with the usual commotion, Alma Aldershoff arrived with her daughter, Leona Croft. Mrs Aldershoff was leaning heavily on her stick. Her bony white hand seemed scrawnier than usual. It resembled a claw. She looked frail, as if she had aged suddenly. As if she had been defeated somehow, or simply given up. He wondered what had happened to her in the last twenty-four hours to so diminish her.

Mr Stirling noticed too, on greeting them, that Mrs Croft was carrying the dreaded Ouija board in its distinctive blue box. He very much hoped that she did not intend to use it.

'I'd like to see Miss Tate alone.' Mrs Aldershoff announced this in her usual lofty tone. Mr Stirling was surprised to feel relief that her voice retained its punch.

'Are you sure, Mom?' Mrs Croft asked, her thin face crinkling with concern.

'I'm sure,' her mother replied curtly. She did not go on to explain why. But Alma never felt the need to explain anything, and her daughter wished she hadn't asked.

'Of course,' said Mr Stirling. 'Why don't you come into the dining room and I'll introduce you.' Mrs Aldershoff sniffed her approval and followed him across the hall and through the double doors.

Pixie saw Mr Stirling approach with a frail-looking woman leaning on a walking stick and knew at once that she must be Alma Aldershoff. She was birdlike in stature, but formidable in gaze, which settled sharply on Pixie with ill-concealed surprise. It must have been her pink hair, she deduced. From the conventional manner in which the old lady was dressed, it was not inconceivable that Pixie would come across as alarmingly quirky.

'May I introduce Mrs Aldershoff,' said Mr Stirling in a formal voice. 'And her daughter, Mrs Croft. Pixie Tate and Ulysses Lozano.' Both Pixie and Ulysses got to their feet. Alma Aldershoff had the air of a queen and both felt compelled to show her due respect.

Pixie shook Mrs Aldershoff's hand. It was bony and cold. 'It's a pleasure to meet you,' Pixie said.

The elderly woman appraised Pixie with a hawklike regard and did not return her smile. 'I hope you are good at your job,' she said, and then added, 'Much depends on it.'

Leona Croft's demeanour was apologetic and Pixie sensed that her mother had dominated her all her life and even now, in her sixties, she had not learnt how to stand up to her. 'It's lovely to meet you,' Mrs Croft said, and she shook Pixie's hand with a limp hold.

'Give Miss Tate the box, Leona. The table, please, Mr Stirling.'

Pixie took the box Mrs Croft gave her. She suspected it contained the Ouija board, but she decided to wait until Mrs Aldershoff mentioned it before she made a comment. Mr Stirling showed Mrs Aldershoff and Pixie to a table at the far end of the room and pulled out an armchair for the older woman. 'Put the box on the banquette,' Mrs Aldershoff said to Pixie, waving her bejewelled fingers as to a servant, and sank into the chair with a groan.

Ulysses invited Mrs Croft to join him while they waited, and taking the chair Pixie had vacated she glanced anxiously over at her mother.

'Pixie will look after her,' said Ulysses kindly. 'She's experienced at this sort of thing.'

'I do hope so,' said Mrs Croft, turning her eyes back to Ulysses. 'She's been acting very strangely recently. I'm not sure what's got into her. One minute she's the autocrat she's always been and the next minute she's as terrified as a mouse.' She sighed. 'It's good of you both to fly out from London.'

Ulysses grinned and her face softened and smiled with him. 'Are you kidding? It's a joy. I wouldn't have missed coming here for the world!'

Mr Stirling reluctantly left the room. He would have liked to spend more time with Ulysses, but work did not allow it. He needed to go to his office and prepare for the meeting with Tanya and the marketing team. He hoped that whatever Alma Aldershoff and Pixie Tate were up to, they would be discreet.

Mrs Aldershoff handed Pixie her walking stick as if Pixie were a lady-in-waiting and settled into the armchair. Pixie admired the silver dog's head in order to put the other woman at ease, for she seemed tense and suspicious, and then leant it carefully up against the wall. 'It was my grandfather's,' Mrs Aldershoff told her, lifting her chin. 'William Aldershoff, who built this mansion.'

'It's beautiful,' Pixie replied and slipped onto the banquette opposite.

'It was made especially for him in London.'

'How lovely to have something of his to remember him by.'

Mrs Aldershoff sniffed. 'Oh, I never knew him. He died before I was born.'

Pixie wished she were as charming as Ulysses, then she'd have more chance of getting the woman to break into a smile. The waitress came to the table and Mrs Aldershoff ordered a pot of tea. Pixie, who had already had a cup of coffee, ordered a glass of orange juice. 'Tell me about Lester,' she asked gently once the waitress had gone.

'I see Mr Stirling has filled you in,' said Mrs Aldershoff, arching her thin eyebrows.

'I linked into Lester myself last night,' Pixie informed her. 'Dapper man in Edwardian dress.'

Mrs Aldershoff's lips curled a little in surprise and Pixie got the feeling that if she won her trust, the woman might crack a bit to reveal a soft centre, like an egg. 'Dapper. That's the word my grandmother used for him,' she said quietly. 'Dapper. Yes, he *was* dapper.' She paused a moment, for that word brought her grandmother back to her. She could almost smell her floral perfume. 'I never met Lester. But I do have a photograph of him.' She unzipped her handbag and took out a white envelope. Pixie noticed that her burgundy nail polish was chipped, which seemed odd because everything else about her was so immaculate. 'This is the only photograph I have of him,' she said, handing Pixie the envelope. 'On the day of his engagement to my sister, Esme, who was twenty-two years older than me. Lester was Viscount Ravenglass. He owned a large estate in Hampshire and a townhouse in Mayfair. His father died when he was twenty-three years old, and he inherited the title and the properties that went with it. His marriage to my sister lasted barely four years. They had no children. She divorced him and came back to New York, not before he spent all her money.' She laughed wryly. 'He became an alcoholic. That's all I know. I have no idea why he's here. He came to New York to court Esme, but after their marriage he never returned. My mother sold this house when I was fifteen, after my father died.' She smiled sadly and swept her watery eyes about the room. 'I'm sure Mr Stirling told you, but this was once my home.' She frowned and her shoulders dropped. 'Feels like another life now. So long ago.'

Pixie could relate to that. She hadn't been back to her home since leaving it as a child and moving in with her grandmother. She wondered whether, were she to revisit that house, it would *feel* like home. She didn't think it would. She'd been too young, and too unhappy. Like Alma Aldershoff, that time belonged to another life.

She took the photograph out of the envelope and studied it closely. Lester had a distant expression, as if he was distracted, and he looked very serious. But then people never smiled in those old photographs. Early photography was a lengthy process that required the sitter to remain still for several minutes. It was no surprise that no one wanted to hold a smile for that long. 'I tried to make contact with him in the drawing room yesterday,' she told Alma. 'But he was having none of it. I'm not sure whether that's because he's unable to communicate or because he doesn't want to. I gather he made a right mess of that room.'

The light returned to Mrs Aldershoff's eyes. 'He did. It was terrifying. It was as if I'd unleashed a poltergeist.'

'You certainly unleashed a very unhappy spirit.'

'I've brought the board,' said Mrs Aldershoff suddenly, as if Pixie's readiness to believe her story gave her confidence to share it. Pixie lifted the blue box off the banquette and placed it on the table. 'I was trying to contact my father but got Lester instead.' Mrs Aldershoff sniffed with frustration. 'I'm not sure how that happened. The board belonged to my grandmother, you see. She knew how to use it. I should have paid more attention, but I wasn't really into that sort of thing.'

'I see,' said Pixie thoughtfully. 'But you're into it now?'

Mrs Aldershoff looked bashful. She paused while a waitress brought the tea and orange juice, and then resumed speaking, lowering her voice. 'I need to contact my father,' she said, lifting the delicate china teacup to her lips. 'I need to ask him something. There's something he knows that no one else knows. It's important to me.'

'What do you need to ask him? Perhaps I can help you there.'

Mrs Aldershoff sighed. 'Maybe you can. I don't know what you people can and can't do. You see, my grandfather bought a very precious diamond in the late eighteen-nineties and hid it somewhere in this house to keep it safe. My father, his son, was the only member of the family who knew where it was hidden, but he died without sharing that information with anyone. He wanted a son, but he got me.' She sniffed again and pulled a face. 'I was a great disappointment to him.' Pixie noticed hurt inflicted long ago darken Mrs Aldershoff's face and felt her heart swell with compassion. She, too, had grown up without her father's love, but for a very different reason. She pushed the thought away and concentrated on the elderly woman. 'Anyway, I'm certain it's here somewhere. I need to know where it is. I thought, if I could contact my father, he might be able to tell me. It was a last resort. Foolish, really.' She pulled a small key on a gold chain out from beneath her blouse. 'This fits into a lock somewhere. But a key is useless without a keyhole.'

'I've heard about the Potemkin Diamond,' said Pixie.

Mrs Aldershoff laughed bitterly. 'Everyone knows about the

diamond. It's one of those urban myths. Everyone has a theory. Some say my grandfather buried it in the park and hid a map in the house. Others that he buried it at our cottage in Newport. But I know it's here. I just know it.'

Pixie did not want to disappoint her, but she felt compelled to tell her the truth. 'I used my dowsing crystal yesterday with Mr Stirling,' she said. 'As far as I can tell, the diamond is not in the house.'

Mrs Aldershoff's eyes flashed suddenly. 'It *has* to be here,' she retorted. 'My grandfather wouldn't have hidden it anywhere else but here. It has to be here, don't you see?'

'Maybe I'm wrong,' Pixie conceded quickly, but she knew she wasn't.

With a trembling hand, Mrs Aldershoff lifted her teacup to her thin lips and took a sip. Pixie observed the gold jewellery and coiffed hair, and sensed beneath the refined veneer a deep weariness. Alma Aldershoff was not long for this world.

The old lady put down her teacup and her thin shoulders slumped beneath the padded jacket, which suddenly looked too big for her small frame. 'My great-grandson died of a brain tumour. He was only five. A dear little thing. He was very special to me.'

'I'm sorry,' said Pixie with feeling.

'So am I. That little boy had something. I don't know what it was. I cherished him more than I've ever cherished anyone. Then he died.' She shook her head and sighed laboriously, as if it hurt her chest to inhale. 'I've been thinking about death a great deal recently. We all know that's where we're headed, and yet somehow we believe it won't ever happen. Well, I'm in my nineties now, so I can't pretend it's something that only happens to other people, because I'm staring it in the face.' She fixed Pixie with eyes that revealed both her sorrow and her fear. How different she was now to the grandiose woman who had shaken her hand not even an hour ago. 'Tell me, Pixie, what is this life for?'

The shell had indeed cracked, and Pixie saw her soft and tender centre, and her heart went out to her. 'That's the biggest question there is,' she replied gently.

'But you people have all the answers, don't you?'

'I think I have *some* answers, but I certainly don't have all of them.'

'Well, what do you *think* it's all for? Why are we here? Why am *I* here?'

'To live the best life you can, and to learn,' Pixie said simply, picking up a small silver spoon from the table and toying with it. 'That's what it's all about. You're here because you chose to be here. You chose all the obstacles and challenges because you needed to grow. Before you came down here, you worked out a plan. Whether you've stuck to that plan is anyone's guess. But you had a plan. A list of things you needed to do, people you needed to have relationships with, things you needed to experience. Well, that's what I believe.'

'Will I be judged when I get up there? I mean, will they rap me on the knuckles and tell me I've done a bad job? You see, I haven't got much time left to put things right.' Mrs Aldershoff's eyes watered and she averted her gaze, dropping it to her teacup.

Pixie felt the impulse to reassure her and reached out to touch her hand. It was still cold. 'No one judges you, Mrs Aldershoff, but *you*.'

'So, I've just let *myself* down then?'

'I don't know. Have you?'

The old lady took a staggered breath as if struggling to breathe beneath a great weight that lay upon her chest. 'I can't say this to anyone else, but I can say it to you, because you don't know me and I can tell from your eyes that you're a good person.' She blinked a few times and lowered her voice to a whisper. 'I've been selfish. I didn't realise how selfish, until I lost my great-grandson. Then I woke up. It was as if I had been hit between the eyes by a light. It was revelatory, actually. Biblical. Sounds silly, but I cried for the first time in eighty years.' Her voice softened and the lines on her brow deepened. Her shiny blue eyes lost their focus and hovered somewhere about the surface of the table. 'I watched him die, you see, and I cried.' She put a hand against her heart. 'I *felt*, and I *hurt*. And I realised then that I had never truly felt or hurt before. And then I thought of all the people in my life that I had hurt. People who had loved me.' She looked steadily at Pixie. 'My great-grandson was the first person I had ever really loved, and he was taken from me. The moment I learnt to love, I lost it. That's not fair, is it?'

'If your great-grandson hadn't died, you might never have learnt that lesson. Maybe part of *his* plan was to leave the world early to teach people like you something important about themselves. We all have our purpose, Mrs Aldershoff.'

The elderly woman looked at Pixie and her eyes took on a feverish sheen. 'I need to find that diamond,' she said. 'There was a time when my family was one of the richest in America, but we're not rich any more. I took it all for granted and lived a grand life, but I was never happy. I know that now. I thought I was happy, but I was always dissatisfied. I knew something was missing, I just didn't know what it was. Joshua, that was his name, my great-grandson. He made me realise a terrible truth – that I didn't really love my own daughter or my granddaughter. Not properly. Not in the way mothers and grandmothers are meant to love. Selflessly.' She smiled sadly. 'Isn't that a terrible thing to confess?'

'It's honest,' Pixie replied.

'It's a terrible thing to realise. I'd rather not have worked it out, but it's been tormenting me ever since. I never had time for them. I only ever made time for myself.'

'As a child, did *you* feel loved?'

She waved the question away. 'Oh, I was very self-sufficient. I didn't need to feel loved.'

'Yes, you did. We *all* need to feel loved, Mrs Aldershoff. How else do you learn how to love if you're not shown by your parents?' A lump lodged itself in Pixie's throat. It was unexpected and she swallowed hard. This wasn't about her. But at the mention of not being loved by one's parents, Pixie couldn't help but think of herself.

Mrs Aldershoff shrugged. 'My parents were too busy with their own lives.'

'As were you.'

'It's true. I was.'

'You simply repeated your parents' example. You might have gone through your whole life just repeating that familiar pattern, but you've gone beyond it. That's commendable. That's probably what you came here to learn.'

'Better late than never, I suppose.' Mrs Aldershoff chortled bitterly. 'Well, now I want to put things right. I haven't got much time left. My life is nearly over. Goodness, I'm almost a hundred. No one should live this long! I want to put things right before I go. I *need* to put things right.'

'I would say that the fact that you *desire* to do so is in itself putting things right.'

'It's not enough. I must find the diamond and then I can leave a legacy that's worth something. Will you try to find out where it is, Pixie? While you're sending Lester on his way, will you try to speak to my father and ask him? You people can do that, can't you?'

'I'll try,' said Pixie. 'But the dead aren't often forthcoming about material things. Where they dwell, material things have no value.'

'Take the board with you,' said Mrs Aldershoff, tapping it with her long nails, fired suddenly with enthusiasm. 'I have a feeling that Lester is somehow connected to it. You see, a couple of nights ago, I took it out. I wasn't going to use it again. I was much too afraid to do that. But I took it out to look at it. I had it on my lap when Lester came out of nowhere and sent it flying across the floor. I know it was him. I got that cold feeling I got when we were in our seance. Well, he gave me the fright of my life. Anyway, it got me thinking. Lester came here only once, when he courted my sister. There's no reason for him to be connected to the house, but perhaps he's connected to the board. After all, it's the board that gave him a doorway into our world, isn't it, and then when I took it out again, he made it jump right off my knee. Don't you think it makes sense?' She pushed the blue box towards Pixie. 'Take it and see if you can speak to my father, Walter-Wyatt Aldershoff. You'd be doing an old lady a wonderful favour. I'd be so grateful. I'll die in peace. And you'll solve a mystery that no one else has been able to solve.'

Pixie put her hand on the box. Mrs Aldershoff had a point. The Ouija board did seem to be significant, and, if she needed to slide back to Lester's time, the board might be just the object to link her to him. 'I'll do my best,' she replied. She couldn't promise more than that.

Pixie and Ulysses accompanied Mrs Aldershoff and Mrs Croft into the hall. 'Are you going to make contact now?' Mrs Aldershoff asked Pixie.

'I'm going to give it a try.'

'I hope you do a better job than that other medium Mr Stirling invited over.'

'Oh, Mother,' said Mrs Croft. 'The poor man did his best.'

'His best wasn't good enough, Leona,' retorted Mrs Aldershoff. She turned to Pixie. 'You remember what I told you?'

'Of course.' Pixie quickly reassured her.

'Mr Stirling can call me when you're through.'

Mrs Croft put her hand beneath her mother's elbow as they set off towards the front door. Pixie saw Mrs Aldershoff pull it away and heard her strident voice, now back to its usual timbre. 'I don't need help, Leona. I'm not dead yet.' Indeed, the hope that Pixie might find the whereabouts of the Potemkin Diamond seemed to be giving her something to live for.

Pixie took the Ouija board and the white envelope that contained the photograph of Lester and Esme into the Walter-Wyatt drawing room and settled into one of the sturdy upholstered chairs. Ulysses locked the door behind them and then placed one of the chairs in front of it just to be safe; he wasn't going to take any chances after the last time, when Pixie was wrenched out of her trance by a naughty child. Pixie having a seizure on the floor was not something he wanted to see again.

'Did that box belong to Lester Ravenglass?' he asked, watching her place it on her knee and spread her fingers over the lid.

'Not exactly, but he's definitely trying to use it to communicate with us. With luck, this photograph of Lester,' she waved the envelope in the air, 'and the Ouija board will be enough to link me to him. Together with my intention, the law of attraction should send me back to his time to find out why he doesn't want to move on.'

'And if it doesn't?'

She shrugged. 'I'll come back and try again.' She pulled a nervous face.

'Are you ready for this, Pix?' he asked,

'As ready as I'll ever be,' she replied and gave him a wan smile. When it came to timesliding, it was impossible to know what would happen in the past, just as it was impossible to predict what would happen in the future. She couldn't even predict who she would be. It all depended on the law of attraction, her intention and the object she held in her hands. At least she knew Cavill wouldn't be there this time to distract her from her purpose. She was certainly not going to lose her heart in the search for Lester Ravenglass.

'I'll be right here waiting for you, as always,' Ulysses reassured her. 'But if you could make it quick so we can head out to see the Rockefeller Center this afternoon, I'd be grateful.'

Pixie laughed and wriggled back into the chair. 'Oh sure, I wouldn't want to keep you from having fun!'

Ulysses put on his earphones and switched on his iPad. Pixie knew he'd be watching an Ingrid Bergman movie for the umpteenth time. He checked his watch. 'It's ten to eleven,' he said. 'See you on the other side.'

Pixie nodded, then closed her eyes and took three conscious breaths. She imagined a silver cord extending from her solar plexus, the place just beneath her ribcage, and wrapping around the Ouija board and the white envelope, connecting her to them.

She focused her mind on the photo of Lester Ravenglass, with his faraway expression and tousled hair, and put out the desire to slide back into the past to uncover what it was that kept him stuck in the Aldershoffs' mansion, unable to move into the light. She felt the familiar heaviness wash over her limbs and the quiet thrumming in her ears. But just as she floated gently out of her body and slipped through the veil of time, it wasn't Lester's face that was held in her mind, but Cavill's. She saw his twinkling blue eyes and the affection in them. She saw his mouth that always looked as if it was about to break into a smile. And she felt her heart expand with love and ache with a deep and searing longing.

Cavill.

Past

Chapter Eight

I open my eyes to find that I'm in a breathtakingly elegant oak-panelled drawing room, sitting at a square table with two formally dressed men either side of me and a voluptuous, bejewelled woman seated opposite. I'm holding in my small hands a fan of cards, but I have no idea what game we're playing. I can only play racing demon, but this is definitely not that!

I'm seized with panic. I don't know who I am, where I am, and who these people are that are seated around this table studying their cards. I have taken over the body of someone, a woman, but I know nothing about her. Once again, I feel as if I've been thrown onto a stage, in front of an expectant audience, but I have forgotten my lines and which part I'm playing. Fears shoot through my mind, but I don't have time to consider them. One is more urgent than the others: I have a duty to the woman I possess. I mustn't let her down. But I have no way of finding out who she is.

Immediately, I feel the squeeze of a corset about my torso and glance down at my dress. Judging by the style, and the one worn by the woman opposite me, I estimate that it's later than my previous slide to 1895. I would guess that it's Edwardian England and this time I'm a lady. That's a novelty. I've never been a lady before! I think of Cordelia Pengower and decide that in order to be convincing, I must imitate *her*.

I run my eyes around the room, taking everything in. There are tables and chairs scattered about, and armchairs and sofas, upholstered in green and gold, arranged around a marble fireplace, but there are few people occupying them. I wonder whether I have slid back to the Aldershoff during the Gilded Age. Somehow, it doesn't feel like a private home in Manhattan. It feels more like a country house hotel in England. There's something oddly familiar about it, as if I've seen it before, in a photograph, perhaps. It's dark outside the tall bay windows, so it must be night-time. Perhaps the other guests have gone to bed. The ceiling is high and lavishly moulded. The place looks as if it's been modelled on Versailles. *Are* we at Versailles? Surely not. Frantically, I try to work it out while, at the same time, breathing consciously to calm my hopping nerves. I know from my history degree that Napoleon chose not to settle in that palace, but in Paris instead. So, we're definitely not at Versailles. That's a relief because I don't speak French. I do hope these people speak English! There's something unusual about the room, though, but I can't put my finger on it. I don't have time to figure it out. I'm in the middle of a card game I don't know how to play. What the hell am I going to do?

I try to catch my reflection in a silver teaspoon that lies on a saucer beside an empty teacup. Brown hair, pink face, the indigo and black feathers in my headdress, all distorted in the concave curve of the spoon. Not helpful.

I turn my attention to the woman sitting opposite me. She's stout with thick auburn curls pinned in an updo and a spectacular diamond necklace sparkling above the low neckline of her black dress. She wears an extravagant spray of black feathers in her hair and heavy diamond-and-pearl drops on her fleshy earlobes. Her big eyes are the colour of honey and brimming with vivacity and warmth. I can tell at once that she's an intelligent, straight-talking woman with a good sense of humour. She's the kind of woman who doesn't care what people think of her and is not afraid to speak her mind. One of those gutsy feminists, like Emmeline Pankhurst, blazing the trail for women's rights. She has about her an air of rebellion and courage, and I know that I like her.

The two men at the table are studying their cards. They're wearing black tailcoats with stiff white shirts and bow ties, but they're very different. One is middle-aged, thin-faced and serious, with bright china-blue eyes and round spectacles on the bridge of a strong nose. His brown hair is greying at the temples and swept off a high forehead creased with worry lines. He is still handsome in a rugged way. The other is young with a clean-shaven, angular face, pale blue-green eyes and full, sensual lips. Really, he is so good-looking – he might even put Ulysses in the shade! His light-brown hair is tousled and falling over a wide brow. He pushes it back and I notice the gold signet ring on his little finger and then the diamond studs on his shirt and the sapphire cufflinks on his cuffs. They glint sharply in the electric lights. He might be young but he's wealthy. As I stare at him, he lifts his eyes languidly off his cards and grins at me, the familiar, playful grin of someone who knows me very well. At that moment I realise who he is. He's Lester Ravenglass – young and fresh, before alcohol and unhappiness takes their toll. How different he is from the solemn man staring out of the photograph Mrs Aldershoff gave me. Now his expression is playful and full of fun.

'No luck tonight, Aunt Constance?' he says, looking at me from under his brows.

I'm an aunt! I glance at my hands in surprise. I cannot tell how old I am, but I see to my dismay that I'm not young. I might even be as old as forty!

The auburn-haired woman laughs heartily and winks at me in collusion. 'I've only known Miss Fleet two days, but I can tell you, Ravenglass, that your aunt is a dark horse. Just when you think you've got her, she'll whip out an ace!' She speaks with a southern American drawl, but her laugh is universal and delightfully contagious. I laugh too, because of the raffish way she arches her eyebrows and smiles, but also at the absurdity of the situation in which I find myself – I'm Miss Constance Fleet, poised to make a move in a game I know nothing about. How the hell am I going to wing it?

Just then my attention is drawn to a man pushing out his armchair near the fireplace a short distance from us. He gets to his feet and says something to the two elderly men seated with him.

My heart stops.

I recognise him immediately, even before I see his face. I would recognise him anywhere, even in a crowd of thousands. His back is towards me, but I know him, every inch of him, for he is engraved deep into my memory, into my soul. It's Cavill.

Cavill.

What on earth is *he* doing here? How did this happen? A sudden understanding stuns me, like an arrow of fire burning through my consciousness. Did my love for him, by the law of attraction, draw me to him? Did it somehow pull me back through time like a powerful magnet? Did the universe, God, higher power, whatever one wants to call it, somehow engineer for us to be reunited? But I'm confused. Am I here for Lester Ravenglass or for *me*?

I want to run to him. I want to forget my purpose – and I almost do – and throw my arms around him. To feel him solid and alive in my embrace. Oh, to press my cheek to his and tell him that I'm back. I never thought it was possible. I saw his gravestone in the chapel yard in St Sidwell and mourned his death. Those dates 1867-1943 are carved into the wound in my heart. But he's alive and he's here! However, the realisation that I am not Hermione Swift, that I'm not even Pixie Tate, but Constance Fleet, hits me like a slap in the face.

He won't know who I am.

I feel lightheaded, as if the very floor is moving. Indeed, it's as if the room is moving. I grab the edge of the table for balance. Of course, Cavill won't recognise me for I'm Miss Constance Fleet, not Hermione Swift whom he loved and subsequently married. The realisation that he won't know me is overwhelming and I put down my cards. 'I'm feeling faint,' I declare in a voice that sounds nothing like mine – it's lower and richer. I push out my chair.

What if Hermione Swift is *here*? What if we come face to face – me, Pixie, and the body I inhabited, staring back at me? What will that feel like? A prickly heat crawls over my skin and nausea churns in my belly.

I don't want to know.

'My dear, you have gone very white,' says the woman, alarmed.

'Is your hand so very bad, Aunt Constance?' jokes Lester.

'Perhaps you ought to retire,' suggests the older man kindly. Like the woman, he's American. 'Mrs Brown, perhaps you'd better escort Miss Fleet to her room.'

'Most certainly, Mr Rowland. Come on, my dear. Let's get you to bed.' She stands and both men stand with her.

I get to my feet, but feel strangely unsteady. It's as if the earth beneath my feet is rocking. 'Thank you,' I reply. 'I'm sorry I can't finish the game. I don't know what's come over me.'

'Defeat.' Lester laughs, but not unkindly.

'You're forgiven, my dear Miss Fleet.' The older man smiles at me sweetly. 'There are four more days to go before we arrive in New York. Plenty of time to play cards.'

New York? We're going to New York? I look around in bewilderment and then, with a jolt of panic, I realise why the room looks strange. Why I feel as if the floor is rocking. Because it *is* rocking. We're not in an hotel or a country house. We're on a ship. A magnificent ship. It truly *is* a palace. 'We've been at sea for two days already,' says Lester, frowning at me. 'One would have thought you'd have found your sea legs by now!'

Mrs Brown comes round the table and takes me by the arm. She has an air of efficiency as if she's used to bossing people around and being obeyed. Mrs Brown . . .

I go cold suddenly as I'm hit by another flash of comprehension.

Mrs Brown. A vast ship. New York. 'Molly Brown?' I mutter incredulously, nausea rising again. Surely not!

She flinches and gazes at me with concern. 'Well, no one calls me by that name, my dear. My friends and family know me as Maggie. Molly, indeed! Come, let's get you to bed. You've taken a nasty turn.'

The unsinkable Molly Brown. Dear God, we're on the *Titanic*!

We make our way towards the door. My legs feel as if they belong to someone else, which, I suppose technically, they do! I'm in 1912, over one hundred years from where my body sits in the Aldershoff Hotel in the present. I shake my head, trying to keep my thoughts on Constance, and the room I'm in now that gently vibrates from the rumble of the engine room far below. Cavill is making his way to the door as well. We are bound to collide. I see him crossing the room and I can't take my eyes off him. He's still tall and handsome, but more mature. Yes, his flaxen hair has darkened and is greying at the temples, his face is thinner, his skin weathered; time has robbed it of its bloom, but not of its charm. He's not the young man I knew, but an older, more seasoned version. What is Cavill Pengower doing on the *Titanic*? I wonder, then, whether I haven't slid at all but am suffering a horrendous nightmare.

Cavill reaches the door first and stands aside to let us pass. He smiles politely and those achingly familiar eyes rest upon my face with not even a glimmer of recognition. 'After you, ladies,' he says, bowing. Then a look of concern softens his expression. 'Are you all right, Miss Fleet?'

I cannot answer. My throat is as rough and dry as bark.

'Miss Fleet is not cut out to be a sailor, Mr Pengower,' says Mrs Brown with a chuckle, ushering me past. I gaze up at him, searching his face for a sign, for a flinch, for the smallest hint of perception, but there is nothing of the soul connection I believed there to be – I *hoped* there would be. There is only civility and respect given to a woman whose acquaintance he has made, perhaps only recently. *Do you not know me?* I cry out in my mind. My temples pound with the force of keeping those words contained in my head.

Our conversation from a different lifetime floats into my mind. It's like a vaporous cloud I want to hold on to but can't. I question now whether it ever happened.

'Will we recognise each other when we no longer have our physical bodies? Will we recognise each other when we are made of light?'

And his reply. 'Of course, I will recognise your soul. I'd recognise your soul if it was a ray of light among a thousand rays.'

But he has *not* recognised it. He has not recognised it at all.

Mrs Brown escorts me past the grand wooden staircase, which looks remarkably similar to the replica in James Cameron's famous film. It's the same with its magnificent glass dome, wood-panelled walls and clock. They must have copied it to the smallest detail. Now I know why the room looked so familiar. As Mrs Brown leads me across the marble floor and on through a door and down a carpeted corridor, I realise with mounting panic that this ship is going to hit an iceberg in two days' time – I believe the tragedy happened on the fourth day of the journey across the Atlantic and we have already been at sea for two.

It's going to hit the iceberg and sink.

And I am on it.

We reach a white-panelled door and I fumble in the silk bag I'm carrying for the key. I imagine it must be in there and I'm right. Mrs Brown takes charge and puts the key in the lock, but she needn't have bothered. The door is not locked and opens easily. A maid in a black dress and white apron is turning down the big canopy bed nestled into the embrace of the wall. She looks up from her work and a shadow of apprehension darkens her face. 'Ma'am, is everything all right?' she asks. Like Henry Higgins, I place her accent in the East End of London.

'Miss Fleet has taken a turn, Ruby,' Mrs Brown informs her, and I wonder how she knows the name of the maid and the whereabouts of my cabin. 'She's like *The Princess and the Pea*, feeling the motion of the water on a boat this size,' she continues in her strident, humorous tone. 'Really, to me it feels as solid as my home in Denver.' She laughs. 'I'm sure you'll feel better in the morning, my dear. You just need a good night's sleep. Perhaps a thimble of rum.'

I turn to Mrs Brown. I want to tell her that the ship is going to sink and that she's going to be heroic, manning an oar and urging the crew in the lifeboat to go back and rescue those in the water. But I cannot – and what would be the point? She wouldn't believe me. Everyone believed the Titanic to be unsinkable. I wonder what becomes of Constance Fleet, this woman whose body I've slid into? Does she survive? And what of Cavill? I realise with a shudder that I've never considered the possibility of dying while in a slide. If I don't manage to get off the ship in time and return to the future, what will happen? Will I remain in a limbo state between life and death? Will I be lost in time? Are Cavill and I destined to die together? His gravestone at St Sidwell stated that he died in 1943, but what if I've altered destiny by triggering once again the law of attraction and bringing him to me. I've changed the date of his death once before. What's to stop me doing it again?

Mrs Brown leaves, closing the door softly behind her.

Ruby is a young woman with a pretty, round face, pebble-grey eyes and a pointed chin. Her shiny brown hair is swept off her forehead and tied in a bun. She looks at me with kindness. 'Let me help you out of your dress,' she says and comes towards me with the confidence of a person who is doing a job she knows well. I realise she must be Constance's personal maid, and has been, perhaps, for some time.

I catch myself in the standing mirror and examine the body I've slipped into. It's not beautiful like Hermione Swift – it's sturdier and not as tall, but Constance is appealing none the less. I imagine she's in her forties, but it's hard to tell for people age differently in these times. Her hair is soft brown and greying. She wears it up, as is the fashion, curled and pinned, with a crimped fringe falling over a low brow. Her eyes are hazel, deep-set with dark lashes. They're intelligent, bold, unafraid – even with *me* staring out of them I can tell that she's formidable. Her nose is strong and straight, and her lips neither full nor thin but somewhere in between. She's a woman who smiles a lot for she has laughter lines around her mouth and eyes, and a sharp jawline and chin that denote determination. Yes, she has a determined chin. I don't imagine she's the kind of woman who allows people to push her around.

As Ruby unbuttons my dress and unties the laces on the back of my corset, I take a moment to reflect. The problem is that I don't know what sort of woman I am. At least with Hermione Swift I could be anyone I wanted to be, because I arrived at St Sidwell Manor as a governess whom no one had previously met. But this is a different story. Constance is known. Besides her name, Miss Fleet, which suggests she's not married, I have no information about her at all. Is she quiet, or is she brassy and bold like Mrs Brown? I feel an overwhelming sense of helplessness – I've got myself into this, but I don't know how I'm meant to behave. I pull myself together. I've done this before on previous slides. I can do it again. I just need to focus and think laterally.

'Thank you, Ruby,' I say. 'I'm sure I'll feel better in the morning. I'm not used to being at sea.'

She laughs. 'It's probably the excitement, ma'am. This is the biggest boat the world has ever seen and we're on it. It's quite something, isn't it?'

'It certainly is,' I reply. I wonder whether Ruby survives. Or does she, with the other fifteen hundred people, die a horrible death. Does Constance?

One thing I know for sure is that Lester survives the *Titanic* disaster. But at what cost? Something terrible must happen over the next two days to keep him trapped in the Aldershoff a century later. Is that what I'm here to discover?

Ruby opens a drawer and takes out a leather-bound book and hands it to me. 'Are you too sick to write your journal tonight?' she asks.

I stare at it in astonishment. It's tied with ribbon and thick with pages. Pages that might contain information I need to know about Constance's life, her thoughts, her dreams and desires. It's exactly what I need in order to navigate my way through this bewildering drama. What luck! Of course, it was very common for people to keep diaries in those days – I've read a few myself and they're wonderfully detailed and vivid. But I'm thankful to Constance for having one.

I take it eagerly, my heart swelling with gratitude. 'I will write it.' I sit at the dressing table so that she can take the pins out of my hair and brush it. The cover of the diary depicts forget-me-nots and daisies. I stare at them, hope building in my chest. This might not only contain information about Constance Fleet, but about Lester Ravenglass too. Nothing happens by chance. There's a reason why I'm here, on this ship, at this time. I have to trust the higher power. I'm on the *Titanic* because I *need* to be here to carry out my purpose, otherwise I wouldn't be here.

Before the maid leaves the room, I ask, 'Ruby, if you didn't know me, how would you describe me? What sort of woman am I?'

She frowns, her face full of doubt. Then she grins and the doubt is dispelled. 'Is this a game, ma'am?'

'I suppose it is. Yes, a game. We were playing it in the drawing room after dinner. I'd like to know how *you* would respond.'

She bites her bottom lip and narrows her eyes. 'Well, ma'am, I would say that you're strong-willed and . . .' She hesitates. 'Brave.' She laughs nervously, fearful perhaps that she's being too familiar.

'Brave?' I ask.

'Well, other women feel they have to marry and have children, don't they? Most women need a man to look after them. But you're not like them. You're independent. It takes a lot of courage to live your own life, if you don't mind me saying, even though your father was Viscount Ravenglass. It takes guts to go it alone.'

My mind seizes upon the information like a thief. So, my father was Viscount Ravenglass – he's dead, of course, and so is his son, because Lester is a lord, which makes *him* the current

Viscount Ravenglass. That means that their family name is Fleet, hence I am the *Honourable* Constance Fleet, sister to Lester's late father. English titles are complicated, but I understand them, having studied history. 'I appreciate your honesty,' I say at last, because Ruby is standing in the doorway, waiting for me to respond.

She nods, relieved. 'I hope you sleep well, ma'am. I suspect we'll have another day of sunshine tomorrow,' she adds. 'It's thrilling to be in the middle of the ocean, isn't it?'

I struggle to find the words to reply. She has no idea what horror lies ahead.

But I smile back, as I must. I'm not here to change the course of history, even though I wish I could. 'Thrilling,' I say, feigning excitement. 'A grand adventure. You sleep well, too, Ruby.' Knowing it will be first-class women and children off the boat first, I promise myself to make sure that Ruby comes with me.

Before I settle down with the diary, I explore the bedroom for clues as to what sort of person I am. I rifle through Constance's clothes – she has so many dresses, I wonder how she managed to pack them all into suitcases. I open a glass pot of cream placed on the dressing table and try it on the back of my hand. It has the silky texture of Nivea. I spray perfume into the air and sniff it: tuberose, heavy and sweet. I look at the books Constance has brought with her, searching for more clues about this daughter of a viscount. *Love and Marriage* by Ellen Key, *The House of Mirth* by Edith Wharton and *The Suffragette* magazine are stacked on the side table, with her jewellery neatly arranged in a red velvet case beside them; can they possibly be *real* diamonds? Constance Fleet is a very rich woman. If she's not married, her wealth must have come from her father, Lester's grandfather, Viscount Ravenglass. I wonder why Constance is travelling to

New York with Lester. I hope the diary will enlighten me before I have to face Lester, and everyone else Constance knows, in the morning!

I seize upon a copy of the *Atlantic Daily Bulletin*, which is typed on A4 white paper and dated April 12th. It lists weather on board, a review of the markets, world news, sporting news, et cetera. But I'm most interested in the date. We have been at sea two days already and have two days to go before the ship will go down. My calculations are correct.

I'm about to climb into bed with the diary when I notice something hard and square-shaped lying beneath a dressing gown thrown over a chair in the corner of the cabin. My heart lurches. I hurry over and lift the gown to reveal the familiar blue box that contains Mrs Aldershoff's Ouija board.

It didn't belong to Alice Aldershoff, at least not originally. It belonged to Constance Fleet!

My heart is now thumping in my chest. I'm wide awake. I no longer feel sick but revived by the mystery now unfolding before me. Constance survives the *Titanic*, for how else would her Ouija board end up with Alice Aldershoff? And Lester survives too, for he dies later, in England. So, whatever happens aboard this ship in the next two days is key to him being earthbound later, in spirit. I'm clearly here to find out something or I wouldn't be here at all. How am I going to do it when I don't know what I'm looking for?

I climb into bed, settle myself against the pillows and pull the diary towards me. Cavill Pengower steals into my mind then, and my heart burns with a terrible disappointment. I thought there was no chance of us meeting again. I'd accepted that. Sure, it hurt, but I had managed to endure it and get on with my life. When I agreed to this job, I anticipated a brief and dispassionate slide. How wrong I was! Here I am on the *Titanic*, of all places, with Cavill, of all people, and he doesn't know who I am. Unless I discover in the next forty-eight hours what I'm here to find out, I'm going to have to experience the terror of being on the *Titanic* as it sinks and suffer the pain of being in the same place as Cavill but unable to reach him. It's like a nightmare and I long to wake up. My courage flags suddenly. I'm not sure I can go through with it. It's too hard. I could slide back and tell Mr Stirling that the task is an impossible one. But that's the coward's way and I'm not a coward. I haven't been given this gift of timesliding to bail out the moment it gets tough. I feel duty-bound to help him and Lester. I cannot allow Lester's misery to go on simply because of my lack of nerve. I can't do it.

I rally and push Cavill out of my mind. There's no point wishing things were different. He doesn't recognise me – why would he? And I cannot enlighten him. There's only one thing to do: concentrate wholeheartedly on my mission.

I open Constance's diary to the first entry and am surprised to see that it doesn't start on the first day of this year, 1912, but on 11th June, presumably of the previous year, 1911. And I laugh to myself at the first line she writes in her slanted, flowing hand:

Three reasons to be infuriated by L.

I imagine she means Lester. I'm going to have to get used to her unfamiliar penmanship, which is typical of its time and quite hard to read. The book is fat, stuffed with leaflets, letters, dance cards and opera tickets. I cannot possibly get through it all in one night. I will have to find the relevant entries and sweep my eyes over the rest.

I settle back against the pillows, wide awake now, my wits sharp. I have always loved a diary. With mounting anticipation, I'm transported back into the past.

SECRETS OF THE STARLIT SEA

The diary of the Honourable Constance Fleet

Sunday, 11th June, 1911

Three reasons to be infuriated with L.

1. Lester and I had a row this morning over breakfast. My dear brother is dead just over a year and my nephew has taken it upon himself to gamble and carouse away his inheritance. I have noticed that the Constable has vanished from the green drawing room here at Broadmere and even though Lester has tried to mask its disappearance by hanging the Landseer in its place, I am not fooled. JE NE SUIS PAS IDIOTE! I grew up in this great house and know every inch of it by heart. But what can I do? He owns the estate now and has no sense of duty towards it, only a blind impulse to satisfy his own selfish desires. Why, dear George would turn in his grave were he to see how his son is squandering his fortune and how this magnificent house is going to ruin! But, oh, how Lester loves striding about as the new Viscount Ravenglass. If he's not careful, he won't have an estate to go with that title, and then he'll be sorry! Bertha is unhelpful. She only thinks of the next party, the next card game, the next win – or, in her case, loss, because she's as brainless as a hen – and is a terrible example to her son. I am in despair. Broadmere will not survive into the next generation if Lester continues to shirk his responsibility. Once again, I gave him a piece of my mind and he raised his voice, as he is wont to do when he finds himself cornered, and retaliated with spite. 'Women should know their place,' he told me unpleasantly. 'If only you had a husband, Aunt Constance, then you would know yours.'
2. Which brings me on to my second point: women's rights. Lester is as terrified of my political activism as Asquith is of Emmeline Pankhurst. I have become quite vociferous in stating my position and am proud to be a member of the WSPU and a suffragette. Lester seeks every opportunity to put me in my place, but I will not be cowed by a twenty-five-year-old whose strongest argument against women being given the vote is a belief, sadly not uncommon, that due to our lunar cycles, we cannot be trusted not to go mad once a month. I can just imagine the inane

conversations he has with his peers in White's Club. Truly, pigs have a grander intelligence than they do.

My dear brother was of the same mind as me. He saw the value of women's contribution to society and believed they should have the same status and rights as men. It is a tragedy that his wife is content to leave the management of every aspect of her life to men. She is simply not interested in voting or even in having her opinions heard. Were she inclined to get off her lazy behind and visit the workhouses like I have done, and seen the pitiful conditions where desperate women and children are treated with less respect and compassion than animals, she might be motivated to do something about it. The only way we can change the sorry state of the poor is in law. Men are not interested in alleviating the suffering of those in need as women are. Indeed, we are far more compassionate. If we had political power, society would be greatly improved. It is something we must fight for. As long as Bertha has money to spend and pretty dresses, she cares not about her rights as a human being.

I rounded on Lord D and the young Marquess of S when they dined with us at Broadmere last week, after they agreed that the government should indeed put a stop to force-feeding suffragette prisoners who go on hunger strike but only so that they are left to starve themselves to death instead. IMBÉCILES! Indeed, the heartlessness of the comment left me breathless. 'They must learn that their acts of vandalism will not get them anywhere,' said Lord D. What a pompous man he is, and ugly too, I might add.

I told them that since we have started throwing rocks through windows the government has, indeed, started to panic. 'We have tried to hold discussions and meetings and peaceful processions, but to no avail,' I said. 'Now we have resorted to vandalism. It is the only way to be heard. Suffragettes will continue to fight for equality until we get it. It is as simple as that and the government will try, as they have tried throughout history, to crush ideas that cannot die, in the usual heavy-handed way. Unfortunately, they never learn from history.'

L was not amused. 'Men have been the dominant gender for thousands of years,' he said, as if that was an intelligent argument.

'And why do you think that is, my dear Lester?' I asked with a smile. Before he could answer, I said, simply, 'Brawn.' When the three of them looked at me blankly — none of the other ladies were brave enough to support me and chose to drop their eyes onto their pudding plates — I added, by way of an explanation, 'For thousands of years, muscles were required for communities to survive. That is no longer the case. We have automobiles, farm machinery and any number of devices to take the place of men's brawn. When it comes to brains, I would even go so far as to say that women's are more effective. There would be less poverty and more compassion if women were in power.' I laugh now to recall it. I unleashed three furies and none more furious than L, who has quite a temper.

'Pay no attention to this cat mewing,' he said, quoting Lloyd George. 'With respect, Aunt Constance, women having any power beyond the nursery is as likely as man walking on the moon.'

My reply to that was, 'We shall see.'

3. My trusty informer, Ruby, has more information on Glover — the dastardly valet! She took my brooch into Hatton Garden to be repaired. As she passed the pawn shop, whom did she see in there, but Glover, pawning items surely pilfered from his master's dressing room. She went in to confront him and her eyes seized upon the cufflinks he was sporting. COMME UN CHAT, Ruby misses nothing! Lester's cufflinks! There was no mistaking them. The gold-and-sapphire ones that belonged to his dear father. The audacity of the man is beyond belief. Ruby commented upon them and Glover, in his usual supercilious way, looked at her down his long nose and replied, 'I am doing Lord Ravenglass's bidding, if you don't mind. I am sure you have business of Miss Fleet's to attend to.' When I informed Lester, he told me to mind my own business. Glover is his valet and his responsibility, he argued. I said he should dismiss him and employ someone trustworthy. There are plenty of good valets to be found. Indeed, they are two a penny. Besides, Glover has only been in service to Lester for eight months, certainly not long enough to make himself indispensable. Which makes me suspicious. What does Glover have on Lester? Is he privy to immoral behaviour? Lester is a ladies' man, to be sure, and quite likely reckless in his adventures. Is there something that Lester has done, which he fears Glover might expose? If there is something unseemly in Lester's life, I must find out what it is and deal with it before it comes into the light. Nothing must be allowed to

ruin his reputation if he is to marry a suitable girl, which he must. The very survival of Broadmere as the Ravenglass family seat depends on it. Am I the only member of this family who holds the same values as our ancestors? Grandpa Hume, dear Papa and dear recently departed George loved Broadmere with all their hearts, and so do I. Oh, if only I had been born a boy!

Monday, 12th June, 1911

I must take another lover. I have grown tired of Romeo. Inconceivable at first, for how I longed for those magic hours between CINQUE À SEPT, when I could forget myself in his kisses and indulge my desires in a most unladylike fashion. I found him handsome and amusing, and he made me laugh, but he is now petulant and brings his complaints to my bed, which is tiresome. Less of a Romeo now and more of a Rusty! I am not the least interested in his gripes. Let us be frank, I do not cherish Romeo for his conversation! Indeed, familiarity breeds contempt. Once, the clandestine nature of our rendezvous simply made them more exciting; however, now I am bored in spite of the danger. I must find a new paramour. How they are stacking up: Prospero the Brigadier, boastful Petruchio, silver-tongued Fool, and Benedick with the dreamy brown eyes . . . none of them lasts. TANT PIS. I am not made for one man alone. It is not long before ennui sets in and I must discard them like matches whose flames have died and are, as a consequence, no longer fit for purpose. With careful navigation, I have managed to keep them sweet. The secret to ensuring their discretion is to keep the door of possibility open a crack, thus ensuring they remain loyal – and hopeful. I am aware that I possess neither youth nor beauty, but I do have charm and exuberance, and a spark of outrageousness, which most women lack, and many men admire and secretly crave. I do not want a husband – I have no need, being independently wealthy – but I have physical yearnings. Yes, I must cast my eye about for a new lover and deal kindly with poor lovelorn Romeo.

SECRETS OF THE STARLIT SEA

Wednesday, 14th June, 1911

Emmeline Pankhurst is a formidable woman with a vision she holds firm and aloft. In truth, nothing and no one will turn her from her path. I admire her greatly. The WSPU has planned a glorious march through the city on Saturday, five days before the King's coronation, to put pressure on the government to grant votes for women in the Conciliation Bill. It does not go far enough, of course, proposing to give the vote only to propertied women, but it is a start. We can build on that. I do believe it will go through. We seem to be making wonderful progress at last.

Met with Romeo and let him down gently. I pretended that Bertha had reported hearing our names whispered in the same sentence at Lady J's salon and that I cannot afford a scandal. I am amused. Bertha wouldn't hear such a rumour if it were shouted into her ear. She is much too busy thinking about herself. Romeo, having much to lose himself were our relationship to come into the light, has retreated like a terrified squirrel scampering up a tree. Handsome he may be, but he's no MacDuff!

Lady J's salon. On the lookout for a new paramour, but no one new to behold. Only the same, familiar faces. Dull, dull, dull. London is too small. Perhaps I must return to Paris for another season. Yes, I can easily see myself with the Count of Montecristo or D'Artagnan. Would that not be AMUSANT?

I found myself at the same table as Lester and ended up partnering him at bridge. That game, being my strength — I do not believe there is a shrewder player than I in our PETIT MONDE — induced Lester to express his most sincere gratitude for my aptitude and cunning, for we made a mockery of our opponents and collected some impressive winnings. Nothing to Lester, really, for he likes to gamble big. I do not. I intend to live into grand old age with my wealth intact. I dare say, Lester will marry someone with a bottomless pit of gold. I do hope so, for he will need it. Still, we were friends tonight and that made me surprisingly happy. I do love my nephew. I simply wish that he were more sensible. As for Bertha, she is a sorry sight. She drinks too much and most often loses at cards. Indeed, for London's most enthusiastic gossip vultures, the Viscountess Ravenglass is surely a juicy meal. But I must be grateful that she is not yet interested in flirtations and as for marrying again, that appears unlikely. The manner in which she gambles away her money will put off any prospective suitor with more than one brain cell and a desire to hold on to his fortune. She sent my dear brother to an early grave, God rest his soul. I trust no sensible man will go near this most misguided and foolish of widows!

Saturday, 17th June, 1911

What a glorious day! Forty thousand suffragettes marched from Westminster to the Albert Hall dressed in white in support of the poor suffragette prisoners languishing at His Majesty's pleasure in Holloway. What an exhilarating experience it was to be among the marchers. The atmosphere was peaceful but determined, and included many different suffrage societies. Never before has there been such a procession. There were floats, banners, fancy dress, all led by our own brave general, Flora Drummond, on horseback. Women came from all corners of the earth and from all walks of life, united in our common goal. VOTES FOR WOMEN. What a turn out! What a triumph! The route was ten people deep with spectators and bystanders. The PM can no longer claim that most women are not interested in being given the vote! Bertha, I imagine, was at home, filing her nails, but so many of my dear friends were out in force. We women number over half of the nation's population. We are loyal subjects of the King. We deserve, no, we demand, to be heard!

Tuesday, 20th June, 1911

I am wild with excitement. I have met Orlando — I rather fancy myself as Rosalind, being quick-witted and formidable. To be sure, she is my favourite character in all of Shakespeare's plays. But let me start at the beginning. I am almost too agitated to write. Indeed, my pen is trembling in my hand. But I will take my time and draw it out, because I am quite smitten and now the world looks different!

It was a hot evening when I arrived at Bertha's coronation party. I have never known a hotter June. A thick haze hung over Hyde Park. The air was sugar-scented, the light soft as the sun sunk in the sky and the moon, like a giant grapefruit, assumed her place. There could not have been a more perfect setting for our encounter. COMME C'EST ROMANTIQUE!

London is thrumming with activity, for the coronation is but two days away. Bertha has decorated her garden with Union Jack bunting and embellished little cakes with golden crowns. Her box hedges were clipped to perfection and the purple delphiniums had never looked so lavish. Indeed, her garden is ravishing. She takes pride in collecting people and, to be sure, everyone was there. She was crowing about the three dukes: Bedford, Beauford and Marlborough, and many other big beasts besides, who had graced her celebration, but I was more interested in Lady V, who is a keen fellow member of the WSPU. She and I had an interesting conversation while Bertha fluttered from duke to duke like a butterfly high on nectar.

Lester, raffish in a straw boater, jaunty striped jacket and lively sea-green waistcoat that brought out the unusual colour of his eyes, did look mightily handsome. He was on excellent form. We were enjoying some lively repartee when my eye was drawn to a group of guests I did not know. A gentleman, three pretty young ladies and an older woman of about my age who had the imperious gaze of a duchess. They had just come out of the house and were standing at the top of the steps that led into the garden. I assumed, at first sight, that they were a couple with their three daughters, but, mercifully as it turned out, I was quite wrong. 'Who are they?' I asked Lester, my interest piqued by the gentleman who stood out on account of his height. He had greying, mouse-brown hair, a gentle gaze and a slight stoop — there was something about the sensitivity of his expression that drew my eye.

'They, my dear Constance, are the Aldershoffs. One of the richest families in America. They own one of the most valuable diamonds in the world! Imagine that! A Russian diamond, no less. Mother has recently added them to her collection. You see the beauty that stands a little to the left of her aunt?' I most certainly did. She was fine-boned and flaxen-haired, with a waspish waist and an elegant deportment. 'She is Esme Aldershoff, daughter of Walter-Wyatt and Alice of New York. Is she not lovely?'

'She is a picture of loveliness,' I replied. 'The gentleman — is he Walter-Wyatt?'

'No, he is a cousin of Esme's mother, Alice. His daughter is the plain one in the pink dress, on his right.' The mention of his daughter made my heart sink. Where there is a daughter, there is sure to be a mother.

'And the older lady is his wife?'

'She is Walter-Wyatt's sister, Mrs Willesden. They have all been in Italy.' I was relieved that the gentleman and Mrs Willesden were not a married couple.

'Does the gentleman have a wife?' I asked, trying to keep the hope out of my voice.

'Widowed, some years ago,' said Lester.

'How very tragic,' I replied, but I admit that, apart from compassion for his motherless daughter and for his loss, I felt a twinge of joy for myself. EST-CE QUE C'EST MAUVAIS? 'Do introduce us,' I said.

The group descended the steps, and Lester and I weaved through the throng to meet them. One or two people attempted to attract my attention, but I was not to be diverted. I was single-minded in my desire to meet this intriguing gentleman, to whom I had already given the heroic name Orlando! I was not to be disappointed. He is every bit the Orlando of fame.

Mrs Willesden — Hope is her name — has the steady, lofty gaze of a woman who is used to being respected and admired. Her face is handsome, her nose long and straight, her lips thin but not unattractive. She is elegant and expensively dressed. When I commented upon her dress, she was quick to tell me that it was from Worth. Of course it was! I do not imagine she gets her dresses fashioned anywhere else but in Paris. Her daughter is winsome yet inferior to her cousin Esme in both looks and manner. Orlando's daughter is shy with a long face and her father's gentle eyes. I sensed she was accustomed to being overshadowed by her cousins and content to remain so. I do believe she is a few years younger than they are, which perhaps accounts for her timidity. In any case, I was not interested in the girls and was only too happy to leave them to Lester and offer the gentleman my hand. No sooner did he take it than I was ready to offer him my heart as well, and most enthusiastically. It was quite extraordinary. I have never been so taken with anyone in my life. It was as if I had suddenly awoken from a sleep.

I have experienced lust and plenty of it, but romantic love? That has always eluded me. Was I now, at the grand age of thirty-eight, going to experience it for the first time? Could he be Orlando to my Rosalind?

SECRETS OF THE STARLIT SEA

Wednesday, 21st June, 1911

I called upon Bertha this morning for a postmortem. As I suspected, she was still in bed when I arrived at midday! I'm surprised the din outside her windows did not wake her up. London is truly the gayest of cities in its pre-coronation excitement. The route from Buckingham Palace to Westminster Abbey is already lined with people who have camped out for days in order to secure the best views of the King and Queen. No one is a stranger. It is as if we are all friends and, as I walked around Hyde Park so as not to arrive too early at Bertha's, I found myself chatting to all sorts of people. I'm sure, after the coronation, we will retreat into our own little worlds again and the spirit of unity and friendliness will be lost.

Bertha wafted into the drawing room in a peach-coloured tea dress with her greying hair fashioned in the style of a Greek goddess. She looked worse for wear indeed, her hair was already falling away from its pins. She sank into a chair with a loud sigh and reached for her cigarette box. I told her what a triumph it had been, and she listed with misty eyes the dukes who had deigned to attend. Truly, she could not have been less interested in everyone else. I let her rabbit on, but I was restless and could barely sit still. There was only one person about whom I wanted to talk. He will shortly be returning to America and I am desperate to engineer a meeting before he leaves. I needed to persuade Bertha to invite him to Broadmere.

At last, I brought up his name. 'Very charming,' she said absentmindedly.

Not to be deterred, I added quickly, before she could swing the conversation back to the dukes, 'Would it not be nice to invite Mrs Willesden and her party to Broadmere? Esme Aldershoff is after all an heiress and Lester is in want of a wife with a fortune. Indeed, Broadmere depends on it.'

I had struck a chord. Her beady eyes glinted greedily. 'Really, Connie, you are more conniving than I.' She smiled hungrily and put a cigarette to her lips. I could see her busy mind whirring with possibilities. 'Lester and Esme Aldershoff. Why did I not think of that myself? She has enough money to put an entire new roof on Broadmere! Can you imagine how fabulous it will be when my Lester, Viscount Ravenglass, and his lovely viscountess explode upon the New York scene?' She turned to me with great affection. 'Why, Connie, my dear, you are truly wonderful. Wonderful! What would I do without you? Yes, Lester and Esme Aldershoff. Fortunately, she is a beauty. Why, I have already heard him comment on that. We are halfway there. Let us not waste a moment. They must come and stay, at the soonest. I will write to Mrs Willesden at once!"

Now my mind is whirring with possibilities. If Lester and Esme decide that they like each other, then a trip to New York will be a certainty and I shall go with him. I will see that it happens. Bertha loathes travelling and will not accompany him. That leaves me. My excitement is growing already. Now I need to focus my attention on Esme and encourage her to fall in love with Lester. She must know only of his advantages and none of his shortcomings. When he wants to, he can turn on the charm. No one can resist it. It is important, therefore, that Lester and I are friends. I will call a truce and argue with him no more. In fact, he will find me most agreeable. AU TRAVAIL!

Tuesday, 11th July, 1911

At last, Orlando has come to Broadmere! I am proud to show off our family home. It is, indeed, magnificent. We took a carriage drive around the estate and he was charmed by the beauty of the gardens, the park and the lake, designed by none other than Capability Brown himself. I think that impressed him more than anything else. Mrs Willesden said that she had never seen a more lovely view when we picnicked on the hill overlooking the Test. Esme likened it to a ribbon of silver and Lester, who I believe is quite taken with her, declared that she must surely be a poet. His mother must have had a word with him for he is very attentive to her. I have not yet managed to get Orlando on his own, for in typical Bertha style, the house is full of London's most dashing and there is so much going on – croquet, tennis and other games. But I am gradually making his acquaintance. He does not talk about himself and I sense that he would not want one to refer to his late wife. Poor motherless child – my heart does go out to his daughter. How difficult her life must be without a mother to guide her. I cannot help but imagine myself in that role. I think I would rise to the occasion most successfully. I do not take to small children — they are always under one's feet — but an older daughter would suit me well. She is still young enough to be moulded to her best advantage. With a little help, she could be quite pretty.

I have not breathed a word about women's votes, and Lester and I are getting on well. Esme likes him, that is plain to see. Her winsome blue eyes light up when she looks at him and the colour flourishes on her cheeks. She is lovely to look at and has an air of nobility. She will make a perfect viscountess — and keep her wayward husband in the style to which he is accustomed, and his mother too, of course. What a pair they are, but I think young Esme Aldershoff might very well be their saviour, and mine, because no place is dearer to my heart than Broadmere. Golden memories shine out of every corner — my darling brother's memory being the brightest of them all. How I miss him. How he would suffer to see his home threatened by his wife and son's excesses. Had the estate been left to me, I would have run it wisely. But even if I had been born first, it would have passed into George's hands because he was a boy. There is something fundamentally wrong with a society that so woefully neglects one half of its population. We are all equal in God's eyes — why not in man's?

Wednesday, 12th July, 1911

I finally managed to get Orlando on his own and for long enough for me to make a good impression. He wanted to ride and I volunteered to accompany him in order to show him more of the estate. I am an accomplished horsewoman, and he was impressed when I showed him that I am not afraid of galloping at a pace. I grew up on a horse. Sitting in the saddle is second nature to me. As we walked side by side, I asked him about his tour of Italy. It sounds as if they have had the most wonderful time. He was entertaining when it came to Mrs Willesden. She sounds bossy, not that he made the slightest accusation. Only she insisted on the girls having tutors wherever they went. Apparently, it is important in her eyes that they grow up to be 'renaissance women', by which she means receiving a well-rounded education. In the words of his daughter, in Florence she hired the 'enthusiastic' Signor Pazzi to teach them painting, 'dull' Signor Bardi to enlighten them in monotone about architecture, and 'doddery' old Professor Antinore to lecture them on literature. He laughed and said that by the end of each day, the girls' heads were dizzy with so much information they were likely to soon forget. 'It was just as bad when we got to Rome.'

He asked me what it was like to grow up here, in this beautiful place, and I told him about my brother and laughed fondly at the games we had played as children. He, also, has experienced too much loss. I could see the anguish in his eyes. He was attentive and sympathetic in the way only someone who has suffered can be. I did not bring up the subject of his wife. I don't know him well enough. It would not have been appropriate, but I long to kiss away his sorrow.

He is devastatingly attractive, but not in the way my usual paramours are. He is reticent, quietly spoken, guarded. He doesn't prance and show off. There is a depth to him, an inner strength, a gentle confidence. He feels not a need to impress. But he does impress, simply with his charisma and charm. And he has gravitas, a weight about him, that is irresistible. I find him most sincere and intriguing. I think he is very intelligent and wise, which is more than I can say for my recent AMANT.

I want to see more of him, but he is leaving for New York in a week. Given the opportunity, I think I could well and truly lose my heart to him.

Thursday, 13th July, 1911

I am growing immensely fond of dear Esme. She is a delight. Innocent, sweet with a wonderful sense of humour and CHARME. She has fallen in love with Lester — that is blindingly obvious. I do hope he reciprocates in the same tone. I would hate for her tender heart to be broken. She is naïve and idealistic — must be a Pisces! She is wealthy, that is not in doubt, but she has qualities that an older person such as myself is equipped to appreciate. I do hope Lester appreciates those qualities too and that he isn't just seeing a lovely pot of gold. She deserves better than that.

I notice in her a fine intelligence, which, if honed, might grow to be formidable. We discussed women's right to vote and she was very interested in what I had to say.

I was careful, however, not to fill her young mind with too many ideas, knowing as I do how opposed Lester is to such concepts.

Bertha demanded that I entertain her guests and I could not very well object. It started at dinner. Spiritualism is all the rage and everyone seems to have had a paranormal experience. Lady P recounted a tale about being almost dragged out of bed in some Scottish castle she stayed in when she was a child. Sir B claimed to have seen the ghost of his father — the old man had appeared in his room one night, only for Sir B to be told the next morning that his father had passed away, just around the time his spirit had appeared to him. Lester claimed to have heard footsteps in his bedroom in this very house, but I'm sure he only said that for Esme's benefit. She was quite gripped and wanted to hear more stories, so Bertha took it upon herself to announce that I own a spirit board. Indeed, I do. It was given to me by my dear mama, who has taught me well. Bertha made it sound as though I communicate with spirits on a daily basis. Lester made a quip about witches and stakes, and I retaliated by saying that I'd flown down to Broadmere on a broomstick, at which everyone laughed heartily. But I could not avoid holding a seance. Bertha demanded it and Esme begged me. I agreed and the entire party packed into the library, including Orlando who appeared intrigued. I did not want him to think less of me and was relieved that he was as game as everyone else. I lit a candle in the centre of the round table and the two young ladies, Bertha, Lady P, Lady K and I took the chairs. Everyone else stood around, eager to see what was going to happen.

I placed the board on the table and explained how it worked. I made it very clear that spirit boards are not games. One does not do it for fun. An air of solemnity and reverence is crucial in order not to attract a nasty entity. Nasty entities, once allowed in, can linger. I said a prayer of protection and the room went quiet. You could have heard a mouse scratching beneath the floorboards. I told the ladies to gently rest a finger each upon the planchette.

Then I asked if there was anyone present who wished to communicate with us.

We waited.

It was not long before the planchette moved, causing the girls to gasp in amazement.

Everyone remained still as the name was spelled out.

BUNGIE

'Does anyone know a person of that name?' I asked.

A surprised voice piped up from the back. It was Sir B. 'Good Lord,' he said with a chuckle. 'Bungie was my dog!'

Thursday, 20th July, 1911

Alas, Orlando has left for America and I feel thwarted. I can do little else but think of him. Esme, however, has remained in London with her aunt. Bertha is delighted, because it is on account of Lester that the girl has stayed. I do believe an engagement will be announced very soon. Perhaps then I can accompany Lester to America. Or Mrs Pankhurst, who is planning a trip to attend the Annual Convention of the National American Woman Suffrage Association in the autumn. Like a sailor on a sailboat, I will set my rudder and aim for the States. Nothing happens in life unless one puts one's mind to it and makes it happen. And I am truly tired of London. COURAGE, Constance!

Sunday, 23rd July, 1911

Attended a lovely service with Mrs Willesden and Esme, who are missing their church in New York. The latter is doe-eyed in Lester's company. Truly, she is very taken with him, and he with her, I do believe. Although, one can never tell with Lester! He is such a selfish man. However, I do think even the most selfish of men would find his heart grow soft in the company of dear Miss Aldershoff. She has grace and charm, and a lively spirit too. The more I get to know her the deeper my affection for her grows. I do hope she will inspire in L a sense of responsibility and duty. ON NE PEUT QU'ESPÉRER.

I have rather taken my eye off my purpose as a champion of women's rights. All I seem to be able to think about is Orlando. I am in unfamiliar territory and find it most unsettling. Romeo is trying to find a way back in and I am doing my best to keep him out, without offending him. Truly, they are all inferior to Orlando, every one of them. I am even considering moving to New York for a while. How amusing it will be to spend a season in another city, and one as gay as New York. I know I will be welcome at the Aldershoffs'.

Friday, 1st September, 1911

Lester and Esme are engaged – pending her parents' permission, of course, which they will surely give when Lester travels to New York to meet them! What excitement! What joy! Bertha is beside herself. Those greedy eyes are gleaming at the thought of the Aldershoff wealth coming her way. I cannot help but feel reassured. Broadmere will be saved and the Ravenglass name salvaged from the impending scandal that has, by good fortune, Lester's title and handsome face, been averted. Lester will now have to curb his gambling, and do his duty and dismiss the odious Glover. This ugly chapter must end now.

Esme will return to America before Christmas and Lester will follow at the end of the shooting season, in February, to meet her family. I'm not certain why he doesn't follow her sooner. Surely, love is more important than shooting pheasants? But perhaps therein lies the answer: Lester is not in love. Why did I think him capable of it? He is only interested in himself! PLUS ÇA CHANGE! Apparently they have very long engagements in America. It might even last a whole year! How tiresome! Then they will marry here at Broadmere, in the family chapel, and I will do my best to guide dear Esme as she learns to be mistress of a grand estate. I know Bertha will be no help at all, and neither will Lester. They will be too busy thinking of themselves. It is a shame dear Mama is too old.

Oh, the disappointment! Mrs Willesden told me that Orlando is not in America, but travelling on business. She says he has interests in South America. She also told me that since losing his wife he has been aimless. Poor, darling man. I know I can make him happy, if only I am given the chance. But I cannot very well chase him around the world! I must be patient, as an angler is in pursuit of a big fish! ET QUEL POISSON MAJESTUEUX!

Chapter Nine
RMS TITANIC
Saturday, 13th April, 1912
Day 3

I open my eyes, startled by the unfamiliar room and then by my unfamiliar body. I look down at my hands, which are those of a woman in her late thirties, and am reminded that I'm not Pixie Tate, but Constance Fleet. I'm propped up against the pillows and the diary is open on the quilt. I must have fallen asleep while reading it. I panic. I was going to read the recent entries so that I could bluff my way through today. But now I have no time. Once again, I'm going to have to wing it!

I feel a gentle vibration rising up from beneath me, causing the bed to tremble slightly, and remember suddenly that I'm on a ship. But not just any ship. I'm on the *Titanic*. I take a deep breath as the horror of it comes back to me and remind myself that I've slid and that I have a mission to carry out and must not lose courage.

I sweep my eyes over the room. Sunshine is slipping through the gaps in the curtains, gently illuminating the wood-panelled walls and furniture, and the Ouija board placed on the chair. I know now that the board belonged to Constance and that is why I have possessed *her*. At least I'm familiar with Ouija boards. If asked to use it, I'll know what to do.

I remember then that Cavill is on the ship.

Cavill.

I sit up in alarm as details of the evening before come flooding back. How is it even possible? But it is. He is here. I feel a deep ache in the core of my chest. I never thought I would see him again and now it will be impossible to avoid him. I'll have to be on my guard and not let my feelings show, because I'm not Hermione Swift. I'm Constance Fleet and *she* is in love with the American she calls Orlando. *I* am in love with Cavill Pengower. We have completely different objectives. However, at least when it comes to love, I know exactly how she is feeling.

But I'm not here for *me*. I'm here to find out what happens to Lester Ravenglass. I must put my own feelings aside and commit to my mission. But, oh, what I would give to be Hermione again and for Cavill to wrap his arms around me!

There's a knock at the door.

'Come in,' I reply, and Ruby enters. Her cheeks are rosy, her energy vibrant. She's happy to be on the *Titanic*.

'It's a beautiful day, ma'am,' she says, opening the curtains and shaking me from my reverie.

'It's glorious.' I push Cavill from my mind and climb out of bed.

I hand Ruby the diary. She puts it in a drawer. I go to the washstand and brush my teeth using tooth powder that's in a glass bottle. My reflection in the mirror startles me. I'm still groggy with sleep and blink a few times to focus. Nothing is familiar. It's taking me a while to get into character. I stare at the strange hazel eyes gazing back at me and search, once again, for *me*, Pixie Tate, hiding somewhere behind them. But there is no trace of her. It's a shock to see my face. It no longer has the bloom of youth, but the lined, loose skin of a woman in middle age. I run my fingers over my cheek and then pull it towards my ear to smooth out the slack jowl.

'Is everything all right, ma'am?' Ruby asks. She's frowning at me.

'I'm getting old, Ruby,' I tell her, drawing away from the mirror with a sigh. I'm relieved I won't be Constance Fleet for ever.

Ruby smiles as she takes a skirt and blouse out of the wardrobe. 'We all grow old in the end, don't we?' she says blithely. *She* won't grow old for years. Maybe she won't grow old at all? I shudder at that thought. Will *she* make it off this boat? 'How about the green? It matches your eyes.'

'The green will do nicely.' She helps me dress and I turn so that she can tie the corset at the back. I feel as if I'm putting on a costume for a play. I suppose, in a way, I am. As Ruby pulls the laces, I reflect on the diary and Constance's involvement with the suffragettes, and imagine how she must hate to wear such restricting clothing. 'How is everything below stairs?' I ask Ruby. I'm in the dark, grappling for light. I don't even know what I'm looking for. But whatever it is, it's *here*, or I would not have slid to this time and place.

She pulls a face. 'Mr Glover is throwing his weight around again,' she says. 'You know what he's like.'

I know from the diary that Glover is Lester's valet, and that Constance suspects him of theft. 'What's he doing now?' I ask, injecting a little impatience into my voice to give the impression that I'm well aware of Mr Glover's antics.

'There's a fair bit of jostling for position down there, and Mr Glover, of course being the *valet of a viscount*, thinks he's better than everyone else. He wants to mix only with those serving aristocracy and wants me to do the same.' She shakes her head in exasperation.

'But you don't listen to him, surely?'

'No, you know what he's like. He has ideas above his station, that one.' She fastens the little covered buttons on the back of my blouse. Then her hands stop working and she lowers her voice. 'You know you asked me to keep an eye on him?' she says softly.

'I do,' I answer.

Our eyes meet over my shoulder in the mirror. 'Well, last night, he was gambling again.'

I'm not sure how to respond. So, I encourage her to say more. 'Go on.'

'With Lord Ravenglass,' she adds.

I frown. 'Lord Ravenglass was with the servants?' I know enough about the *Titanic* to know that it would be unusual for Lester Ravenglass, a first-class passenger, to fraternise with the valets.

'He was, ma'am. In the saloon of all the places.'

She resumes the buttoning-up of my blouse. I try to think of something to say that won't betray me. 'He must have gone down after I'd retired to bed. Do you know how long they were playing for?'

'No, ma'am. I went down to look for Miss Bird, Mrs Straus's maid. That's when I saw them. But Miss Bird had retired, so I left them at the table and went to bed myself. It was later when I heard singing. I don't know what time it was, but it was late. I poked my head out of the door and saw Lord Ravenglass and Mr Glover coming down the corridor. They were merry.'

'Merry?' By that, I assume she means drunk.

'Yes, ma'am. They were very merry indeed.'

I know from Constance's diary that she suspects Glover of having some kind of hold over Lester. Might Lester have a gambling addiction, and Glover is enabling it? Is Glover pawning Lester's valuables to pay his debts? Lester has already sold a

Constable – how much money is he losing at the card tables? I wish I had had time to read more of the diary. I decide to jump ahead when I go back to it and see if I can find out more of what's going on. I sense Glover plays an important part in this drama.

Ruby pins up my hair and then places a flamboyant feathered hat on my head. I look like I'm going to a garden party rather than breakfast on a ship. She opens the door for me. I turn to thank her, and she grins and points at the door opposite. 'I imagine his lordship is sleeping it off,' she says with a giggle. Well, at least I now know where Lester's cabin is.

As I walk down the corridor towards the dining room, I reflect on Ruby. She and Constance must have an intimate relationship, judging from the way the maid talks to her mistress. She's relaxed and gossipy, and clearly a confidante if Constance has asked her to keep an eye on her nephew's valet.

Just as I'm crossing the foyer, Cavill comes up the stairs. I catch my breath. My heart lurches and my whole body stiffens. I feel like a deer caught in headlights A moment passes before he sees me. I remind myself of the role I'm playing and the importance of not letting Constance down. I must remember that I am her. Who knew that timesliding required Oscar-worthy performances?

Cavill's face registers recognition and he arches his eyebrows. 'Good morning, Miss Fleet,' he says.

'Good morning,' I reply, and smile.

'I trust you feel better?' he asks. How strange it is to look into his eyes and see not a glimmer of affection, compared to when I was Hermione Swift and he gazed at me with love.

'Much better. It takes a bit of getting used to, this ship.'

He frowns. 'I barely feel it moving, it's so large.'

He reaches me and we stand face to face. Constance is shorter than Hermione was, so Cavill appears taller now. 'I have never been on a ship of this size,' I say, which is stupid as there hasn't ever been a ship of this size before.

He looks at me steadily and I don't shift my gaze but look right back at him. My stare must be either inappropriate or surprising, because his expression changes and he appears confused. There follows a giant pause. It's as if we are suddenly both lost for words. He clears his throat. I blink, search frantically for something clever to say, but find nothing. At last, he fills the silence. 'Allow me to escort you into breakfast,' he says.

'Thank you,' I manage, relieved. 'I must say, I'm ravenous. Must be the sea air. I could eat a whale.'

He looks at me in amusement, and laughs. My spirits rise at the sight of his face breaking into a smile, and I laugh with him.

'I dare say they serve whale, Miss Fleet,' he replies. 'They seem to provide every kind of dish on this ship.'

'And fish,' I add because it rhymes, and slip my hand around his arm, dizzy from the solid feel of him beneath his jacket, this man whom I thought I would never see again. With a jaunty step, I walk beside him into the dining room.

It is busy with passengers. The ladies are clothed in elegant dresses and hats, the gentlemen in suits. There's an atmosphere of delight. The very air quivers with it. No one can imagine what's going to happen. The windows are frosted, but one is open and I glimpse through it blue sky and sunshine, and the flat navy sea that stretches uninterrupted all the way to the horizon. I feel a terrible sense of dread. It all looks so benign and beautiful. But in two days' time, this magnificent ship will be at the bottom of the ocean.

I sweep my eyes around the room. I cannot believe the beauty of it. The white walls embellished with pretty mouldings are more stunning than could ever be captured on film. It's unbearable to think of it disintegrating on the seabed. Unbearable to think of the vast quantity of people who will go down with it. My gaze passes over the faces of the passengers and crew, and I wonder how many of them will die. I suffer a moment's dizziness. I'm looking at a room full of ghosts.

Mrs Brown is waving at me from a long table by the window and I decide to focus on my mission and not on the inevitable sinking of the ship. If I'm to do my job well, I must remain firmly in the present. I wave back and we make our way towards her. I can't help but notice that she's wearing an incredibly extravagant hat for breakfast; it makes me think of the hat of Edward Lear's Quangle Wangle Quee. I try not to laugh, turning my grin into what I hope is a serene smile. She's seated with other passengers and I panic, for I don't recognise any of them. Am I supposed to be acquainted with them?

Cavill and I part, and I watch him walk to the other end of the table where a young blonde woman of about sixteen is turning to him expectantly. He takes the chair beside her. I look at them both. The likeness is remarkable – the same angular jaw and cheekbones, the same sensitive blue eyes. She must be his daughter. *Hermione's* daughter. I glance quickly at the other faces in search of her, but she's not here. My heart starts up again at a terrific pace, pounding hard against my ribs. Surely Hermione will join her husband and daughter, and then I will have to meet her. I feel sick.

I'm about to sit down when I catch Cavill's daughter's eye and she gives me a gentle smile. It's a smile of collusion. I wonder what the nature of her relationship is with Constance. Surprised, I return her smile and then greet the men who have politely got to their feet.

'Are you feeling better, Connie?' I turn to the vivacious Mrs Brown. If she calls me Connie, do I call her Maggie? I know not to call her Molly now.

'Much better, thank you,' I reply, taking the chair beside her and sitting down.

'Mr Gilsden was just telling us that they are hoping to reach New York a day early, weren't you, Mr Gilsden?'

The man sitting opposite me has a moustache like a pair of raven's wings. His watery grey eyes are enlarged behind his spectacles. 'I spoke to the captain at dinner last night and he says we're sailing at twenty knots,' Mr Gilsden replies, lifting his chin importantly and looking at me with his steady, watery gaze. It's as if the colour has been washed out of his irises. 'He said they'll get it up to twenty-two knots. I dare say he wants to beat all expectations.'

Mrs Brown whistles. 'That's mighty fast,' she says. I notice one of the ladies opposite grimacing at the unladylike whistling. The English must think the American woman coarse. I think she's fabulous. She pops a grape into her mouth and chews it cheerfully. 'Oh, no. Here comes trouble,' she adds under her breath. I follow the line of her gaze and see an elderly woman making her way towards us. She's as stout as a teapot in a mauve dress and matching hat. Her face is pinched with anxiety. 'It's Mr Gilsden's mother, Connie,' whispers Mrs Brown in my ear. 'Don't listen to a word she says – she'll put you off your breakfast.'

'I apologise in advance,' Mr Gilsden says in a low voice. 'I'm rather wishing I had left her in Winchester.'

I'm curious to hear what this woman is going to say. She looks harmless enough. There is a spare seat beside Mr Gilsden. A waiter pulls it out for her, and she sits down stiffly opposite me and Mrs Brown.

'Well, Mrs Gilsden, you kept us safe last night.' Mrs Brown is teasing her, but I don't know what about. The American chuckles and her large breasts rise and fall, and the feathers on her hat wave up and down. Everything about her is lively. Her bright eyes dance with mischief, but not meanness. Not at all. Mrs Brown's smile is full of warmth and affection. 'I'd say it's time for bed for you,' she adds, lifting her teacup to her curling lips.

Mrs Gilsden sniffs. She does not find anything amusing in Mrs Brown's playfulness. 'I should never have come,' she says and her thin voice quivers. 'I told you, Archie. You should have left me in England.'

'Mother, let's not go through this again,' Mr Gilsden replies tersely. 'It's day three of our voyage and, if the captain is right, we will arrive in New York in just three days' time. We're jolly nearly there.'

'Imagine naming a ship *Titanic*!' she exclaims. 'It's an affront to the Almighty.' Her eyes, as watery and colourless as her son's, widen with fear. 'It's like a red flag to a bull. This ship will never make it to New York. I just know it.'

I go cold. She's absolutely right, of course. But how can she know?

'Then why did you come?' I ask.

Mrs Brown laughs and puts a plump hand on mine. 'Mr Gilsden is heading to Canada to start a new life, Connie. He couldn't very well leave his mother behind, now, could he?'

Mr Gilsden looks sorely tried. 'Why don't you stop this silly nightly vigil and join in with the rest of us? There's plenty to do on this ship. We could go for a nice walk along the deck. The weather is fine today.'

Mrs Gilsden purses her lips. Her face is very white. 'I will go to bed after breakfast and join you for dinner. I will not stop my nightly vigil until we arrive in New York. Who is going to wake you up when the ship starts sinking?'

I gasp so loudly that Mrs Brown pats my hand. 'Don't panic, my dear. This ship is unsinkable, everyone knows that.'

I pick at a bowl of baked apples, but I don't have the stomach to eat. The menu is impressive. There's stewed fruit, Quaker oats, all sort of eggs, mutton, lamb, bacon, sausages and kidneys, scones and buckwheat cakes. It's as abundant as the menu in the Aldershoff Hotel. I peek at Cavill. He's in conversation with his daughter. I'm struck by the tender way he looks at her. His face is full of affection and he listens attentively to everything she says. I remember him looking at *me* like that – or rather at *Hermione*, only I was behind her eyes, looking out. I'm a mere acquaintance to him now, another passenger on the boat.

Then why am I here? Why is *he* here with me? Nothing happens by chance. If I just needed to find out about Lester, surely I would have been pulled back to Broadmere. The law of attraction brought me to *this* time and place. To Cavill. There *has* to be a purpose behind it, or it would not be. What is the connection between Lester and Cavill?

Cavill looks up then and we catch each other's eye. I hold his gaze for what feels like a long moment. I sense bewilderment in the uncertain way he is looking at me.

Lester appears then and I tear my gaze away. He stands behind me and places a hand on my shoulder. 'Good morning, ladies, gentlemen,' he says cheerfully. 'Aunt Constance.' He moves to take the empty chair beside Cavill. The two men greet each other as friends. I wonder whether they have perhaps enjoyed an evening at the card table, too. He then engages in conversation with both Cavill and Cavill's daughter, and I notice the young girl's cheeks burning as he directs a question at her.

Lester doesn't look at all hungover. His face is aglow with delight, as bright as the dawn. But then he's young. I meet his eye and he grins. 'Ravenglass looks like the cat that's got the cream,' says Mrs Brown under her breath.

'I wonder what the cream is,' I reply, feeling completely out of place and out of rhythm with everyone else. Constance is a spirited, independent and outspoken woman. I'm not doing her justice. 'But knowing my nephew, he will lap it all up,' I add, not knowing what the hell I'm talking about.

Mrs Brown laughs. 'Even young Miss Pengower is putty in his hands. Is no one immune to his charm?' she asks.

I recall the diary and suspect that Lester is heading out to New York to court Esme Aldershoff, whom he later marries, and Constance is accompanying him in the hope of bumping into Orlando. I imagine Lester, being a ladies' man, flirts with anything in a dress!

'Where is the girl's mother?' I blurt this out before realising that Constance would likely know – after all, they've already been on the Titanic for two days. I hold my breath for the answer, hoping I haven't put my foot in it.

Mrs Brown's face turns solemn and she frowns. 'Why, don't you know, Connie? Pengower's wife died some years ago. He's a widower.'

I should be pleased to hear this, but I feel only compassion for him. Not only did he suffer the death of his nephew and sister-in-law, but he lost his wife too. When I met him he was an insouciant, carefree man in his twenties. Now that nonchalance is gone, and I understand why. He's a man in his forties who has endured too much loss.

My gaze falls softly upon him. 'How terribly sad.'

Mrs Brown's frown deepens. 'You're really not yourself today, Connie. Perhaps you should rest a little. Read a book in the sunshine. The ocean isn't agreeing with you.'

'Oh, I'm fine,' I protest. 'But I shall take your advice and rest all the same.'

After breakfast, I return to my room. As I walk down the corridor, I see a man leaving Lester's cabin. It must be Glover, his valet. I'm surprised by how tall and handsome he is. He must be about twenty-five with luscious blonde hair and a long, angular face. His eyes are deep-set and pearl grey, his eyebrows thick and straight. There's something sly about the curve of his mouth, however, that belies his beauty. Something menacing. Constance is right to be wary of him. I can sense immediately that he's not to be trusted. He's carrying a pair of Lester's shoes in one hand and draped over his arm is a tailcoat and white shirt. He recognises me and smirks. There's something distasteful in the lofty way he looks down his nose at me. 'Good morning, Miss Fleet.' He over-emphasises my name as if mocking me, and those pale eyes stare at me with an intensity that makes me uncomfortable.

'Good morning, Glover,' I answer tartly. He looks surprised that I've even acknowledged him and hesitates as if expecting me to say something more. When I say nothing, he frowns. He looks at me with the same bewildered expression as Mrs Brown. I'm obviously not doing a very good job at playing Constance Fleet.

I enter my room and close the door behind me. I take a deep breath. I need to know what's going on and the only way to do that is to read more of Constance's diary. I decide to take it out onto the deck and read it in the sun. I find a coat in the wardrobe and pull out a fur stole. The stole is horrendous. It's made out of some sort of animal, and not just one. I most certainly won't be wearing *that*! I throw it back in the wardrobe, I'd rather catch cold.

I head outside. The air is bitter. The sunshine gives little warmth, but it's bright and cheerful, and bounces off the waves in golden stars. I walk up the deck and notice at once the stunning view. It's deliberately free of lifeboats. My fury mounts. I know the history of the *Titanic*, of course, but being here, on the *real* ship, walking the *real* decks, makes the folly of the design even more acute. If Alexander Carlisle had thought more about the safety of the ship's passengers rather than the aesthetic of the first-class promenade, so many more lives would have been saved.

I lean on the railing and gaze into the blue. The sky is vast, melting into the sea in a hazy line so that you can barely see where the water ends, and the great space begins. I drop my eyes into the foam churning at the base of the ship a hundred feet below me. I'm lost. I don't know what I'm doing here or for how long I'll need to remain. Will I slide back before the ship sinks? Somehow, I doubt it. Lester is stuck in the mansion in New York. I fear *that* that is where I must go. But why didn't I slide there directly? Why am I here, on the *Titanic*? On the bloody *Titanic* that is shortly going to sink.

What is my purpose here?

I've been brought to this time and place, but have no idea what to search for. Lester and I have barely spoken. His valet is obviously a menace. How is it possible that a hotel in New York in 2014 harbours an earthbound spirit who just happens to be connected to Cavill Pengower? And I am called in to release him.

The coincidence is incredible.

Unless the common denominator is not Cavill Pengower, but me! Could I have started something beyond my understanding when I first met Cavill, seventeen years ago? My head swims as I consider this. Am I the reason that Lester and Cavill are together on this boat? After all, it's because of me unwittingly preventing Cavill from travelling to South America and dying on the journey that he's alive today. I did what I'm not supposed to do: change events that impact the future. But instead of dying young, Cavill married Hermione and they had a daughter. I realise then the enormity of what I've done. I've impacted the future and brought his daughter into the world.

'Isn't it immense?' I would know that voice anywhere.

I turn to see Cavill standing beside me. My heart throws itself against my ribs and I straighten with a jolt.

'I'm sorry. Did I startle you?' He smiles down at me and I'm bewildered. He's looking at me now with a completely different expression on his face, and I don't know why.

'I was miles away,' I reply.

'Finding your sea legs,' he says.

'Of course.'

'Josephine has just told me how kind you were to take the trouble to talk to her yesterday. She said you were very reassuring. Thank you.'

I assume he's talking about his daughter? I wonder what the hell did Constance do for her to warrant his thanks. 'Please. No thanks are necessary.'

He rests his forearms on the railing and looks out to sea. The sun warms his face, but it emphasises too the lines etched upon it. The face I knew had no lines at all. He takes a breath. 'She has never got over her mother's death,' he says. He keeps his gaze trained on the horizon. It's easier to speak about feelings when one isn't making eye contact.

'I know,' I reply. 'I don't think a young person ever gets over that kind of loss.' My mind flicks to my own mother, whom I haven't seen since I was a child. She's not dead, but she just as well might be. Something in the view, or in the fact that Cavill, whom I thought I would never see again, is standing right beside me, causes my throat to constrict with emotion. After what my mother did to my father, she has no right to make me miss her.

'I'm sorry about your mother. I believe you were very close to her.'

For a second I'm confused. But only a second. I remember who I am. Constance Fleet. He's referring to Constance's mother.

She must be dead. I take a breath. It's not difficult to convey Constance's sorrow when my own heart is suddenly engulfed in sorrow of my own. 'I was close to her,' I say. 'But I know that those we lose never leave us. That they're still with us in spirit.'

'Wise words.' He nods, but still his eyes don't leave the horizon.

I decide to take a gamble. I know I shouldn't. I take a breath, teetering on the brink of doing what's right and satisfying my curiosity. 'You know I met your wife, Mr Pengower.'

He turns to me now and frowns. 'You did?'

'Yes, I wasn't going to mention it. When she was a governess. Long ago.'

He chuckles. He looks at his hands. 'Yes, she was a governess. Not many people know that.'

'She was lovely. You must miss her very much.'

'I do,' he says. 'Our time together was short. But everything changed after my nephew disappeared.'

'Little Felix. I remember hearing about that tragedy.' I pull my coat tightly around me and shiver. It feels as if my discovery back in 1895 was only moments ago. But for Cavill, seventeen years have passed.

'Yes, the house of Pengower has suffered too much loss.' He looks out to sea again.

'*You* have suffered too much loss,' I tell him, and I can hear the emotion causing my voice to rise.

'Life is not always fair,' he says with a shrug.

'It's not meant to be fair. It's meant to challenge us. We have to accept what it throws at us, both good and bad. Without sadness, we cannot experience joy.'

He looks at me steadily and those blue eyes seem to penetrate the physical, piercing my very soul. 'You know, Miss Fleet, my wife once talked like that. She was deep and wise, like you. But Felix's disappearance changed her. She lost her faith. After he vanished, she didn't talk like that any more. In fact, she didn't recall that she ever had.' He frowns, trying to make sense of something that, from whichever angle he views it, cannot be understood.

I'm aghast. So, he *did* notice a difference from when I inhabited Hermione's body to when I left it. For a moment I'm speechless. I want to confess, to tell him who I am, who I *really* am. But I can't. He would never believe me. Worse, he would think me mad.

'It must have been the shock,' I manage to whisper.

'Yes, I suppose it was,' he agrees sadly.

We both throw our gazes onto that misty line and leave them there. Just me and Cavill. He doesn't realise, as he searches for the woman he loves out there in the blue, that she is standing right beside him.

After a while, Cavill leaves me to go and find his daughter. I watch him go and wonder why he came out to speak to me. Was it just to thank me for being kind to Josephine? Or was it for another reason. I realise I must get back to Constance's diary if I'm to even begin to answer the many questions I have. I find a quiet spot and recline on one of the deckchairs with a blanket thrown over my legs, and open the diary. This time, I don't dally with the distant past. I start with day one on the *Titanic*, Wednesday, 10th 1912.

The diary of the Honourable Constance Fleet

Wednesday, 10th April, 1912

At last, we are on the great TITANIC, Lester and I. I was beginning to worry that Lester was not wholly committed to his fiancée. He was dithering so. There was always some excuse as to why he couldn't travel. Something important to do in

London, or Broadmere, or an invitation he couldn't decline. But here we are, on our way to America, on this magnificent ship.

And, oh, what a splendid ship she is. Indeed, she is the largest ever built, and I'm sure the most beautiful. It is thrilling to be travelling on her maiden voyage. I did try to persuade Bertha to come, to conquer her fear of boats, but she dug in her heels and refused to even consider it. She said she has a fear of water if it is deeper than a bath! QUELLE FOLIE!

The scenes at Southampton docks were extraordinary. Crowds of people waving off their loved ones and the enormous decks of the ship teeming with passengers. It is really quite a challenge to take in the sheer size of the vessel! The excitement was palpable, the cries a roar! Then the giant funnels belched out smoke and off we went, accompanied by a flotilla of small boats, keen to see us off into the big blue sea.

To my dismay, L has insisted on bringing G with him, which is not only extravagant but exasperating, as I have to suffer him and I find him odious. When we were planning the voyage, I suggested that L travel without a valet, but he would not hear of it. What is a viscount without his valet, he argued, and I suppose I do agree with him on that point. If he is to marry Esme Aldershoff, he must at least play the part of a man of means. If the Aldershoffs knew the truth about his dwindling fortune and shameful habits, I'm sure they would call off the engagement at once. I do hope Esme not only fills up the family coffers, but rescues Lester from himself, and instils in him a sense of duty and decorum.

Glover must know that I mistrust him for he gives me surly looks. I have taken to ignoring him completely. I do not condone his influence over my nephew. He is a bad egg and he makes me feel increasingly uneasy. I fear Lester is leaving himself open to blackmail, or something of the kind. He is young and foolish, and Glover, albeit young too, is streetwise and wily. I must listen to my intuition for it has never let me down. What worries me more than anything is that I would be the last person in whom Lester would confide were he to find himself in a precarious position. I need to win his trust so that he can turn to me for help. Besides his hopeless mother, I am the only close family member he has. We have been at odds over my involvement with the suffragettes. I must make more of an effort to put those differences to the side.

My cabin is delightfully comfortable, and the crew are both gracious and polite. Wherever one looks there are helpful people in uniform waiting to be of service. I feel as if I am in a large house party of society's most elite. Among the passengers is John Jacob Astor, the American millionaire, and his wife, Madeleine. They have brought their dog with them called Kitty. They are well acquainted with the Aldershoffs, and Lester and I have already struck up a friendship. They have suggested we go to Newport. The Aldershoffs have a house there — indeed, it seems that Newport is the place to be in the summer. I very much look forward to seeing it and meeting new people. Truly, I have grown tired of London. New people beckon me like a bright beacon of lighthouse to a weary traveller.

Speaking of new people, I have taken an immediate liking to a boisterous and vivacious American lady called Mrs J.J. Brown (her husband is not with her). Her friends call her Maggie. She is from Denver, Colorado, and is immensely wealthy. She has opinions and is not afraid to voice them, and in the most strident tones. I have noticed that the English ladies turn up their noses at her, but I enjoy her confidence and vitality. She has ESPRIT! We took tea together in the Café Parisien, which is so pretty with its view of the ocean and French trellising. I was delighted to notice that the ivy and creeping plants that climb up it are real. CHARMANT! The food is excellent, and we feasted on scones and eclairs. Maggie told me that the Aldershoffs have an enormous mansion in Newport. They call those palaces 'cottages', which is wonderfully ironic. It's not as large as Beechwood, which is the Astor's 'cottage', but it's mighty impressive. Maggie was very interested to hear about Emmeline Pankhurst and impressed with my involvement in the WSPU. She says that if EP goes to America again, she will offer to host a party for her. I cannot wait to tell EP. I'm sure she will go down very well across the Atlantic!

We stopped at Cherbourg to pick up passengers. Tomorrow we will stop at Queenstown and then head out into the wide-open sea. PALPITANT!

Drinks before dinner was lively. Lester is in his element, charming all the young ladies. He certainly takes a shine to Americans. I am anxious to get him into the arms of his fiancée. He rarely speaks of her and seems easily distracted by other young women. We should never have left it so long but travelled out in January. The sooner we get to the Aldershoffs' house, the better. He needs to see Esme again to remind him of her beauty and grace, and of where his duty lies. And I need to see to it that his eye does not stray on this ship! There are many Americans here who know the Aldershoffs. Lester must arrive without the slightest stain on his reputation!

A rubber of bridge after dinner. I partnered Lester and won. Maggie says she will partner Lester tomorrow in order to split us up. She claims we have an unfair advantage being related. I like Maggie very much.

Thursday, 11th April, 1912

I found a free desk in the writing room and set about penning a letter to Bertha on vellum paper embellished with the White Star Line company's red flag. As I was sealing up the envelope, I noticed a shy young woman at the next-door desk surreptitiously squirrelling away postcards in her bag. She noticed me watching her and blushed to the roots of her hair. Poor dear was most embarrassed to have been caught. I reassured her by commenting that it would be rude not to take souvenirs, and she gave me a charming smile in return. She is called Isabella Norris and is here with her mother. Her father died and they are starting a new life in America. When she mentioned her father, her big eyes welled with tears and she looked utterly bereft. My heart went out to her, poor child. She told me that the worst of it was that she never got to say goodbye, because he was killed in an accident. I told her about my spirit board and her tears dried at once. She was most curious and asked whether she could try to communicate with her father. I suggested we have a seance in my cabin after lunch. She took my hand and thanked me, and asked most specifically not to tell her mama, who considers spirit boards the work of the devil. I promised her that I would tell no one. She asked if she could bring a friend and I told her that she could.

We stopped at Queenstown to pick up passengers. Most were steerage passengers on their way to the New World. I took my letter to the post office and then went up to stroll along the promenade deck. There was a chilly breeze, but the sea was only mildly ruffled. I wrapped my coat about me and went in search of

Maggie. Instead of Maggie, I found Lester smoking by the railing and watching the grey coastline of Ireland looming out of the mist. It takes the breath away with its beauty. 'Aunt Constance,' he said when he saw me. 'What devilish things are you up to?'

I couldn't help but laugh. Lester's smile is winning. I told him that there is only room for one devil in this family and that's him.

He offered me a cigarette. It isn't ladylike to smoke on deck, like a sailor – indeed, Mother would turn in her grave if she knew I was indulging in such an unbecoming pastime, but I accepted all the same. I do so loathe those kinds of conventions. In fact, I rather relish defying them. I popped one between my lips and Lester lit it. He asked whether I was going to grill him about Glover again. I told him I didn't fancy wasting my breath. 'You're no longer a boy. You're not my responsibility. If you don't mind him pawning your possessions, as well as wearing them, that's your business.'

He laughed and changed the subject, commenting on, 'Poor, troubled Ireland,' but there was no feeling in his words. He is not one to feel empathy, being so unutterably selfish. I thought Ireland beautiful, so green and lush and wild. He said it's like a sinking ship. 'You'll watch the rats deserting it now in their droves. Leaving it to sink and heading for uncertain futures on this unsinkable ship. I'm not sure what they hope to find in America. It might be nothing more than a mirage. Smoke and mirrors. Perhaps they had better stay at home.'

I told him I thought they were brave. They have so little, but they're not afraid to try their luck on another shore, so far away. Many will be leaving their families and friends and their homes for ever. At least he and I will return to our beloved Broadmere.

He looked at me slyly and added, 'With a great fortune to restore it.'

I felt a twinge of concern then. It was the flippant, careless way he said it, as if Esme were simply a pot of gold to be mined. I asked him whether he loved her. He replied, much too hastily, that he did. Then he stuck out his bottom lip and accused me of not considering his feelings and asking Esme whether she loved him. 'Do I not count for anything?' he said, and I found myself patting his arm and consoling him as if he were a boy, all the while knowing I was being played.

The craggy hills of Cork came into focus, clearly defined against the big blue sky. 'There she is, your beautiful Ireland,' he said. 'Like a lovely-looking potato that's rotting on the inside.'

I told him off for being such a cynic and we laughed. I do so enjoy my nephew when he is spirited. It pains me to think of him making wrong decisions and suffering the consequences. I do wish my dear brother were alive to guide him.

We stood together and watched as the TITANIC drew close to the land and then dropped anchor. Small tenders went out and returned sometime later with passengers, luggage and mail. Shortly, we were joined by Maggie, beaming cheerfully from beneath an extravagant black hat embellished with what might easily have been mistaken for long-tailed widowbirds. Their feathers flapped in the wind, giving the impression that they were about to launch themselves off the brim and fly away. 'Hello, Connie. Hello, Ravenglass,' she trilled in that merry way of hers that is so infectious. She told us that she had just been having tea in the Café Parisien with Mr Andrews. He asked her to let him know if there was anything she could think of that would make the voyage more comfortable.

I asked her if she managed to come up with anything, for I most certainly couldn't. She gave a sniff and said that she would have to think of something simply to indulge him. She said he's like a lover who can't take his hands off his paramour — well, I know what that is like!

Maggie went on to tell us that she had found a squash court and a Turkish bath, and even a gymnasium, although she and I couldn't imagine why anyone would want to go in there.

'Oh, I can see you on one of those mechanical bicycles, Mrs Brown,' Lester exclaimed with a laugh. 'Or the electric horse. Woe betide the horse that tries to buck you off!'

Maggie laughed with him. She has a wonderful sense of humour. 'You're a mischief, Ravenglass!' was her response. But Lester's gaze was drifting to the wealthy young widow who has been attracting a great deal of attention on account of her exceptional beauty and playful eye. I noticed him talking to her yesterday evening, before dinner. She's called Delia Finch and is what many would call 'fast'. Mrs Finch was now walking towards us with a swish of her skirts and a flick of her hips, and a determined glint in that playful eye. I sensed trouble, but Maggie insisted that I go inside with her to browse among the goods some Irish merchants had brought aboard for our amusement. I didn't want to leave Lester and Delia Finch alone together, but had no alternative. Maggie was most determined. When she's like that, I don't imagine anything can allay her. She suggested I buy something for Alice Aldershoff. Ireland is famed for its linen, after all.

Maggie brought up the Potemkin Diamond, and mentioned the preposterous myth of being able to see the face of Catherine the Great in the flaws. People are so simple-minded to invent something like that, and to believe it. At least Maggie had the sense to laugh at it. She told me that the gem is one of the most valuable diamonds in the world and that she has it on good authority that Walter-Wyatt wants to leave it to a son. What a delightful gossip she is! But he's unlikely to have a son now, for Alice is almost forty. Maggie glanced at me slyly and suggested that he might leave it to Lester.

I hadn't thought of that. Really, it had not even entered my mind. But I can just picture Bertha's face enlivening at the smallest hint of that famous diamond ending up at Broadmere, as a Ravenglass heirloom. She's like a greedy magpie, going berserk at the sight of anything that shines!

Maggie told me that the diamond is no longer on display for Walter-Wyatt has hidden it where no one will ever find it. That's very sensible. I would think a gem of that value is just begging to be stolen. I said I hoped he'd show it to me while I'm there. It would be a pity to leave without seeing it.

'A great pity,' Mrs Brown agreed. 'But I suspect he'll want to show it off. After all, that's why he bought it in the first place.' I had to laugh at that. MAGGIE NE MÂCHE PAS SES MOTS!

I was returning to my cabin to freshen up before luncheon when who should I bump into in the hall, but Orlando! What an extraordinary coincidence! He boarded the ship at Queenstown! What luck. We are travelling to New York together. How MAGNIFIQUE that we will have time to get to know one another, because we are confined to this ship with nowhere to escape for three or four more days. 'How lovely to see you again, Miss Fleet,' he called out, and his smile was wide and genuine, and so very handsome. I told him that I was travelling with Lester, and he congratulated me on his engagement to his cousin Esme. 'We must raise a toast to your nephew,' he said, and I replied that Lester would very much enjoy that.

'I will take great pleasure in telling him that you are here,' I said. Then, as I made my way to the dining room, I realised that Lester really must behave himself now and not allow a whiff of scandal to besmirch him. Orlando is Alice Aldershoff's first cousin, and the man upon whom I have set my heart. Lester must be above reproach.

I had lunch in the dining room with Lester, Maggie and Mr Gilsden, whose mother was asleep, having been up all night, keeping watch in case the ship ran into trouble and started sinking. I was relieved that Lester had not invited Mrs Finch to join us, although she might well have declined. The Earl and Countess of N appeared to want to join us, until they saw Maggie presiding loudly over the table in her gaudy hat. At that point, they nodded politely and glided towards a table for two at the other side of the room. I didn't care, I find Lady N as sour as an old lemon and am much happier in the company of the exuberant Maggie Brown.

I searched the room for Orlando – Lester is most eager to see him – but did not find him. He must have been dining in the Café Parisien. I was disappointed, but reassured myself that we have days on this ship in which to get better acquainted. The fact that he is here has breathed new life into me. I feel energised and excited, and optimistic about my stay in America. Now I have found Orlando, even the dullest things look gilded.

We dined on chicken Lyonnaise, green beans and creamed carrots. Really, the cuisine is exceptional, and to think they manage to provide it all in the middle of the Atlantic! I did not enjoy a glass of wine on account of my imminent seance with Miss Norris. I know not to mix alcohol with spiritual practices. It is imperative that one is always clear in mind and good of heart and intention, otherwise one might draw into one's domain a lost soul from the lower planes. One does not want to do that!

Mr Gilsden did not drink either, for he was going to make up a rubber of bridge after luncheon with Lord N, Sir J and Lester. Lester, on the other hand, enjoyed a couple of glasses of chilled Sauvignon, declaring that he is always luckier at cards if he has been tranquilised aforehand with wine. I did not argue with him for it isn't my place, but, judging by his dwindling fortune, that method is clearly not working for him. I hope they will be sensible and not play for excessive amounts of money!

After luncheon, I made my way back to my cabin. As I turned to unlock my door, the door to Lester's cabin behind me opened and out stepped Glover. When he saw me, a supercilious look spread over his face and he greeted me insolently, clipping the consonants of my name and looking at me with an impertinent gaze.

I have taken to ignoring him and it has given me great pleasure to do so, but unfortunately, at that moment, I needed him to bring a chair from Lester's cabin into mine, for the seance. I had to step down off my high horse in order to give him instructions. He carried them out with a petulant expression on his face, as if I was asking much of him. As soon as it was done, I went to my cabin and closed the door behind me. How I hate him with his conceited air and impudent tongue. Once we return to London, I will most ardently insist on his dismissal. It wouldn't be fair on Esme Aldershoff to have him roaming their new home and potentially thieving. No, there will be no argument — the man has to go.

Miss Norris arrived a short while later, accompanied by her friend, Miss Livingstone, who is from Oxfordshire and travelling to America with her mother and aunt. They were quivering in the corridor like a pair of young horses in the starting gate, their cheeks flushed with excitement. I invited them in and they sat at the little round table I had pulled into the middle of the room.

They looked terrified.

'You need not be afraid,' I said, closing the door and locking it. 'The spirit board is simply a way of allowing those with no voice, to have a voice.' I told them that Lester accuses me of being a witch. I'm flattered, of course. I wish I WERE a witch, then I could put spells on people I do not like. Believe me, there are plenty of those I would relish turning into toads and rats. Glover, for one, would make a very fine rat.

The girls laughed more easily after that and settled into the chairs.

'Tell me about your father?' I asked Miss N.

Golden sunlight streamed in through the porthole and settled gently upon the girl's face, endowing it with an angelic radiance. 'He had a kind face,' she replied, and my heart went out to her, for she looked so sad. 'He loved books and used to read me stories when I was a child. He was a man of few words and was quite eclipsed by my mother, but when I had him to myself, he would talk without pause, delighting in my complete attention.' At that moment Miss N's eyes welled with tears. 'I miss him, Miss Fleet,' she said.

I reassured her, telling her what my dear mama always told me. That those who love us on the other side, simply want to let us know that they live on. They don't have special messages necessarily, because they have left the material world behind and no longer care for it. But they care for us and want us to know that they are watching over us and loving us from another dimension. I told her that I was sure her father was no different.

The two young ladies watched with curiosity as I opened the board in front of them. Miss L asked if she could touch the planchette. I explained what it was for, then took the opportunity to make them aware of how very difficult it is for spirits to communicate with us. If it were easy, everyone would be doing it. Spirits are made of light. We are made of matter. There is a big difference between the frequency of their realm and ours. The spirit board does not always work. I hoped it would today.

I performed the usual rituals, then we closed our eyes and I said the prayer of protection. After which, I told the girls to rest their forefingers gently on the planchette. I asked Miss N for her father's name. She said it was Francis. I took a deep breath and centred myself. Then I asked Francis Norris to make himself known.

It didn't take long.

We all felt the temperature drop. To be honest, I was surprised at how quickly it fell. I noticed that the girls barely dared breathe.

The skin on Miss N's arms suddenly rippled with goosebumps and her eyes shone with tears. 'Oh, Miss Fleet, I can feel him,' she said, the colour deepening in her cheeks. 'I can feel him beside me.' So affected was she by the presence of her father that she didn't notice the planchette move slowly and laboriously onto the letter H.

The letter H?

I asked her if her father answered to another name. A nickname, perhaps. Miss N frowned and looked puzzled. 'No, he was Francis or Frank,' she said. Then who is H? I wondered.

At that moment, Miss L piped up. 'My grandfather's name was David Harry Livingstone. Might the spirit be he?'

I cleared my throat, feeling bad for poor Miss N who so wanted to contact her father. 'Are you David Harry Livingstone?' I asked.

The planchette moved slowly and hesitantly onto the word No. It was clearly finding it hard to communicate.

Miss L was disappointed, as was I. 'Give us another letter for your name,' I asked. I repeated the question three times as the planchette did not move. Finally, it carried the fingers across the board to the letter P.

'H or P – might your father have had a middle name beginning with either of those letters?' I asked Miss N. She shook her head. I looked at Miss L. She shook her head too. It wasn't going well.

I sensed that the spirit's energy was faint. It was taking a great deal of effort for it to manipulate matter. A few minutes passed during which nothing happened. But eventually the planchette slid once again onto the letter H, where it remained, most determinedly.

None of us could work out who it was and consequently the afternoon was dispiriting. I explained once more that sometimes it works, but most often it doesn't. Tant pis. Perhaps we can try again in New York. Being on water might not be conducive to spirit communication. I wish Mama were here, so I could ask her.

Tonight, Lester did not cover himself in glory. I do wish he would not linger so at the side of Mrs Finch. She is a widow in search of a new husband and has the unmistakeable air of a gold digger. I can spot them a mile away! I managed to drag him from her on the pretext of taking him off to see Orlando. But no sooner had they found one another, than Lester sprang back to Mrs Finch's side and the two of them engaged in a conversation that looked both intimate and secretive. I was furious. Dinner was at a long table with various new friends, among them, Maggie, Orlando and the dreaded Mrs Finch. She has her claws in Lester and is intent on keeping them there. She claimed, very loudly, that Lester kindly offered to escort her on the voyage, as is custom for men to do with unaccompanied ladies. Kind, indeed! I was having none of it. 'My dear Mrs Finch,' I replied, equally loud, but in a crisp, cold voice. 'I am afraid my nephew is already escorting me.' Well, she could find nothing to say about that and Lester could hardly deny it. Maggie and I laughed about it later as we took our chairs at the bridge table. As Orlando had agreed to play with us, Lester was compelled to make up the four. He played very badly, partnering Maggie, and Orlando and I won.

Orlando is quite solemn, but I believe I am lightening him up. Every time he smiles, I feel I have won something precious. Patience and endurance will reap their rewards. Is it not so with the pearl in the oyster shell?

Chapter Ten
RMS TITANIC
Saturday, 13th April, 1912

I close Constance's diary. That was her final entry before I slipped back in time. There's no point in *my* writing in her place because this book might very well go down with the ship. Everything will go down with the ship. Besides, I couldn't for the life of me emulate her writing.

On a positive note, I think I have worked out who Orlando is. Constance gives her lovers Shakespearean names. Therefore, this mysterious man must be Mr Rowland, for that is the name of Orlando's father in *As You Like It*. Orlando is also Italian for Rowland. I remember that from my English literature class at school when we studied that very play. It's too much of a coincidence that both names are in the same play, and Mr Rowland was once again beside Constance at the card table when I arrived and possessed her last night. He's also American and is very friendly with Lester, which he would be being related to Esme Aldershoff. Now, of course, I'm in a quandary. *I* love Cavill. I want to seek him out, talk to him, spend time with him. But Constance has *her* heart set on Mr Rowland and I must do right by *her*. I can't ruin things for her by cold-shouldering him. I must encourage him as she would do. I'm not here for me. But how I wish I could forget my duty, my purpose, and indulge my own desires!

I allow my gaze to wander over the deck. There are couples promenading arm in arm, and the odd dog trotting contentedly over the decking on a lead. An old man leans on the railing and looks out to sea. A small girl plays with her rag doll, a couple of boys with a ball. In a way it's a privilege to slide back in time and see how people lived, how they dressed, how they behaved.

There's no point in returning to my cabin as I'll discover nothing in there, so I decide to go to the Café Parisien and see if I can find Lester. *He* must be my focus. I have to try to sweep all other distractions aside. Time is running out and I must do my best in the limited hours that remain to find out what could possibly have happened to Lester that causes his tormented soul to create havoc in the Aldershoff Hotel. And that is all.

The café is very much like a café in Paris and just like Constance described in her diary. The walls are white with real ivy climbing up the trellising and a green carpet covering the floor. It's light and airy, and full of people sipping tea and coffee and eating cake and éclairs. I'm amazed at how quickly one gets used to things that only a short while ago were strange. It doesn't surprise me now to see women in elaborate hats, lace blouses and long skirts. Some are wearing dresses that we, in our time, would consider too smart even for a ball. The men are in suits with stiff collars and polished shoes. I've never liked a moustache. I'm glad they're not fashionable where I come from. They're much too fashionable here! Even young men who can barely grow facial hair are cultivating them. Teeth are a major difference too. We take our dentistry for granted, but few people here have straight teeth and many old people have none at all! It makes me laugh to think of those historical dramas on television where the actors have perfect white smiles. That is not the reality at all!

I'm relieved to find Mrs Brown at the corner table. She's sitting with two women I haven't met before. I assume they're mother and daughter. Both are plump with auburn hair and white, freckly skin. The mother's lips are thin and downturned, whereas the daughter's are pink and pillowy – life has not yet disappointed her. Mrs Brown waves me over with an enthusiastic flick of her bejewelled hand. I smile, feigning confidence I don't feel because I have no idea whether or not Constance knows them. As I'm about to introduce myself, the mother says, 'Your nephew is creating quite a stir among the ladies, Miss Fleet.' She gives a disapproving sniff.

So, we are acquainted. I smile back at them, raising my eyebrows in mock exasperation at my 'nephew's' antics, then sweep aside my long skirt and sit down. 'Oh, really?' I reply. The women are American, like Mrs Brown.

I notice the younger woman's cheeks burning at the mention of Lester. The older woman continues in a hard and strident voice. 'If I were Miss Aldershoff, I would be nervous indeed.'

I laugh to play for time as Mrs Brown calls over a waiter and orders a fresh pot of tea. 'I don't think Miss Aldershoff has anything to be nervous about,' I say. 'My nephew's heart very much belongs to her.'

I spot the younger woman's smile falter slightly and I sense that she rather fancies Lester herself. Well, he *is* handsome – there's no doubt about that.

Mrs Brown chuckles and pops into her mouth a glazed cherry from the top of her slice of sponge cake. 'Lester is spoilt for choice, that's the trouble,' she says, chewing with pleasure. 'He's rich and titled, with the face of a Greek statue. If I were a young woman, I'm sure I would lose my heart to him too. Why is he marrying so young, Connie? A man of five and twenty shouldn't be tied down, but out playing the field with all the other young bucks!'

The older woman flicks open her fan and waves it vigorously

in front of her face. She looks at me expectantly, hard eyes brimming with condemnation. I try to think of how Constance would reply. She's a straightforward, straight-talking woman who rather enjoys being unconventional. What would she say? I'm about to cobble together some sort of reply when Mrs Brown comes to my rescue.

'Just because he's marrying young, doesn't mean he's retreating into retirement, Mrs Norris. Miss Aldershoff is going to have to learn to turn a blind eye.' Ah, so she's Mrs Norris and her daughter must be Isabella who tried to make contact with her dead father via Constance's Ouija board.

'Mrs Brown!' Mrs Norris exclaims, horrified. She turns to her daughter and a look of concern darkens her face; it's clear she would rather her child did not hear such things. 'That's hardly the behaviour of a gentleman,' she snaps.

I cut in. 'Oh, I'm afraid I think that is *exactly* the behaviour of a gentleman – at least, an English gentleman.'

Mrs Brown smiles at me in agreement and those black feathers on her hat give a little flutter. 'That is the problem with arranged marriages,' she says. 'We in America marry for love while you in England marry for estates and titles and money. Therein lies the fault. I wouldn't trust a handsome young aristocrat as far as I could throw him, unless I was absolutely certain I had his heart.'

Mrs Norris purses her lips. 'Isabella, don't listen to these two. They're joking, of course.'

Isabella gazes at me with wide, innocent eyes. She knows nothing of the freedoms we women in the modern age enjoy. I appreciate more than ever women like Constance Fleet and Emmeline Pankhurst who fought so hard to win them.

'It's a man's world,' says Mrs Brown.

'Not for long,' I say. 'We suffragettes are making great progress in England fighting for women's rights.' I can't resist, so I add, somewhat rashly, 'One day we'll have a female prime minister, you'll see.'

I see Mrs Norris is one of those women who are happy with the status quo, like Bertha Ravenglass. 'I can think of nothing more alarming than a woman meddling in politics,' she says with a derisory sniff. 'Men are much better equipped both intellectually and physically to run a country. I know where my duty lies.'

I'm sure Constance would have much to say about that, but I decide not to challenge her. I'm not here to change her mind.

'What is Miss Aldershoff like?' Isabella asks in a quiet voice, and I realise that this is the first time I've heard her speak. I don't imagine, with an assertive mother like Mrs Norris, that she gets many opportunities to be heard.

'She is charming and beautiful,' I respond, recalling her description from Constance's diary.

'With a backbone of steel, I hope,' interjects Mrs Brown. She arches her eyebrows. 'With a husband like Ravenglass, she's going to need all the strength she can get.' Isabella frowns and Mrs Brown answers her silent question. 'My dear child, if you were to marry an English aristocrat with a large estate full of servants you must manage, and customs and traditions you know nothing about, you would need a backbone of steel too. The English are not like us Americans at all. We simply share the language. They have a formality that we don't care for, and they're completely tied to their history and habits, and are most inflexible. Poor Miss Aldershoff is going to have to learn a great deal, as well as suffer the inclement weather. I can't think of anything worse than presiding over a shooting weekend in November, and very likely in the rain!'

By the soppy look on Isabella's face, I sense that for Lester, she would give anything to be presiding over a shooting weekend in any weather.

'Isabella will not marry an English aristocrat if those are their morals,' says Mrs Norris. 'She will marry a man who respects and cherishes her, like her sisters have done. Besides, I couldn't bear her to live across the sea. That would be too much. I haven't endured the vicissitudes of motherhood only to send my daughter to the other side of the world!'

'She's a treasure, Mrs Norris,' says Mrs Brown kindly. 'You keep her close.'

'Oh, I intend to, Mrs Brown. Poor Mrs Aldershoff. Her only daughter will be leaving her to live on the other side of the Atlantic,' Mrs Norris replies with a sigh. She puts a gloved hand on her breast and shakes her head mournfully. 'How will she bear it?'

'Because her daughter will be Viscountess Ravenglass,' I say with a laugh.

Mrs Brown laughs with me. 'That will be consolation indeed.'

I catch Isabella's eye and she gives me a complicit smile. I wonder how much she would give to live on the other side of the Atlantic to her mother.

When we leave the restaurant, Mrs Brown cups my elbow in her generous hand. 'Are you quite all right, Connie? You're unusually quiet.'

'Am I?' I ask. I thought I was doing rather a good job of being Constance, but clearly not.

'You are not quite yourself.'

I realise that I'm going to have to explain the change in Constance – Mrs Brown wouldn't believe me if I told her the truth. 'Between you and me, Mrs Brown . . .'

'Maggie,' she says, frowning. The very fact that I have misnamed her justifies her comments, and her eyes scrutinise me with concern.

'Of course. Maggie. To be honest, I have been feeling a little off for the last couple of days. It might be the motion of the ship or my worries about Lord Ravenglass.' I give her a meaningful look.

She nods slowly. 'Say no more, Connie,' she replies, lowering her voice. 'That Ravenglass is a liability, for sure. You need to get him up that aisle as quickly as possible.'

'You're so right.'

'Before he causes a scandal.'

I inhale through my nostrils and feign anxiety. 'I worry about Miss Aldershoff, too. I only hope Lord Ravenglass truly loves her.'

Mrs Brown laughs heartily. She thinks I'm joking. 'You kill me, Connie!' She pats my arm. 'The only person Ravenglass loves is himself! No woman can compete with that!'

We wander up the deck. Coming towards us is Mr Rowland. Behind him, leaning on the railing looking out to sea in the company of Josephine and another young woman I don't recognise, is Cavill. I'm torn. I want to go and talk to him, but I suspect, by the keen look on Mr Rowland's face, that he's about to speak to us. My heart sinks. I can do nothing but oblige.

'Good day to you, ladies,' he says, doffing his hat. 'Are you having a fine morning?'

'We are, indeed,' Mrs Brown replies heartily.

'Might I join you for a stroll?' He looks from Mrs Brown to me, his blue eyes shining with enthusiasm, and then Mrs Brown chortles in that easy manner of hers and says, 'I must return to my cabin, so I will leave you both to enjoy the sunshine.' She smiles broadly and strides off, the feathers on her hat dancing cheerfully. I wonder whether Mrs Brown is colluding with Constance. Does she know how she feels about Mr Rowland – Orlando? Is she deliberately leaving us alone together?

Mr Rowland offers me his arm, and I do my duty and take it. I have no alternative than to make polite conversation. I'm aware with every step that I'm leaving Cavill behind me. 'Isn't the weather just lovely,' I say, turning to look at Cavill again. As I do, he turns his head and our eyes meet. It's for a moment only, a fleeting moment that is quickly over. But I'm electrified.

'We are fortunate. Every day, sunshine,' says Mr Rowland and I have to tear my eyes away. I can feel Cavill's gaze still on me as I set off into the wind. 'And what a pace we're keeping. I do believe we will reach New York a day early.'

'Is that so?' I ask vaguely, trying to concentrate on him and shake off the lingering feeling of Cavill's eyes locked on mine.

'I heard Mr Ismay instructing Captain Smith to take her up a notch. Thrilling, isn't it!'

'Is that wise?'

'Mr Ismay wants to beat all expectations. He's an ambitious man, Miss Fleet.'

If only Mr Ismay knew how dangerous his ambitions are, but he can't imagine the disaster that is just over a day away. And I can't tell him!

'We're almost flying,' I reply flatly, turning my eyes to the horizon and feeling a sudden pang of sorrow for all the lives that will be lost. I wonder whether Mr Rowland makes it off. And Cavill . . . It's too awful to think about.

'I do hope I may call on you in New York,' he says.

'Of course, you may,' I answer, hoping that he makes it there. 'You'll know where to find me,' I add, because he's Alice Aldershoff's cousin.

'I most certainly will.' He chuckles. 'No one can miss a house that size!'

'I can't wait to see it. I've been told so much about it.'

'Oh, it's mighty big. You won't be disappointed. And they

entertain lavishly. In fact, I would go as far as to say that Mrs Aldershoff gives the best parties in New York!' He smiles across at me. 'I do believe you enjoy a party, Miss Fleet.'

'Tell me, what do you like best about the city?' I ask, in order to avoid talking about myself. He's delighted by my question and, as he begins to describe the opera, the music, the grand social scene and the habits and customs of the people, I feel as if I'm in an Edith Wharton novel.

As we make for the door to take us back into the ship, I notice Lester deep in conversation with a woman I have not seen before. They are wandering slowly up the deck, and she has her hand in the crook of his arm. She's beautiful. Even from a distance I can see that. Her face is angular, her eyes long and striking, framed with thick black lashes. Her lustrous brown hair is pinned up and crowned with a playful hat. She's slim. In fact, her figure is the classic hourglass shape so admired by Edwardians, and her purple-and-black dress, which seems demure with the lace buttoned high at her throat, is actually quite brash. By the vivacious way she moves her gloved hand and tosses her head when she laughs, I suspect that she is Mrs Delia Finch, the widow Constance believes is a danger to Lester's reputation. He does seem quite taken with her.

Mr Rowland and I part in the hall, and I'm left wondering what to do. What would Constance do in this position? Would she intervene? Would she leave them to it?

Just then, Josephine Pengower rushes up to me with the young woman she was talking to earlier on the deck with her father. But Cavill is nowhere to be seen. 'Miss Fleet,' she says, standing before me now with her father's eyes and smile. My heart lurches at the resemblance. 'Emma has been telling me about your spirit board,' she says, lowering her voice and looking at me directly.

'I told her that the letters spelt out were *H* and *P*,' says the girl who must be Miss Livingstone – Emma Livingstone.

'Those are my mother's initials.' Josephine's eyes shine hopefully. 'Hermione Pengower.'

When I read the diary, that did not occur to me. I'm astonished. Constance thought the seance had failed. It hadn't. It was just that the wrong spirit had come through.

'I was wondering whether you might do it again, for me.'

I don't hesitate. I know that Constance would leap at this piece of information. 'Let us meet in my cabin after lunch,' I tell her.

The girls smile. 'Thank you, Miss Fleet,' says Josephine and she touches my arm. I sense an intimacy between Josephine and Constance, and wonder how that came about.

They set off down the grand staircase and I head outside with the intention of breaking up Lester and Delia, but when I cast my eye down the promenade deck I find that they are no longer there.

I am reunited with Lester and Mrs Brown at lunch in the Café Parisien. We are joined by Mrs Norris and Isabella, Mr Gilsden, whose mother sleeps during the day, and Mr Rowland, who eagerly takes the chair beside mine. I turn my eyes to the door with a pang of longing, but Cavill must be having lunch with his daughter in the dining room. I turn my attention to my companions and concentrate on the part I'm playing.

'What have you been up to this morning, Ravenglass?' Mrs Brown asks Lester, and when he replies, there is no mention of Mrs Finch.

I meet with Josephine Pengower and Emma Livingstone in my cabin after lunch as planned. I realise I need another chair and knock on Lester's door. When no one answers, I try the knob. It's locked. I notice a steward at the other end of the corridor and summon him in a manner that would make the Honourable Constance proud. 'I need to borrow a chair from my nephew's cabin,' I tell him in an imperious tone. 'Would you be very kind and unlock the door?' He doesn't hesitate and unlocks it at once. I slip inside. It's similar to my cabin with a large bed, wood-panelled walls and a window opening onto bright blue skies and sunshine. As the steward carries the chair across the corridor to my cabin, I take the opportunity to look around. Light falls onto the quilt and the objects on the chest of drawers. There doesn't seem to be anything unusual – simply, the normal things a man might have in his bedroom. It's tidy too. Immaculate, actually. Lester's black shoes are neatly placed beside the chair. They're so shiny, they look wet. His evening dress is pressed to perfection and arranged on a hanger on the door of the wardrobe, ready for tonight. His silver-backed brushes and combs are laid out on a linen towel side by side, and three bottles of unidentifiable liquids stand in a row. Nothing is out of place. I can see that great care has gone into keeping Lester's belongings clean and orderly.

The steward returns and coughs, giving me a signal to leave the cabin so he can lock it. It's then that I notice the woman's glove on the bedside table. It's a long white one. It stands out because it isn't placed with care, but in a messy mound. It's the only thing in the entire room that has been carelessly tossed aside.

Isn't it a little strange for a man to have a woman's glove in his bedroom?

I return to my cabin and the job at hand. The glove bothers me. Is it Delia Finch's glove? Could it be? Is a liaison with this woman the reason I'm here on the Titanic? Is this what I'm meant to witness?

We sit around the table. I light the candle and lay out the board. I don't need to explain to Emma Livingstone how it works, and, as Josephine doesn't ask, I assume that she, too, is familiar with it. I say the prayer and, with my eyes closed, imagine the room filled with light and love. This raises the energy and makes it easier for spirits to reach us. Then I ask specifically for Hermione Pengower. This is strange, as it was only a short while ago in my time that I possessed her. Now, as I feel her come close, bringing with her a draught of cold air, I wonder whether she has any idea who I am.

'Are you here, Hermione Pengower?' I ask. It doesn't take long. She has been here before, and this time she is stronger. That might be due to the altered energy in the room, or to the presence of her daughter. I sense an urgency about this spirit. She has something specific she wants to say.

The planchette carrying our three fingers moves across the board to the word *Yes*.

Josephine lets out a gasp. Emma stares wide-eyed at the planchette.

'Can you feel anything?' I ask Josephine.

She closes her eyes, determined to feel her mother's spirit. 'The room has gone cold,' she says.

'That's normal,' I tell her. 'Your mother is with us. I can feel her close. Are you happy, Hermione?' I ask.

The planchette slowly moves onto the word *Yes*. Both Josephine and Emma are in awe of the force that's moving it. They know it's not their doing.

'Do you miss us?' Josephine asks suddenly and her eyes fill with tears. The planchette glides over the board and settles, surprisingly, onto the word *No*. Josephine frowns, crestfallen. 'You don't miss us at all?' she asks.

I cut in. 'Is that because you are with your husband and daughter in spirit?'

The planchette moves back onto the word *Yes*. This time more easily. Josephine's face relaxes again.

'Do you have a special message for your daughter?' I ask. I know it'll get difficult now, because it takes a lot of energy to spell out words and I don't feel Hermione has very much.

There's a long pause. For a while nothing happens. The girls watch the planchette expectantly.

L O V E

'You love her,' I say and smile tenderly at Josephine. The tears are now slipping down her pale cheeks, leaving shiny trails.

'I love you too, Mama. So very much,' she whispers.

'That's really all they ever want to tell us,' I say, knowing that Constance and I both agree on that. In that moment, I realise how similar we are and am awed by the law of attraction that has brought us together. 'Love is all we take with us,' I add, and watch Josephine's cheeks flush pink.

To my surprise, the planchette starts to move again, a new vigour giving it a sense of urgency. From letter to letter, it staggers.

S T Y C L S T O C

I write down the letters and then take a moment to work them out. 'Stay close to C,' I say at last, interpreting the abbreviations.

'What does that mean?' Josephine asks.

'My name begins with C. Constance.'

'Can we ask her to be clearer?' says Emma, who has not spoken for a while.

'Of course,' I reply. 'We can try. Why must she stay close to C, Hermione?' I ask.

The planchette vibrates. I feel the energy in the room intensify. The temperature seems to drop further. I sense that she is now becoming agitated, perhaps at her own ineffectiveness.

B O A T

'Are you telling Josephine to stay close to me on this ship?' I ask.

No

'Are you telling her to stay close to *me*, Constance?'

Yes

'On this ship?'

No

'Then on what ship?'

B O T

'Boat?'

Yes

'On what boat must she remain close to me?'

The planchette picks up speed and races over the letters.

B O T

B O T

B O T

I take my finger off the planchette. 'I think that's all we're going to get out of her,' I tell them.

'I don't understand,' says Josephine, putting her hands in her lap.

I understand perfectly. When the ship sinks, she wants me to make sure Josephine gets into a lifeboat. But I can't let on that I know what's going to happen.

'Me neither,' I say. 'But remember that she is seeing our world from a different perspective. Everything will become clear. Just keep it in mind. Perhaps we will meet again in New York and take a boat together somewhere. Maybe her advice is not for now, but for a time in the future.'

Josephine nods. Then her frown vanishes and she smiles broadly. 'The important thing is that I felt her, Miss Fleet. And she communicated with me. She is always with me. I won't forget that. Whenever I miss her, I will remind myself that she is with me in spirit. I am so grateful to you. Thank you. What you have given me today is so special.' She brushes away a tear with trembling fingers. 'I only wish I could tell Papa, but I cannot. He wouldn't understand. He might even get cross. But Mama is not in the ground at St Sidwell, but right here with us.'

I take her hand and squeeze it. 'Those we love and lose never leave us. I promise you that. Love never dies. It connects you for ever in an unbreakable bond.'

Chapter Eleven

That evening, Ruby lays out my dress for dinner. It's a long teal blue number, sparkling with sequins. She has run me a bath and I wallow in the hot water, which I imagine is pretty impressive for a ship in 1912. We take those kinds of things for granted, but I know most houses in England do not yet have indoor plumbing!

My mind wanders to Cavill. How I long for him. But I'm imprisoned in the body of another woman. He has no idea who I really am. I wasn't Hermione, either. Even if I told him the truth, he wouldn't believe me. And even if I managed to persuade him, then what? It would achieve nothing. It might induce him to hate me for having deceived him. I can do nothing but love him from a distance.

Ruby is adept at putting up my hair. She uses fake hair pieces to pad out the style and pins it onto the back of my head. I imagine that if we were in Constance's home rather than on a boat, she might use heated tongs to curl it, but there's no way of doing that on this ship. The effect is elegant, however. Constance is a handsome woman. I only wish that I were a wit so that I could do her justice. Having read her diaries, I realise that she's much cleverer than I am, and funnier too. Plus, I don't speak French. I will just have to blame seasickness for my lack of *esprit*.

'Mr Glover is placing bets on the speed of the ship and on

the time of arrival in New York,' says Ruby with a disapproving sniff.

'I daresay my nephew is doing the same,' I reply.

'Of course. I do not imagine Mr Glover is betting with his own money.'

'No, you're right about that.' I've learnt from Constance's diary that Glover encourages Lester to gamble.

'Mr Glover will bet on anything.'

'So will Lord Ravenglass.' We both laugh.

I leave Ruby in the cabin to tidy up, and step into the corridor. I glance at Lester's door and remember the glove on the chest of drawers. The glove that may or may not belong to Delia Finch. Tomorrow night the *Titanic* will sink and I'm no closer to finding out why Lester's soul becomes earthbound. So far, besides a possible addiction to gambling, and maybe a flirtation with a beautiful widow, there is no indication of what exactly triggers his terrible unhappiness. He marries Esme Aldershoff, who presumably repairs the roof of their family home and refills the coffers. There's a strong chance that Glover takes advantage of him somehow. Perhaps he has something on him that he uses to blackmail him. I'm not sure. Constance is certainly worrying about that. Perhaps the trauma of nearly drowning is the trigger. But then why am I here now? I could have simply slid back to tomorrow night and witnessed the sinking and Lester's experience, but I didn't. I slid back to *before*, to give me time . . . time for what? What am I supposed to witness?

There are cocktails in the lounge before dinner. Everyone is mingling. It's like a film set. Women in long, elegant dresses with feathers in their hair and gloves up to their elbows are laughing and sipping champagne out of crystal flutes. Diamonds sparkle at their throats and on their earlobes. The men are in black tailcoats, with stiff white collars and white bow ties. The band is playing music, and the air is filled with perfume and the fizz of jubilation. I search the faces for Cavill and, with a lurch of my heart, spot him. He's tall, so he rises above everyone else, but my gaze would be drawn to him all the same.

I can't approach him. I must keep Constance in mind and do nothing to embarrass or compromise her. I suppose I should be looking out for Mr Rowland. I really don't have the will to do that while Cavill is in the room. I don't know who he and his daughter are talking to, and I don't imagine it's appropriate for a single woman to bound up to an unattached man, although, judging by Constance's diary, no one would be surprised if she did. However, the atmosphere here on the *Titanic* is formal and stiff. As with Hermione, I will eventually slip out and go back to my own time, leaving Constance to face whatever situation I have left her in. That's another responsibility I have to consider. It's impossible to tread without leaving footprints, but I must try to make them as shallow as possible.

Instead, I turn and look for Lester. I spot him in conversation with the woman I believe to be Delia Finch. She's wearing an olive-coloured dress, sparkling with sequins and adorned with lace. I notice too that she's wearing long white gloves like the one in Lester's bedroom. But then, so are most of the other women. Long white gloves are as common as corsets!

I approach Lester and a shadow of irritation passes across his face. He's none too happy to be interrupted. But as Constance Fleet, I must interrupt him, for he's engaged to Esme Aldershoff and nothing must induce a scandal or prevent the marriage from taking place. I know that much from Constance's diary. I know she would do the same.

'Mrs Finch, may I present my aunt, the Honourable Constance Fleet?'

Delia Finch appraises me like a panther before a racoon, but I lift my chin and endeavour to hold my own as I'm sure Constance would, although I know Constance would do a better job of it. 'It's a pleasure to meet you,' I say.

'The pleasure is all mine,' she returns frostily and smiles the smug smile of a woman who knows she is younger and more beautiful than me and is determined to make me feel inferior.

'My aunt is a strict chaperone,' Lester says and there's a nasty edge to his voice. I sense he's already had too much to drink. He doesn't seem quite himself. 'She is here to check up on me, are you not, Aunt Constance?'

Delia laughs flirtatiously, holding the champagne flute in front of a beautiful but cruel mouth. 'If I were your aunt, Lord Ravenglass, I would keep my eye on you too.' They hold each other's gaze, and I feel excluded and uncomfortable. I wonder what Constance would say. I don't believe she would be easily rattled or diminished.

'Now why would I need to check up on *you*, Lester? I would say you are all bark and no bite. And every dog must be indulged up to a point, don't you agree?' I'm satisfied with that. I hope Constance would be too. 'Are you travelling alone, Mrs Finch?'

'I am. I'm sure you will agree, travelling without a chaperone gives one great freedom.' Her smile is complicit as she locks her panther's eyes with his. 'I am confident that, were I to fall overboard, a gallant gentleman might dive to my rescue.'

'How are you in cold water, Lester?' I ask, hoping to dampen the sparks flying between them.

'I would brave it for Mrs Finch,' he says. I'm sure Constance would have a sharp and witty comeback, but my mind feels dull. I snatch at the only advantage I have.

'What will you do if the ship hits an iceberg and sinks? You'll have to save the both of us.' I smile at him defiantly, but I feel guilty for even alluding to what is to come.

Lester pulls a face. He thinks my joke is absurd. 'Isn't it lucky then that the *Titanic* is unsinkable.'

'There is no ship in the world that is unsinkable,' I say seriously. 'It is only a fool who claims it is so.'

'The fool is she who underestimates the power of man,' he says with surprising rancour. I baulk at his sexist comment and cannot resist a sharp retort.

'The power of *man* is limited, my dear Lester.' My patronising tone is worthy, I hope, of the very spirited Constance Fleet. 'It is a naïve and arrogant man who believes he is stronger than nature, and God.' With that, I take my leave and go and find Mrs Brown. My blood is boiling. I've seen a less attractive side of Lester Ravenglass tonight. He's like a wasp capable of a nasty sting if he wants to hurt. I don't know what's got into him. If I were Esme Aldershoff, I'd find someone else to marry.

Delia Finch's tinkling laughter follows me as I weave my way through the throng. I despise women like her who believe their beauty sets them above those less physically blessed.

We dine in the à la carte restaurant, known as The Ritz. It's a smaller room than the dining room, with panelled walls and mirrors that give the illusion of space. I'm seated at a table with Mrs Brown, Mr Gilsden and his mother, the Norrises and Mr Rowland.

Lester has chosen to sit with Delia Finch and a grand-looking couple I haven't met. The husband has fluffy sideburns known as mutton-chop whiskers, and the wife is wearing a supercilious expression and a diamond tiara. I'm glad Lester's not sitting with me, because I'm still smarting from his comment. I remind myself that I'm not here to start a fight, but to witness what unfolds. It's not easy to resist getting drawn into drama. The trouble is, I don't know whether Constance and Lester are used to having these kinds of skirmishes or whether this one is unusual. I don't want to make life difficult for Constance when I leave her. Constance, as much as I know of her, is a woman who stands her ground and will not be disrespected. I must try harder to do her justice.

I'm interested in the dynamic between Lester and Delia, however. Surely, being engaged, he shouldn't be hanging out so much with an unattached woman! Is this budding relationship going to cause problems when he gets to America?

I search the faces for Cavill, but he hasn't come through to the à la carte restaurant yet. Or perhaps he's chosen to eat in the dining room instead. I feel a sense of panic. Tomorrow night this ship will sink. I've barely had a moment to speak with him, besides our brief chats when he arrived and on the deck. I have to engineer another meeting somehow. There's so little time left. Shortly, I will slide back and leave him once again. I can't do that knowing I missed opportunities to be with him.

I curb my frustration and turn my attention to Mrs Brown, who is sitting next to me because we are five women and two men. 'Connie, you need to take your nephew in hand,' she says and gives the green feathers in her hair a toss in Lester's direction. I see he's grinning at the young widow who Constance believes is out to steal him. 'Isn't that what you're here for? You want to be careful. This ship has eyes and ears and big mouths too!'

'I know. I'm not sure what to do.' I sigh inwardly. That doesn't sound very like Constance!

'New York is a small town and some of its residents are here.' She arches her eyebrows. 'Walls have ears too,' she adds with significance.

I'm not sure what she means. 'Indeed?' I question, hoping she'll explain.

She's only too ready to. 'He was having a row earlier with his valet. Didn't you hear, Connie?'

'No, I didn't.'

She lowers her voice. 'As I was on my way to dinner, I passed his cabin and heard him shouting. Really, if one has to shout at one's valet, it's time to exchange him for a new one.'

I'm astonished. How come I didn't hear? I must have been in the bath, perhaps. 'I did notice he was out of sorts,' I reply.

She sniffs. 'Like a bear with a sore head. Well, you can count on Mrs Black Widow to soothe it!' Her toffee-brown eyes widen in mock horror. 'You've got to get a grip on him, Connie, or it'll end badly, I tell you. Viscount or no viscount, no one approves of improper behaviour.'

She's right, of course. Not for the first time, I wonder what Constance would do.

Dinner is delicious. There are copious helpings of caviar, and a different wine for each of the nine courses, if one so desires to eat that much food! In my corset, I feel full almost immediately. I drink only a small glass of wine, even though as Pixie Tate I'm more than a little partial to it and have often gone through an entire bottle on my own! But tonight, I must remain sober and alert.

After dinner, we go to the first-class lounge for a rubber of bridge. My mind scurries like a mouse in a maze trying to find a way out of it. I cannot feign dizziness again, but neither can I play bridge, so what am I going to do? I have to do something or everyone will think it extremely odd. I know from her diary that Constance Fleet is a very good bridge player.

We find a spare table. Mrs Brown takes the chair opposite

me, and Mr Gilsden and Mr Rowland seat themselves on the chairs between us. Mr Gilsden's moustache is so comical that for a moment I'm distracted by the urge to reach out and touch it. The flamboyant black wings look like they're stuck on with tape.

'I hope you're on form tonight, Connie,' says Mrs Brown, eyes shining at me with their usual good humour.

'Let's play racing demon,' I suggest. 'I'm so terribly bored of bridge.'

Mrs Brown arches her eyebrows. 'Racing demon?' She glances at the men. 'Now that's a game I haven't played in a while. What do you say, gentlemen?'

'I think it's a capital idea,' Mr Rowland replies, and smiles at me appreciatively.

Mr Gilsden twiddles the wing of his moustache between his thumb and forefinger. 'How original of you, Miss Fleet.' And so it is. We play a couple of games, and I win, not just once, but twice. I might not be accomplished at the piano. I don't speak any language besides my own, and I'm a poor dancer, but I'm a fiend at racing demon. I think of Ulysses then, sitting in the Walter-Wyatt drawing room, keeping me safe. How often the two of us have played racing demon long into the night.

'Well, I can see why you wanted to play racing demon,' says Mr Rowland, impressed. 'You haven't given us much of a chance.'

'You played like the devil, Connie,' exclaims Mrs Brown heartily. 'But that was the point, wasn't it?'

I laugh with her and begin to gather up the cards for another game when my attention is diverted by Cavill, who is crossing the drawing room. I watch him keenly. He's making his way towards the door. He cuts a dash with his height and quiet glamour. I know instantly that I must seize this moment. I might not get another chance to speak with him, at least, not when he's alone. I rise suddenly and the two men stand with me, which is customary when a lady leaves or arrives at the table. 'I will only be a minute,' I say. 'I need to powder my nose before the next game. Shuffle the cards, Maggie.' And I hasten across the room.

I reach Cavill in time to see him heading through the door onto the deck.

I follow after him. The cold hits me like an icy wall. I had not expected it to be this bitter. My breath mists on the air and I shiver, for I'm not wearing a coat and my dress is flimsy.

I join him at the railing. He turns to me in surprise. 'Miss Fleet! Are you not cold?'

'I needed air,' I reply lamely, taking a breath. It burns my throat. 'Forgive me. I saw you come outside and went after you. I didn't want to be out here alone. I hope you don't mind.'

'Of course not.' He takes off his tailcoat. 'You must put this on or you will catch your death.'

'Thank you.' I allow him to help me into his coat. 'Now *you* will freeze,' I tell him, and it takes every ounce of self-control to resist the desire to wrap my arms around him and nuzzle into the crook of his neck.

'When I start to go blue, we can go back inside.'

'All right.' I turn my face to the stars. They're exceptionally bright tonight, like golden flecks from a sparkler. My throat tightens. I feel the warmth of his body in the tailcoat and the smell of him envelops me, and I can't help but think of the precious times I basked in his embrace, in his kisses, and the tightness in my throat begins to ache. Overwhelmed by the knowledge of what is to come, I want to cry at my helplessness.

I cannot allow him to die. I just can't. Not when I believe I brought him here.

'I dreamt last night that this ship sank,' I tell him gravely.

'You and Mrs Gilsden.' He dismisses my fear with a chuckle.

'What if we're right?' I venture.

'Dreams are just dreams, Miss Fleet. It's natural to be anxious in the middle of the ocean. But you have no reason to be. This ship is—'

'Unsinkable.' I cut in grimly. 'I know. That's what they all say. But there are icebergs out there and we might easily hit one.'

'I trust our captain,' he says. 'Captain Smith won't let that happen. You should be enjoying the voyage, not worrying about things that are so unlikely to happen. This is the most magnificent ship in the world, and the fastest. We'll be in New York before you know it and then you'll wish you had savoured every moment.'

How much more can I tell him without putting the future in jeopardy? I want to save him, but I cannot tell him the truth without potentially saving everyone, and that is tampering with the past and changing the future. I can't do that. This ship *has* to sink and that's all there is to it.

'Just look at that sky,' he says, and gazes up at it. His profile is silhouetted against the luminous blue and I want to trace it with my fingertips, that wide forehead, that patrician nose, that dimpled chin, those sensual lips. The crow's feet that fan into his temples, deeper now, are so familiar to me, I know exactly how they would feel beneath my touch. For a moment I forget who I am. It's just me and Cavill, two people who love each other, standing together on the deck of a ship. But an icy breeze brushes my cheek and I drop my eyes to the black water below. I'm hoping for the impossible. Hoping that Cavill might be able to see beyond the body of Constance Fleet standing before him and remember me. Remember us.

I think of the miles of water beneath the hull. Of the silent tomb on the seabed where in just over twenty-four hours this ship will meet its final resting place. And the feeling of dread overwhelms me.

'I must go back inside,' I say at length, and take off his coat. He looks at me and smiles.

'And you're going blue,' I add with a laugh. 'So, you'd better put this back on.'

He takes the coat. I hold his gaze. He looks deeply into my eyes and then a frown furrows his brow, and he looks as if he's about to say something. I arch my eyebrows questioningly. There's a sudden intimacy in the way he's observing me. Could it be that he's finding something familiar there? Am I wrong to hope?

He seems to change his mind then, and the tension dissipates. 'You had better get into the warmth, Miss Fleet,' he says, threading his arms into the coat.

Reluctantly, I leave him there. As I return inside, I wonder what it was that he was about to say.

Chapter Twelve

I hasten to the card table where my companions are waiting for me. I glance about for Lester, but he hasn't come into the lounge. Neither has Delia Finch. There are many places they could be, and they might not be together. We resume our game. I win again. But I don't feel at all triumphant. There's an anxiety growing in my belly. I recall Mrs Brown's comment about Lester shouting at Glover before dinner and sense a drama building. When Mr Rowland suggests we go back to bridge, I declare that I'm tired and retire to my cabin.

Ruby has turned down my bed. She helps me out of my dress and corset, and then leaves me alone. I'm at a loss. I pick up Constance's diary and decide to read as much as I can this evening. There must be clues within its pages – after she left Broadmere, and before she boarded the *Titanic*. But just as I climb into bed, I hear a strange sound in the corridor. A muffled thump, followed by hushed whispering.

I put my dressing gown over my nightdress and open the door a sliver. My heart is hammering against my ribcage. I hover, uncertainly, behind the door. A moment later, I see two figures fall against the wall at the far end of the corridor. The lights are dimmed in the ship's corridors at this time of the evening, but I quickly recognise them. Glover and Lester. They're unsteady on their feet, holding on to each other for balance. They're like a pair of schoolboys returning from a dare, laughing into their hands. They do not look like master and servant, but brothers up to no good. I imagine they've been downstairs, gambling. Their cheeks are flushed, their eyes shiny. They're enveloped in the whiff of cigarette smoke and alcohol. Lester's teeth are very white as he smiles unevenly. I quietly close the door, barely daring to breathe, as they open Lester's door and disappear inside.

My fingertips are still clutching the brass handle. I can feel the pulse throbbing at my temples. It's nearly midnight. I wait for twenty long minutes, my back pressed against the door, until I'm certain that Glover must have left his master's cabin after helping him undress.

Gingerly, I open my cabin door a crack. The corridor is now empty and silent. Only the soft vibration of the engines deep in the bowels of the ship can be felt beneath my feet. I step out and cross the corridor to Lester's door. I press my ear against the wood. I hear barely audible muffled voices. Lester is not alone. My mind immediately springs to Delia Finch. Can she be in there? Is Lester that reckless? Is she?

I feel a compulsion to go inside. I don't know what I'll say when Lester sees me. I suppose I could pretend I'm sleepwalking or in need of something to ease a headache.

For a moment I fear that he might have locked the door, but I needn't have worried. He's much too drunk to think of that. I turn the knob and push it. It opens easily. The small amount of light from the corridor spills into the room, throwing a triangle of gold onto the carpet. I quietly step inside.

There's movement in the bed. Beneath the quilt a lump resembles a great beast rising and falling, a bulky shadow in the dimness. The beast groans and sighs. My eyes adjust and I realise then what it is. Not a beast at all, but two people. Lester and Delia.

I stare in astonishment. My mind is racing. How did she sneak in so fast? What will the consequences of this liaison be?

The quilt stills. Two pairs of eyes pop out and stare back at me, glinting like silver.

I catch my breath.

They do not belong to Lester and Delia, but Lester and Glover.

Lester and Glover are making love.

I'm rooted to the spot with shock. I cannot tear my gaze away. The two men, dazed with both surprise and intoxication, gape back. Then Lester breaks the tension. 'Constance?'

Mortified, I back away and flee to my cabin. I close the door behind me and lock it with a shaking hand. Then I lean against it, panting as if I've run a marathon. My mind is racing with a dozen possibilities. The blood now pounds against my temples. Lester and Glover are lovers.

What have I done?

So, after all his flirting with Delia Finch on board this ship, it turns out that Lester is secretly gay. I want to laugh at the absurdity of it – to think that I thought Delia Finch was a threat to Esme! And that long white glove lying on his bedside table is not a smoking gun at all! It must be Esme's. A love token – one I don't imagine Lester much cares for. How wrong was I! Lester isn't under Glover's thumb. He's his lover!

Everything is now falling into place. Glover wears Lester's cufflinks not because he's stealing from him, but because Lester gave them to him. Glover isn't pawning Lester's valuables for himself, but more likely on Lester's instruction. The valet is overconfident and arrogant because he's sharing Lester's bed and has Lester's ear and his affection. But Lester is playing a dangerous game. Love – if indeed it is love – can very quickly turn to loathing. If it goes wrong, the man could ruin him in a heartbeat. In 1912, being gay is a crime. It isn't decriminalised for another fifty-five years.

Does it go wrong?

Another thought springs to mind. If he's in love with Glover, that might explain why Lester wasn't *that* keen to travel to America to see Esme Aldershoff. He kept putting it off with one excuse after another. Who delays seeing the woman he loves because it's the shooting season? Perhaps he's sabotaging his engagement on purpose by flirting with Delia Finch, because in his heart he doesn't want to marry at all.

I feel sorry for him then. For both of them. Gay relationships are commonplace in my time; in fact, same-sex marriage has just been legalised in the UK. But now, in 1912, theirs is an impossible love – and I know what that feels like.

I feel as if I'm beginning to make headway at last. The drama that condemns Lester's soul to remain earthbound must have taken place inside the Aldershoffs' house. That much is clear. The reason I slid back to *this* moment was to witness Lester's relationship with Glover. That is also clear. I sense I'm on the right track, but there is still much to discover.

And what of Cavill? What is he doing here? How is it that Lester and Cavill are both on the *Titanic*? It must surely be because I've started something with Cavill that I cannot stop. As the old traveller woman in Cornwall told me in 1895, 'Love will *always* bring you back.' Has the power of love brought us together again?

I slip into bed, but I'm far from sleepy. My mind is frantic. I feel as if it's a messy bundle of threads I'm striving to untangle. I try to imagine how Constance would feel were she to have found her nephew in bed with his valet. Pixie Tate thinks nothing of it, but Constance Fleet is a woman of her time. She'd be horrified,

I imagine, and fear for his engagement as well as his reputation were the truth to come out. Having read her diary, I know that she's concerned about Esme's happiness. Upon Esme's happiness rests her own, because she has her sights set on the girl's cousin. If Lester hurts or disappoints Esme, Orlando will certainly not look favourably upon his aunt. If the marriage doesn't happen, where will Lester find the fortune to sustain Broadmere?

I decide to skim the diary to see if I can find out whether Constance had suspicions about Lester's sexuality. Would she really be so worried about his valet if she didn't suspect theirs to be an unusually close relationship? She might not write about it overtly in these pages – after all, would she use nicknames for her lovers if she didn't fear someone might read it? But she might allude to it in some way.

I scan the entries, searching for the name Glover, or the letter G, which she sometimes uses. There are many references to him. She spends a lot of time at Broadmere with Bertha and Lester, and Glover seems to be an ongoing concern. For a man who has only worked for Lester for eight months, he's certainly made his mark!

At last, I find one sentence that surely confirms my growing suspicion that Constance has known all along about their affair, and that that is at the root of her preoccupation with Glover. On the 10th of January 1912, she writes:

I walked past Lester's dressing room. The door was ajar. I had a direct view of the two young men. There was something about the way Glover was brushing lint off Lester's shoulder that gave me pause for thought. Sometimes one has to really look hard at something to see it for what it is.

Knowing what I know, how am I going to behave when I see Lester in the morning? How would Constance behave? Would she have it out with him and tell him their relationship has to end? Would she insist he dismiss Mr Glover? Or would she ignore it and hope that his secret would never come to light?

When I slip back to my time, Constance will remember nothing.

With that in mind, I decide it's best to pretend that it didn't happen. That's the only way I can safeguard Constance. Lester's secret must go down with the ship.

I awake to a resplendent dawn. The rising sun gently bathes the flat sea in a soft, cold light, and catches the tiny shards of ice that dance on the air and glitter prettily. I look out of the porthole and think of what is to come. When the sun rises again, this ship will not see it.

It could not be a more beautiful morning, or a more fateful one.

Lester does not appear at breakfast. I imagine he has a horrible hangover. I sit at a table with Mrs Brown, who is as cheerful as ever. 'I couldn't resist, I've gone for the baked apples and scones again,' she tells me with relish. 'Tomorrow I'm going to try something else.' She picks up her coffee cup and puts it to her lips. I want to tell her that tomorrow there will be no breakfast, at least not on the *Titanic*. She'll have something hot to drink on the *Carpathia*, the ship which will rescue her and the other fortunate people who will manage to escape in the lifeboats. But tomorrow, everything we see and touch will be at the bottom of the ocean.

I still can't get my head around it. A part of me hopes I'm wrong and that it won't happen. That, somehow, the ship won't hit the iceberg. A *tiny* part of me is tempted to change history and prevent the disaster, but that part has no courage to power it. It's nothing but a fantasy without substance. I'm never going to do it. I know I won't. I can't hop about time and change things as if it's a game. What if I were to change something that had a chain reaction that altered my *own* existence? What if my actions caused *me* to cease to be? I hadn't thought of that!

Lester doesn't appear for the church service that takes place at eleven in the dining saloon. He doesn't appear after, either, so I decide to walk out on deck. It's a strange, unsettling feeling to know that something terrible is about to happen and that you can't do anything to stop it. Or warn anyone about it. Or, indeed, avoid it. I can feel every second passing, drawing every single person closer to the terrible night ahead, and no one on this boat but me knows what is coming. I pace the promenade deck in agitation and as I round the stern of the ship, I'm pleasantly surprised to find Josephine on a deckchair, reading a book in the sunshine. The sky is as blue as lapis, the ocean as calm as a lake. There's nothing but water as far as the eye can see. Water, deep, cold and deathly.

Josephine invites me to join her. I put my feet up on the deckchair beside her and cover myself, as she has, with a blanket. Few people are on deck at this time. Everything feels still and expectant, as if the world is holding its breath. I know *I* am.

'Have you noticed there are no birds?' says Josephine pensively. I'm reminded at once about her father's love of sketching. When I was Hermione, he gave me his sketchbook when we parted. In it he had drawn all sorts of birds – gulls, cormorants, puffins. He loved ducks best of all.

'We're very far from land,' I reply. 'I suppose only migrating birds cross the Atlantic.'

'How do they sleep, do you think?'

'On the wing.'

She laughs incredulously. 'Really?'

'I don't know. I'm just guessing. Your father loves birds, doesn't he?' I can't help but speak of him. The next best thing after *being* with him, is *talking* about him. I hope she doesn't ask me how I know.

'Yes. He used to sketch them,' she replies wistfully, as if remembering something that happened long ago.

'He doesn't any more?' I ask, curious as to why not.

She sighs and shakes her head, bemused. 'I think his life got too busy.'

'How can one be too busy to do something one loves?'

'Life got serious. At least, that's what he tells me. *I* sketch,' she announces with childish enthusiasm. 'Papa gave me his crayons and I draw sometimes. I'm not sure I'm as accomplished as he is, but I enjoy doing it.'

'I think the important thing is to do things one enjoys and not worry about what other people think.'

'You're so right, Miss Fleet. One is constantly comparing oneself to others and it can, at times, be disheartening.' She pulls her blanket up to her chin. 'Have you noticed how cold it is suddenly?'

'I have. The very air is glittering with ice.'

'Pretty, isn't it? Like fairy dust.' She laughs. 'You know it gets bitterly cold in New York in the winter.'

'Have you been to New York before?' I ask.

She looks surprised. 'We *live* in New York,' she says slowly. Then she laughs. 'Are you teasing me, Miss Fleet? For you already know we live there.'

I turn my face to the sea and try to cover my mistake. 'Of course, I know you live in New York. What I meant was, have you been to New *England*? It gets bitterly cold there, too. Sometimes the sea even freezes. Imagine that!' I'm gabbling, but I think I've recovered the situation.

She shakes her head. 'No, we have not been there, but I would like to. We usually spend the winters in Europe.'

I want to ask a dozen questions now – how long have they lived in New York? Why did they leave St Sidwell? How did Hermione die . . .? but I'm afraid I'll put my foot in it again. I have no idea what Constance knows already.

I have no choice but to change the subject to one that is safe. 'What have you enjoyed most about this voyage?'

She narrows her eyes and considers the question. 'Oh, there are so many things . . .'

I turn my eyes once more to the sea. The smooth, benign sea. And the ship sails on, full steam ahead, in a direct line to devastation.

I'm relieved when Lester finally appears for lunch. I'm at the table with Mrs Brown, Mrs Norris and Isabella, when he strides up in his usual confident manner. He smiles politely and greets us with a bow. I notice he does not look at me directly. He's trying to act natural, but beneath his insouciance is a tacit nervousness. Isabella's face flushes and even the humourless Mrs Norris becomes animated. Only Mrs Brown is herself, teasing Lester in her habitual way and tossing her head as she laughs. Mrs Brown is not concerned about being indelicate. I suppose that's one reason why Constance likes her. From her diaries she seems to be a woman who doesn't much care for convention.

Lester takes the seat beside mine and then accompanies Mrs Brown to the buffet. I choose mutton chops and mashed potato from the menu. They return with plates of roast beef. The food is exceptional. As we eat, the energy between Lester and me relaxes a little. I presume that he's relieved I'm not cold with him, or cross. I act as if nothing untoward has happened. I hope he doesn't ever bring it up. I really don't want to leave Constance in an awkward predicament.

'I have enjoyed a close game of squash with Pengower,' Lester says and there is not a hint in his voice of the mocking tone he adopted with me the evening before. 'For an old man, he's surprisingly quick about the court.'

'Isn't it splendid to have a squash court on board a ship!' Mrs Brown exclaims.

'Good Lord, they have truly thought of everything,' says Mrs Norris, dabbing the corners of her mouth with a napkin.

'There's barely enough time to enjoy it all,' Lester adds.

'Well, I would rather we arrived as scheduled on Wednesday,' says Mrs Brown. 'I haven't worked my way through even a tenth of the breakfast menu. I am yet to try the Yarmouth bloaters, whatever they are.' She laughs cheerfully.

'They are smoked herrings, Mrs Brown,' says Lester.

'They're delicious,' I add, because I feel I should say something. I wish I didn't know what I know.

'I don't ever want to leave,' Isabella gushes, and she turns her doe eyes to Lester, who smiles at her. The colour burns in her cheeks and she drops her gaze towards her plate.

'I don't either,' he says. 'Why would anyone want to leave? We have everything we need right here. I think I might use the gymnasium and have a Turkish bath this afternoon. Make the most of the facilities while we're on board. How about you, Aunt Constance?'

We lock eyes for the first time since last night. An understanding passes between us. He's not going to mention it, and neither am I. The corners of his mouth twitch. He holds my gaze. Challenging me to look away first, but I don't. I hold his gaze right back. 'I think I will do exactly what I have done every afternoon since we left Southampton,' I tell him coolly.

'I will promenade the deck and enjoy the sunshine.'

He nods, satisfied with my response. There is no change. I want to reassure him of that. I don't know how Constance would react, so turning a blind eye is the only option open to me.

That afternoon, I continue to play the part of Constance Fleet while I wait for night to fall and the iceberg to loom out of the dark. I feel as if I'm waiting for the executioner's axe. The sun shines, the ship steams on through a flat, benign sea, and life continues as it has for the last four days. No one can anticipate or imagine what is about to happen. Only me, alone with the dreadful knowledge. Face to face with fate.

The gong sounds and I go and change for dinner with a rising sense of dread. Ruby has put out my best dress, for tonight is a special night. 'You look pale, ma'am,' she says, the skin pinching between her eyebrows. 'Are you quite well?'

'I'm fine,' I reply. 'I'm not sure the ship agrees with me, even though I can barely feel it moving.'

She smiles, relieved. 'A nice warm bath will make you feel better,' she says, going into the bathroom. I hear the gush of water as she turns on the taps. The scent of lily of the valley wafts out with the steam. I stand there, wondering what to do with myself. I feel almost paralysed with fear. The sense of impotence is overwhelming. Then I'm struck with an idea.

'Ruby,' I say as she comes out of the bathroom.

'Yes, ma'am?'

'Will you wait for me in my room from around eleven thirty, please?'

'Of course.'

I know I can't change or influence the past, but I can't let Ruby drown. The ship hits the iceberg sometime around midnight, if I remember rightly. I convince myself that Ruby would very likely have been in her mistress's bedroom, turning down her bed and waiting to help her out of her clothes anyway, so I'm probably not changing anything. I'll make sure that I'm dressed warmly, and that Ruby is with me when I go out onto the deck.

Tonight, everyone is dressed in their very finest. I wear a crimson-coloured dress with black satin gloves to my elbow. Rubies shine at my neck and in my ears, and diamonds and black feathers adorn my hair. I refuse to wear the mink stole, even though Ruby puts it out for me. There are more jewels on display tonight than in the Burlington Arcade. So much lace and silk and pearls and fur. It's a dizzying sight. The men are in white tie and tails, with diamond studs in their waistcoats and cuffs. Pocket watches hang on gold chains and shoes are polished to a high shine. The air is thick with perfume and the atmosphere quivers with excitement. We sip champagne and mingle in the reception room before dinner is served in the restaurant. I smile and converse while my stomach churns with dread. We are only hours away from tragedy. What am I going to do about Cavill? I have changed the future for him once already. Would it hurt to change it again?

To my pleasant surprise, Mrs Brown has taken control of the table and invited Cavill and Josephine to join us. She has placed Cavill at the end between his daughter and Mrs Norris. Lester is opposite me beside the now innocuous Delia Finch, in spite of Mrs Brown asking Delia to sit between Isabella and Mr Gilsden. Mrs Brown complains to me in a loud voice, 'Some people really are the limit!'

I am placed between Mr Rowland and Mr Gilsden. Mrs Gilsden is on her son's other side. We are a large table of eleven.

I have no appetite, but I know I must eat. There are many courses and copious amounts of wine. Tonight, I decide to allow myself more than one drink. Dutch courage. I'm going to need it. I'm going to have to witness this ship sinking and hundreds of people drowning. I know that most of the men on board perish. Will Cavill be among them? I don't know that I can face the horror.

My sips turn to gulps, and I feel my head swim and my body relax. I feel more confident and less afraid. I watch the waiter top up my glass as I bring it time and again to my lips. My head tells me I need to be focused, my heart tells me I need courage. I have one eye on Cavill and little by little I lose concentration. I am taken over by a liberating sense of reckless abandon.

It is over dessert that the conversation turns to literature and then to poetry. Everyone names their favourite authors. When it comes to me, I wave my half-empty glass in front of me and announce that I want to recite a poem. Mrs Brown smiles with delight. In her eyes, I see respect. Now I am the Constance Fleet she first met – bold, unconventional and witty. In this moment I feel every bit her. Perhaps I'm being more me. Perhaps, deep down, Constance and I are more alike than I realised.

'I'm going to recite *The King's Breakfast*.' I turn to Cavill. He's staring at me with a puzzled look on his face. Does he remember when, as Hermione Swift, I recited this poem by A. A. Milne and claimed it as my own composition? Does he remember?

Of course he does. He remembers every moment of those precious days, before I left and Hermione became herself. Before she changed.

I begin to recite the poem, knowing how reckless I'm being. But these final hours might be the last I ever spend with Cavill, and this poem is the only thing I can think of that only he and I will recognise.

I put on the voices, just as I did when I was Hermione in the drawing room at St Sidwell Manor. I mimic the deep, gravelly voice of the King, the high-pitched tones of the Queen, and the west country accent of the Dairymaid. I even do an impression of the Alderney cow. My cheeks burn, my heart races and I feel a wonderful swell of triumph because reciting poems is, besides racing demon, one of the only things I do well. Everyone is enthralled. They are watching me with wonder and delight, as if I'm the most talented woman in the room. I ride on the wave of their admiration. I ride on the wave of Cavill's confusion. He believes his wife wrote it. He can't fathom how I know it. And for a blissful moment I am her again.

I look different, but I'm reciting it just as I did back then when I was Hermione, with the same voices, the same accents, and the same intonation. Cavill stares at me dumbfounded, his face drains of colour, his lips part. When I finish, he's the only person who doesn't clap. He barely blinks, so complete is his horror.

I realise then that I've gone too far. That's not the effect I was hoping for.

Mr Rowland, who clapped the loudest, volunteers to recite a poem too, and soon everyone is joining in as he recites something they're all familiar with, except me. I've never heard it before. Cavill doesn't take his eyes off me. I allow mine to be swallowed into his gaze. I wonder then whether he sees me. Whether he *really sees me*, Pixie Tate. And after two glasses of that golden, delicious wine, I dare to believe. Can it be that he recognises my soul?

At ten thirty, some of the guests retire to bed, while others make their way to the men's smoking room for port and cigars, or to the lounge to play cards. In around one hour, the ship will hit the iceberg. I remember Hermione's words the afternoon Constance and Josephine used the Ouija board and decide to keep Josephine close. Cavill detains me as I make my way through to the lounge. 'That poem,' he says. By the strange look on his face, I can tell he's really rattled.

'Yes?' I reply, now wishing I hadn't recited it. I didn't intend to upset him.

'How do you know it?'

'Someone very close to me used to recite it,' I answer quietly.

'Indeed.' He swallows and when he speaks, his voice is husky. 'I've only ever heard it once before.' He shakes his head, as if trying to rid it of an unsettling thought. 'It was as if . . . when you were reciting it, you were just like . . ..' He hesitates, his face tormented.

'I was just like . . .?'

His blue stare penetrates mine searchingly, but he doesn't complete the sentence.

I put a hand on his arm, sorry suddenly that I've hurt him. I can never explain the truth. All I've done is given him pain. Seeing him so distressed causes me pain too. I want to tell him that I love him, that I might look different on the outside, but inside I'm the same woman who lost her heart to him in 1895. But I can't. He would think me mad.

Instead, I try to repair the harm I have done. 'I'm a good mimic,' I say, smiling at him kindly.

I leave him because I don't know what else to say. I know he recognises something in me, but can't put his finger on what it is. He can't imagine the truth. But his soul recognises *my* soul, I'm sure of it.

I'd recognise your soul if it was a ray of light among a thousand rays.

Do you, Cavill?

Present

Chapter Thirteen
The Aldershoff Hotel

Mr Stirling waited for Tanya Roseby and her assistant, Lara, in the hotel lobby. He glanced at the door to the Walter-Wyatt drawing room and hoped that behind it, Pixie was getting rid of the ghost. He certainly didn't want her to come out in the middle of his meeting and declare that she'd failed – he didn't want Tanya to know anything about Lester Ravenglass.

It was busy this morning. People were arriving, others checking out, and guests were setting off to spend the day sightseeing and shopping or hanging out in the restaurant drinking coffee. The hotel wasn't full, but the level of reservations was respectable. He really needed Tanya to agree to represent them in order to encourage more visitors from the UK. Her public-relations company was the best in the business and was certain to boost bookings. And bookings really needed to be boosted; competition in New York was fierce.

Mrs Aldershoff had been and gone, which was a blessing. He didn't want the old lady to scare Tanya off with her talk of ghosts and that dreaded Ouija board she carried with her all the time. He knew she would be back because she'd want to know whether Pixie had succeeded. And this building having been her family home gave her a sense of entitlement that she milked. He just hoped she wouldn't reappear before he'd finished his meeting. Goodness, there were many Pooh traps to be avoided today, he thought.

The elevator doors opened and Tanya and Lara stepped out. Tanya always managed to look sumptuous. In her usual pale cashmere with a camel-hair coat hooked casually over her shoulders and gold earrings shining from beneath her glossy blonde bob, she radiated stylishness. Her assistant looked businesslike in a grey herringbone trouser suit and cream silk blouse. They both carried expensive tote bags and an air of success. Mr Stirling, who appreciated glamour, watched them approach with a swell of admiration. He wanted them to represent the Aldershoff more than anything, not only because Manson & Roseby was the best, but because Tanya and Lara were absolutely the right image for the hotel, and image mattered very much to Mr Stirling.

'Good morning, ladies,' he said, smiling broadly. 'I trust you slept well.'

'We did,' Tanya replied, smiling back. 'The bed was like a cloud!'

'It's hard getting out of a cloud,' Lara added with a laugh.

'I'm glad to hear it,' Mr Stirling replied, relieved that Lester Ravenglass had not made an appearance. 'I thought it would be nice to have the meeting in the bar over a cup of coffee.'

'Marvellous,' said Tanya, following him across the lobby. 'What a beautiful room,' she exclaimed when they entered. 'So flamboyant. I love the murals.'

Mr Stirling showed them to a discreet table in the corner. 'I was determined to restore the mansion to its former glory. As you know, it's had various incarnations. Fortunately, the bones of the place were never destroyed.'

Tanya put down her tote bag, slipped the coat off her shoulders and settled onto the banquette with a satisfied sigh. 'It must have been stunning as a private house. Can you imagine!'

'Alma Aldershoff, who grew up here, is a regular visitor,' said Mr Stirling, pulling out a chair for Lara and then sitting down beside her. 'Her mother sold it when she was fifteen. I don't think Mrs Aldershoff has ever got over it.'

'Hard to see your home as a hotel,' said Lara, crinkling her pretty nose. 'Strangers wandering about rooms that were once yours. Weird.'

'You know it's haunted,' Tanya said to Mr Stirling.

The air stilled around him suddenly. He stared at her in horror. Completely wrongfooted, he did not know how to respond, except to deny it, most ardently. 'Oh no,' he replied, feigning nonchalance. Disappointment hit the bottom of his stomach like a stone fallen from a great height. 'There are no ghosts in the Aldershoff.'

'Oh, there are,' Tanya insisted. 'I saw one last night. Quite exciting. I love a ghost.'

'You do?'

'Oh, yes. Don't you, Lara?'

'Not really,' Lara replied with a shrug. 'I don't believe in them.'

'Well, I do. There most certainly was a ghost in my bedroom last night. It didn't hang around for long, sadly. It was like a hand in the wall. Strange.'

Mr Stirling rubbed the back of his neck, which was prickling with anxiety.

'Creepy!' Lara exclaimed.

'Not at all,' said Tanya. 'It didn't scare me in the least or surprise me. I'd expect a ghost or two in a house this old. In fact,' she added with a grin, 'I'd be disappointed if there wasn't one.'

'It's not old by English standards,' said Mr Stirling, waving over the waiter to order the coffee. 'It was built in eighteen seventy-two. Modern by European standards.'

'Long enough for the odd ghost to get trapped and stick around.' Tanya looked at Mr Stirling with a pensive gaze. 'You know, I think we can use this. You wouldn't believe the amount of people who book hotels just because they're haunted.'

Mr Stirling was alarmed. 'You don't think it would put people off?'

'Not if it's done carefully.' She knitted her fingers beneath her chin and narrowed her eyes ponderingly. 'No, if it's done right, it could be just the thing to set you apart from everyone else!'

Mr Stirling hadn't thought of that. His spirits spluttered back to life with cautious optimism. 'Go on,' he said. 'I'm interested to hear how you see it.'

He wondered, just for a moment, whether he should rush into the Walter-Wyatt drawing room and stop Pixie sending the ghost away.

Alma stood by the grave of her great-grandson, Joshua. He was buried in a quiet spot in the shade of a maple tree. Being early autumn, the leaves were already turning a vibrant cerise colour and falling like tears onto the grass below. Joshua's headstone was a simple one, with the inscription bearing his name and dates, and the words: *Most beloved, we held you in our arms for a little while, but we'll hold you in our hearts forever.* On reading those words again, Alma's eyes filled with sorrow and spilled onto her cheeks, leaving glistening rivulets in her face powder.

Leona, who had been parking the car, came up and stood beside her mother. For a while she said nothing. Joshua had been her grandchild and his death had hurt her as much as it had hurt Alma. But it hadn't changed her so radically, for Leona had never been afraid of feeling and had always openly displayed emotion without shame. Her mother's reaction had surprised her. For as long as she could remember, she had never seen Alma cry. In fact, Alma had sniffed derisively at anyone who did. She was scathing of the 'touchy-feely' modern world where reality television shows demanded that their contestants pour out their hearts without any restraint. But now Alma was pouring out hers and Leona was finding it a little alarming.

'He's with Jesus now,' she said at length, hoping to comfort her mother. She would have put an arm around her if she'd been anyone else, but Alma was not a demonstrative woman. Indeed, public – or private – displays of affection were anathema to her.

Therefore, Leona was surprised when her mother took her hand and squeezed it tightly. The other hand gripped the silver dog's head of her walking stick. Leona was astonished. The hand felt cold and strange in hers. But on some deep level, a forgotten part of her warmed. 'You all right, Mom?' she asked.

Alma nodded. 'I haven't been a good mother to you, have I?' she said suddenly.

'Oh, Mom. That's not fair.' But Leona knew it was true. Alma's social life had always come first. She'd never shown much interest in Leona when she was growing up. Alma certainly hadn't been there when she'd needed her. Being a mother herself, and, for five brief years, a grandmother, Leona knew that love was shown in the small things: the moments of intense listening, the stroking of fevered brows, of bruised knees, the application of plasters, sun cream, antiseptic. The many tiny but vital demonstrations of caring that make a child feel valued. Alma hadn't been present for any of them.

But Alma knew. In her heart, she knew. 'You don't need to pretend. I know I wasn't. I've taken a long hard look at myself lately and I'm not very happy with what I see.'

'I think you're taking Joshua's death very hard,' Leona said. 'You need to let him go now.'

'On the contrary. Joshua has done me a favour. He's given my life a point. It never had a point before.' She sighed heavily. 'It's only a pity that I've realised now when I'm about to leave the world.'

'Don't say that, Mom.'

'I'm nearly a hundred, Leona. How long do you think I've got!' Her tone was sharper than she'd intended it to be. 'We all have to go sometime,' she added, more gently.

'Very well. Then don't waste the time you have left in mourning.'

'Now that's sensible and I agree with you.' She turned her eyes onto Leona and looked at her with an unwavering, penetrating gaze. 'I want you to promise me something.'

Leona nodded warily. She wasn't comfortable talking about death.

'If this woman, Pixie, doesn't find out what's happened to it, I want you to look for the Potemkin Diamond.'

'Mom, it's never going to be found.'

'Not true. It's in the hotel somewhere, I know it. I don't want you to give up.'

Leona smiled indulgently. 'I probably won't use a Ouija board to look for it.'

'No, that didn't work out for me, did it? But you will try, won't you? Promise me that, Leona. And when you do find it, I want you to build a hospice in Joshua's name, here in New York. The Joshua Litton Hospice, so that children can have the care they need when their illnesses are terminal.'

'You don't want it in your name?' Leona asked. The Alma Aldershoff she knew would most certainly want to bask in all the credit.

'No, I want it to be in his name. In Joshua's. That's very important, because it will be he who has inspired it, and I'll be long gone. I want this to happen more than anything, not for me, but for children like Joshua.' She drew her lips into a thin line. 'I want to do something good for someone else for once. Better late than never!'

'I'll do my best.' Leona reassured her softly.

'If we hadn't squandered our fortune, I could have done it myself. But we have nothing to give now but our good intentions, and they're not enough to build a top-of-the-range hospice! I wish . . . oh!' She sighed again, this time with frustration. 'We were once one of the wealthiest families in America. What a waste. What a goddamn waste.'

Leona had never heard her mother swear. 'Money's not all it's cracked up to be,' she said diplomatically.

'It's everything it's cracked up to be if it's used wisely. We didn't use ours wisely at all.' Alma let go of Leona's hand. 'So, you find the Potemkin Diamond, if it's the last thing you do, and you build that hospice. If you don't, I'll haunt you like Lester Ravenglass.' She grinned playfully. 'And I'm sorry I was a selfish mother. I admit it now. I was a selfish mother.' She gave a sniff and set off up the gravel path. 'But if you find that diamond, I can atone for all the bad I've ever done.'

Leona wanted to tell her that the word 'sorry' – another word she had never heard her mother utter until now – was enough.

After the meeting with Tanya and Lara, Mr Stirling returned to his office feeling both relief and optimism. Tanya was a shrewd woman with a talent for looking at situations from unusual angles. Her ideas had been carefully thought out, weighed up and presented with eloquence and intelligence, and he was impressed. Manson & Roseby would indeed be the perfect company to promote the Aldershoff in the UK. He hoped that Tanya would agree. Wouldn't it be ironic, he thought to himself as he sat in front of his laptop, if one of the reasons why she chose to represent them was Lester Ravenglass's ghost haunting the place!

He scrolled down his emails, but his mind drifted to Pixie and Ulysses, and he wondered how long they would take to complete the job. He had no idea what was involved or how much time was customary. Glancing at the digital clock in the right-hand corner of his screen, he could see that they had been in the Walter-Wyatt drawing room for almost two hours. He hoped that Pixie was managing to move the spirit on, and not taking advantage of his ignorance and watching a soap opera instead! Hamish McCloud had seemed genuine enough, for he had come highly recommended and hadn't asked for a fee when he couldn't get rid of the poltergeist, and he presumed the College of Psychic Studies was a reputable place, but still, how on earth would he know if the ghost had gone? He wasn't one hundred per cent sure that it had been there in the first place. It would be Pixie's word, and he'd have to believe it and pay her, irrespective of evidence. After all, how could it be proven? He took off his glasses and rubbed the bridge of his nose. Was he a gullible fool?

He thought of Ulysses then and hope flared in his chest. Whether or not the pair were charlatans, he was exceedingly happy to have met *him*. It had been a long time since he had felt drawn to anyone in that way and the feeling was unnerving and exciting at the same time.

He tried to answer a couple of emails, but he was too distracted to concentrate. Instead, he went onto the internet and began to search for Ulysses Lozano to see what he could find. When he found one of his social media pages, he expanded the first photograph and leant back on his chair. Ulysses was possibly the most beautiful man he had ever seen. He rested his hand on his chin, gazed into those beautiful green eyes and let out a deep sigh. There was no harm in dreaming.

He was seized by a crazy idea. It really wasn't the sort of thing he did, and he'd be mortified if someone caught him doing it. But it was too compelling an idea to resist. He got up from his chair and left his office. He wandered purposefully through the hall, nodding and smiling at the members of staff who stood about on duty. He stopped to make small talk with the doormen, and then wandered nonchalantly into the street. The sun bathed the pavements in a warm golden light. A couple with a black Labrador strode by on their way to the park. A trio of girls in Lycra jogged lightly over the tarmac. The usual noise of road works, police sirens and traffic rose into the air with the evaporating rain from the night before. Mr Stirling put his hands in his pockets and sidled up to the window of the Walter-Wyatt drawing room, behind which Ulysses and Pixie were supposedly hard at work.

The curtains were drawn behind the glass and there were railings separating the pavement where he stood from the wall of the building. He couldn't get close. But on keener inspection he could just make out, through a sliver of a gap where the curtains hadn't quite joined, Pixie sitting on a chair with her back straight, her hands on her knees and her eyes closed. He was relieved to see that she wasn't whiling away the time watching Netflix. He moved his head a little to find Ulysses, but regretfully the gap wasn't wide enough. As it was, he only managed to get a partial view of Pixie.

He sighed. He'd love to know what Ulysses was up to. What exactly was his role in this enterprise? Well, he wasn't going to get any answers standing outside. He wandered back into the hotel. There was nothing for him to do but wait.

Past

Chapter Fourteen
RMS TITANIC
Sunday, 14th April, 1912
Day 4

The hands of the clock on that famous staircase move inexorably towards ten thirty. Most people retire to their cabins. The more robust men gather in the men's smoking room, while others head in the direction of the card tables. I walk through to the first-class lounge and glance outside the windows where the promenade deck is empty of passengers and bitterly cold. I can't see anything beyond the deck but darkness. However, I know that shortly the iceberg will glide by like a large windjammer, its sail white in the starlight, and those on the bridge will hold their breath. It will seem like a near miss. Indeed, those two men in the crow's nest will breathe sighs of relief, but not for long. Beneath the water, the ice will rip a great big hole through the hull and so seal our fate.

Cavill, Josephine and I settle into easy chairs placed around the large marble fireplace. Mrs Brown and Mr Rowland join us, and a steward takes our orders for drinks. Cavill suggests that Josephine retire to bed, but I encourage her to stay. My eyes flick to the clock on the mantlepiece. In just over an hour, or thereabouts, the ship will hit the iceberg. I need Josephine to stay close to me.

What of Cavill? How will I save him when they will only allow women and children into the lifeboats? I've seen the films. I know what happens. I've watched the crew turning the men away. How can I leave Cavill to die? What can I do to help him? Surely, I'm not altering the future any more than I have *already* altered it, by saving him from dying seventeen years ago. At least that's what I tell myself. What harm would it do to save him a second time?

I remain in the chair while Mrs Brown entertains the group with a story about the time she found a goat in her drawing room. I only half listen. A horrible sense of dread settles upon me like a cold and heavy blanket. There is nothing I can do now to save Cavill. It's too late. The rudder of history is set, and it will not change its course.

Cavill gazes at me with fiercely penetrating eyes. They seem to bore into me, as if searching for my deeper self. But he will never know the truth. He might die tonight, never knowing that the woman he loves is right here beside him. That thought depresses me further.

Mr Rowland is now telling a story of his own. 'Speaking of goats,' he says, his lips curling into a smile, anticipating the laughter to come. 'I know a man who had a pet goat called Rafferty and he allowed him to sleep on a mattress in his bedroom. He awoke one morning to find the goat had climbed onto his bed and placed his head upon the pillow.'

Mrs Brown laughs loudly. 'Did he mistake it for his wife?'

Cavill laughs then. It's too ridiculous, but it breaks the tension between us and I can't help but chuckle in spite of my misery. 'Good Lord, Mrs Brown,' Cavill exclaims. 'I would hope there was enough of a difference to tell them apart!'

I notice Josephine has dozed off in her chair. Her head is resting gently on her shoulder and she's breathing softly. Cavill rattles the ice in his whisky glass.

Emboldened now, Mr Rowland embarks on another anecdote. A waiter leaving the room drops a teacup and the clatter of it hitting the floor makes me jump. Josephine doesn't stir, but Cavill leans forwards in his chair. 'Are you all right, Miss Fleet?' he asks in a low voice, while Mr Rowland continues, oblivious. 'You seem nervous.'

'I have a sense that something terrible is going to happen,' I whisper. I want to say more. I want him to know that I love him, that I always will.

Cavill looks puzzled. 'You know you have nothing to worry about, Miss Fleet.' He smiles bashfully. 'If I can be so candid, you make me a little nervous, too—'

Before I can reply, the subtlest sensation of a jolt causes the *Titanic* to shudder, like a shiver rippling through it. I'm surprised that something so devastating begins with a barely perceptible bump. The ice in Cavill's whisky glass trembles. He stares into it and frowns. I look up at the clock; it's 11.40 p.m.

And so it begins.

Josephine wakes up suddenly. 'What was that?' she asks. Her eyes dart to her father. 'Papa?'

Mrs Brown has barely noticed. 'Mr Rowland, what did the poor woman do with the pig?' Mr Rowland hesitates a beat, as if sensing something is amiss, but then continues with his story.

Just then a man runs into the lounge cradling a large chunk of ice. 'Look at this!' he exclaims gleefully, cheeks pink with cold. 'There are loads of it on deck. We missed an iceberg by a foot! A foot, I tell you!'

Cavill turns to me. 'It was likely just a scrape. There's nothing to worry about. Captain Smith is a seasoned mariner. He will be aware of icebergs and avoid them.'

'We didn't miss it.' I stand up. 'We need to go and put on lifejackets.' My voice is quivering with fear.

'My dear Connie, aren't you being a little over-dramatic?' says Mrs Brown.

'I don't think one can ever be too cautious,' I reply.

Mr Rowland gets to his feet, eager to be of service. 'Allow me to find one for you, Miss Fleet.'

'Thank you, Mr Rowland, but I must go and find my maid. Josephine, you come with me.'

I can tell from the expression on Cavill's face that he thinks I'm overreacting. But he doesn't know what I know. None of them do.

I leave the room with Josephine, leaving Cavill staring after me in bewilderment. Right now, there is no indication that the ship has hit an iceberg, merely scraped one. No crew members are telling people to put on lifejackets. Passengers are still sleeping soundly in their beds and the boat powers on. They are unaware of the seriousness of what has just happened. Of the chaos to come. I wonder as I hurry down the corridor to my cabin whether I will see Cavill again.

Ruby is waiting for me in my bedroom as instructed. She's surprised to see Josephine with me. 'Is everything all right, ma'am?' she asks, wringing her hands anxiously.

'No. Everything is far from all right,' I reply. 'You must come with us.'

She looks alarmed. 'Did you feel the ship judder?' she asks. 'Is that what this is about? Has something happened?'

I'm about to answer her when the ship goes quiet. The continuous vibration that has accompanied us throughout the voyage has stopped. They have turned off the engines.

Ruby's eyes jump from Josephine to me. 'What's going on?'

'We need to wrap up,' I tell them. 'It's going to be freezing cold on deck. Take anything of mine, Ruby, to keep you warm. You too, Josephine.'

Ruby hesitates. She's wondering whether I'm overreacting. She might even suspect I've had too much to drink. 'Can't we stay inside?' she asks in a small voice.

'No. We're all going to have to go on deck. The lucky ones will get into lifeboats.'

'Lifeboats?' Josephine is alarmed now. 'Surely not.'

'Surely, yes,' I tell her firmly. 'Now put this on.' I toss her the fur stole that I have refused to wear. She drapes it over her shoulders gingerly, still doubtful whether I can be believed. 'I know you think I'm making this up. But I'm not. This ship has hit an iceberg and will sink in a couple of hours. Don't ask me how I know. I just do. You'll see I'm not a fantasist when the crew come around handing out lifejackets. Now come on.'

Josephine's lips tremble. Ruby's eyes well with tears. Without a word we wrap up as best we can in Constance's fur coats and shawls. My eye catches the Ouija board lying on the table and I grab it. Perhaps that's what Constance did, for it survives and ends up with Didi Aldershoff. At least in salvaging it, I'm doing one thing that I know is right. As I make for the door, I feel a soft hand on my arm. Josephine looks at me with different eyes. The eyes of someone who has just seen the dawn. 'That's what Mama meant when she said the word "boat", isn't it?' she murmurs.

'Yes,' I reply. 'Your mother was warning you to get into a lifeboat.'

'Then we must heed her warning,' she says, eyes burning with newfound zeal. 'What about Papa?'

'He must also find a place on a lifeboat.'

She nods, satisfied. She doesn't know that it will be women and children only who are permitted places. She doesn't know that most of the men on this ship will perish.

When we reach the grand staircase, people are milling about the foyer in confusion. Some have put coats over their pyjamas and nightdresses. Others are in bathrobes and boots. Some are in fur coats and slippers. They look incongruous, like bewildered sheep. There's talk of the ship hitting an iceberg and everyone has noticed that the engines have stopped, but, at the very worst, they believe we will be motionless for a short while only before the engines can be restarted and we can proceed with our journey once again.

Lester saunters into the foyer as if he's entering a cocktail party. He's still in his evening dress. I imagine he's been in the smoking room, playing cards, or in the lower regions of the ship, gambling. 'What the devil is going on?' he asks with a grimace, frowning at Ruby who he believes shouldn't be here, in the first-class foyer. 'Why have we stopped?' He has the entitled air of a man affronted by a vulgar and unnecessary disturbance.

Mrs Brown appears in a mink coat and hat. *She* has the air of a general on the point of marshalling her troops. 'You were right, Connie. We all need to buckle up! They say there's nothing to worry about, but I don't believe them. We've hit an iceberg and that is never going to be good, whichever way you look at it.'

Lester frowns. 'This is all highly irregular,' he says, eyeing Ruby again.

'You need to wrap up warmly,' I tell him. 'It's cold out there.'

'Good Lord,' he says with a sigh. 'You're like Chicken Licken, Aunt Constance, clucking away that the sky is falling in.'

'The sky *is* falling in, Lester,' I reply coolly. But I don't need to worry about him because I know he survives. I'm more concerned about Cavill. I search the faces for him but can't see him anywhere.

A steward weaves his way through the throng handing out life vests. He gives one to me. 'You must put this on, madam,' he says, then turns to Josephine, Ruby and Mrs Brown. 'This is simply a precaution. Nothing to worry about. We've lost a propeller, that's all.'

We help each other into the life vests, tying the cords tightly.

'I'm going out to see the fun!' exclaims Mr Rowland, pushing through the crowd to get out onto the promenade deck. 'Will you accompany me, Miss Fleet?'

'You go ahead,' I tell him, wanting to remain with the women.

'It's a great adventure,' he says heartily. 'I want to enjoy every minute of it.'

Mrs Gilsden appears, ashen-faced, with her son. 'I told you this would happen!' she wails. 'Why didn't anyone listen to me?'

'Don't be ridiculous, Mother. There is nothing to worry about – an officer told us so. Consider it like a fire drill. We'll be moving again in no time, you'll see.'

'Come on, Connie,' says Mrs Brown, giving me a nudge. 'Let's go and see what's going on.' The four of us head outside.

The night is beautiful. The sky is alight with stars, the sea as calm as a lake beneath it. The air sparkles with thousands of tiny ice diamonds that catch the glowing lights of the liner. It looks magical. There's no indication of the impending horror. No one is panicking.

But they will.

The ship is dead in the water. Only the huge funnels continue to puff out steam, but soon they too will go quiet. 'Nothing to see out here,' says Mrs Brown with a sniff. 'Better to go back into the warm.' She turns and marches towards the door to the foyer. I remain on deck with Josephine and Ruby.

'Do you really think they'll have to launch the lifeboats?' Josephine asks anxiously. 'No one seems to be worrying.'

'They're not worrying yet. But they will.' I look at Ruby, who hasn't said a word since we left the cabin. She's shivering inside one of Constance's fur coats. It's much too big for her. She looks like a miserable bear.

'There you are, Josephine.' It's Cavill. He puts his arm around his daughter. 'Come, let's get you out of the cold.' He turns to me. 'You too, Miss Fleet. You'll catch your death of cold out here.'

'I think we should stay on deck and wait for them to launch the lifeboats,' I reply.

He smiles sympathetically, if a little impatiently. 'My dear Miss Fleet, I don't think it will get to that. Come, let's go inside. Please. There's nothing to worry about.'

Oh, but there is.

'I will come and find you as soon as they are launched,' I say, and he shakes his head.

'Very well, Miss Fleet. We'll be in the lounge.'

He turns and leaves me, taking Josephine with him. I watch him go. There's nothing I can do to convince him that I'm telling the truth. I have to wait it out. Soon the drama will begin in earnest and then he'll believe me.

I wander the deck with Ruby trailing beside me, shivering and bewildered. I hear a man tell his wife that it's all a fuss about nothing. 'This ship is unsinkable. Everyone knows that,' he says, and chortles into the icy air. People are leaning on the railing, gazing cheerfully into the still water below, or out at the vast, endless sky that twinkles and shimmers innocuously. Steerage passengers are playing football with chunks of ice on the third-class deck below, their breath misting like puffs of smoke in the cold. I hear laughter as a pair of boys throw ice at each other like snowballs. It all seems innocent and fun. But on the bridge, they will know that it isn't. They will be wondering what the hell they are going to do and sending out SOS signals to any vessels in the area that can come to their aid. Captain Smith will be panicking.

He doesn't know that he'll go down with his ship, but he must, at this point, realise that there's a strong chance of that happening. He knows there are insufficient lifeboats aboard. He must be feeling sick.

It's the quiet before the storm. The inhale before the dramatic exhale that will send this ship to the bottom of the sea. I know I can slide back and avoid the tragedy. I can leave them to it – leave Constance to it. I don't have to experience this nightmare – for that's what it is, a nightmare. I remind myself that this crisis has already happened. That it's in the past. Nevertheless, in my perception, it's happening now and I'm at the heart of it. Nightmare or reality, it makes no difference, because I'm really going through it. But I don't slide back. I choose to remain. I choose to live through it. I choose to do my job and try to release Lester's soul. And I can't leave Constance now, in the middle of this chaos. I have a duty to her too.

I search the faces for Lester and Glover, but I can't find them. I know Lester survives, but what of Glover? Does he survive too? Might Lester somehow manage to get him off the ship and to safety?

Some of the passengers decide to return to their cabins. Others are enjoying the excitement and wandering about the decks in search of more information. No one seems to think there's anything to worry about. But gradually the atmosphere darkens and the truth of the situation becomes frighteningly clear.

People leak out onto the deck, having been roused from their beds by their stewards, dressed in warm clothes and lifejackets. Some are carrying small bags as if they're embarking on a weekend away to a country house. There's less jollity now, no sense of thrill. Talk of water rising into the lower decks turns doubt into fear. Those who returned to their cabins to retrieve their valuables have now hurried back up, having discovered that their rooms are flooding. Alarm spreads through the passengers like an airborne virus. Stewards hand out life vests with more urgency and order everyone onto the boat deck. Panic takes hold with its cold and relentless fingers. The ship lists. A woman shrieks. The sound punctures a hole in the beautiful night and allows the ugly truth to seep in: the great *Titanic* is sinking.

Chaos ensues. Members of the crew swarm around the lifeboats, lifting off the canvas covers and making them ready to lower into the sea. 'I'm not getting in one of those,' says Ruby in a tremulous voice.

'Yes, you are,' I tell her. 'If you don't, you will drown.'

'But this ship is unsinkable. I heard them say it. Not even God could sink it.'

'Well, that enormous iceberg is going to sink it, so you'd better be brave and do as I say.'

She stares up at me in distress.

Members of the crew begin to call the women and children forward to board the lifeboats, but they are reluctant to be separated from their men, and many don't believe it's necessary. In spite of all the evidence to the contrary, they are convinced the ship will stay afloat. I push Ruby forward. '*You* go,' I tell her.

'Not without you, Miss Fleet!' she exclaims. Her eyes are wild with terror.

'I'll be right behind you. Don't worry about me. If I don't board this one, I'll board another. I just need to find Josephine. I promised I'd look out for her.'

'Her father will do that,' says Ruby. 'Please come, Miss Fleet.'

I push her forward and the man in uniform, who might be the famous officer, Lightoller, helps her into the boat. She's unsteady, but she makes it in and sits down, rigid with fear, clutching her coat about her. I wonder whether they would give women and children priority in my time, or whether equality would dictate first come, first served, whatever gender.

People gather anxiously, waiting to board. Husbands push their wives forward; sons encourage their sisters and mothers with words of reassurance that they'll be reunited soon; one or two passengers scoff that this is all folly and return to the warmth. 'It's much safer on this ship than in that little boat!' comments an elderly man, who turns around and makes his way back inside. His remark creates doubt that ripples through the throng, causing some to follow after him.

I notice Mrs Norris and her daughter, Isabella, hurrying towards us. They're eager to join Ruby and the few others sitting anxiously in the boat. Isabella's face is rigid with determination while her mother's sags with uncertainty beneath a purple-feathered hat. 'Don't worry, Mama,' Isabella says boldly, giving her her hand. 'I'll look after you.' How the tables have turned. 'Let us through!' she shouts and the men part respectfully. I think of my own mother then and my chest aches with longing. Longing for love to replace the resentment that attempts to push its way into my heart. I wonder, if she and I found ourselves in a similar situation, whether I would forgive her. Whether I could. The vision of the bloodied knife floats before my eyes, and my father's convulsing body on the floor, and she remains unworthy of my forgiveness.

The band has assembled on the boat deck and begun to play ragtime. They will all drown. It's too awful to witness. But I know not one of them will survive. Right now, no one believes that will happen. No one knows that there are not enough lifeboats for everyone. They will realise soon enough and then the real panic will set in. I don't want to witness it. I don't know that I can.

With a frantic sense of urgency, I leave Ruby and set off in search of Josephine. I hurry about the boat deck, my eyes jumping from face to face, but she's nowhere to be found. I then make my way to the starboard side. Here, men are being allowed into the boats if there are no more women and children to take the places. I see through the throng of people a familiar face in one of the boats as it's being lowered perilously down the side of the ship. It's Glover. He catches my eye and holds it, as if challenging me to denounce him. I wonder how he managed to get in there. But then I notice his attire. He's dressed like a gentleman in Lester's clothes. He's even wearing Lester's top hat. Where *is* Lester? Why isn't he in the boat too? I tell myself that I don't need to worry about him. That he survives. Then a horrid thought takes hold.

What if Lester only survived the *Titanic* sinking because Constance saved him?

I feel sick suddenly. I don't know what to do. Am I meant to save him? Or if I do, will I commit someone else to the depths of the ocean?

Panic rising into my throat, I scurry about looking for Josephine *and* Lester. As I search the faces for both, I know, deep in my heart, that I'm really looking for Cavill. That I'm hiding that truth even from myself.

The ship is seriously listing now and we seem to be much closer to the ocean. People are beginning to lose control. Cries and screams pierce the air. I can see some of the lifeboats rowing out, their oars churning the water into waves and ripples that catch the starlight and glitter. The boats seem very small out there in the dark and they're far from full. Why the hell don't they fill them to capacity? I need to get into one before there are none left. I cannot allow Constance to die on this ship. That is *not* her destiny, I'm sure of it.

At last, I find Cavill and Josephine back on the boat deck.

Their anxious faces burn orange in the glow of the rockets now breaking into a million golden stars in the sky.

Josephine cries out. 'Miss Fleet.'

'Constance!' That's the first time I've heard Cavill use her first name. But there's no time to dwell on the significance of that small change.

'I'll take Josephine into one of the lifeboats,' I tell him. 'But we have to be quick.'

'And Papa.' Josephine clings to him. 'I will not leave Papa behind.'

He embraces her. 'It's all right, my darling. I won't leave you,' he says, but I know he's going to have to.

'Stand back, stand back, women and children *only*.' The order is a blow. They're not allowing men into the boats on this deck. Brawls are breaking out. I sense there's going to be a rebellion. It might get nasty.

'We could risk it and run round to the starboard side where they were permitting men to board,' I suggest. I panic then that we'll miss the opportunity on both sides. Wouldn't it be prudent for Josephine and me to just get into this one while it's here? I'm torn between saving Constance and trying to save Cavill. I make a hasty decision. I'll try to save them both.

'Let's go!' Cavill shouts over the clamour of arguing men and the boom and hiss of rockets. He grabs his daughter's hand and hastens back into the ship with a determined stride. I follow him, searching all the while for Lester. We cross the foyer, pushing our way through bewildered people who don't know where to go or what to do. Everywhere we look there are people doomed to drown. When we reach the lifeboats on the starboard side we discover, to our frustration, that they are now only allowing women and children, and barring the men with increasing force. I hesitate. I want to accompany Josephine onto a lifeboat, but I want to save Cavill too – and what about Lester? Where the hell is Lester?

Mrs Brown's voice crashes through the din. 'Connie! Come on, get in!' She stands up in the boat and waves at me frantically. I see her feathered hat flapping above the throng like a startled black hen.

'I'm not going without Papa!' Josephine shouts. Then she begins to sob. 'I can't leave Papa. He's all I have in the world!'

Cavill embraces her fiercely. 'You must go, my darling. I will find you. I promise.' He kisses her wet cheek. 'Do it for me.' His voice breaks. The sorrow in his eyes cuts my heart in two as he looks upon the face of his child with love, knowing now that he will likely never see it again.

He once looked at me like that.

I shove that thought aside. This isn't about me.

I hesitate. What do I do? Do I go with Josephine, or search for Lester? What if Lester has already departed in another lifeboat like Glover did? And I mustn't forget Constance. I need to get her onto a boat or *she* will drown. I must take care of *her*.

Josephine is pulled away and bundled roughly into the boat where she slumps on the seat beside Mrs Brown. She stares up at her father with glassy eyes.

I'm left no choice but to go with her and hope that Lester has made it off the ship.

I turn to Cavill. 'I will look after Josephine,' I tell him, gripping the lapels of his coat. 'If you don't make it, I'll be her guardian. I promise.'

'Thank you, Miss Fleet . . . Constance. I wish . . .' His shoulders drop.

'Connie!' shouts Mrs Brown, more urgently now. The boat is almost full to capacity. I need to get in at once.

'Listen to me, Cavill,' I command in a voice that I don't

recognise. 'There are collapsible boats on this ship. You have to find one and get into it.' I remember then, in a flash of memory, the baker who survives hours in the freezing water because he's drunk on whisky. 'Down as much whisky as you can to keep warm. You have to trust me on this. Whisky, lots of it. The *Carpathia* is going to come to the rescue, but not in time to save all these people. If you follow my instructions, you might make it.' He stares at me, that bewildered look on his face again. Only this time he's not arguing, but listening attentively. 'And you must find Lester.'

He nods. The defeat in his eyes vanishes and is replaced by a gritty determination. 'I'll find Lester,' he replies. 'And the collapsible boats.'

'Connie, hurry!' Mrs Brown's voice rises above the cacophony. They're already lowering the lifeboat.

I'm still clutching the lapels of Cavill's coat. I don't want to let him go. Not again! There's so much I want to say, but no time, and he wouldn't understand anyway. My throat tightens and my chest aches. This might be the last time I see him. I gaze into his stricken eyes and I feel an overwhelming sense of defeat. 'Save yourself,' I say in a rasping voice. 'Please, Cavill, save yourself.'

Hands grab me and pull me forcefully towards the lifeboat. Everyone is losing patience.

As it's lowered, Cavill's face is momentarily lit up by another flare exploding into the black sky. He looks from me to Josephine, and then he is gone.

Chapter Fifteen

The boat carrying me, Josephine, Mrs Brown and about twenty other passengers is lowered down the side of the sinking ship. The creaking sound as it swings from the davits causes some of the women to cry out in panic. There are only about fifteen feet now between the deck and the ocean. It's a shock to see how far the ship has sunk. The *Titanic* will soon be gone and, if Cavill and Lester don't find a collapsible lifeboat, they will go down with it. Perhaps Lester has found his way onto another lifeboat. I pray that he has. I pray that I haven't let Constance down and abandoned her nephew to drown. If I have then I will have changed history. Who knows what sequence of events I will have started?

As we descend, we can see through the portholes the water flooding the rooms and churning about the furniture. It's a terrible sight witnessing the destruction of those exquisitely decorated and crafted cabins. I look up to see a couple in lifejackets and fancy hats leaning on the railings, watching us impassively. Their faces are eerily white in the starlight. I wonder whether they have chosen not to be separated and are resigned to their fate. Or perhaps they hope the ship won't go down. I suppose everyone is hoping the ship won't go down. But tonight, hope is as useless as prayer.

The passengers in the lifeboat are strangely quiet. Wherever we look, there is panic and chaos. It's too much to take in. There are already people thrashing about in the water. People jumping overboard. People trying to swim, trying to survive, holding on to anything they can find that's in the sea. And we can't save them. Not a single one of them. I feel a dreadful mixture of relief and guilt that I am safe and dry in the boat, and a crushing feeling of helplessness and sorrow for those who aren't as lucky. I want to slide back to my time and save myself from having to see and hear, but I don't. I've come this far. I can find the courage to see it through.

The lifeboat touches the water with a splash and the ropes are swiftly untethered. It takes a while for the crew seated by the tillers to get the hang of the oars, but after some awkward and out-of-step rowing, we gradually pull away from the stricken ship. Josephine is crying. Her pitiful sobs accompany the wet sound of lapping oars. Mrs Brown is silent for once, staring with round, incredulous eyes at the extraordinary sight of the enormous ship slowly disappearing into the Atlantic, when everyone believed it to be unsinkable. There are twenty-five of us on board. No one speaks. Everyone is stunned with horror. Most have left loved ones behind. They must know now that those poor souls will likely perish. No one wants to watch the drama, but we can't tear our eyes away.

The sound of human panic and incongruously uplifting music from the band fades to a dull roar as the distance between us and the *Titanic* widens. The passengers who are stranded on board are little more than black silhouettes, except for the stewards whose white jackets occasionally shine in the electric lights of the ship. The *Titanic*'s bow gradually dips and the stern rises. It seems to be sinking faster now. Those black silhouettes are running up the deck, away from the wave which, with the motion of the submerging ship, rolls towards them, engulfing many. Then the lights flicker and go out. The magnificent ship is like a giant rock outlined against the deep indigo sky.

I think of Cavill and Lester. I can't bear to imagine what they must be going through, if they are indeed still on board. People are throwing themselves into the sea. Others are scrambling up and down the deck, but there is nowhere to go. Nowhere to flee. There is only water and death. From where we are watching, they look as small as ants and just as helpless. I know from history that there are some who decide to die in their beds, and a great number of third-class passengers who are locked behind grilled gates and confined to die in their quarters. I feel an overpowering sickness in my heart.

The bow sinks lower into the ocean, the stern climbs higher into the sky. The giant black propellers are lifted out of the water and glisten sharply. The sea swamps the deck and rises to swallow the bridge. One of the funnels collapses and crashes into the water. People swarm around anything solid that might stop them from falling to their deaths as the deck slopes more dramatically and makes it impossible to remain standing.

There's a thunderous roar as the ship cracks like a branch and breaks in two. Those giant propellers come crashing down onto the water, crushing all the people splashing about beneath it. 'Dear God!' mutters Mrs Brown. She pulls Josephine against her fur coat and the girl buries her face and covers her eyes. For a moment the stern, torn from the rest of the ship, bobs about like a duck with its head in the water. There's an excruciating pause as we hold our breath, anticipating the end. Then with increasing speed, the final part of that great ship slides beneath the waves and disappears for ever.

'She's gone,' says one of the crew. He looks at his watch. 'It's twenty minutes past two.' It's taken two and a half hours for the ship to sink.

It's a terrible sight, that empty black space where, only minutes ago, the *Titanic* dominated the view. The stars, as pretty as an advent calendar, continue to twinkle serenely. Yet beneath them is suffering and death.

Screams drift on the still, icy air. The sea churns with hundreds of thrashing arms as people fight for their lives in the freezing water.

'We must go back,' says Mrs Brown. 'We can't leave them to drown. We must go back!'

'No! That is folly!' a woman protests shrilly. I recognise her voice at once. It's clawing and pitiless, the voice of a woman who will always think of herself first: Delia Finch. 'They'll swamp the boat and we'll all drown. It would be madness. Madness. Don't you see? We will not go back.'

'Those are your husbands and sons out there. We've got to do something!' Mrs Brown insists, looking at each passenger in turn, but most look away. They are too afraid of being overwhelmed and drowning as well. 'We can't sit here and watch them die. We must do something.'

And so the legend is born. Maggie Brown immortalised into the fabled heroine 'The Unsinkable Molly Brown'.

She is right, of course. What about Lester and Cavill? What about the other men? 'We must go back,' I exclaim, but I know they won't row back. The boat falls into guilty silence. Even the children are mute. The clamour of drowning people goes on and on, minute after agonising minute. When will it end?

Josephine is now too shocked to cry. All we can do is watch helplessly and wait for it to be over.

*

It's quiet now. The sea is as flat as a reservoir, and as silent as a grave. The thrashing in the water has stopped. There's only stillness and a strange, desolate calm. I gaze up at the shooting stars that whizz through the darkness in streaks of silver, and pray that Cavill has made it. That Lester has made it, too. So many have died – among them, the poor captain who has gone down with his ship. It's hard to take in a tragedy of this scale.

I know, of course, that we'll be rescued. I want to reassure the others in the lifeboat, but I must not. I just whisper to poor Josephine, who is numb with cold and grief, that I'm sure help is on its way. Mrs Brown, in her unique style, organises the rowing because we must take it in turns to give the crew a rest. I volunteer in order to keep myself from freezing. Two women hold the tillers in place while Mrs Brown and I row. None of us knows where we're headed, but it seems futile to sit in the middle of the sea and do nothing.

Time passes. The exertion gives me something to focus on and warms me a little. Occasionally, we see the green glow of flares launched from other lifeboats and hear the calls as survivors hail one another in the dark. The light illuminates fleetingly the icebergs that are scattered among the bobbing lifeboats. It's hard to distinguish them. There's a little small talk, words of comfort, the sharing of brandy from a flask, a blanket offered to a child who is whimpering with cold. I anticipate impatiently the lights of the *Carpathia* that will soon loom out of the dawn, for I have never in my life been so cold. But the sky is black and there's no sign of the sun. It seems as if the night will go on for ever.

At last, a faint light can be seen on the horizon twinkling above the waterline. The boat rises and falls on the swell, causing the light to disappear and reappear in a tantalising game of cat and mouse. 'There's a ship out there,' I say through chattering teeth.

'It's a star,' says Delia Finch dogmatically.

'No, it's a boat and they're coming to rescue us,' I argue.

'I'd put my money on Connie,' says Mrs Brown, who is able to inject a timbre of humour into her voice even in this dreadful hour.

'She's an optimist,' says one of the crew.

'You'll see,' I reply quietly. But I don't feel smug. Even though I know we will be rescued, the wait is unbearable. We are cold, traumatised and desperately sad.

We fall into silence as everyone fixates upon the light, which gradually grows brighter and brighter until it finally reveals itself as a ship. I want to say 'I told you so' to Delia Finch, but I don't have the energy to score points. I'm numb with cold and fatigue, and a strange humility. I'm an imposter, for although I'm sharing this moment with these people, I'm not truly a part of it. I shouldn't really be here. I'm an actor in a play and I will eventually step off the stage. But my grief for Cavill is real and that enables me to share their loss with genuine sorrow.

The other boats have seen the light too. Tiny fires glow as survivors burn letters, hats, newspaper – whatever they can find – and wave them in the air to attract attention. Cheers float over the water with cries of relief as the night gives way to a purple-and-orange dawn. Its beauty is an affront; how can there be such splendour in the wake of such tragedy?

We draw up to the precipitous side of the *Carpathia*. She's a White Star Line ship, not unlike the *Titanic*, only smaller and less grand. One by one we climb the ladder to safety. I make sure Josephine goes before me. She's trembling and so shocked with cold and grief that she can barely hold the ropes. As for me, my legs are numb too, and wrapped in my long skirt, it's a challenge to make it to the top. We're greeted with blankets and hot drinks and disbelief; no one can believe that the great *Titanic* has sunk. The rising sun shines golden onto the faces of survivors, but there's little warmth in it, or pleasure. I'm among those who search for their loved ones. But as more lifeboats reach us and offload their passengers, my hope dwindles. Lester and Cavill are not among them.

Josephine is sobbing. She stays close to me as we wander about the deck, our eyes scanning the faces for those of the man we both love. I spy Glover, huddled over a mug of something hot. He's still wearing his master's hat and astrakhan-trimmed overcoat. His face is half obscured behind the collar, which he has pulled up to hide his identity. I don't blame him for pretending to be a first-class passenger. It's appalling that second- and third-class passengers were considered less valuable and turned away from the boat decks. People are people and should be treated equally. Besides, the lifeboats weren't even full to capacity. Glover used his ingenuity and saved himself. I applaud him. I wonder whether Constance would applaud him, or whether she would condemn him as deceitful?

Ruby finds us and throws her arms around me with a cry of joy. 'You're safe, ma'am. We are truly blessed.' I'm grateful that she made it and embrace her fiercely. We stand at the railing and gaze out onto the ocean, which is now sparkling beneath a clear blue sky. Icebergs glow pink and mauve, and glitter in the emerging dawn. On the horizon, a pale crescent moon appears and starts to rise. Hope ignites in my chest as more lifeboats row towards us from every side. They are woefully short of passengers. Had they filled them to capacity, so many more lives would have been saved. I strain my eyes for Cavill and Lester. But with each boat that draws up beside the *Carpathia*, my hope fades. There's no sign of them.

I fear then that I have somehow changed history and that

Lester might not have survived. In which case, whatever happens in the Aldershoff house that later keeps him trapped as an earthbound spirit *won't* happen. Will I slide back and find him gone, because he was never there? I can't get my head around it and my anxiety mounts. Every one of my actions, however small, will alter history. I can't avoid it. The question is, how big has my impact on Lester been?

Hours seem to pass. I notice that some of the survivors are now coming up soaked to the skin. They must have swum out to the lifeboats or been picked up when one of the lifeboats returned to look for survivors. I'm astonished they've made it. A few of them are surprisingly calm. Maybe they're in shock.

Then two faces I recognise look up from one of the last lifeboats to reach the *Carpathia*. It's full of men who appear as if they've literally been fished out of the sea. Their clothes are frozen stiff and their hair is white with frost. They're bedraggled, grey-faced and shivering.

Cavill and Lester.

I can't believe it. The relief is overwhelming. My vision blurs as my heart aches with the sudden joy that overwhelms. They're alive! They've been saved! I grip the railing tightly to stop myself from sinking to the floor, for my legs have lost all feeling, and I restrain myself from crying out, for I mustn't lose sight of the part I'm playing. Of who I am. Constance.

Josephine shouts, 'Papa!' and he lifts his weary eyes. When he sees his daughter leaning over the railing, his face collapses with emotion that he cannot contain. He smiles at her, and then laughs as she begins to wave, not like a young woman, but as a child who has just discovered her precious father is alive.

I watch this tender moment and share in their joy. After the horror of the sinking *Titanic*, this rare glimpse of happiness is like a precious gift.

'Lester!' I exclaim, and Lester sees me and nods cheerlessly. He has clearly been through a terrible ordeal. His face is ashen, his clothes clinging to his body. He's shivering madly. He must be so cold. He looks forlorn and bedraggled.

The sound of that name reaches Glover. A moment later, Lester's valet is leaning over the railing a short distance from us, gazing down at his master, his face aglow with elation. I watch him in wonder. Never has a face expressed such love as his, in this rawest of moments, and I realise that not only Constance, but I too, have misjudged him. Misjudged them both. Glover and Lester love each other. There is no doubt and I find my heart swelling for them too.

The two men gaze at each other with an unbearable restraint. I turn my attention back to Cavill because I feel as if I'm intruding on something immensely private. And it gives me pain to witness two people for whom love is so cruelly forbidden.

The men climb up the ladder and into the *Carpathia*. When Cavill appears, his daughter runs to him and throws her arms around him. She sobs into his frozen lifejacket, then gives him her blanket, wrapping it about him gently. I leave them alone. I don't want to intrude and it wouldn't be my place anyway. I remind myself that I'm Constance Fleet and give my attention to Lester.

Lester clambers stiffly over the railing and allows me to embrace him. He feels frozen solid, as if he's made of ice. 'I'm glad you're safe, Connie,' he murmurs, and there's genuine affection in his hollow, bloodshot eyes.

'And you, dear Lester,' I reply.

'We are two of the lucky ones. Hundreds were not so lucky.' His gaze clouds with desperation. 'Gilsden and Rowland didn't make it . . .' He shakes his head with despair. But he can't speak any more.

Glover appears and holds out a blanket, and a member of the crew offers him a hot drink. He throws the blanket around his shoulders and takes the mug gratefully. He and Glover then move away to talk somewhere quiet. I watch them, heads together, and sense the deep affection between them. This is a rare moment when they can simply be two young men who have survived a great tragedy. Soon they will have to revert to master and valet, and the wretched duplicity will resume.

I'm longing to know what happened, and why Lester and Cavill are soaking wet. I wonder whether they were among those men who clung to the hull of the upturned lifeboat. Whatever took place out there on the ocean, they're lucky to be alive.

A service is held in the main lounge. A clergyman leads it, thanking God for those who survived and praying for peace and rest for those who lost their lives. I sit with Mrs Brown, Mrs Norris and Isabella, and Delia Finch, who has barely said anything since she boarded the *Carpathia*. Lester and Glover are not among us. There are very few men. I think of poor Mr Gilsden, and his mother who mourns him, and Mr Rowland – Constance's Orlando. Constance will be devastated when she learns that he didn't survive, that he's gone. She had her heart set on him and I feel terrible for her, for she is yet to wake up to that dreadful reality.

As we huddle together, a bedraggled, traumatised congregation, the engines vibrate through the ship and the *Carpathia* sets off for New York.

After the service, I find a couple of deckchairs in the sun and sit with Ruby. It's mid-morning now. The shadows are gone and the world around us is brightly coloured again. The sea is a sapphire blue, the bergs that rise out of the water a glaring white, seemingly innocuous in the daylight. Golden rays shine onto the ripples that pucker in the wind and ignite a blazing trail all the way to the horizon. We are grateful to be warm.

'How many people died, do you think?' Ruby asks solemnly.

'There were lifeboats for only a third of the passengers,' I tell her, shaking my head at the appalling negligence. 'And most of those boats left only half full.'

'Why didn't they have more lifeboats?'

'Because they never believed the ship would sink. And they didn't want to ruin the first-class promenade deck by blocking the view with more boats.'

Her eyes shine with tears and she looks out at the flat ocean. 'All those lives lost because of a view. I can hardly bear to think of it.'

'It will go down in history as one of the greatest tragedies.'

'And one of the most senseless.' She turns to me, her pale face bathed softly in sunlight. 'Thank you for looking after me, Miss Fleet. If it wasn't for you, I might be at the bottom of the sea with all those other poor souls.'

I smile at her warmly. I've only known her a couple of days, but I'm truly fond of her. 'I wasn't going to leave you, Ruby.'

'You're very kind, ma'am. I'm sure many people thought only of themselves.'

'You're family.'

She blinks at me in amazement. I don't imagine many mistresses would consider their servants family. Her eyes drop to her hands and she takes a deep breath. A moment passes during which neither of us speaks. Finally, she nods thoughtfully and lifts her gaze to the horizon once more. 'You're the only family I have, ma'am. Your words mean more to me than you could ever imagine.'

I put my hand on hers and squeeze it. She's too overcome with emotion to smile.

*

Cavill finds me sometime later, leaning on the railing, looking out at the vast expanse of ocean. It will take a couple of days to get to New York. I wonder how much longer I'll need to stay in this time. I trust that when the moment comes to leave, I'll recognise it.

'Miss Fleet, I want to thank you,' Cavill says, slipping in beside me. He's so close, our arms are almost touching. I look into his weathered face, at the lines and shadows that grief has left upon his skin, and feel ever more urgently the longing to stop this charade and tell him who I am.

'I thought you'd died,' I say softly. 'How did you escape?'

'I wouldn't have survived if it had not been for you.' He looks across at me. His face is sombre, the frown lines deep upon his brow. 'I did as you said. I raided the bar in the smoking room and downed as much whisky as I could manage without losing consciousness. I found Lester on the boat deck, trying to bribe his way onto a lifeboat. He wasn't having any luck. There were no lifeboats left. I thought we were doomed.'

'So, what did you do?'

'I did what you told me to do. I persuaded him to come with me and we went in search of a collapsible lifeboat. How did you know about those?'

I shrug. 'I talked with the crew. You learn a lot of things if you talk to people.'

He nods slowly, weighing up my answer, but I can tell that he knows there's more to it. 'We found a collapsible but were unable to get it upright. The water was coming in too fast. It was mayhem. So many people trying to get aboard and then it slipped away, into the waves. I managed to swim out to it and climb onto the hull. Lester was right behind me. I pulled him up beside me where we clung on for dear life. If it hadn't been for the whisky, I believe I would have died of cold.' He knits his fingers and stares at them as if working out how best to formulate his next question. I know what's coming and frantically try to think of a good answer. 'How did you know about the *Carpathia?*' Before I have time to reply, he adds. 'You see, I can't make you out, Miss Fleet. You knew something terrible was going to happen. You were right. Was it just female intuition?' He turns to me, and his blue eyes are full of confusion. 'And you called me Cavill. You called me Cavill in a way that was strangely familiar.' He shakes his head and throws his gaze onto the waves churning below us. His frown deepens. 'Perhaps grief has made me find echoes of my wife where there are none.' His voice cracks and it's as if he's now talking to himself. 'But you're so very like the woman she once was.'

At those words, my chest tightens as if crushed by a great weight. How I want to tell him the truth. That I'm not Constance, or Hermione, but Pixie Tate. To tell him to look deep into my eyes and find me there.

I'd recognise your soul if it was a ray of light among a thousand rays.

I see the muscles in his face harden as he fights to control his emotions.

'I *know* you,' he murmurs emphatically, his gaze digging into mine, probing, seeking. 'I don't know why, or how, but I do. Who *are* you?'

I can feel tears stinging and struggle to hold them back. 'Don't ask me that. You would never believe me.'

'Try me.'

'I can't.'

'You must.'

I hesitate. His familiar eyes hold me in their thrall and I feel myself sinking into them, weakening. Surrendering.

Perhaps I can disclose a fundamental truth he *can* believe, without compromising Constance. 'I will tell you one thing and one thing only.' My heart is now thumping wildly, hitting my ribcage like a hammer.

'What?'

He leans in.

'You are very dear to me.'

With those words I hurry away through the clusters of survivors who are gathered on the deck. Tears blur my vision so that all I see are great brush strokes of greys and black, like a painting smudged in the rain. I need to get away from Cavill before I tell him too much. I curse my weakness and remind myself of what I'm here to do. Who I'm here *for*. I need to find Lester and get off this boat as swiftly as possible. I must put Cavill out of my mind now and concentrate on my mission. I haven't slid for *him*. I've slid for Lester.

It's Lester's soul I must save. That is my only job.

Chapter Sixteen

The following two days I manage to avoid being alone again with Cavill, for I have already said too much. My focus is Lester now and I set my mind to my mission with a renewed sense of purpose. I'm not here for me. I'm here for *him*. Therefore, I make sure Mrs Brown is with me, or Ruby, or Josephine, or even Mrs Norris and Isabella. We remain in a tight group, clinging to one another for solace, grateful to be alive but mourning those hundreds who were not so fortunate.

At last, on the second evening, I seize the opportunity to speak with Lester alone. It's sunset. The sky is streaked with pink and orange, the water glistening beneath it like ink. He's standing on deck, leaning on the railing and smoking a cigarette, deep in thought. His face is serious, his hat pulled low over his worried brow. I suspect he doesn't want to be disturbed, but I need to talk to him. There's nowhere we can be private, but there are quiet places where we won't be overheard. This part of the deck is one of them, for it's fiercely cold and windy, and few passengers want to be outside. They are desperate, sick of the ocean and waiting impatiently for dry land.

I walk up to him, wrapping my coat tightly about me. 'It's beautiful, isn't it,' I say, turning my face to the setting sun.

He nods dolefully. 'The dogs bark and the caravan moves on,' he says flatly.

'Are you all right?' I ask him.

He sighs. 'There's always going to be a degree of guilt for having survived when so many drowned.'

'You have nothing to feel guilty about. You were lucky. And you were brave,' I tell him. 'You didn't deny anyone a place on a lifeboat. Mr Pengower told me.'

He nods again and says nothing.

'How did Glover get into a lifeboat and not you?' I ask.

He hesitates, losing his gaze on the foam frothing below us. 'I gave him my coat, scarf and hat, and told him to pretend he was me. I wanted to save him, Connie.'

'I see.'

A muscle throbs in his jaw. He takes a long drag on his cigarette. I sense he's uncomfortable talking about Glover. I don't imagine I'm going to get the full story. He'll fob me off with something close to it, I suspect. After all, he knows that Constance doesn't approve of his valet. 'Glover and I had a disagreement earlier in the evening,' he tells me. 'I left him in my cabin and went up to dinner. After the ship hit the iceberg, I went into the smoking room with the intention of drinking myself into oblivion. I thought I'd wait it out. I didn't realise it was serious, you see. Then they were allowing only women and children onto the lifeboats, and I knew that Glover . . .' He looks at me steadily, his gaze intense. 'Joe,' he adds with emphasis. He waits for my reaction, but I remain impassive. 'I knew that there was a good chance that Joe wouldn't get a place. So, I went to find him. I wasn't going to leave him on the ship. Judge me as you see fit, Aunt Constance. You will never understand. I wasn't going to let him drown.' His shoulders stiffen defensively. 'He had a brief opportunity when a woman refused to board without a man. He took it. Good for him, I say. If he hadn't, he wouldn't be here now and I'd have no one to press my clothes.' He chuckles bitterly at his lame joke and draws again on his cigarette.

'Do you want one?' he asks, reaching into his coat and taking out a blue enamel cigarette case. He studies it pensively. 'This is all I brought with me. All I have left.'

'I won't, thank you,' I reply.

He frowns. 'How unlike you, Aunt Constance, to refuse a cigarette. I would have thought that now more than ever you needed one.'

'You only have a few left. I wouldn't want to deprive you of one,' I say. I can't bear the taste of cigarettes.

There's a long silence as he chews the inside of his cheek and stares thoughtfully at the sea. At last, he lets out a puff of smoke and takes a sharp breath. 'What you saw on the *Titanic* . . .' His voice trails off. He doesn't know how to word it. I try to imagine what Constance would say. I know she and I would likely differ very much in our opinions of sexuality, and I must stay true to her.

'You know you're going to have to dismiss him, don't you?' I say.

Lester looks at me. He blows smoke out of the side of his mouth as he considers my question. I wait for him to reply, but he turns away and casts his eyes onto the water.

'You can't marry Esme and carry on with Glover,' I tell him. 'You're playing with fire. You're putting yourself in his power. That's imprudent. Surely, you realise that? A man in your position—'

'It's none of your business, Aunt Constance.'

'Oh, I think it is every bit my business. Esme loves you and trusts you.'

'And I will be a good husband to her.'

'With Glover lurking like a shadow in the background? I think not. Besides, you have the reputation of your family to consider. Your mother, me . . .'

Lester's face turns from thoughtful to furious in a moment. 'I will not speak of this any more,' he snaps.

I have touched a nerve. 'Very well.' I pat his arm in a maternal way and lower my voice. 'You are lucky it was only me. Imagine if Esme catches you like that. What then? It cannot happen. You know that, don't you? It must not. Society doesn't allow it. One day, I hope, it will, but right now it's too dangerous for you, Lester. You could lose everything.'

He snatches his arm away and tosses his cigarette into the water, then stalks off in a huff, leaving me standing there in the wind, wondering where those words came from. I don't even believe them. But they are the sort of words Constance might say, and I must try to stay in character.

*

The *Carpathia* arrives in New York on the evening of the 18th of April. The Statue of Liberty comes into view, shining brightly in front of the twinkling lights of Manhattan. It's a reassuring sight after the loneliness of the Atlantic and many people break down and cry. I'm standing beside Mrs Brown. 'It's going to get nasty now,' she says, shaking her head portentously. The quay is crowded with people and members of the press, eager to get the first testimonies from survivors. 'I wouldn't want to be Bruce Ismay,' she says, referring to the chairman of the White Star Line who is the highest-ranking official to make it off the *Titanic*. 'I think he'll wish he'd gone down with the ship like poor Captain Smith.'

'I think many will be made to feel guilty at having survived,' I reply diplomatically. Although I don't imagine Glover will feel remotely guilty for anything.

'Ismay has been hiding out for the last three days in the bowels of the ship, but he's going to have to break cover now. Can't you just see the headlines? He's going to be called a coward for having abandoned the ship when there were still plenty of women and children on board. He's going to be hounded like a fox.'

'I feel sorry for him. I'm sure, if I were in his position, I'd have saved myself as well. It takes a lot of courage to turn down the chance of survival.'

'He should have taken it like a man,' Mrs Brown replies obstinately. I imagine, if she were Bruce Ismay, she'd have thrown herself into the sea without a thought.

We say goodbye to each other and to our fellow passengers. I am sad to part with Mrs Brown, but feel privileged to have spent time with such a legendary figure. Shame I won't be able to boast about it in the future! I embrace Josephine tightly and feel a sudden pang of regret. We have grown close over the last few days and I'm loath to part with her too. I don't imagine I'll see her again. She, on the other hand, is confident that I will. 'We will call on you as soon as we can,' she says. I suppose society in New York is small, therefore she and Constance are likely to find themselves in the same circle of friends. I envy Constance that. I will slide back and *she* will live on in this time, with these people of whom I have grown so fond, who I will have to leave.

I want to embrace Cavill too, but I have to conduct myself in the manner of an Edwardian lady, with moderation.

'Goodbye, Mr Pengower,' I say, and give him my hand. My heart weighs heavily in my chest, for I know this is the final time I will lay eyes on him, and I can't bear it.

He takes my hand and gives a formal bow. There's no hint of regret or sorrow in his eyes. He, too, is sure our paths will cross again. But he cannot imagine the century that will separate us.

'I hope you settle into New York,' he says. 'The Aldershoffs will look after you well.'

'I'm sure they will.' I search his face for a trace of the intimacy we've shared, but there's nothing but politeness.

'Until we meet again,' he says, and we join the throng of passengers walking down the gangplank.

Lester and I are met by Walter-Wyatt Aldershoff himself in a chauffeur-driven racing-green motor car with huge round headlights that resemble a pair of giant frog's eyes. It stands out from the crowd like a diamond among stones. Ruby and Glover are to travel behind in another car of the same make and colour. Besides my Ouija board, we have no luggage.

Neither Lester nor Constance have met Walter-Wyatt before. From Constance's diary, I know that Lester's engagement to their daughter, Esme, was overseen by William-Wyatt's sister, Hope Willesden. Lester is meeting his soon-to-be parents-in-law for the first time.

Walter-Wyatt is tall and thin with shiny black hair and intelligent blue eyes that look upon us with curiosity from behind a pair of wire-framed spectacles. He's serious and stiff in an expensively tailored three-piece grey suit and fedora hat. He has a mild stoop as if he's self-conscious about being tall. 'Boy, am I happy to see you!' he exclaims when we present ourselves, having spotted the chauffeur holding up a cardboard sign with our names on it. That's one thing that hasn't changed! He shakes Lester's hand with a strong and confident grip. 'Lord Ravenglass, Miss Fleet, I'm glad you made it off the ship.' He takes off his hat and bows to me, yet completely ignores Ruby and Glover, who are shown into the awaiting vehicle by a driver dressed in green livery to match the car, black leather gloves and a black cap. 'Luggage?' he says, looking around for our suitcases.

Lester shrugs. 'Everything went down with the ship,' he replies.

Walter-Wyatt looks astonished. 'Good God, was there so little time?' He clearly hasn't a clue of what has happened. 'Well, let's get you back to civilisation.'

We climb into the back of the car and settle onto swish leather seats. It's really the most exquisite car I've ever been in. Walter-Wyatt rides in front with the driver, but swivels round to talk to us. 'It's been all over the papers,' he says, and I sense he's been rather gripped by the tragedy. I wonder whether he knows about his wife's cousin, Mr Rowland, who drowned. As he doesn't mention him, I decide not to tell him. Perhaps lists of survivors haven't been made public yet. Anyway, it's not for Constance to inform him of Mr Rowland's death. 'First they were saying that everyone survived, and that the *Titanic* was being towed to Halifax! Then they said it had sunk and very few people survived. I want to hear what really happened.' He pumps us for details and I let Lester do all the talking. I'm much more interested in looking out of the window at the city of New York. How different it is to the one I recently arrived in.

Manhattan is ablaze with electric lights. The magnificent skyscrapers for which the city is so celebrated soar into the night sky. Even though it's not yet the shiny glass forest that it later becomes, those brownstone giants are nonetheless impressive and beautifully designed. What strikes me at once is the lack of clutter on the roads. There are no ugly bollards or traffic lights, telephone boxes and public bins. No lurid markings to mar the asphalt such as zebra crossings, yellow lines and white zigzags. Some roads don't even have pavements. Still, it's a sophisticated city; there are golden streetlamps and shiny shop fronts, grand public buildings and townhouses, but the place looks more open and less advanced than in my time. I feel nostalgic looking at it like this, through the lens of the future. It feels strangely unreal, as if I'm on a film set, which isn't surprising considering the number of movies I've watched that are set in this period. It's a city in frenetic development. There's a great deal of construction work going on. High-rise towers are in the process of being built and they will form the dramatic skyline of the future. Right now, they're hidden behind scaffolding, and no one can imagine how glorious they're going to be.

Down here, the streets are busy; horse-drawn carriages clatter over asphalt, and, in some streets, rattle over cobblestones. Buses travel along tramlines, clanging their bells to alert pedestrians in their way. There are plenty of motor cars belching black smoke out of their exhausts, but few are as grand as this one. It's noisy too, but with a different kind of sound to the one I'm used to: there's the bellowing of klaxons, the screeching of whistles, the whirring of motorcar engines and the clippety-clop of hooves. It's late at night, but the streets are lively and full of activity. I realise then that New York has *never* slept.

Lester doesn't want to talk about the *Titanic*. He's gripped by the sights outside his window, this being the first time he has been in America too. He manages to divert the conversation by asking Walter-Wyatt to point out buildings of interest. I imagine Ruby and Glover are just as thrilled to see this new city, and feel huge relief that we are safe, on solid ground, not aboard a sinking ship.

We pull up outside what later becomes the Aldershoff Hotel. It's not a hotel now. It's a private house, Walter-Wyatt's house, built forty years ago by his father, William, who, as I recall, is dead. Alma is yet to be born. Walter-Wyatt lives here with his wife, Alice, and their only child, Esme. My mind turns then to the Potemkin Diamond. I won't go out of my way to find it – where would I begin? But I'll keep my antennae alert just in case I find clues to its whereabouts. Walter-Wyatt has inherited it and only *he* knows where it's hidden.

It's night, but I can see in the glow of the streetlights that the trees have already started to sprout their new leaves. Some are already in blossom. The sweet scent of warming earth and burgeoning plants is carried on the breeze with the odorous smell of horse manure. The big door is opened by a butler who, on greeting us, reveals himself to be English. We are shown into the house. I catch my breath. It's even more impressive than the hotel. When Mr Stirling explained that he had worked hard to keep the integrity of the original home, he was right, he had, and he did a good job. But the original house is infinitely more remarkable. The grandeur takes my breath away. I stand in the hall and look around in wonder. It's like a mini-Versailles with the elaborate trompe l'œil on the ceiling and the giant murals painted on the walls and bordered with gold frames. Chandeliers dazzle above us with hundreds of glass crystals that drop like tears from a great height, and the magnificent staircase dominates the hall with a bright-scarlet runner and intricate iron balustrade.

A woman appears on the landing and glides down in an indigo-blue dress. She's strikingly pretty with light brown hair loosely pinned up in the Edwardian fashion, a flawless, creamy complexion enhanced with a touch of rouge, and a very small waist. Her smile is blithe and carefree. She must be in her late thirties. 'You poor darlings!' she exclaims in a languid American accent, putting out her hands to take mine. They're pale and delicate, and shining with gems. 'Was it dreadful? You must be tired and hungry.' She smiles warmly and looks me up and down, not unkindly. 'My dear Miss Fleet—'

'Please, call me Constance After all, we are soon to be family.'

She smiles, pleased. 'Constance, then. You must want to

change out of your travelling clothes.' She looks at her husband. 'Has Henderson arranged for their luggage to be taken to their rooms?'

'There is no luggage, Alice. Apparently, it all went down with the ship,' he replies. I notice that the butler has handed him the walking stick Alma uses. I recognise the silver dog's head handle. I find that curious, because he doesn't have a limp, and he's young. Perhaps it's part of a gentleman's attire, like shirt studs and cufflinks. He runs his thumb over the furrows of the dog's jowl as if caressing a beloved pet. 'Everything went down with the ship. Imagine that! Not a thing left.' He's clearly enjoying the drama. 'Lester, may I call you Lester?'

Lester nods. 'Of course, if I may call you Walter-Wyatt.'

'Everyone calls me Walter,' he corrects. He turns to his wife. 'Lester and Constance are going to have to buy a whole new wardrobe.'

Alice beams happily. 'How exciting!' She turns her bright brown eyes to me. 'I'll summon my dressmaker tomorrow to run you up a few outfits. In the meantime, we'll go shopping. If you've lost everything, you'll need to start from scratch. I know just the places to go. Lester, you can borrow from Walter until his tailor can fix you up.' She evidently has no understanding of the horror we have both been through. Neither does Walter-Wyatt. 'Esme will see you tomorrow. She's relieved, as we all are, that you survived the disaster. Why don't I show you your rooms and then I'll send up some supper. It's late and you'll be wanting to bathe and go to bed. I can't wait to hear about your adventure, but perhaps you'd rather tell us tomorrow, when you're rested.' I'm astonished that they consider it an adventure, as if it's all been wonderfully exciting.

'That's a good idea,' I reply. I suddenly feel overwhelmingly tired. It's exhausting keeping up this charade. There are so many pitfalls if I'm not on my mettle. I glance through to what in the present day is the Walter-Wyatt drawing room and think of Ulysses in there, keeping an eye on me. I wonder how long I've been in trance. The room is totally different now, more like a library full of bookshelves.

Alice's smooth brow furrows. 'You know, they say John Jacob Astor died on the ship. You'd have thought he'd have gotten into a lifeboat, wouldn't you? I can't imagine why he didn't.'

I'm too weary to put her straight but wonder once again whether she knows about her cousin, Mr Rowland. If she does, she's doing a very good job of hiding her grief.

Walter-Wyatt can't get enough of the tragedy. 'There weren't enough lifeboats, my dear. Can you imagine what a dreadful oversight!'

'Well, if you think a ship won't sink, why would you bother with lifeboats?' she replies with a shrug.

Lester is bored of the subject and perhaps as vexed as I am by their lack of understanding of the scale of the tragedy. 'Why, indeed?' he agrees politely.

'Those jackasses have egg on their faces now,' Walter-Wyatt adds, chuckling. 'I'll leave you now and look forward to seeing you in the morning. I hope you both sleep well.' He calls after his wife. 'My dear, we are expected at the Johnson Stokes' in half an hour.'

'I will be ready,' she declares. I'm surprised they're going out so late. It's well after ten o'clock and it looks like their evening is just beginning.

Alice lifts her skirt and leads us up the grand staircase. 'The newspapers are full of it, you know,' she tells us in her soft, breathy voice, repeating what her husband said in the car. 'No one can talk of anything else, especially Walter. Such a riveting drama. Everyone said it couldn't sink. Well, they look a little foolish now, don't they? I can't imagine the horror, so many people will have lost everything. You know, you can't replace jewellery that's been handed down the generations. You simply can't. It breaks my heart to think of it rotting on the seabed. Just awful.'

'I think most survivors will mourn the *people* they have lost,' I tell her.

'Oh, of course, that too.' She dismisses *them* with a wave of her elegant hand. I'm beginning to get the measure of Alice Aldershoff.

Lester trails behind us, exasperated by Alice's conversation and seemingly unimpressed with the house. I suppose, having been brought up in an English stately home, to him this building is regrettably nouveau.

She shows us to our bedrooms, which are opposite one another, like on the *Titanic*. The serene luxury of her home is a world away from the one we've just inhabited. It's an oasis, a bubble, and I'm relieved to be in it. The big double bed looks so inviting, I long to dive into it and go to sleep. Ruby is nowhere to be seen, but the blue box has been placed on the bed.

'Your maid is being shown to her quarters upstairs,' Alice continues. 'She'll be well looked after and can tend to you tomorrow.' She pulls a gold cord, which hangs like a donkey's tail beside the bed. 'In the meantime, one of my maids will look after you and see that you have everything you need. I can lend you nightclothes and toiletries. You poor dear, Constance. I can't imagine what it's like to lose all your beautiful things.'

I couldn't give a damn about my beautiful things and I don't imagine Constance would either. But I agree that it is dreadful, just to humour her.

She looks at the blue box. 'What's that?'

'It's a Ouija board,' I tell her. 'A spirit board.'

Her eyes widen with delight. 'To communicate with the

dead?' she asks, reaching out and unclipping it. She lifts the lid. When she sees the board, she gasps. 'Would you look at that? How splendid.'

'Sometimes it's possible,' I reply.

She laughs. The laugh of a woman who has no cares. 'Oh, let's have some fun tomorrow.' She turns and takes my hands in hers again. 'I'm just so happy you're here. I'm sure we're going to love Lester just as much as Esme does. And how good of you to come with him. I'm just sorry his mother wasn't able to make the trip. Although, in light of what's happened, she had a lucky escape. I have arranged a party in Lester's honour in Newport next week, so that he can meet our friends and family. In fact, I have arranged many events. I want to show you both off – my daughter's fiancé, Viscount Ravenglass, and his aunt, the Honourable Constance Fleet. It's thrilling, really, that you're both here. Even more thrilling that you were on the *Titanic*. Everyone is going to want to hear about it. But I will make sure they don't tire you out. We have a darling cottage by the sea and will leave New York as soon as you are both rested.'

Alice leaves me alone at last to head out to her party. My head is spinning from her chatter. I realise that she hasn't heard about her cousin's death, and feel sorry that she will soon learn the terrible news. Carter, a young Irish maid with curly brown hair and freckles, runs me a bath in the most over-decorated bathroom I have ever been in, and then goes off in search of a nightdress and toiletries. I wallow in the warm, scented water, taking in the big Venetian mirrors, elaborate mouldings and white marble, and wash away the trauma of the last few days. It seems strange to be here in this beautiful house where everything is shiny and new, after having languished in the freezing cold on a lifeboat, watching the great *Titanic* sink. I remind myself that this is not my reality, that I'm living a dream and that I can return to my own time whenever I want. It's too easy to lose oneself in the drama and I must not let that happen. I mustn't forget who I really am and what I'm here for.

I eat vegetable soup and bread alone in my bedroom. The silk curtains are drawn and besides the distant rumbling of the city, the house is quiet. I think of Cavill and my heart aches for him. Now I know that our paths are unlikely to cross again, I'm anxious to discover what happens to Lester and then slide back to my own time. I'm weary of living this drama.

I put my head on the soft pillow and slip into a dreamless sleep.

The following morning, I'm awoken by Ruby, who's wearing a borrowed uniform. Her white apron is pristine over a long black dress and she's wearing a white cap on the back of her head. She's clearly pleased with her new outfit for she has a bounce in her step as she crosses the floor to open the curtains. Spring sunshine pours into the room, bringing into light the elegant French furniture and pretty floral wallpaper. The bedroom is exquisite. I imagine it's even more exquisite than the Ritz! It's large with a high ceiling, and everywhere the eye travels there's something lovely to look at: Persian rugs, china lamps, pretty paintings, chairs upholstered in silk, and a charming chaise longue at the end of the bed. I notice a vase of white peonies on the dressing table. Even they are extravagantly big and beautiful. I can't help but marvel at how these wealthy Gilded Age people lived. It's beyond anything in my experience. It seems to be beyond anything Ruby has experienced either, for she chatters on about how gorgeous it is.

Ruby has brought me a skirt and blouse to wear. I don't imagine they belong to Alice because I wouldn't fit into anything of hers; she's as petite as a doll. As I dress, I can't help but turn my nose up at the unattractive beige-coloured skirt and white lacey blouse. I wonder where Alice found this unappealing ensemble. I have no choice but to wear it, as I have nothing else. I do need to buy new clothes, but I don't have any money. It's not like I can nip out to a cashpoint, or transfer funds from my UK bank account with my phone. I have no idea how anything is done here, in this time – and I can't let my ignorance show. I just have to hope that Alice will take charge and look after me while I'm being Constance. It can't be for much longer.

Ruby looks me up and down, and I can see the dismay on her face.

'I look a sight,' I tell her with a sigh.

I can tell she's trying to think of something positive to say. 'It's not that bad, just plain when you're a lady who loves colour.'

I smile at her. 'You're very diplomatic, Ruby. I think your uniform is more exciting than this dowdy ensemble.'

She laughs and smooths her white apron with her hands. 'It's nice, isn't it? Maybe I should wear a uniform like this when we get back home.'

'I'm sure they'll let you keep it.'

'I hope so.'

'Tell me, how is everything downstairs? Are the servants nice?'

'Miss O'Donnell, Mrs Aldershoff's lady's maid, is very kind. She's Irish, you know. She left her family in Cork to come here. She hasn't seen them in six years.'

'That's a long time.'

'And Mr Henderson, the senior butler, is English. He's strict, but he has lots of servants to manage, so I suppose he has to be firm. Then there's Mrs Farkas, the housekeeper. She's from Hungary. There are lots of immigrants here, you know. Mrs

Farkas is kind too. So far, everyone has been kind. They're all curious to know what happened on the *Titanic*.'

'And Glover? How is he?'

She shrugs. 'I haven't seen him, ma'am.'

I wonder then whether he spent the night in Lester's bed. Surely, he wouldn't be that reckless. 'Oh. Well, I hope he's being treated well too,' I add casually.

'I'm sure he is,' she replies. 'They're not like English people who are suspicious of foreigners.'

As I leave my room, Lester is leaving his. I spy Glover through the gap in the open door and wonder again whether they've spent the night together. After what they've both been through, and survived, it would be natural to want to stay close. Glover catches my eye and glowers. There's real hatred in his gaze. I suppose he knows it was me who caught them in flagrante on the *Titanic*. Perhaps he's worried about what I'll do with that information. Lester doesn't smile. I suppose he's still cross with me for suggesting Glover be dismissed. 'I trust you slept well, Aunt Constance?' he says tightly, closing the door behind him. I imagine he's wearing borrowed clothes as well, but his are well cut and dashing, even though they don't have his usual flair for colour and design. I suspect they belong to Walter-Wyatt who must wear the same size. They're both tall and slim.

'I did sleep well. I trust you did, too.' We set off down the corridor together. 'It's some house, isn't it?' I say, trying to make conversation but sensing from his closed energy that it's going to be a challenge.

'I'm not so easily impressed,' he replies in a lofty tone. 'It's like theatre; there's nothing authentic about it at all.'

'You're hard to please, Lester.'

He sighs. 'Stuffing a house full of antiques to give the

impression of heritage and history does not fool me, Aunt Constance. I'm surprised, your critical eye is usually less forgiving.'

'I like it. It's magnificent and I appreciate magnificence.'

'It's fake and I abhor pretentiousness.'

'What would you prefer, that they had bought everything in America? Even Broadmere is full of French and Italian antiques.' I have no idea, of course. I'm just guessing. But I'm proved to be right, for he doesn't contradict me.

He stops at the top of the stairs and lowers his voice so the servants won't hear. 'Broadmere was first built in fifteen forty-seven and then remodelled by our ancestors in seventeen thirty-six into the house that stands today. It has had over one hundred and fifty years of embellishment. One hundred and fifty years of Ravenglasses adding to its splendour with every grand tour they made. This house is merely forty years old, and they think that by imitating the great English mansions and French châteaux they will fool people into believing them to be an *old* family. Well, I tell you, my dear aunt Constance, that they haven't fooled *me*.'

He sets off down the stairs at a trot and I follow him.

'By the by, what *are* you wearing?' he says, and the tone of his voice confirms my own judgement – this outfit is decidedly *un*attractive.

When we enter the dining room, I'm surprised to see so many footmen attending Walter-Wyatt, who presides over the long table with his face buried in the *New York Times*, and a young woman I recognise immediately as Esme. Constance's diary was very descriptive. She is indeed beautiful and elegant. 'Lester!' she exclaims, getting up with a smile. Her cheeks flush prettily and she holds out her hands for him to take. She's dressed in a charming blue dress trimmed with white lace. I remember from the diary that she visited Broadmere, so she knows Constance.

'My dear Esme,' I say when she turns to greet me.

'Oh, Miss Fleet, I'm so relieved you both made it off that ship. What a horrible time you must have had.' I can see a large photograph of the *Titanic* on the front page of Walter-Wyatt's newspaper and a grim headline in bold black print. Walter-Wyatt closes it and stands up to greet us. 'Good morning, Constance. Good morning, Lester. I'm reading all about the disaster, but I feel ahead of the news having the two of you here to tell me what *really* happened.'

'It's all a bit of a blur now,' says Lester languidly, sitting down and flicking out his napkin.

'But you were one of the lucky few,' Walter-Wyatt continues. 'Astor's son is offering a reward for anyone who has news of his father.'

'I'm afraid he'll keep his money. John Jacob is at the bottom of the sea,' says Lester.

'With so many others,' I add, an echo of the horrible scenes in the water reverberating in my memory. 'I doubt many men survived.'

'How did you survive, dear Lester?' Esme asks, and she has the same shallow gaze as her mother.

'He managed to climb onto an overturned lifeboat,' I tell them, thinking of Cavill.

Esme gazes at him with admiration. 'Oh, you're so clever, Lester, dear.'

'I cannot claim to be clever, merely lucky,' he replies.

Esme smiles. 'I disagree. I think you're clever, and brave.'

Lester can't help but swell with pride. The corners of his pretty lips curl into a smile. 'I thought I was a goner, to be honest,' he says, brightening. 'I thought my time was up. It focuses the mind somewhat, out there in the dark with nothing but sea all around you and an unsteady boat that threatens to roll you off at any moment. But we made it against all the odds. I can tell you one thing, that water was damned cold. It felt like I was being stabbed by a thousand knives.'

Esme gasps. 'A thousand knives,' she repeats. 'How simply dreadful. I cannot imagine!'

Walter-Wyatt is lapping it up. His eyes widen behind his glasses and he gazes upon Lester with interest. 'You'll have to tell everyone your story. They'll be dying to hear it,' he exclaims enthusiastically. 'Why, to have survived to tell the tale, you must have been *exceptionally* brave.'

Lester asks one of the footmen for eggs and toast, and watches while the young man fills his cup with coffee. Then he sits back with his wrists on the white tablecloth and looks at Walter-Wyatt steadily. 'I will tell my story to anyone who wants to hear it, if you show me the Potemkin Diamond.'

Walter-Wyatt grins. 'The Potemkin Diamond, eh? Well, sure. I'll show it to you after breakfast.'

'Where do you keep such a valuable jewel?' I ask, thinking of Alma Aldershoff and her yearning to find it.

Esme giggles, dabbing the corners of her pretty mouth with a napkin. 'Oh, we'd all like to know that, Miss Fleet!'

'My late father, William Aldershoff, designed special hiding places all over this house in which to conceal his valuables. You'd be surprised at the ingenuity of some of them. He was both playful and shrewd. He used to say the least safe place in a house is a safe.'

'Well, that's obviously the first place a thief will look,' I say.

'That's right.' He smiles. 'Therefore, he had no respect for safes. Wouldn't have one in the house, or in the cottage.'

'How very cunning of him.'

'I can tell you that the Potemkin Diamond is hidden in the most brilliant hiding place of all. I am the only person who knows where that is.'

'But surely, you must tell Esme, in case . . .' I don't want to be rude. I think of Alma and plough on. 'What if something happened to you. Take the *Titanic* as an example. One can never know what destiny is going to throw at one.'

'I've considered that,' he replies with a grin, and settles his shrewd eyes onto Lester. 'All will be revealed in good time. I'm young and healthy. I'm not going anywhere.'

The way he looked at Lester was significant. I ask myself whether he intends to bequeath the diamond to him following his marriage to Esme. I remember Alma telling me that he wanted to leave it to a boy, so that would make sense.

I turn to Lester and see that his face has gone quite pink. *He certainly hopes so.*

I turn back to Walter-Wyatt and wonder whether he wears the little key beneath his clothes, and where the lock might be.

After breakfast, during which Alice does not appear and Esme returns upstairs, he leads us into a small sitting room decorated in rich purple and green. 'Now, you wait here and I'll go get it.' He leaves the room and crosses the hall, his stick making loud tapping noises over the marble floor. I can see through the crack in the door that he's going into one of the drawing rooms on the other side of the house. It could very well be the room that is currently the dining room in the Aldershoff Hotel.

'I wonder where he hides it,' I mumble, longing to take a look around.

Lester grins. 'Are you planning on stealing it, Aunt Constance? Now that would do more than repair the ailing roof at Broadmere.' He chuckles, casually lifting up a silver photograph frame and peering into the faces within it. However, behind his veneer of not caring, I sense he's busy imagining what it would mean to own that precious gem.

A moment later, Walter-Wyatt returns with something in his

hand. He goes to the round table in front of the window where the room gets the most light, and gently lays down a silk handkerchief. Lester and I stand either side of him. Walter-Wyatt, conscious of the gravitas of the moment, pauses for effect. His hand hovers over the handkerchief. Lester and I lean in, eager to see this most famous of diamonds, gifted to the Empress of Russia no less. Then, slowly, his fingers peel back the folds like the petals of a waterlily. I cannot help but gasp with wonder. Displayed before us, sparkling with splendour, is the Potemkin Diamond.

Lester catches his breath. 'It's exquisite,' he says, his eyes widening with amazement. He's gone very red, and his eyes are shining like Bilbo Baggins' at the sight of the ring.

'It really is extraordinary,' I agree. I hadn't anticipated it to be pink, or so big. It's the size of a grape. 'What an unusual colour. It's the colour of bubblegum.'

Walter-Wyatt looks at me and frowns. 'And what the devil is bubblegum?' he asks.

I realise then that I've made a faux pas. Bubblegum has clearly not yet been invented. 'Oh, it's like a boiled sweet, but you chew it,' I reply smoothly. 'Maybe it's an English sweet.'

Fortunately, Lester is too busy staring into the shining facets of the diamond to contradict me. I imagine his mind is conjuring up all the things he could do were it his to sell.

Might the diamond have been his had he not divorced? I wonder.

'Incredible,' Lester murmurs. 'And it really belonged to Catherine the Great?'

'It did indeed. If you look hard enough, you can see her face reflected in the flaws.'

I stare into it, but see nothing but the gleaming facets.

'May I hold it?' Lester asks, reaching out his fingers.

'Of course. Go ahead. But don't put it in your mouth and chew it!' Walter-Wyatt laughs. Lester doesn't. He's quite serious. He picks it up and holds it to the light, and then he blows the air through his cheeks. 'It's the most beautiful thing I've ever seen.'

Walter-Wyatt folds the diamond away in the handkerchief and takes it back to the drawing room. 'I didn't see a face, did you?' Lester asks.

'No. I think it's a myth.'

'I dare say they made it up themselves to make it more interesting.'

'Isn't that how all myths start?' I hear Walter-Wyatt's stick on the marble floor as he makes his way back to the drawing room, and drop the subject.

Shortly, Alice floats into the sitting room upon a wave of lilac, accompanied by Esme. I suppose Alice has eaten breakfast in her bedroom. 'Good morning,' she says, smiling blithely at us. 'I do hope you slept well.'

'Lester's just been telling us how he saved himself by climbing onto the hull of a lifeboat that had turned over,' says Walter-Wyatt gleefully.

Lester smiles. 'Yes, Alice, you'll be pleased to hear that we both survived the cold water, me and your brave cousin.'

I panic. It's not true. Mr Rowland did *not* survive. I put a hand on Lester's arm to deter him. Alice is smiling, so is Walter-Wyatt. Neither have a clue that Mr Rowland perished. 'Lester, dear, her cousin did *not* survive,' I say in a quiet but firm voice. I can feel my face burn. I'm horrified to find myself in the position of being the one to tell them that he drowned.

Alice turns to me and a rare frown puckers her brow. 'It's all right, Constance,' she says. 'I got word from them at dawn. We are so relieved; they both survived and are due here at any minute. The girls can't wait to see each other.'

I'm confused. Who was Mr Rowland if he wasn't Orlando? I look from Alice to Lester, then to Walter-Wyatt. There's an awkward silence. I don't know what to say. Have I missed something?

Then, blessedly, we are interrupted by the sound of the doorbell. I follow Alice and Walter-Wyatt into the hall. I don't dare glance at Lester, who stands back to allow me to pass. I can feel his contempt without having to see it reflected on his face.

The butler is holding open the huge doors and being handed a gentleman's hat. A young woman is running towards Esme, smiling and laughing.

I stare in astonishment.

Cavill and Josephine.

Chapter Seventeen

I'm blindsided. I stand gawping at Cavill in stunned silence. How could I have got it so wrong? How did I miss that Orlando was Cavill all along? Why did I assume he was American? I have no time to process all the information, to replay the events of the six days. One thing is for certain, however – this changes *everything*!

If Constance is in love with Cavill, then I am free to love him too! The revelation makes me dizzy with happiness.

Cavill greets me with a warm smile. No wonder he didn't make a big deal out of parting yesterday. He knew we'd be re-united today. 'Miss Fleet,' he says, and runs his eyes over my dress. I feel self-conscious suddenly that I look dowdy. I wish I had something more elegant to wear. For the first time on this slide, it really matters to me how I look.

I laugh to mask my embarrassment. 'Alice has kindly lent me some clothes . . .'

'We are all lucky to be alive,' he says seriously, and I realise that he couldn't care less what I'm wearing. 'To say nothing of the joy of being warm and dry,' he adds with a grateful smile.

Josephine embraces me affectionately. Her eyes are damp from her reunion with her cousin Esme. 'Oh, Miss Fleet, it is good to see you again.'

'Josephine could not wait,' says Cavill to Alice with an affable shrug.

'I'm seeing everyone with fresh eyes.' Josephine laughs. 'I will never again take life for granted.'

Alice looks stunned. She can't imagine why they're making such a drama out of the reunion. She laughs in a slightly patronising way. 'Goodness, what a delightful scene. Come, let us go into the drawing room.'

'We want to hear all about it, Cavill,' says Walter-Wyatt, putting a hand on Cavill's back. 'Lester says you were both in the water. I bet that must have felt like a thousand knives!'

Lester offers Esme his arm and she slips her small hand around it and gazes up at him adoringly. He turns to me. 'What on earth has got into you, Connie?' he whispers.

I shrug helplessly. 'It must be shock,' I reply, shaking my head. 'I don't feel myself at all.'

He sighs and walks into the drawing room with Esme. I follow, feeling massively discombobulated, but at the same time elated.

Constance and I love the *same* man! How can that be possible?

The drawing room is sumptuous and very large. Vast windows are framed by flouncy crimson curtains that are trimmed with frills and tassels, and God knows what else. Huge carpets are woven in gold and red, and the walls are panelled and painted to match. The effect is stunning. I've never seen anything so grand, and so overdone. Everywhere I look, I see dollar signs. I can't help it. A room like this in my time would cost a fortune. I can't imagine what it cost William Aldershoff.

I sweep my gaze around the room and wonder where the Potemkin Diamond is hidden. It must be in here somewhere. However, there are a million places it could be. The room is cluttered with furniture and objects, sculptures and paintings.

I imagine it's hidden somewhere in the bones of the room, for William Aldershoff had secret compartments incorporated into the design of the architecture as well as into the furniture. I don't imagine he would hide such a valuable diamond in something that could be easily moved. Therefore, it must be in a concealed cavity in the wall, or in the bookcase, or beneath a floorboard. A cavity that requires a key to unlock it. It's intriguing, but I'm not going to waste any time on it. I'm not here for Alma Aldershoff, but for Lester. And, as far as I was able to tell with my dowsing crystal, the diamond is not in the Aldershoff Hotel, so it really is of no consequence whether it's here now.

Music is playing on the gramophone. A man with a high voice is singing against the crackle of the record. I have no idea who he is. We seat ourselves on French-style armchairs upholstered in crimson damask silk. They are stiff and not particularly comfortable, but suit the people who sit in them whose corsets and formal clothing would make slumping in modern chairs impossible. Alice settles onto an equally beautiful but formal sofa. Maids bring pots of tea and cake on trays, and footmen hover, awaiting instructions. They look comical to me in their livery and I want to laugh. They're so serious, like the beefeaters who guard the Tower of London. It would be an amusing challenge to see if one could get them to crack a smile.

Josephine is far more confident in the company of her family. Her words tumble out in a torrent of descriptions. She tells them how sumptuous the *Titanic* was and how charming all the other passengers were. She mentions the Astors' dog and then her voice trails off as she voices her concern that many animals must have drowned when the ship went down. Alice and Esme listen to every word, eyes wide with excitement and lips parted, riveted by each detail, however small. Walter-Wyatt listens with mild interest to the descriptions of the ship itself and the people on it. He grows animated, however, the moment Lester and Cavill take up the story and describe the moment the great hull scrapes the iceberg, then he gives his full attention to the tale, firing questions at them in his quest to experience vicariously every enthralling minute of the tragedy. Cavill's face is grave as he describes the drama. He doesn't mention Lester trying to bribe a member of the crew to let him board the lifeboat, and he keeps the information I gave him about the collapsible boat and the *Carpathia* to himself. Only once does he catch my eye, and a tacit understanding passes between us like two violins playing the same phrase.

Cavill and Lester have bonded over their experience out there on the ocean. As one finishes a sentence, the other picks it up in a seamless narrative. When they reach the end of the story, the room falls into silence. I think Walter-Wyatt and Alice are imagining that beautiful ship at the bottom of the sea with all the valuable and precious things that sank with it. They're visualising the wealth lost in the sand and marvelling at the extraordinary twist of fate that sent the supposedly unsinkable ship to its horrible end. Esme's eyes are damp, and she reaches out her hand and takes Josephine's. I'm touched by her compassion. She doesn't get that from her parents. I think of Alma then, yet to be born, and understand how she must have felt growing up with parents who were so unfeeling. Parents who were disappointed that she wasn't born a boy.

At length, Walter-Wyatt announces that he's going to take Lester to his club, the Knickerbocker. Esme takes Josephine by the hand and they set off for a walk in Central Park. To my surprise, Cavill turns to me and invites me for a drive. 'As it's your first time in New York, Miss Fleet, I would like to take this opportunity to show you something of the city,' he proposes.

I agree. After all, Constance is soon to be a part of his family.

Personally, I want to get out of the house; Alice and Walter-Wyatt Aldershoff are dreadful.

Alice reminds me that her dressmaker is coming to the house at noon. 'You mustn't miss it or you won't have a suitable dress to wear for Lester and Esme's engagement party next week, or, for that matter,' she turns up her pretty nose, 'anything else.'

Cavill glances at his gold pocket watch, which hangs on a chain in his waistcoat. 'That gives us plenty of time,' he says with a wide smile. 'I will make sure Miss Fleet is delivered back to your door with time to spare.'

A maid brings me a hat, a pair of gloves and a parasol. Alice looks me up and down and cannot disguise her distaste. Nothing matches. 'The sooner we get you to a shop, the better,' she says as I endeavour to put on the hat in front of the mirror.

'I'm more concerned about what's *inside* the clothes.' I laugh, for what do I care, now I know that Cavill isn't at all put off by my mismatching clothes.

Alice corrects me. 'That might be so in England, but, here in New York, a woman's clothes are of the utmost importance. It says everything about her.' She notices me fumbling with the pins and asks the maid to help me. I'm not used to wearing anything other than a bobble hat. Alice probably writes me off as an English eccentric.

Cavill summons one of the horse-drawn carriages that wait in a long line beneath the trees beside the park and offers me his hand so that I can climb in. 'This is a good way to see the city,' he declares, settling onto the leather seat beside me. The driver sitting up on the box cracks his whip and the big carthorse sets off with a plodding gait.

The sun shines brightly onto the city and I put up my parasol, then turn to look at Cavill. We are alone together at last and we are free to love each other without inhibition. Constance, certainly, had no inhibitions in that department. He rests his eyes on mine and smiles, a smile that is both intimate and open. A smile that brings back to me those many precious moments at St Sidwell Manor when we were candid and honest about how we felt. 'Welcome to New York,' he says. 'Now, allow me to show you all the things I love about it and then I'll tell you what I miss about home.'

I gaze around in wonder. Every detail is gripping to me, coming as I do from the future. Motor cars and trolleys are just becoming the norm, and horses and carts still prevail; the clip-clop of hooves blends with the ticking of engines, the tinkling of bells and the screeching of whistles. There are no traffic lights, so people cross the streets where and when they want. Nothing moves very fast, however. There's a languor that doesn't exist in my time. It's pleasant to be a part of it, this gentle, unhurried pace. The air does not smell of fumes, and I get occasional whiffs of hyacinth and gardenia, which are carried from the park on the warm spring breeze.

Birds clamour in the trees among delicate, phosphorescent green leaves that have only recently unfurled. Women walk arm in arm in long skirts and elaborate hats, but I'm struck by how many more men there are in the streets than women. And there's a marked uniformity to their dress that's so different from my time. Three-piece suits, white shirts, ties and hats. It's easy to spot a gentleman from a builder and a lady from a maid; the way people dress says everything about their status in society. Alice is right about that. It cannot be disguised.

The pavements teem with people. I notice a uniformed nursemaid pushing a pram down the pavement, two young children skipping hand in hand, and a one-legged man hobbling on wooden crutches. While there is colour, there are no brash tones and there are yet to be giant billboards advertising merchandise in flashing lights. The advertisements that currently exist are muted and seem to be written on the flat sides of buildings: *Washington Crisps* and *Cross, London. Leather Goods and English Gloves.*

Cavill is quite transformed from the serious man he was on the *Titanic*. There's a lightness to him now, as if he's appreciating everything around him with renewed vigour. He's more the young man I fell in love with at St Sidwell. He even looks at me in a different way. With affection. Perhaps, because we have shared such a dreadful experience, he feels bonded to *me* as well as Lester.

Or is it something else? Is he beginning to see the real me behind the disguise?

'May I call you Constance?' he asks after a while, and he looks at me askance and his lips curl into a knowing smile. 'After all, you did call me Cavill.'

I laugh. 'I might remind you that you called me Constance on the ship. But I'll permit you to go one step further. You may call me Connie.' I smile back flirtatiously.

'Very well, Connie. I'm happy to have some time with you alone.'

I recall telling him that he was dear to me. Now I know that Constance feels the same, I need not be so restrained. 'I'm happy to be alone with you, too,' I reply, and I feel startled by my candour. I have been so restrained, until now.

'May I be direct with you, Connie?'

'I would be disappointed if you were not.'

'When we met last year, I was grieving for my wife,' he says. He turns to me and frowns. 'I didn't *see* you.' He runs his eyes over my face, as if he really is seeing it afresh.

I catch my breath. 'And you see me now?' I ask, barely daring to hope.

He nods slowly. 'That evening when you came out onto the deck, and I lent you my coat. Something changed.'

'It did?'

He nods and again frowns, as if he can't quite believe it himself. 'I saw you with different eyes, Connie. It sounds mad, I'm sure, but I felt, that night on the deck, that I knew you. I don't mean in the way two people meet socially. Of course, I knew you like that. I mean that I found in you something I hadn't seen in you before.' He smiles diffidently now and holds my gaze. His eyes fill with tenderness. 'I liked it.'

He reaches across and takes my hand. 'I liked it a lot.'

I look down at my hand in his. It's small in his large one. I feel the tears stinging my eyes and blink to hold them back. I can't believe that I have been given another opportunity to love him, and to be loved in return.

'When I said you are dear to me, I meant it,' I tell him softly.

He squeezes my hand. 'I never believed I would say this again. But you are dear to me too, Connie.'

Then he lifts my hand and, with gentle fingers, slowly unbuttons the glove, exposing the skin on my wrist one button at a time. It looks quite naked with the kid leather peeled away, and I catch my breath. He doesn't say a word. He brings my wrist to his lips and presses them against it in a kiss.

True to his word, Cavill returns me to the house on Fifth Avenue in time for the dress fitting. He helps me out of the carriage and bids me goodbye, bringing my hand to his mouth and brushing my glove with his lips. I can barely climb the steps to the front door for the elation that causes my head to swim. I'm full of excitement but also anxiety, for I know I'm heading down a familiar path once more, which can only lead to heartbreak. I will have to slide back and leave him again. Is a moment of bliss worth a lifetime of pain? Am I so reckless that I will allow myself to suffer so?

And what of Cavill? Will he go on and marry Constance? Has that already happened, without my intervention? Or is it because I have embodied Constance that he has fallen in love with her? Have I altered history once again?

I force myself to think of Lester. But, oh, how I wish I could be here simply for Cavill.

Mrs Varga, the dressmaker, brings boxes of trimming, lace and ribbons, buttons, sequins and strappings, and a couple of young assistants to help her. Alice greets her warmly but ignores the assistants as if they're invisible. The two girls carry the boxes into a drawing room I have not yet seen. It is as extravagantly decorated as the others, with floor-length pale-blue silk curtains embellished with gold fringes and arranged in swirls and drapes and goodness knows what else over a thick wooden pole. The walls are covered in paintings and the ceiling is adorned with white mouldings and an enormous chandelier, which hangs from a large rose in the centre. The marble chimney surround is laden with ornaments and porcelain vases of white roses. On the floor are exquisite rugs woven in blues, yellow and gold to match the curtains. The girls lay things out on the table, which has been cleared for this very purpose. They work like ghosts, saying nothing and moving about the room with a silent tread. Mrs Varga is middle-aged with greying hair, an aquiline nose, and full, sensual lips. She measures me and then, with Alice's help, for she's really an expert in this department, we choose the patterns from a book Mrs Varga has brought with her. Mrs Varga has the weary, haggard look of a woman who works every hour God gives her. She must have been beautiful once. From her accent I deduce that she's an immigrant, from Poland or

Hungary, I presume. The contrast between her rough hands and Alice's smooth ones is remarkable. Alice delights in each decision as if the skirts, blouses and dresses are for her. She demands that they are run up immediately and Mrs Varga reassures her that the first pieces will arrive the following morning, which is Saturday. I imagine the workers are going to be toiling through the night! I'm sure Alice Aldershoff is one of Mrs Varga's most valuable clients.

When the women leave, I turn to Alice and sigh loudly, sinking onto the sofa – that really was a marathon! 'How often does she make dresses for you?' I ask.

Alice chortles disdainfully. 'My dear Constance, I rarely employ her. I order most of my dresses from Worth in Paris at the start of each season. Don't you?' She frowns.

'Oh, Bertha does, of course. But I have a wonderful dressmaker in London,' I retaliate, not sure where Constance and Bertha get their clothes. 'The tailoring in London's West End is exceptionally good.'

Alice pulls a doubtful face. 'I suppose the Paris salons have ateliers in London.'

'They most certainly do.' I'd love to tell her that in the future there will be a train that connects London to Paris, and online shopping with next-day delivery, plus a very efficient returns policy. That would wipe the superior look off her face.

A three-course lunch is served in the dining room at the long table, which is covered in glass vases of bright pink and white peonies. We are joined by three other couples who are as hungry to hear about the *Titanic* as Walter-Wyatt and Alice are. Lester and I are getting rather good at telling the story. We're a double act. It appears that Lester has forgotten his animosity towards me for he's his usual jovial self again. I notice that his story has been embellished. He recounts how it was *he* who saved Cavill Pengower, and others besides, by clambering aboard an overturned lifeboat and pulling to safety those struggling in the water. I bristle at the lie, for it was Cavill who saved *him* and not the other way around.

Whenever he mentions Cavill's name, I can feel my cheeks burn. The words of the gypsy woman come back to me, louder than ever. *Love will* always *bring you back.*

Will it *always*?

Lester doesn't disclose the fact that his valet donned his master's clothes in order to be given a place in one of the lifeboats. There's already growing public disapproval of the men who saved themselves when there were still women and children awaiting rescue. Viscount Ravenglass, who didn't rob anyone of a place, is deemed a hero, and he's milking every ounce of admiration. He certainly won't allow the truth to interfere with a good story.

They wouldn't consider him a hero if they witnessed what *I* witnessed in his cabin the night before the ship sank. How well he hides who he really is. How sad that he has to.

'The cries and screams of hundreds of drowning people will haunt me for the rest of my days,' he says gravely, and the room goes quiet as they appreciate how truly terrible it must have been.

That afternoon, Alice takes me shopping. She changes her clothes, donning a primrose-yellow dress of such splendour one could be forgiven for thinking she's off to a ball. Diamonds sparkle on her earlobes and around her neck. I'm sure, if she wasn't wearing gloves, they would sparkle on her fingers too. I am like a thrush beside a very beautiful parrot, but I don't really care. As far as my mission goes, it doesn't matter what I look like and it appears that Cavill likes me just the way I am.

Alice takes me to a milliner to buy hats and gloves, and then by chauffeur-driven car to Saks on Herald Square. I'm well enough informed about New York to know that Saks later becomes an enormous department store on Fifth Avenue. Others will mushroom, like Bloomingdales, Barney's and Bergdorf Goodman. But right now, Saks is one of the very few to exist and Mrs Aldershoff is obviously a very extravagant client for they welcome her as if she's the Queen.

We are escorted around the floors by the manager, an obsequious man with a tidy moustache and greased back hair, and a retinue of young boys in livery who scurry about like hounds at a hunt. The store appears to have come to a standstill just for Alice. She waves her gloved hand here and there, and items are carried away and wrapped up in tissue paper and tied with ribbon. I realise how very important she is. Everyone stares at her as if she's a movie star – if they had iPhones they'd be taking her photograph and asking for selfies, but she ignores them like a horse ignores flies. She's focused on what she's doing and clearly enjoying herself very much. In the end she doesn't pay, she just sweeps out leaving the parcels to be delivered straight to her home. I assume a monthly bill is sent to the house. She probably doesn't even see it. God knows how much she's spent.

I'm on the point of climbing into the car when I spot Emma Livingstone walking up the pavement towards me with a woman I assume is her chaperone. 'Miss Livingstone!' I exclaim.

Her face lights up when she sees me. 'Miss Fleet! What luck!'

I hurry to her and take her hands in mine. 'Are you all right?'

'I have nothing to wear,' she replies with a shrug. 'I'm having to buy clothes or I'm not fit to be seen in public.'

'Likewise,' I reply. 'Everything we owned is at the bottom of the sea.'

She lowers her voice. 'I'm glad I've bumped into you,' she says quietly, glancing around furtively. 'You remember Mrs Gilsden?

Her son didn't make it and she's desperate, poor dear. I wonder, would it be presumptuous of me to ask whether you might be able to give her a seance, with that spirit board? Like you did for Josephine. I think it would give her comfort to know that he lives on.'

I could give her a seance without the Ouija board, but I must stay true to Constance. 'Of course.' I tell her to wait while I consult Alice, who is sitting in the back of the car fiddling impatiently with her purse and watching keenly the people in the street, probably making sure no one is more elegantly dressed than she is. When I mention the board, her eyes sharpen and she seizes upon the idea with enthusiasm.

'This evening at six,' she says. 'We will hold a seance in the library. How thrilling.' I can see her mind whirring with the names of people she will invite.

'I will come with Miss Pengower,' Emma says when I tell her, and I hope that Josephine will bring her father.

I climb into the car beside Alice. For the first time, I'm actually grateful that I will have something nice to wear.

Chapter Eighteen

I'm sitting at the dressing table while Ruby styles my hair. Constance has good hair. It's thick and lustrous, and Ruby pins it up with skill. Edwardian women don't wash their hair very often, but they brush it a great deal, with boar-bristle brushes. She's pleased to have borrowed some meshing from Alice's lady's maid to beef up the style, and the effect is impressive. It looks like I have much more hair than I do. She's also borrowed a kind of pomade that gives it shine. I'm fascinated to discover that Edwardians put as much product in their hair as we do.

I hope to see Cavill this evening. The thought fills me with excitement so that I can barely think of anything else. My heart expands and my whole being is flooded with a delicious warmth as if my veins are being pumped with treacle. But it doesn't last for long. The reality of the slide dampens my exuberance. I will lose him again. It's only a matter of time. I would laugh at my delusion if it wasn't so tragic. How can I lose something that I don't have? Cavill has *never* been mine. He loved Hermione. For a short and blissful time, I slipped in behind her eyes and soaked up his love as if he was giving it to me, Pixie. As if he was recognising something special beyond Hermione's face and personality, as if he was seeing *me*. Now I'm Constance Fleet and it's happening all over again. He's falling in love with *her* and I'm hoping that he's really recognising *me*, shining through her. But how can he when he doesn't know there's any difference to be seen – that there is any separation between the physical and the non-physical. Even if I explained it to him, he wouldn't understand it. He'd think I'd lost my mind.

I'll see him tonight and I'll just have to be grateful for that. For these brief and fleeting moments together. They're all I'm being given. I have no choice but to love him from afar. I suppose that's better than not loving him at all.

I tear my thoughts away from Cavill. 'How is everything downstairs?' I ask Ruby.

She slips a spray of blue feathers into my hair and fastens it with pins. 'It's mayhem,' she answers, grinning at me in the mirror. 'Miss O'Donnell has lost her Japanese golden thread and is turning the place upside down in search of it.'

'What's Japanese golden thread?'

'She says it's the finest gold thread in the world, for embroidery. It was in her sewing box, but now it's gone. It's real gold, you know.'

I shouldn't be surprised that Mrs Aldershoff's dresses are woven with real gold! 'Oh dear.'

'And Monsieur Barbier is a tyrant in the kitchen,' she continues. 'He's never happy. His mouth goes down like a bulldog's, and he grunts and groans and shouts at the kitchen maids.'

'It sounds very lively down there.'

She laughs. 'It's mayhem. Everyone's jittery. I don't know why.'

'And Glover?'

She sighs and pulls a face. 'Oh, I don't know what's going on with him, ma'am,' she says, coming round to pin onto the collar of my indigo dress a glittering diamond-and-sapphire brooch borrowed from Alice.

'What do you mean?' I ask, my interest piqued.

'He's nervous and bad-tempered. I don't know what's got into him. Ever since we were rescued by the *Carpathia* he's been on edge, like he's afraid of something.'

I wonder whether Lester has told him he'll have to seek employment elsewhere. 'Perhaps he feels guilty for having survived when so many died,' I suggest. 'The men who were saved in lifeboats are being given a hard time. Take Bruce Ismay, for example. He's being savaged by the press for having taken a place on a lifeboat while women and children were still on board, hoping to be rescued. Although, to be fair, I don't know why one life is worth more than another, simply because of a person's gender. People should be treated equally whatever their sex and status.'

She smiles at me through the mirror. I must seem crazily idealistic to her. 'The world is never going to change, ma'am,' she says simply. 'There is always going to be a difference between men and women, and rich and poor, isn't there? It's the way it is.' She shrugs. 'Everyone below stairs wants to hear Glover's story, but he won't talk about it and I say nothing. It's not my place to tell his story.'

'Very wise. He'll get over it.'

She nods. 'He'll have to.' She puts her soft hands on my shoulders. 'You look lovely, ma'am.'

'Thank you, Ruby,' I reply, and get up off the chair. 'I feel much better in this dress.'

I stand at the top of the flight of stairs with the blue box in my hand. The stair is the *pièce de résistance* of the house and is sublime with its elaborate gilded balustrade and crimson runner. There's something about the way it sweeps down in a curve that's very harmonious and pleasing to the eye. I don't think I've ever seen a staircase to better it. Mr Stirling was wise not to alter it when he designed the Aldershoff Hotel. It's the only part of the building that has remained exactly the same. I run my eyes over the panelled walls and into the grand hall below, and feel privileged to be witnessing the place as a private house. There are few as splendid as this that have survived into the twenty-first century. These magnificent private homes were either converted into museums and public buildings, or demolished. It's fascinating to see how the Gilded Age millionaires lived. It's a world away from my own experience. I doubt I will be here for much longer. I'm eager to see Cavill, and yet the anticipation of saying goodbye is already causing me pain in my heart. A part of me just wants to leave and get it over with.

I put my hand on the balustrade and walk carefully down the steps, holding the blue box in the other hand. I'm aware of tripping on my long skirt and kick it out as I descend. I wouldn't want to stumble and fall. It's a long way to the hall. I can hear voices. Guests have already arrived for the seance. I can smell cigarette smoke wafting out of the drawing room and hear the low murmur of voices.

I hover a moment in the doorway to the drawing room and my eyes immediately find Cavill. He rises above the others, even Lester who is tall. I'm relieved he's come. The room feels full now that he's in it, and charged with a heightened energy. He's talking to Walter-Wyatt. I watch the two of them, aware that time is running out and that soon this scene will be nothing but a memory replayed in the Aldershoff Hotel when I've slid back. When once again I nurse my aching heart and struggle to bear an unbearable sorrow.

Cavill lifts his eyes, and they settle on me with an intimate and familiar warmth. His face softens into a colluding smile.

I smile back discreetly and allow myself to be sucked into his gaze so that everyone around us fades into a blur. It's a brief moment but it has an eternal quality about it that makes it feel so much longer. I'm transported back to St Sidwell Manor, to the window seat in my bedroom, Cavill and me, gazing at the stars, and at each other, and not a sliver of light between us.

He turns his attention back to his host and the connection is dropped, but not lost. We have declared ourselves now and I know it is what Constance would wish. When she wakes up, she will be exactly where she wants to be. There's a certain satisfaction in that.

I join the group of women who stand together like a flock of hens in their fine dresses and jewellery, and try not to allow my gaze to stray.

Alice is quivering with nervous excitement. Her energy is intense, her eyes bright and alert. She seems not to be listening to the conversation, but feigning interest, nodding and smiling distractedly. Her attention slides to the big double doors every few seconds, as if anticipating the arrival of someone very important. I wonder who that might be.

There are only nine of us in the room. Esme is demure in an ivory-coloured lace dress and stands talking to Lester, who seems quite taken with her. If he's faking affection, he's doing a very good job of it. I wonder whether the sight of the Potemkin Diamond has focused his mind and he now knows what he must do. Perhaps that is why Glover is in such a bad mood. Emma Livingstone has brought Mrs Gilsden, whose eyes are raw and swollen. Her distraught face is very white against the high collar of her black dress, and my heart goes out to her for her loss. Children should not die before their parents. Parents should not have to endure that pain. Josephine is lovely in pink and pale green, and looks as fresh as a tulip beside her. Mrs Gilsden is intrigued when I show her the case that carries what they call the spirit board. Alice tells us that Walter-Wyatt doesn't like seances but that he's staying on account of his mother. 'She's squeezing us in between engagements,' Alice informs us keenly, and now I know why she's nervous. Her mother-in-law, the celebrated Didi Aldershoff, is about to arrive.

Shortly, a footman appears in the doorway and announces Mrs William Aldershoff. The room goes quiet. A reverential hush falls over the group. Alice flutters across the floor, her skirts swishing loudly as they trail over the Persian rug in her wake. I catch Cavill's eye again and his expression reflects his amusement at the arrival of a woman who is quite obviously a diva. I'm surprised that no one else has picked up the silent communications passing between us. To me, it sounds like cymbals.

Didi Aldershoff darkens the doorway in an elaborate black silk-and-lace dress. I remember that her husband has only recently died, so she must still be in her mourning clothes. She has not scrimped on diamonds, however. On her breast glitters an enormous brooch in the shape of a rose, and diamonds sparkle in her ears and at her throat. Her dove-grey hair is curled and pinned up in an elegant bouffant. Crowning it is a small diamond tiara that twinkles in the light like ice crystals. She must be in her late fifties, but her figure and posture are those of a young woman; only her grey hair gives away her age, for her skin is barely lined. Everything about her face denotes a formidable character. Her cheekbones are high and pronounced, her jawbone square and sharp, her almond-shaped eyes a deep midnight blue, framed by thick black lashes and eyebrows that arch in fine, symmetrical crescents. She smiles when she sees her daughter-in-law and that's when I'm struck by her beauty. It's arresting. She's every bit as stunning as her reputation professes her to be. What's more, she radiates charm, and her energy fills the room as if she's emanating a bright internal light. I'm sure, when she decides to turn it off, that she can just as easily suck the energy out of the room and leave it in darkness. Her charisma is electrifying, but it's a little scary too. Alice is certainly uneasy in her presence. I can tell by her body language that this is the woman she most wants to please.

Alice brings her over to me and introduces us. 'Miss Fleet was on the *Titanic*,' she says, hoping that that might impress her mother-in-law. It doesn't. She couldn't be less interested in the *Titanic*.

'My daughter-in-law tells me you have a spirit board,' she says eagerly, holding me with her mesmeric gaze. I feel like a mouse in the thrall of an eagle.

'I do. I'm going to try to make contact with Mrs Gilsden's son, who died on the *Titanic*.'

She's not interested in Mrs Gilsden, either. 'I would like you to make contact with my husband, William Aldershoff. Is that possible?' she asks. Judging by the expectant look in her eyes, I imagine for her *anything* is possible.

'If he wants to come through, he will,' I reply.

She nods, satisfied with my answer. 'He died very suddenly. We had no time to say goodbye.'

'There is no reason to say goodbye,' I tell her, and I feel Alice stiffen at my side. I suppose everyone usually agrees with Didi Aldershoff. 'Because you have not been parted,' I add. 'He is still with you, even though you can't see him.'

'That is all very well in theory,' she says. 'But I would like to hear that from him.'

'We shall see. Some spirits find it hard to reach us for our vibration is very dense down here, and they are very fine. If he can, I'm sure he will.'

'My husband was a remarkable man, Miss Fleet. He will make himself known.' She turns to Alice. 'Let us begin. I'm expected at Mrs Oelrichs' at eight.'

I have not yet spoken to Cavill, but I'm aware of him all the time. Aware that he's in the room, breathing the same air as me. That should be enough, but it isn't. I want more. Oh, how my heart *longs* for more! There is no time, however. I follow Alice and Didi across the hall to the library, which later becomes the Walter-Wyatt drawing room. I'm acutely aware of Alma Aldershoff's disastrous seance which happened in this very room. I hope this one will be more successful. There's a central fireplace with an immense marble surround. Above it, a vast portrait of a young Didi in a white silk gown hangs on chains. A pair of bronze dancers dominate the mantlepiece, and in their outstretched hands are tall ivory candles that create golden halos on the painting behind them. The wood-panelled ceiling is mock Tudor and could be straight out of Hampton Court Palace. The walls are lined with thousands of books, arranged neatly on shelves and behind chicken wire in big, arched cabinets. Enormous ferns stand in blue-and-white Chinese ceramic planters, their green fronds drooping prettily. A giant chandelier hangs from a carved Tudor rose painted white for the House of York and red for the House of Lancaster. There's a grand piano at one end of the room, and a desk at the other, placed in front of a large window draped with heavy crimson curtains. In the centre is a round walnut table with six upholstered red chairs.

Footmen pull out the chairs and Alice asks me how I want to arrange the placement. Didi doesn't wait to be seated, but sits down beside me and puts her hands on the table, knitting her fingers together expectantly. I ask the other women to come forward. There are only enough chairs for the six of us, so

Josephine agrees to stand. Esme, Emma and a snivelling Mrs Gilsden take their seats. Walter-Wyatt, Lester and Cavill stand behind us to observe. Cavill is so close I can feel his body heat on my back. I tell myself to concentrate, to get into the zone. I can't let Mrs Gilsden down. She looks so unhappy. Didi has barely said a word to her. I imagine she considers the woman beneath her. I hope William Aldershoff will come through. I'd hate to see Didi disappointed. I'm not sure Alice would forgive me!

I put the case on the table in front of me and unclip it. When I lift out the board, there's a collective gasp as if it has magic powers. The truth is less exciting. It's simply a tool with which to allow Spirit to communicate. Contact can be done with anything – tea leaves, tarot cards, crystals, runes – it's much more about the medium than the device they use. In my case, I don't need the Ouija board. I can communicate with spirits with relative ease, depending on the energy and will of the spirit. But I'm not Pixie Tate. I'm Constance Fleet, so I must play my part, right up until the end.

I put the case on the carpet and lay the board on the table. I have a piece of paper and a pencil so that I can write down any messages that are spelt out. Then I ask one of the footmen to close the curtains and to light a candle and place it in the middle of the table. I'm expecting Lester to crack a joke, to undermine the effectiveness of the board in some way, but he doesn't. I imagine he's respectful of Mrs William Aldershoff, even a little scared of her perhaps. Or maybe he's wary of looking cocky in front of Esme, who sits trembling in front of him like a nervous foal.

I ask the women to place their hands on the table and to spread their fingers wide. I close my eyes and say a prayer of protection. 'In the name of God, Jesus Christ, the Great Brotherhood of Light, the Archangels Michael, Raphael, Gabriel, Uriel and Ariel, please protect us from the forces of evil during this session. Let there be nothing but light surrounding this board and its participants and let us only communicate with powers and entities of the light. Protect us, protect this house, the people in this house and let there only be light and nothing but light. Amen. You may open your eyes.'

I select three women – Didi, Alice and Mrs Gilsden – to put a finger lightly on the planchette, for if we all do it we will make it too heavy. I explain what will happen if a spirit wishes to communicate. I make it very clear that everyone must remain calm and focus on their heart centres. It's imperative that the energy in the room is raised high so as not to attract an entity from the lower astral. We don't want any nasties. I glance at Lester. How ironic that he later becomes one.

Then I ask specifically for Mr Gilsden to come forward. I close my eyes and focus on the man I met on the *Titanic*. I feel the temperature drop around me, especially at my feet. Then the cold builds, until the room feels icy.

A vision appears in my mind. I see Mr Gilsden in his life vest trying to swim out to a lifeboat. I feel his desperation and his terror. He's freezing and growing increasingly weak. He stops swimming and bobs there as helpless as a cork before surrendering to his fate and leaving the world like a wisp of vapour rising into the starlit night. I sense a great wave of relief and then a profound feeling of peace and love.

I open my eyes, startled by the vision I've just seen. But no one is looking at me. They're staring at the planchette, willing it to move. 'We are in the presence of a spirit,' I say quietly, because I feel very strongly a man's energy and it doesn't belong to the living ones standing around the table, but an old soul who has long passed. 'Who are you?' I ask, for it's most certainly not Mr Gilsden.

The planchette moves from letter to letter, dragging the three fingers with it. I notice the women's eyes widen with astonishment for they know *they* are not moving it.

ROBERT

'Who is Robert?' I ask, looking at Mrs Gilsden hopefully.

Mrs Gilsden takes a sharp breath. 'My father, Archie's grandfather. It must be he.'

'Are you Mrs Gilsden' father, Robert?' I ask.

The planchette moves to *Yes*.

Mrs Gilsden begins to cry and presses her handkerchief to her mouth to smother her sobs.

I sense then why Robert has come through. 'Is Archie with you, Robert?' I ask.

RESTING

'Is Archie resting after his ordeal?'

Yes

'Is he happy and at peace?'

Yes

'Do you have a special message for your daughter, Robert?'

LOVE

'Oh, Papa. I love you, too. You can't imagine how much I miss you. Please take care of Archie. Please take care of my son.'

I see a vision of Robert laughing and feel I must pass this on. 'I'm being shown a man in a black frock coat with a white collar. He has a sweeping moustache, rather like Archie's, and spectacles that hang on a long chain. He's holding a bible.'

'Yes, that's Papa,' Mrs Gilsden states keenly. 'He was a vicar.'

'That makes sense then. He's laughing. He's telling you not to worry. He and Archie are both where they should be. Everything is as it should be. He says you must live your life with joy and love, and not waste time mourning your loss. He and Archie are not lost to you; they are simply out of sight, for now.'

Mrs Gilsden nods. Her cheeks are shiny with tears.

'That's beautiful,' Cavill murmurs under his breath. I wonder whether he's thinking of Hermione.

'Ask for William to come through,' Didi demands impatiently. 'I know he will come if you ask him to. William, are you here?'

I know I must do as I'm told, but first I tell them to move the planchette to *Goodbye* to officially close our session with Robert.

Then I do Didi's bidding. 'William Aldershoff, if you are here, please make yourself known.'

It takes only a moment for William's energy to be felt, for, unlike Robert's, William's is fiercely assertive.

Yes

'Oh, my darling William,' Didi exclaims, moved suddenly to tenderness. 'Is that really you?'

The planchette quivers on the word *Yes*.

I link into his energy and see a tall, powerfully built man with a black beard and intense, cobalt-coloured eyes. I perceive his intelligence, which is formidable, and a mischievous sense of humour.

'How can I be sure it is you?' Didi asks. 'Give me proof.'

I see him smile wryly. The planchette moves again.

FIND WHITMAN

'I don't understand,' says Didi. 'What do you mean?'

'Walt Whitman?' Cavill suggests.

'Oh, really, how can that be proof?' says Didi petulantly. 'Walt Whitman?'

'To *find* Walt Whitman?' Cavill adds.

'Who's Walt Whitman?' I ask, assuming he's a friend.

'The author,' Didi tells me. I can tell from her tone of voice that she's surprised I don't know.

I nod. 'Then we must find him.'

'And how might we do that?' Didi asks. 'How can we possibly find him when he's dead?'

Then a thought springs to mind. 'Walter, will you do as he asks and find Walt Whitman in the bookcase?'

'You think that's what he means?' Alice asks, eyes gleaming with fascination.

'Perhaps,' I reply. 'We're in the library, after all.'

Walter-Wyatt takes no time in finding *W* and seizes upon a green book with gold writing. He holds it up for us to see. '*Leaves of Grass*,' he reads out. 'Good God, is this it, do you think?'

'Will you please give it to Mrs William Aldershoff,' I say.

Walter-Wyatt places the book on the table in front of his mother.

The planchette moves again. Every eye focuses keenly upon it.

OPEN

Didi gasps. Now she's in no doubt that her husband is present. With a trembling hand, she lifts the hard cover. To her surprise, there's a secret compartment within, lined in red velvet. Placed in there is an old dollar bill. 'Oh, my Lord!' she mutters, touching it gently. She is clearly stirred. 'This was the first dollar he ever made. He told me he had hidden it somewhere clever. He liked to hide things.' Her eyes well with tears and her voice cracks. She puts a hand on her breast and takes a deep breath. 'He said that he held this dollar in his hand and made a vow, that he would become the richest man in America.'

'Well, he certainly did that,' says Alice, laughing lightly.

'What special message do you have for your wife?' I ask.

LOVE NOTHING MATTERS

'What on earth does he mean?' Didi asks. 'Nothing matters?'

'I think he means that nothing matters, but love,' I tell her. She frowns. 'How absurd!'

'That doesn't sound at all like William,' says Alice.

'How very odd,' Didi mutters, but she's frowning. I wonder whether she's realising that wealth is only an earthly concern. Where William Aldershoff is, material wealth means nothing at all.

The planchette moves again. Another entity has taken over. I try to sense who it is, but William Aldershoff's energy is so strong, it's overpowering it. I focus and try to sense beyond William. I perceive a faint female energy. It's soft and gentle, and coming to me in colours of baby pink and apple green. Yes, I see colours, but I can't see a face.

BEWARE THE STAIR

I'm startled by the warning, and alarmed, suddenly. It's very specific, but cryptic. A part of me wants to ask questions, but I feel an unpleasant darkness creeping into the corners of the room. I make the decision to close the session.

'Goodbye,' I declare loudly, reaching into the table and sliding the planchette to the word *Goodbye* on the board. 'We must draw this seance to a close,' I say quickly.

The women take their fingers off the planchette.

'Whatever does he mean, beware the stair? What stair? And who needs to beware?' Didi looks at me for an answer.

I shrug. 'I don't know. But I do know that that wasn't your husband, but another entity pushing through. Ignore them.'

'Most peculiar,' Didi murmurs. 'Is it me? Do I have to beware of the stair? Is something going to happen to *me*?' I can see that she's a woman who brings everything around to herself.

'No, nothing is going to happen to you,' I reassure her, folding the board and reaching for the blue box. Although, I can't be sure.

I remember the dark energy I sensed on the stair in the hotel and a cold shiver ripples over my skin. *Beware the stair.* What on earth are they trying to tell me?

And I don't know who is giving the warning, or who it is for.

But I sense that I'm finally approaching the reason for my slide.

I glance at Cavill and anticipate my departure with a stab of anguish.

Chapter Nineteen

As soon as the seance is over, everyone makes their way into the hall to depart. Didi is obsessing about the strange warning and says she doesn't feel like dining with Mrs Oelrichs now. 'How can I possibly dine when I fear every stair I encounter?' I've told her numerous times that the warning was not for her, but she won't listen; she thinks everything is about her. 'If only William was here. But I'm alone. All alone.'

Her son tells her patiently that she is never alone, but I can tell he is weary of servicing such a demanding mother. Cavill and Lester jump in to reassure her, and she soaks up their attention like a hydrangea soaks up water. Didi Aldershoff is a woman accustomed to male attention and is an expert at milking it. I realise that she has a suite of rooms here but has been spending her time at their 'cottage' in Newport. She doesn't thank me for the seance, even though her wish was granted and her husband came through and communicated with her. Her displeasure has sucked the energy out of the room, as I knew it would when she decided not to be charming. I think she blames me for the warning about the stair.

She calls for a footman to escort her up to her rooms. He comes at once and offers her his hand. She takes it and grips it tightly. 'I'm not going up or down these without being attended,' she declares, holding tightly to the balustrade with the other hand. 'Beware the stair,' she says with a sniff, giving me a stern look that reminds me, in a flash, of Alma. 'Well, I'm *very* aware.'

Mrs Gilsden is grateful to have had a communication from her father. She's reassured now that her son is safe and well, and lives on in Spirit. I reiterate the fact that those we love never leave us, and she embraces me firmly. 'You are so right, Miss Fleet. How can I ever thank you?'

'Your happiness is thanks enough,' I reply, and watch her depart with Josephine and Emma, who have just said their farewells to Walter-Wyatt, Alice and Esme, who are standing by the door.

The last guest to leave is Cavill. He takes my hand and looks at me with an intensity I haven't seen since St Sidwell. 'Walk with me tomorrow?' he asks, lowering his voice. 'There is something I want to tell you.'

'Tomorrow?'

'In the park. At the grand staircase. Midday?' He runs his eyes over my face, lingering a moment on my lips.

I nod. He smiles, pleased. There is no reticence now, no hesitation, just an acceptance perhaps of the heart's enigmatic longings.

'Until then.' He lets go of my hand and Henderson gives him his coat and hat. He trots lightly down the steps as he did that first time I met him at St Sidwell. I watch him climb into the front of the car, where Mrs Gilsden, Emma and Josephine are waiting for him on the back seat. The driver walks round to the bonnet and cranks the engine to start it. We take it for granted that in our time one can simply turn a key. In fact, many cars don't even require a key, but a button, and bingo! Wouldn't Cavill be astonished by that!

I turn around and walk back inside, and Henderson closes the door behind me.

Tomorrow cannot come soon enough.

That night, Lester and I are included in a dinner party with people called the Havemeyers, and then at a ball at the de Groots', but as I have nothing elegant to wear – my dresses will be delivered tomorrow – I decide to stay behind. Alice approves; she does not want me letting the side down by wearing something unsuitable.

Lester and I wait in the drawing room for the family to come downstairs. Music is resounding from the gramophone once again. The same man with the high voice singing a song about his heart being like a garden. I'm sitting on the sofa. Lester's standing by the fireplace. He has borrowed clothes from Walter-Wyatt again. He looks conventionally elegant with his stiff white collar and bow tie, and diamond studs glinting on his white waistcoat. He offers me a cigarette. 'Are you still not smoking?'

'I'm not,' I reply.

He narrows his eyes, appraising me curiously.

'Who is this singer?' I ask.

He frowns. 'Enrico Caruso.' He stares at me in amazement, as if I've morphed into someone he doesn't recognise, which, I suppose, I have. 'I can't make you out, Aunt Constance. You've been acting very oddly ever since we boarded the *Titanic*. Really, you're not yourself at all. What's come over you?'

'I don't know what you mean?' I'm obviously not winning any Oscars for my performance as Constance.

'You're dull.'

'Excuse me?'

'Sorry to be so blunt, but you've lost your spunk.'

Now that's a word!

'I haven't been feeling myself.' I fold my arms defensively. 'I didn't like that ship and I didn't like its sinking. I'm sure in a few days, I will be myself again.' Surely, the time is approaching for me to leave Constance.

He strikes a match and lights his cigarette. Then he glances at the door and lowers his voice. 'I have told Glover that when we return to London, I will find him another post.' He drops his eyes to the carpet and I can see his jaw tense. It must have cost him dearly to dismiss him. He drags on his cigarette and then exhales loudly. 'He hasn't taken it very well.'

'Maybe you should have waited until you were home before you told him,' I say reproachfully.

'We had a row. He forced my hand.'

Now I know why Glover is out of sorts downstairs. 'You've made things hard for yourself, Lester. You now have an unhappy valet. Might he not become vengeful?'

He takes another puff and shakes his head. 'You're so melodramatic.' But I can tell he's nervous. 'You don't know him like I do.'

'I just know people.'

'You know *dead* people,' he retorts with a chuckle. 'You know, you were remarkable today. Really, I was impressed. There's something in it, to be sure.'

'I'm glad you didn't try to undermine me.'

'Oh, ye of little faith. Come, come, Aunt Constance, why would I want to do that? Esme was impressed too.'

'She's a lovely girl.'

'You don't need to tell *me* how lovely she is. I'm marrying her, aren't I?'

'I can't make you out. One moment you love Glover and the next you're making a full commitment to Esme.'

He flicks ash into the little round dish placed on the

mantlepiece beside him and looks wistful for a moment. 'I've had to choose between love and money, Constance. It's as simple as that. And I've chosen money.'

'How very sentimental of you.'

'Indeed.' He grins, but there's a bitter twist on his lips. 'There was really no contest. Mama would never forgive me if I came home without the bacon!'

Walter-Wyatt has returned from his club and has dressed for dinner. He appears in the drawing room with his cane, as elegant as Lester. 'I hear you're not joining us, Constance,' he says.

'I'm afraid I have nothing suitable to wear.'

'That's a shame. I was hoping to show you off. But Lester can tell his account of the *Titanic*, can't you, Lester? After all, your adventure was one of survival, while yours, Constance, if I may say so, was one of rescue. It's one thing floating about in a lifeboat, but quite another surviving the freezing cold water and clambering aboard an upturned boat. Everyone will want to hear about it.'

'And I will happily retell it,' says Lester.

I smile to myself. I suspect Lester's account of his adventure is becoming increasingly heroic.

Alice glides down the stairs in a pale-pink gown. She glitters with jewels and radiates opulence. In her wake, Esme looks young and graceful in white. I'm glad I'm not going with them for I'd look like a goose beside swans. No one tries to persuade me to come. 'Your dresses will arrive tomorrow, Constance, and then you will be the belle of *all* the balls,' Alice exclaims as she sashays out of the house.

Esme walks out on the arm of her fiancé, who has complimented her on her beauty. They make a handsome couple. With doe eyes she gazes adoringly up at him. I watch them leave the house and a sentence springs to mind: *ignorance is bliss*. In this case it will only lead to heartbreak and divorce down the line. I feel sorry for Esme for marrying a man who would rather be with another man, and I feel sorry for Lester, too, who has to hide who he really is. How perfectly beautiful it looks on the outside, but how tragic it is inside.

I'm thrilled to be left alone. I couldn't face going to parties and having to perform when I'm pining for Cavill and anticipating having to leave him again. My mind is busy trying to work out what he could possibly want to talk to me about and I want some quiet time to process the possibilities. I need to be ready in case he throws me a fast ball.

I climb the stairs. Everywhere there are servants. I can't imagine living like this, being watched all the time. But people like Walter-Wyatt and Alice are used to it and barely notice the people whose job it is to make their lives comfortable. And they rarely thank them.

The door to Lester's bedroom is wide open and Glover is in there drawing the curtains. 'Good evening, Glover,' I say, hovering in the corridor.

He spins around as if I've caught him doing something underhand. His eyes are wild with guilt. 'Is everything all right?' I ask him, wondering at his reaction. There's nothing dishonest about him tidying his master's bedroom. But it would have been prudent for Lester to wait until they were back in England to dismiss him.

'Yes, ma'am,' he replies stiffly, not meeting my eye.

'Have you recovered from your ordeal?' He looks embarrassed. The colour rises in his cheeks. I'm reminded then of how young he is. He's barely reached adulthood and he's survived the sinking of the *Titanic*. If it were my day, he'd be in therapy. 'You've been through a terrible trauma, Glover,' I continue. 'We all have.

To have witnessed people drowning, and that ship going down, well, that's enough to turn a person insane. If you feel guilty for having survived, you must tell yourself that it was your destiny to survive, otherwise you would have perished. It was meant to be.' He's staring at me with a startled look on his face. I don't know whether that's because of what I'm saying, or because I'm speaking to him. Perhaps Constance has never spoken to him beyond the odd salutation.

'Will that be all?' he asks.

I can't make him out. I'd like to say more, to engage him in further conversation, but he's unwilling to talk. 'I will leave you to your duties, then.' I smile, but he turns away and draws the other pair of curtains.

I feel my frustration mount. He should be grateful that I'm being so nice to him, but he's full of resentment. I remind myself that Lester has told him he's to be dismissed. Perhaps he's just sad.

Instead of going to my room, I decide to go downstairs and play the piano. I feel uneasy suddenly. There's a dark energy beginning to build in the house. *Beware the stair. Beware the stair.* I have no idea what that means, and who the message is meant for. Is someone going to fall down the stairs? If so, who?

I'm longing for tomorrow to come so that I can meet with Cavill. But my anticipation is clouded by the knowledge that I can't have him. I will slide back to my time soon and Cavill will be left in the past. When I open my eyes in the Aldershoff Hotel, Cavill will be long dead.

I sense that I'm close to finding out the root of Lester's trouble. I feel my return is imminent. Yet, I have no idea what to look out for. I have to trust that I'll be shown.

Henderson gives me an enquiring look when I encounter him in the hall. I tell him I'm going to play the piano. He asks whether I would like something to drink. A cup of tea, or some hot milk and honey. A bowl of soup. I decline. I don't have an appetite tonight. My belly feels like it's teeming with ants, and none of them know where they're going, or why they're there.

I only know how to play a couple of songs. I was brought up by my grandmother after my father died and my mother was taken away. She had an upright piano in her front room and I taught myself out of boredom. The music made me feel better at times when I felt overcome by despair. I sit on the stool now, lift the lid of the piano and hover my fingers over the keys. Then I begin to play 'Let It Be' by the Beatles. I don't need to look because I've played the tune so many times. I close my eyes and sing. Constance has a good voice, I discover. Not that it's a difficult song. As I get into it, I feel myself relax and I'm taken over by a wonderful feeling of bliss. I enter into a zone that's free of cares and worries, and I bask in it – until I open my eyes and see Didi Aldershoff standing in the doorway, staring at me in astonishment.

I snatch my fingers off the keys as if scalded. I didn't sense her there. What on earth must she think?

She shakes her head as if she can't believe what she's just heard. 'That was beautiful,' she gushes, her face opening into a charming smile. 'What was it? I've never heard anything like it before.'

I shrug. 'Something I made up.'

'Of course you did. What a talent you are. And the words? Did you make them up, too?'

I nod. 'Do play it again. I want to hear it from the beginning.'

She goes and perches on an armchair. I'm left no alternative than to do as she asks. I take a deep breath and commence. As I sing, the servants are drawn to the door. I feel like the Pied Piper of Hamlin luring the rats away with his music. Their faces are alight with wonder. I suppose the Beatles couldn't be more different from Enrico Caruso! When I play the final chord, they all clap. 'Play something else,' Didi demands, but I close the lid. I don't imagine she'll be as impressed by Chris de Burgh's 'Patricia the Stripper'! Those are the only two songs I know how to play.

The servants melt away, muttering to each other. A footman remains, I imagine, to escort Mrs Aldershoff back up the stairs when she's ready.

But she has no intention of leaving now. 'Come and sit with me,' she says, waving her elegant hand at the armchair beside her, her pretty lips curling with pleasure. 'You're a curious woman, Constance.'

I take the seat, sweeping my skirt to one side and settling into the chair. 'Am I to take that as a compliment?' I ask with a smile. Didi is irresistible when she wants to be.

Her bright eyes are penetrating. She's trying to work me out. 'There's something unusual about you that I can't put my finger on. Perhaps it's your Englishness, but, I admit, I've never met an Englishwoman like you before and I've met many.' She lifts her chin, accepting defeat perhaps in her ability to decipher me. 'Who taught you to use the spirit board?' she asks.

'My mama,' I reply, reminding myself that I'm Constance. The music has put me back in touch with Pixie and I must shake her off and assume my role. 'She died recently and left it to me.'

'Can anyone use it?'

'Anyone.'

'Does one need to be trained?'

'Not at all. You just need patience and good intentions. The law of attraction will draw like for like. If you go into it with the intention of creating mischief, that is what you will attract.

Therefore, you must aim for the highest good and attract only benevolent spirits.'

'But the spirit who warned us of the stair. Was that a benevolent spirit or a malevolent one, wanting to create fear?'

'That's a good question, Mrs Aldershoff. I've been trying to work it out. To be honest, I don't know who that was. The message seemed to come out of nowhere.'

'And it wasn't my husband?'

'No, it wasn't. If anything, it was a female energy.'

'You speak of energy, Constance. Tell me what you mean?'

'We are all spirit energy inhabiting these physical bodies in order to experience an earthly life. When we die, we leave our bodies behind as one leaves an old coat one no longer needs. We return home to the spirit dimension, which is simply another frequency of vibration. The slower the vibration, the more solid it appears. A rock, for example, vibrates at a very slow rate. A rainbow vibrates quickly. Spirit vibrates even quicker than that. Everything in the universe is vibration, moving at different speeds, from light and heat to these chairs we're sitting on. They just have different vibrational patterns. That's physics.' She's listening to me intently, her intelligent eyes staring at me as if she's committing everything I say to memory. I sense she's hungry to learn and impressed that I appear so knowledgeable. 'Your husband no longer has a physical body. He's energy.'

'But how will I recognise him when I die and meet him in the next life?' she asks, anxious suddenly.

'He will appear to you as he did in this life, only his body will not be physical. You won't be physical, either. Think of him as a rainbow. You'll both be beautiful rainbows.'

She likes that idea and smiles. 'How do you know so much about physics?'

'I'm not sure I know so much about physics, Mrs Aldershoff. I've been interested in metaphysics all my life.' I hope that's true of Constance. 'I've talked to wise people and read books on the subject. And I was born with a psychic ability.'

Her eyes take me in with renewed curiosity. 'How unusual you are, Constance. You've opened my eyes tonight and I thank you for that. My husband's message to me was to love. Jesus's message to the world was to love. And here we are, surrounded by immense wealth. It seems so important from our perspective, but we can't take it with us, can we? What's it for? William worked hard to make a fortune. He wanted more than anything to be accepted as a great man. In God's eyes, wealth made him neither great nor important. It was inconsequential. Now he understands. He has perspective, because he can look back on his life and see how irrelevant money was. God is love. Jesus is love. We, too, are love, we just don't know it. Isn't that true, Constance?'

'That's exactly what we are and that's exactly why we're here, to wake up to our true natures. To who we really are.'

'And how do we do that? How do we wake up?'

I shrug. 'I don't have all the answers and I'm not enlightened. I'm searching just like you. But I do know how to shut out the noise so that I can connect with the deep part of me that is eternal.'

'Do show me, Constance.'

'When you go to bed tonight, close your eyes and listen to your breath. Be the awareness that is aware of your breathing. The rise and fall of your diaphragm. The feel of air on your nostrils. Cold on the inhale, warm on the exhale. Become awareness. Consciousness. You'll no longer be Didi Aldershoff, widow, mother, grandmother, friend, woman, person. You'll be the awareness beyond all those things. That's the real you.'

She looks genuinely pleased. 'I will try, and report in the morning.'

'It might not come at first, but don't give up. In that state, you'll find the answers you're looking for because you already know them. There is nothing that you don't know.'

She takes my hand and pats it. 'I want to learn to use the spirit board. Will you teach me?'

'Of course, I will.'

'Perhaps we can help others who have lost loved ones on the *Titanic*. Might we do that together, Constance?'

'That's a lovely idea. It would bring comfort to many.'

'I'm so happy you came to New York. I'm so happy we have met. I could have stayed in Newport, but I came here and I'm glad that I did. And I'm glad I didn't go out tonight but talked to you and listened to your beautiful song. I feel a shift inside me. Something magical has happened to me and you have made it happen.'

She stands up. 'It's late. I must go to bed. We will talk in the morning. A carriage ride in the park, perhaps?'

I remember my meeting with Cavill. 'I would like that,' I reply, hoping she's not a late riser like her daughter-in-law.

'Good night, my dear Constance.'

I watch her leave the room. The footman who has stood patiently by the door accompanies her. I wonder whether she has more confidence now on the stair.

I hope that after I've slid back to my time, she won't ask Constance to play 'Let It Be'.

Chapter Twenty

I too go to my room. I ring the bell for Ruby and she comes to help me out of my clothes. I have learnt that ladies who are lucky enough to have maids wear corsets that do up at the back, but those who have to dress themselves wear corsets that do up at the front. 'They're all talking about your singing below stairs,' she tells me as she pulls the laces.

'I'm not very accomplished,' I reply, but I imagine Constance Fleet, being a lady, is very accomplished.

'You're just being modest, ma'am.'

'Nonetheless, I'm glad I've entertained them.'

'And the spirit board. Everyone is talking about that too.'

'What with that and the *Titanic*, we've brought them a great deal of excitement, haven't we?' I say with a laugh.

'Indeed, you have. Is it true that Mr Aldershoff's ghost appeared and gave Mrs Aldershoff a dollar bill in a book hidden in the bookcase?'

I laugh at how quickly stories get exaggerated. 'I wouldn't say that his ghost appeared, but he did communicate through the board and tell us to find a book in the bookcase that contained a dollar bill in a secret compartment.'

Ruby gasps. 'Astonishing.' The laces are undone and I'm free of the dreaded corset. I can breathe freely again. 'Your dresses will be delivered tomorrow and then you can go out,' she says brightly, draping it over the back of a chair. 'They tell me that Mr and Mrs Aldershoff are out every night during the season. But the season is over now and most of their friends have departed for the coast. They have a mansion in Newport. There are picnics and tennis tournaments. It sounds exciting. Mrs William Aldershoff gives a grand ball in July for four hundred people. Can you imagine how wonderful that must be? It's a shame we will be back in England by then.'

'It is a shame,' I agree, although I'll be back in 2014.

I bid her goodnight and go to bed. I allow my thoughts to drift to Cavill like rock doves returning home to roost – whatever the obstacles in the way, they always find their way home. The joyful anticipation of seeing him the following day is tempered by the knowledge that it will surely be the final time. I cannot bear the thought that after tomorrow we might never meet again. Will love bring me back to him another time? Is it possible? If I will it with all my power, might the law of attraction draw me back to him on my next slide? Surely not. It cannot be. And yet I'm unwilling to extinguish the little flame of hope that flickers valiantly in my heart. However, that hope is tempered by the cold reality of being a timeslider. When I see him at midday on those iconic steps, I will be Constance Fleet – and if our paths join on another slide, I will be someone else. Cavill can't imagine Pixie Tate with her pink hair and biker boots, and, if he could, he probably wouldn't fancy her. He will never know the real me and that fills me with sadness. But it is an immutable truth – he will never meet me in my own time.

But what if I do have the courage, or recklessness, to tell him? What then? If I tell him the truth, might he be sufficiently open-minded to believe me? I can prove it, after all, with the thousands of little details that only he and Hermione would know. He would *have* to believe me. What would be the consequences of that knowledge? How would he interact with Constance after I've returned to the future. She won't remember any of the conversations we've had. Perhaps that would be another piece of evidence in my favour. Am I foolish enough to do the unthinkable?

The little flame of hope in my heart grows stronger.

Am I mad enough to do the unimaginable?

I awake to a pair of hands on my shoulders, violently shaking me. My reaction is to fight back, but the hands belong to a man and he's stronger than I am. I open my eyes and see Glover's distraught face staring down at me, his eyes popping out with terror. 'Miss Fleet,' he hisses. 'It's Lord Ravenglass. You have to come at once.'

My mind snaps to wakefulness. My senses sharpen. 'What's happened?' I demand, sitting up.

'He's downstairs in the library. You have to go at once. Something terrible has happened.'

I scramble out of bed. Glover throws me my dressing gown. 'What's he done?' I ask, my stomach clenching with dread, my thoughts scrambling to predict what horror awaits me downstairs. 'Oh, God, what has he done?'

I'm about to discover the reason for my slide. At last, I will know what I came to find out. A sense of purpose grips me and I spring into action.

Glover practically pushes me through the door. 'You have to hurry or it will be too late,' he says, lowering his voice to a whisper. 'I can do nothing for him.'

As I make for the doorway, he looks at me with utter despair. 'I'm sorry,' he says.

My breath catches in my throat. What has he done to Lester?

I lift my gown and hasten down the corridor. The gilded light of dawn is just seeping into the night, glowing through the glass and lighting my way. I reach the top of the staircase at a run. The gold leaf glints on the balustrade. It has an otherworldly quality.

Something catches my ankle. It momentarily bites into my skin. I stumble. I cannot save myself. I reach out to grab whatever I can to break my fall, but it's no good. I fly into the air. I'm falling. Falling.

I feel a sharp bang against my head as it smashes into the banister. Then I'm above my body looking down.

Constance is falling like a ragdoll down the staircase.

BEWARE THE STAIR

I have slid out. I'm suspended in limbo, alert to everything that's happening around me.

It's then that I see Constance. She's not in her body either. She's with me, watching her material form tumbling inelegantly down the steps until it comes to a sudden stop at the bottom, where it lies, twisted and still. A pool of crimson blood flowers around her head and spreads over the marble floor, glistening richly.

She stares at it with a mixture of horror and fascination. It takes her a moment to realise what has just happened. That she is dead. She looks at her hands and moves them. Then she looks down at her feet and moves them too. She understands that her physical body is dead, but *she* still lives. And I wonder whether it surprises her how natural it feels, how very normal, as if she has lived and died a thousand times, only forgotten.

Then she looks at me and slowly an understanding passes between us. She smiles as the truth dawns on her and the veil lifts before her eyes. Her soul has known all along what her human mind did not, that I had taken possession of her. And that, on that deep, eternal level, she had been complicit. Her smile says a thousand words. Her life is complete. She's done what she came to do, and she's ready to step off the stage and return to whence she came. And she's very happy about it.

With joyful surprise she takes the hand that now extends towards her. Pink and green colours shift into focus. A woman materialises like a hologram. I have seen her before. I have *been* her. Hermione Swift. She has come to take Constance home.

It was *she* who tried to warn Constance of danger. First, she warned her daughter of the sinking ship. Then she warned Constance of the stair. But nothing can stand in the way of fate. I realise that now. Not even I with my meddling can alter what is meant to be.

I turn to the stair where Glover is now untying the Japanese golden thread that he fastened across the top step to trip her up. His apology was not for harming Lester, but for killing Constance. There he is, a murderer in the shadows, and the full impact of what he has done hits me hard. I never saw it coming. Probably because I wasn't meant to.

But why did he do it?

And where is Lester?

Present

Chapter Twenty-One

2014

The Aldershoff Hotel

Pixie opened her eyes.

'Did you do it?' It took her a second to recognise Ulysses. To register where she was. He took off his headphones and frowned. 'You all right, Pix?' He shut his laptop and got up off the chair and stretched, letting out a loud groan. He'd been sitting in the same position for too long. 'You look weird. You're not going to freak out again, are you?'

Pixie was aware suddenly that she was not going to meet Cavill in the park, and her heart suffered a sharp pang of disappointment. It felt as if it dropped like a stone into her belly. She put a hand to her chest. She had lost him all over again and the pain was devastating. Her mind flew to their meeting. The meeting that would now never happen. What was he going to talk to her about? What was he going to say? She'd never know. It was 2014– Cavill had been dead seventy years.

It was as if she had awoken from an exceptionally vivid dream – the feelings were still with her, the sensation of falling still reverberating in her consciousness. She took a deep breath and looked around, trying to settle back into this reality. Trying to shake off the feeling of being Constance Fleet, and of experiencing her death. But those energies still clung to her and she hovered uncertainly between the past and the present.

She remembered with a shiver Glover untying the golden thread on the stairs to cover his tracks. The Japanese golden thread that he had stolen from Alice's lady's maid for the purpose of murdering Constance. But why go to such lengths, and risk imprisonment and even death, to kill a woman who was no threat to him?

Or *had* she been a threat?

Ulysses was staring at Pixie with concern. 'You're weirding me out, Pix. Are you okay?'

'I need to speak to Lester on my own, Ulysses,' she told him firmly.

Ulysses dropped his shoulders with relief. 'Gotcha. I'll leave you to it. How did it go, by the way? Was it fun? Did you fall in love again?' He grinned in that infectious way of his, but Pixie couldn't begin to tell him what she'd been through.

'How long was I gone for?' she asked.

He looked at his watch. 'Three hours. God, I need to pee.' He made for the door. 'Did you find the diamond?'

'Diamond?' For a moment she didn't know what he was talking about. Then it registered. The Potemkin Diamond. 'No. No, I didn't find the diamond.' Guilt stabbed her conscience. She didn't want to let Mrs Aldershoff down, but the last thing on her mind right now was the Potemkin Diamond. She'd just been murdered for God's sake!

'Alma Aldershoff will be very disappointed.' He pulled a sad face and chuckled. 'See you in a while. Need a drink? A glass of water?'

She could have done with some vodka.

'Nothing,' she replied, standing up with resolve. 'I need to finish this.'

After Ulysses had gone, Pixie marched around the room, stretching her arms and shaking her hands. She'd been frozen in the same position for three hours and her body ached with stiffness. The nightmare she had lived through had felt very real. She'd experienced death and it wasn't anything like she'd thought it would be. She had barely felt the bang to the head. It had been more like a sound and a thumping sensation rather than a pain. She had scarcely been aware of her body falling down the stairs, so quickly had she slipped out of it. And Constance had slipped out of it, too. She had been there in spirit as well, watching her own death from a safe place above. Pixie doubted she had felt anything either. Did that mean that many who appear to suffer as they're dying have actually already departed, and that what is being seen is simply the mechanics of the physical body breaking down? Perhaps the soul is protected from suffering. That would be a comfort to many people if they knew it.

Pixie replayed the scene in her mind of Constance walking into the light with Hermione. It had been beautiful and she wanted to hold on to it. Hermione had tried to warn Constance of her imminent murder, but it had been no good. Was that because it had been Constance's destiny to be murdered? If that was so, then it shed a new light onto Pixie's timesliding. In spite of Pixie possessing her body, Constance had fulfilled that destiny. It implied that when a destiny had to follow its course, Pixie was less able to alter its direction than she had previously thought. The current that propelled that destiny towards its resolution was too strong.

Did that mean then that Pixie had not necessarily tampered with Cavill's course, but maybe enabled it to change, because that was what was meant to happen? She gathered her thoughts with rising excitement and began to articulate them out loud to better understand them. 'If there is no past, present or future, only a continuous now, then time as we understand it is not linear,' she said as she paced the floor. 'In which case, there is no cause and effect. We only perceive there to be cause and effect in this three-dimensional material world, because otherwise it would be too complicated and we'd all lose our minds. Is it then part of my destiny to alter and influence Cavill's? If it wasn't, would I be able to do it?' In the same way that Constance's destiny was to die, Pixie possessing her body had been unable to alter it. Whatever Pixie had chosen to do that night, she would have tripped on that golden thread. It had been unavoidable.

Pixie had thought she'd been playing with time, like a schoolchild breaking the rules. But perhaps she wasn't playing with it at all. Perhaps she was simply acting out a greater plan. A plan she knew nothing about. A plan devised by a superior intelligence. Maybe she and Cavill had a destiny to fulfil, only not in this life, but in the past. What was the difference? From the soul's point of view, there wasn't one. This time, another time – they were the same. It was all happening now. In which case she would see him again. She sighed heavily. It was a lot to take in and she had no one to discuss it with, because no one but she understood. But that flame of hope sputtered in her chest and grew bigger.

Might she see him again?

Back to the business of settling Lester's soul. She ran her eyes over the room. This was the room where Constance had given her seance. How different it was now. There were no bookcases, no rich crimson curtains, only the fireplace remained with the same marble mantlepiece and the mock Tudor ceiling with the rose, which was no longer red and white, but simply white.

Her experience had not solved the mystery of why Lester's soul was stuck. It had only raised more questions. She had to confront him now and get him to tell her what happened after

Constance was killed. And what part he had to play in her murder.

She sat down again and folded her hands in her lap. She listened to her breath and focused her attention on the gentle rise and fall of her chest, and the air entering and leaving her nostrils – cold as it went in, warm as it came out. Little by little her pulse rate slowed, her thoughts evaporated, and she felt that blissful sense of expansion with which she was so familiar. She became no one, just awareness. Her true, eternal self that had no definition, but was beyond form and was part of everything.

In that dimension her vibration was suitably raised to make contact with Lester, who was stuck between worlds, in a dark limbo of his own making. But to get him to communicate with her, she needed to gain his trust.

Lester, please come forward, I need to speak to you. She didn't say the words out loud, but in her mind, which was now acutely focused on her mission.

She felt the temperature drop. It started around her ankles and built, swirling about her thighs, her stomach and arms, until her ears and nose felt the cold as if an icy breeze were brushing her face. She knew he was present.

Lester. Are you here? I want to help you move into the light.

No response.

I know you can hear me, Lester, because I can feel your energy. It's cold and unhappy. You don't want to be here, do you, yet you don't know how to release yourself. I imagine you're bewildered as to why there are strangers in Walter-Wyatt and Alice Aldershoff's house.

Still no response, but the energy seemed to intensify.

Lester. I know you're here. You can't hide from me. I want to help you.

Still, he remained in the shadows. But she wasn't going to give up so easily. She hadn't gone through all that drama in the past to forsake him now. She hadn't wanted to be so blunt – her approach was always more softly-softly – but she had no choice. Lester *had* to come through and she *had* to speak with him. She couldn't let him down, nor could she let Mr Stirling down. This *had* to work. So, she used the information she had gleaned on the *Titanic* and at the Aldershoffs' mansion to get his attention. *I know you loved Glover, and I know Glover murdered Constance. I'm not here to judge you, Lester, but to help you find your way home.*

At last, his voice responded weakly in her mind, as if he was very far away.

I'm here.

She sensed him better now. A heavy, unhappy energy, like fog that's unable to rise and lingers just above the ground. She kept her eyes shut because that way nothing would distract her and cause her to shift out of focus. It was like tuning into a radio frequency. She must not allow anything to move the dial and cut off the channel of communication.

Do you know that you are dead, Lester?

There was silence. Pixie imagined he was working out what dead really meant because he must have felt very alive.

I know it, he said at last. *If I were alive, I wouldn't be living in such dire poverty.*

Where are you living?

In a dark place. It's cold and damp, and no one is kind. I avoid them.

Don't you want to leave?

I don't know how to leave.

I can help you.

You can't. No one can.

I can.

How can you help me if I can't see you.

Pixie was surprised. *You can't see me?*

Not really. You shift in and out like a ghost.

But you can hear me?

I can hear you.

What do you see?

The room. I see the room and the house. But it's not like before. Now it's different.

You say before. Before what?

Before the spirit board opened a door for me and let me in.

The spirit board let you into our dimension?

If that is what you want to call it. I see beings. They come and go, like mist. You come and go like mist too. But the house. That is clear. I can touch the house. I couldn't before.

Why are you here? You didn't die here, but in England. Why did you come back?

For Constance. Because she died here. Aunt Constance died here, in this house. I cannot leave it. I cannot leave her.

Constance is not here, Lester. She went to the light, where she waits for you now. There is only forgiveness, Lester. Love and forgiveness.

It wasn't my fault. I didn't kill her. I didn't. Glover did.

Pixie sensed his anguish. She knew she had to calm him down before he went on the rampage again and started throwing things around the room.

Of course you didn't. I know you didn't. You weren't there when he killed her.

Did she suffer? His voice was thin and full of torment.

No. Only the initial shock of tripping and falling, but she slipped out of her body with the first blow to her head and then she was free.

I didn't know Glover would kill her. I swear it.

And I believe you.

But I knew that he had.

Did you tell anyone what you knew?

No. I told no one. They thought she had fallen of her own accord.

What happened to Glover?

There was a long pause. For a moment Pixie thought he had gone. Then his voice returned and the sorrow in it tore her heart. *He threw himself off the Brooklyn Bridge.*

I'm sorry.

Not as sorry as I. It was my fault. If I hadn't dismissed him, he wouldn't have taken his life. Oh, God. What have I done? Pixie felt his remorse in the tension building suddenly around her. The same tension that had grown into a rampage and destroyed the room. She needed to keep him calm.

Surely he killed himself because he felt guilty for having committed murder? Perhaps he couldn't live with himself after that?

It was all because of me!

Glover killed Constance because of you?

Yes.

Why?

Because he loved me and couldn't bear to lose me.

And you loved him?

Another pause ensued. Pixie imagined him struggling to admit something that went so sharply against the morals of his time. When he spoke, his voice was flat with resignation. *Yes. Yes, I loved him.*

There is no shame in loving another man, Lester.

Yes, there is. It's against nature.

No, it isn't.

No one understands.

They do now. In my time, men marry men and women marry women, and no one thinks anything of it.

You lie.

I don't lie. It's true. You've been dead over seventy years, Lester.

He was genuinely horrified by that. *I've been here over 70 years?*

You have. This house is now a hotel. It's full of strangers. It's nothing like it was when you were here. The beings you see as mist are guests staying in the hotel.

Men marry men?

Love is love, Lester. The body doesn't matter. It's the heart that counts. In your day your love for Glover was a crime. Today it would be celebrated.

If that is true, it's a miracle.

It's true. People are more open-minded now.

I had to give him up and marry Esme.

And that didn't end well, did it?

I wasn't myself. After Aunt Constance died . . . well, I couldn't forgive myself.

Why? What did you do?

If I've been here a hundred years, *perhaps it is time to unburden my conscience. If I do, I will be released? Is that so?*

It is. You can release yourself whenever you choose. I will show you the way.

Pixie felt his energy lighten at the thought of leaving. Perhaps it was lightening also at the thought of confessing his part in Constance's murder.

Very well. I will tell you everything. If you break your promise, I shall haunt this hotel, if it is truly a hotel, and you will be sorry.

Very well. Pixie hoped his confession would alter his energy sufficiently to enable him to rise into the light when the moment came.

It started with the Potemkin Diamond. One of the most valuable gems in the world. It belonged to Walter-Wyatt Aldershoff. I knew once I laid eyes on it that the Aldershoff wealth was beyond anything I could imagine, and it was going to be mine if I married Esme. She was their only child. She would inherit it all. I saw a bright future. Our home restored in all its glory, and she and I the most desirable couple in London, barring only the King and Queen themselves. I knew I had to dismiss Glover. That our relationship had to end. But if I told him the truth, that fear of being poor far outweighed the fear of losing the man I loved, I knew he would turn nasty. I worried he would take me down with him, out of spite and hurt. I feared he'd ruin my engagement and my future. So, I told him that Aunt Constance was threatening to expose us both if I didn't dismiss him. I told him that if it were up to me, I would keep him as my valet and nothing would change, but that Aunt Constance wouldn't hear of it. She knew our secret and was prepared to risk a scandal by revealing it. Glover was demented with misery, but I never thought he would go to such extremes. He believed that if Constance was out of the way, we would be free to continue as before. Oh, if only I had known how much he loved me! If only I had told him the truth and not thrown Constance to the wolves. So he killed her. But by killing her, he put an obstacle between us that nothing could remove. It not only came between us, but between me and any happiness I could enjoy. Because I knew, in my heart, that it was because of my cowardice that Constance was killed. I could never forgive myself.

And you blamed yourself too for Glover's suicide.

Yes. It was all because of me. I should never have allowed myself to love him. I should have resisted temptation. I was weak and foolish and reckless and . . . His voice trailed off. *God is punishing me for loving a man.*

God is not a person who sits in judgement over you. God is love. It is only we humans who create a God with all the jealousies and petty desires for vengeance that we ourselves have. God is love beyond our understanding. God doesn't punish, you do. You punish yourself. So, stop punishing yourself. You've suffered enough. Forgive yourself instead.

How can I? It might be a hundred years ago to you, but, to me, it seems like yesterday.

The very fact that you have admitted your part in the crime shows that you are ready to forgive. To forgive Glover. To forgive Constance. To forgive you. You came here to experience life with all its ups and downs, joys and sorrows, and to grow. You can either choose to grow wounded or to grow wise. Which will it be?

Wise.

You will return home now and take your wisdom with you. That's the reason you came here in the first place. You're not meant to be stuck in limbo. No one is making you stay here, but you.

I don't understand. If I'm making myself stay here, why can't I set myself free?

You can. But you're weighed down by your negative thoughts and beliefs. You just have to feel the love in your heart. The love for yourself. Feel it, Lester. Be kind to yourself. You came here to learn and you've learnt. You've grown wise. When you stumble, you don't berate yourself for stumbling, do you? You get up and try again. That's what you must do now. Get up and try again. You'll do better next time.

Pixie sensed his energy lighten further.

I want to tell Constance that I'm sorry, and Glover too. I want the chance to make it up to them both.

You will have that chance, Lester.

Pixie opened her eyes.

Lester was there, standing by the fireplace, staring at her. *I see you*, he said, blinking at her in astonishment.

And I see you. He was wearing a three-piece grey suit and bow tie, and a bowler hat on his head. In his hand he was holding a cane.

What do I do now? he asked.

Look around you.

A bright, golden light filled the room, brighter than any electric light could ever be. Brighter even than the sun. Pixie was forced to close her eyes. She saw the light not with her physical eyes, but with her psychic third eye. Then out of the glare came

Constance. She was dressed in bright blue that dazzled like the most vivid sky. She put out her hands. *Come, Lester,* she said. *I've been waiting for you.* And Lester, overwhelmed with emotion, took them.

Oh, Constance! It's really you.

I've always been with you, Lester, only I couldn't reach you. Now I can.

And what of Glover?

Pixie smiled as they both looked at her for an answer. *Perhaps Glover is in a place of darkness as you were,* she said. *Maybe it's up to you to help him forgive himself, as you have forgiven yourself.*

With that the two figures faded, gathered into the eternal light that was home.

Chapter Twenty-Two

Ulysses was sitting in the lobby, glancing at the messages on his phone, when Mr Stirling loomed over him. 'Is it done?' he asked in a low voice.

Ulysses put down his phone. 'Nearly,' he replied. He stretched his arms wide and sighed. 'Pixie's out of her trance, thank God. She's kicked me out so she can finish off.'

Mr Stirling's face showed his utter relief, which in itself revealed the extent of his earlier doubt. 'This is very good news,' he said keenly. 'May I?'

'Please.' Ulysses watched him sit down on the other purple armchair that was arranged around the low table.

'How does she do it?' he asked. 'I mean, it's taken three hours.'

'She goes into trance,' Ulysses said vaguely. He couldn't admit to what she really did.

'You mean she just sits there?'

'Yes, for hours without moving. Quite extraordinary.'

'And what do *you* do?'

'I watch movies.'

'Any in particular?'

'Old movies. Ingrid Bergman, Humphrey Bogart, Lauren Bacall.'

Mr Stirling laughed, his green eyes widening at the recognition of a kindred spirit. 'Me too. What a coincidence. I didn't imagine people cared for old Hollywood any more.'

'I do,' Ulysses replied. 'Give me an old film over a new one any day. It's the dialogue. It's just far superior to the dialogue they write these days. Everything has to be so fast, there's no time to develop the characters. Take a Bogie-Bacall scene – the conversation is snappy, but not short. I must have watched *The Big Sleep* fifty times.'

'Me too. But *To Have and Have Not* is my favourite.'

They laughed heartily as they quoted the famous lines from the film.

Riding high on a wave of enthusiasm, Mr Stirling ordered coffee and the two of them discussed the great Hollywood films of the 1940s and 50s over strong espressos and macaroons. It wasn't long before Mr Stirling insisted Ulysses call him Henry and all formality had been vigorously swept aside. 'You know, I met Lauren Bacall once,' Mr Stirling recounted wistfully, putting down his coffee cup. 'She came here for dinner. You know, she lives in Manhattan. Of course, she was an old lady by then with white hair and those steely blue-green eyes, which had a way of stopping you in your tracks. But she was still beautiful and hadn't lost that sharp wit of hers.' He sighed and shook his head. 'They don't make them like her any more. She's one of the greats.'

Mr Stirling and Ulysses were disappointed when Mrs Aldershoff and her long-suffering daughter stepped into the foyer. The old lady walked slowly, her cane tap-tapping coldly against the marble floor as she made her way towards them. 'Any news?' she demanded, looking from Mr Stirling to Ulysses with her sharp gaze.

'She's just wrapping it up,' Ulysses informed her, draining his coffee cup.

Mr Stirling moved a couple of chairs so that the two women could join them.

Mrs Aldershoff glanced at the big double doors. 'Is she still in there?'

'She is,' Ulysses replied.

'She's been hours.'

'Three,' said Mr Stirling.

'Feels like the whole day,' said Mrs Aldershoff with a sniff.

Ulysses caught Mr Stirling's eye and grinned. 'Not if you're watching an Ingrid Bergman movie.'

Mrs Aldershoff handed her daughter her walking stick and Mrs Croft leant it up against the wall. The elderly lady then sat down slowly and stiffly, letting out a loud sigh when she settled at last, like a roosting hen, into the plush velvet seat. Mr Stirling ordered more coffee and macaroons, but he could have done with something stronger, for Mrs Aldershoff wandered distractedly down memory lane again and began to tell them of the time her father had set up an enormous trainset powered by clockwork on the hall floor and the servants had to step over it to go about their duties. 'It had a lovely green engine, and two fine carriages complete with little seats and doors that opened and closed,' she said in an unusually quiet voice.

Mr Stirling was relieved when Tanya Roseby's cheerful face beamed at him from the entrance. She exchanged pleasantries with the porters and then she and Lara bustled into the hall with a dozen glossy shopping bags hooked over their arms. 'It's amazing how much damage one can do to one's bank account in such a small space of time,' she said when she reached the small group.

'We were lucky to get out of Bergdorf's alive,' said Lara, cheeks rosy from the walk. 'The people selling makeup are like piranha fish.'

'They're all fighting for commission,' said Ulysses. 'They—'

'May I introduce you both to Ulysses Lozano,' Mr Stirling said to Tanya and Lara.

'No need. We met on the plane,' said Tanya breezily.

Mr Stirling was astonished. He'd been so anxious about them crossing paths on the flight. 'Oh,' he said, realising that his fears had been for nothing. 'But you haven't met Mrs Aldershoff and her daughter, Mrs Croft.'

Tanya and Lara shook hands with the elderly lady, awed that they were in the presence of William Aldershoff's granddaughter. 'It's such a pleasure to meet you,' said Tanya. 'I'd love to hear what this beautiful building was like when it was a private house. You must have a million memories. Do share them.'

'Oh, you don't want to hear all that nonsense, do you?' Mrs Aldershoff asked hopefully.

'We really do,' Tanya replied.

Mr Stirling arranged for the bags to be taken up to Tanya's room and then pulled more chairs into the ever-widening circle and ordered another round of coffee and macaroons.

'It was the most beautiful home in New York,' Mrs Aldershoff began. 'More beautiful, even, than the Vanderbilt mansion. That was because my grandmother, Didi Aldershoff, had an eye for beauty and the wealth to fulfil her most extravagant vision.' She inhaled deeply and smiled, which took everyone aback because Alma Aldershoff rarely smiled. 'But in the end, what was it all for? Sure, it made life comfortable, but it wasn't fulfilling beyond that. This is no longer a family home but a hotel. The cottage in Newport is a museum. Ultimately, it was all a great waste of money. I have grown wise at ninety-eight. It's a shame it's taken so long. But I suppose it's better to arrive late than not at all.'

Mr Stirling didn't know what she was talking about. There followed an awkward silence. Everyone sipped their coffee.

Ulysses helped himself to another macaroon. The old woman's gaze lost itself somewhere in the half distance, and Mrs Croft changed the subject and asked Tanya about her business.

Just then, the double doors of the Walter-Wyatt drawing room opened and Pixie stepped out, looking as dazed as a mouse that had been in a dark tunnel for a long time and had just emerged into the light. Mr Stirling jumped out of his chair and strode over swiftly with the intention of cutting her off before she announced her failure to the group, if failure was what she had to report. 'Miss Tate . . .'

Pixie smiled and took a long, satisfied breath. 'Success!' she exclaimed.

'You mean, he's gone?'

'He has.'

Mr Stirling's response was uncharacteristic. So grateful was he that he put his arms around her and gave her a hug. Pixie laughed as his enthusiasm nearly squeezed the life out of her. 'I cannot tell you how relieved I am to hear that,' he said.

'You don't have to,' she replied, wriggling out of his embrace. 'Actions speak louder than words.'

'We must celebrate. Come, Mrs Aldershoff will be very happy to hear your news.'

Pixie stood before the group and looked down at the five faces that turned to her expectantly. 'The resident spirit has moved on,' she announced proudly. None of them could imagine what she had put herself through in order to make that happen.

Tanya's mouth fell open. 'I knew it! Didn't I tell you I'd seen a ghost in my room last night?'

'You did,' Lara replied.

'I don't imagine that was something the hotel were keen to spread around,' said Mrs Croft.

'On the contrary,' Tanya exclaimed with delight. 'I think it's a USP. It's one of the best things about this place.'

Alma clearly didn't know what a USP was, and didn't care. She had more important things to consider. 'How did you do it?' she demanded. 'Do sit down and tell us.' Pixie could tell she was dying to ask about the Potemkin Diamond, but probably didn't want to bring it up in front of strangers. The elderly woman studied Pixie closely, perhaps trying to ascertain whether Pixie had found the secret hiding place.

A member of staff had brought yet another chair and now the group had swollen to seven and was taking up a large portion of the lobby. Mr Stirling had sent someone off to open a bottle of champagne. 'Did you find out what he wanted?' he asked, sitting down again.

Pixie couldn't tell them what she'd experienced on the *Titanic* because no one but Ulysses knew about her timesliding. But she could give them a brief outline of Lester's story. 'Lester did come here, Mrs Aldershoff, before you were born. It was 1912 and he and his aunt, Constance Fleet, were on the *Titanic*.'

Mrs Aldershoff gasped. 'Good Lord. I never knew that.'

'While on the ship, Constance caught her nephew in bed with his valet, Mr Glover. The two men were in love, but Lester was heading out to New York to see his fiancée, Esme Aldershoff, and Constance, being a woman of her time and culture, tried to persuade Lester to dismiss his valet. It would have caused a terrible scandal if Esme had learnt that her fiancé was gay.'

'It certainly would have,' said Mrs Aldershoff. 'So, what happened?'

'Lester told Glover that Constance was prepared to expose them if he didn't dismiss him. So Glover, seeing the removal of Constance as his only salvation, tied a golden thread across the top step of the staircase—'

'*This* staircase?' asked Mr Stirling in surprise.

'This very staircase,' Pixie confirmed. 'Glover woke Constance in the middle of the night claiming that Lester had done something terrible and that she had to hurry down to the library to see him. She ran along the corridor and when she reached the top of the stair, the thread tripped her up and she went tumbling to her death.'

Mrs Aldershoff gasped again. 'Good Lord. She was murdered here in this house?'

'She was,' said Pixie. 'But your parents never knew about it. They thought she had fallen by accident. They had no idea that she had been murdered.'

Mrs Aldershoff shook her head. 'So that's why my mother was so terrified of me falling down the stairs!' she said, riveted by the revelation. 'And Constance's name was never mentioned. This is the first time I've heard it.'

'Lester gave up Glover,' Pixie continued. 'Glover threw himself off the Brooklyn Bridge, either because Lester had ditched him, or because he'd committed murder. Probably both. Lester married Esme but spent the rest of his life in a state of guilt and remorse. He turned to drink, divorced, and died young. It's a tragic story.'

'Was it the Ouija board that brought him back?' Mrs Croft asked.

'Yes,' Pixie replied. 'The spirit board, as they called it, belonged first to Constance's mother. When she died, it was handed down to Constance and survived the *Titanic* disaster. Constance did a seance here in the Walter-Wyatt drawing room the night she was killed. Lester was present. I think the board connected Lester to Constance so that when you tried to contact your father, Mrs Aldershoff, Lester was drawn out of the lower astral and given a portal into our dimension. He wanted help, but didn't know how to ask for it. You see, he was so deeply immersed in his unhappiness that it created a fog of negativity around him, which he was unable to penetrate. He could hear you, but he couldn't see you. He needed to rise out of his trauma in order to connect properly with me. It took time, but I managed to guide him into the light in the end.'

'You are clever, Pixie,' Mr Stirling gushed.

'She never fails,' said Ulysses proudly.

'The truth is that all earthbound spirits want to go to the light. They just don't know how to get there,' said Pixie.

A young waitress appeared with a tray carrying a bottle of Moët & Chandon and seven crystal flutes. 'How fascinating. We can really work with this,' Tanya announced as the waitress handed round the glasses and poured the champagne. 'But I want to hear the story from the beginning.' She grinned. 'Perhaps there should be a book.'

'So, you've decided to represent us?' Mr Stirling asked, looking pleased.

Tanya raised her glass. 'How could I not! This hotel is fabulous. I can't wait to get started.'

'Did you manage to find the Potemkin Diamond?' Mrs Aldershoff asked suddenly, unable to remain patient any longer. 'You did try to contact my father, didn't you?'

Pixie felt bad; she hadn't really tried very hard. Her mission to save Lester had been more important. 'I'm afraid it's not in the house,' she said. The elderly woman's narrow shoulders dropped and she looked so crestfallen that Pixie decided to give her dowsing crystal another go to prove her point. She lifted her carpet bag onto her knee and rummaged around for the suede pouch. 'I'll show you how it works.' She took out the amethyst.

'Ooh, goodie.' Tanya leaned forward in her chair. 'I love this!'

Intrigued, the group watched Pixie rest her elbow on the table and dangle the crystal on its chain between her forefinger and thumb. The crystal had given her an unambiguous no when she had previously asked this question. But she had to do something to show willing. Poor Mrs Aldershoff looked so pitiful. 'Is the Potemkin Diamond in this house?' Pixie asked. To her surprise, the crystal began to move in a clockwise circle. She frowned in confusion as the circle widened and the movement speeded up. When she'd used it the evening before, it had most definitely moved the other way. She couldn't understand it.

'What does it say?' Mrs Aldershoff asked eagerly.

'It doesn't make sense. It says it *is* in the house,' Pixie replied.

Mrs Aldershoff's eyes shone with excitement. 'You see, I told you. I knew it. It's here. Where is it?' She stared hard at the crystal as if it were about to speak.

Pixie put the crystal down. 'I need to work it out,' she said ponderously.

She knew the crystal never lied, so it had to be here, in this house. She thought back to when Walter-Wyatt had gone to get the diamond to show Constance and Lester. He had left them in the sitting room and crossed the hall. She distinctly remembered hearing the tap-tapping of his cane on the marble tiles. A shiver rippled over her skin as she was struck suddenly with a revelation. Walter-Wyatt had returned *without* his cane. He had left it in the drawing room and returned silently across the hall. It had struck her as strange at the time, but she hadn't dwelt on it. The diamond had distracted her. But she dwelt on it now. Why would he have left his cane in the drawing room when he took it everywhere with him?

Pixie looked at Alma's walking stick, which was leaning against the wall. It was the same stick with the silver dog's head as the one Walter-Wyatt had carried. 'When I asked the crystal yesterday, you weren't in the building, were you, Mrs Aldershoff.'

'No, I wasn't,' Alma replied.

'So, if the crystal is telling me that the diamond is now in the building, then it has to be where you are.'

'But I don't have it,' Mrs Aldershoff stated indignantly. 'If I had it, I wouldn't be looking for it, would I?'

'You have the key, right?' Pixie asked.

'I do.' Mrs Aldershoff's hand shot to her chest. The key lay safely tucked beneath her blouse.

Pixie got up. With a rising sense of triumph, she fetched the walking stick. Holding it up to the light, she studied the silver dog's head closely. Everyone watched her in silence. Mrs Aldershoff bit her bottom lip hopefully. Mrs Croft looked as if she couldn't believe Pixie would find anything there. But it didn't take long for Pixie's expression of concentration to break into a smile. 'Oh, my God!' she breathed in wonder. There, under the dog's chin, hidden among the folds of silver, was a tiny keyhole. 'I don't believe it.' She returned to her seat and sat down excitedly. 'May I have the key, Mrs Aldershoff?'

Tanya held her breath. If Pixie had found the Potemkin Diamond it would be one hell of a good story. Mr Stirling looked at Ulysses and the younger man grinned. Ulysses was used to people being surprised by Pixie.

Mrs Croft went to help her mother. She burrowed inside her collar and unclasped the chain. Pixie took the key and inserted it into the keyhole. It was easy to turn. The dog's jaw unlocked with a click and fell open. The group stared in astonishment as the pink diamond was revealed in a bed of velvet made especially to accommodate it.

'Well, I'll be darned,' said Mrs Aldershoff, tears welling in her eyes.

'Oh, Mother!' Mrs Croft put a hand to her mouth.

'The last place anyone would look,' said Pixie. 'Walter-Wyatt was never parted from his stick and now we know why.'

With trembling fingers, Alma lifted the diamond out of its bed and held it in her hand. Her vision blurred as she thought of Joshua, and the diamond became a pink smudge in her palm. 'I've never done anything unselfish in my life,' she said in a thin voice. She looked at her daughter and the fact that Leona's eyes were shining with tears made her own flow freely, seeping into the small crevices on her face. 'But I'm going to do something unselfish now. I'm going to fund a wonderful place for children like my great-grandson Joshua, so that they meet the end of their short lives in a place of comfort and peace, here in New York City. It will be my legacy. The Joshua Litton Hospice.'

'That's a beautiful idea, Mrs Aldershoff,' said Mr Stirling, regretting that he had ever thought of her as a termagant.

Alma's gaze rested on Pixie with gratitude. 'Thank you, my dear,' she said. She could see the surprise on her daughter's face – Alma knew she rarely thanked anyone. Alma then turned to her daughter. 'And I'm sorry I fell short in so many ways,' she said. Leona simply nodded and smiled feebly, too emotional to reply.

'"Love means never having to say you're sorry,"' said Ulysses, giving Mr Stirling a meaningful look.

'I love that film too,' Mr Stirling duly replied with a grin.

'What a load of old rubbish,' said Alma, chuckling through her tears. 'Love means you care enough to say you're sorry. Don't let anyone tell you otherwise.'

And no one could argue with that.

Mr Stirling ordered more champagne, but Pixie got up from her chair. Her head was swimming and she felt exhausted suddenly.

'I hope you don't mind, but I might take a quick walk around the park. I could do with some fresh air.'

She left the group and hurried through the hotel doors into the bright autumn sunshine. She crossed Fifth Avenue, which was busy with traffic. How different it was to a century ago. In those days there'd been horses and carts, carriages, trams and the first motor cars. There'd been no clutter on the roads. Now she noticed the lines painted on the tarmac, the traffic lights, the bollards, the large number of things that hadn't been there in those days. And the sounds of the city – how different they were too. It was extraordinary to think that she had been here, in this very spot, only hours ago, yet a hundred years before. Everyone she had seen was dead. Their lives had been lived and completed, and they had departed. Among them was Cavill. He had departed too. This was the second time she had had to suffer his death, and it wasn't any easier to bear.

She walked through the park in search of the steps where they had arranged to meet. She knew there was no point in going there – she wasn't going to find him, but she couldn't stop herself. She was drawn by a powerful longing that was stronger than she was. Not knowing her way around, she asked a man at a food cart and he told her it was called Bethesda Terrace, and pointed her in the right direction. When she had taken the carriage ride with Cavill, it had been April. The trees had been in flower and the green leaves were just beginning to unfurl. The air had been sugar-scented and invigorated by the aliveness and optimism of spring. Now there was a different smell in the air, the smell of summer dying into autumn, and the leaves were about to turn and fall. It was the end of a cycle. But a new one would begin. That was the same with life. Cycles of death and rebirth, repeated time and again.

It was a balmy afternoon. The sun was warm, the sky above

Manhattan a resplendent blue. It felt good to be outside. A soft breeze brushed her face and played with her hair. She was happy to be Pixie Tate once more. To have shed Constance Fleet, although the memory of her was still acute. She walked fast in her jeans and trainers, no longer constricted by a corset and a long and cumbersome skirt, and she looked around her with fresh eyes seeing everything anew; coming as she did from the past, the present looked strangely unfamiliar.

At last, she reached the two sets of giant sandstone steps that descended at each end of a terrace to a large, round pond below. In the middle of the pond rose a magnificent stone fountain on top of which stood a bronze angel with her wings outspread. Pixie lingered on the terrace and rested her hands on the balustrade. She took a deep breath and closed her eyes for a moment. Had Cavill waited for her *here*? What had he thought when she hadn't come? What had he wanted to say to her? He would have heard soon after that Constance had died. How had he felt about that? It was too presumptuous to hope that he had felt tenderness for *her*, Pixie, but she found herself wondering whether he had perhaps recognised something in Constance that he had found in Hermione, something that was behind the physical appearance of both women. A deep connection that was recognisable but beyond definition. He would not have known what it was, but he might have felt it.

Pixie opened her eyes and let them wander over the fountain and the lake beyond. People were rowing in small boats alongside ducks that glided gracefully over the water. The light caught the ripples in their wake and sparkled. The breeze caused the leaves to oscillate mesmerically so that from where she was standing, they looked like thousands of tiny fairy lights. It was a peaceful scene and it soothed the ache in her heart. She knew she was foolish to pine for a man who had been dead for over seventy years, but her heart had no conception of time, nor did it care about being foolish.

In the dazzling sunlight she saw the tall figure of a man standing with his back to her, contemplating the round pond. Her heart lurched. It couldn't be. Cavill was dead. She was in 2014 Or was she? Her eyes darted to the left and right, taking in the people in modern clothes who were most definitely not from the past. But the man by the pond was so familiar. He was standing in the same way that Cavill stood, with the same broad shoulders and confident stance. Yet, this slide, Cavill had been an older man. *This* man was like a young Cavill. He was wearing a well-cut suit that showed off his slim figure and long legs. He had Cavill's height and his distinctive deportment. She stared, terrified to blink in case the vision melted away. In case it was a trick of her imagination, like an echo from the past that would evaporate if she lost her focus.

Aware perhaps that he was being watched, he turned around.

The disappointment hit her like cold water on her face. He was not Cavill, young or old. He was simply a stranger in the park. But she continued to watch him all the same. Shielding his eyes from the sun, he cast his gaze up to where she was standing on the terrace. He seemed to be looking directly at her. She couldn't see the colour of his eyes from where she was, but she knew they were blue. For a long moment it appeared as if they were staring at each other.

Then he looked at his watch. He sighed with resignation, glanced once more at the terrace, then put his hands in his pockets and walked away.

Pixie watched him saunter off to the right and take the path into the trees. She watched him until he was out of sight, and she continued to watch even though the path was empty. With a heavy heart, she found a tree that was some distance away from the paths and people, and sat cross-legged beneath it.

Dappled sunlight shimmered on the long grass around her, and above, the leaves gently rustled. She rested her head against the trunk and closed her eyes.

I will find a way . . .

Acknowledgements

I have had enormous pleasure in writing the second book in the Timeslider trilogy. These novels are a real challenge to plot, but once I've got my head around the complications of time travel and worked out the various twists and turns, the mystery and love story are great fun to write. Pixie is an intriguing heroine, and I've adored creating her and her sidekick, Ulysses. I'm currently working on the third and final part of the series and I shall be very sad to say goodbye once the story reaches its conclusion.

Glossy novels in bookshop windows do not fly there on their own, so there are many people I would like to thank. Firstly, my agent Sheila Crowley who is my most trusted advisor and friend. We've worked together for over twenty years, and she has stood strong and reliable beside me through thick and thin. She is wise, intelligent, formidable and sensitive, and loves her job, which is why she's so good at it. I thank her for her dedication and invaluable counsel.

I would like to thank my brilliant editor Charlotte Mursell at Orion. We have worked closely together on this series, and I could not have created Pixie's unusual world without her. She led me by the hand as I crafted the very complex plot of *Shadows in the Moonlight*, and continued to help me weave the tale of this book, *Secrets of the Starlit Sea*. She's passionate about the novels she works on and has a real gift for bringing the best out of her authors. I'm so grateful for her boundless energy, enthusiasm and her creative and forensic eye.

Thank you to my dynamic team at Orion: Anna Valentine, Jen Wilson, Sian Baldwin, Leanne Oliver, Snigdha Koirala, Cait Davies, Ellie Nightingale, Victoria Laws, Esther Waters, Paul Stark and Suzy Clarke.

I'd like to thank Sheila's wonderful team at Curtis Brown who work so tirelessly on my behalf: Tanja Goossens, Georgia Williams, Helena Maybery.

I wouldn't be writing at all if my parents hadn't encouraged me from an early age to do what I love. I'm so lucky to have such generous, unselfish and open-minded parents. As a child, my father read me stories by Oscar Wilde, Hans Christian Andersen, Alison Uttley, Kenneth Grahame and A.A. Milne, which inspired in me a desire to tell stories of my own. My parents created a magical world on their farm in Hampshire where I lost myself in my imagination and lived out my fantasies of being Hare, Rabbit and Moley (my sister and I dressing up in hessian cloth from discarded sacks on the farm to fully embrace those roles!) and very often Jane from *The Famous Five*. It was idyllic. The perfect place for my creativity to flower. Like a tree whose gift of fruit is as a consequence of the soil that feeds it, I thank my parents for being at the root of my success.

My husband, Simon Sebag-Montefiore, daughter Lilochka and son Sasha are the greatest source of joy, inspiration and love in my life, and I thank them with all my heart for just being them. Don't ever change!

Credits

Santa Montefiore and Orion Fiction would like to thank everyone at Orion who worked on the publication of *Secrets of the Starlit Sea* in the UK.

Editorial
Charlotte Mursell
Snigdha Koirala

Copyeditor
Suzanne Clarke

Proofreader
Sally Partington

Audio
Paul Stark
Louise Richardson

Contracts
Rachel Monte
Ellie Bowker

Design
Charlotte Abrams-Simpson

Editorial Management
Anshuman Yadav
Charlie Panayiotou
Jane Hughes
Bartley Shaw

Finance
Jasdip Nandra
Nick Gibson
Sue Baker

Production
Ruth Sharvell

Marketing
Cait Davies
Ellie Nightingale

Publicity
Leanne Oliver
Sian Baldwin

Sales
David Murphy
Esther Waters
Victoria Laws
Rachael Hum
Ellie Kyrke-Smith
Frances Doyle
Georgina Cutler

Operations
Group Sales Operations team

Rights
Rebecca Folland
Tara Hiatt
Ben Fowler
Alice Cottrell
Ruth Blakemore
Marie Henckel

Loved *Secrets of the Starlit Sea*?
Then be sure to pick up the first novel in the Timeslider series,
Shadows in the Moonlight!

**A FORBIDDEN LOVE.
AN IMPOSSIBLE CHOICE...**

When **Pixie Tate** is summoned to the wild Cornish coast to investigate a mystery at St Sidwell Manor she senses that something malevolent is hiding in its shadows.

Over one hundred years ago, in the deepest night, a little boy vanished from his bed - and Pixie must find out what happened to him.

But Pixie is no ordinary detective. She has a unique gift: she can travel through time. As she slips back to 1895, secrets are revealed, love affairs exposed and, ultimately, Pixie will be forced to make a devastating choice that will change her life forever...